D0532447

Katie Reus fo... pilfered from her mo... she finally graduated with ... writing thrilling suspense and da... near Biloxi, Mississippi, with her fami... ... not creatu... can usually be found spending time with her family or one of the many ecle... animals they've adopted over the years.

You can find out more about Katie Reus and her books at www.katiereus.com, Twitter: @katiereus or Facebook: www.facebook.com/katiereusauthor.

Praise for *Targeted*:

'Fast-paced romantic suspense that will keep you on the edge of your seat!' Cynthia Eden, *New York Times* bestselling author

'Sexy suspense at its finest' Laura Wright, *New York Times* bestselling author

'Nonstop action, a solid plot, good pacing, and riveting suspense' *Romantic Times*

'Reus strikes just the right balance of steamy sexual tension and nail-biting action . . .' *Publishers Weekly*

Praise for Katie Reus:

'Explosive danger, and enough sexual tension to set the pages on fire . . . fabulous!' Alexandra Ivy, *New York Times* bestselling author

'Sexy alphas, kick-ass heroines, and twisted villains will keep you turning the pages in this new shifter series. *Alpha Instinct* is a winner!' Caridad Piñeiro, *New York Times* bestselling author

'Reus' worldbuilding is incredibly powerful, as she seamlessly blends various elements of legend and myth . . . Her characters manage to both charm and frighten, but the romance between a shifter and a human is the real highlight – it's lusty, heartfelt, and shows that love can conquer all' *Romantic Times* (4 Stars)

By Katie Reus

BOUND TO DANGER
Katie REUS

headline
ETERNAL

Published by arrangement with NAL Signet,
a division of Penguin Group (USA) LLC.
A Penguin Random House Company.

First published in Great Britain in 2014
by HEADLINE ETERNAL
An imprint of HEADLINE PUBLISHING GROUP

1

Cataloguing in Publication Data is available from the British Library

ISBN 978 1 4722 1221 4

Offset in Times by Avon DataSet Ltd, Bidford-on-Avon, Warwickshire

Printed and bound by CPI Group (UK) Ltd, Croydon, CR0 4YY

Headline's policy is to use papers that are natural, renewable and recyclable
products and made from wood grown in sustainable forests. The logging and
manufacturing processes are expected to conform to the environmental
regulations of the country of origin.

HEADLINE PUBLISHING GROUP
An Hachette UK Company
338 Euston Road
London NW1 3BH

www.headlineeternal.com
www.headline.co.uk
www.hachette.co.uk

For my husband, who puts up with my odd
hours and sometimes stressful deadlines.
I would be lost without you.

Prologue

Landing Zone (LZ): area where military aircraft can land.

Six years ago

Cade O'Reilly ran full force through the triple-canopy jungle, the unbearable summer heat and giant mosquitoes barely a blip on his radar as he dodged low-hanging vines and branches. With his M-4 carbine slung over his back and grenades and claymore mines strapped to his jungle BDUs, he was armed to the teeth.

He hadn't planned on needing the extra firepower, but as a United States Marine, he was always prepared for an apocalypse-type situation. Like the fucking Boy Scouts, only well armed. As part of a classified intel unit with the Marine Corps, he often worked with various branches of the government. Including the CIA.

And just like *always*, the jobs he did for the CIA in Central or South America got screwed six ways to Sunday. It was as if he had a homing beacon on him or something when he got in this region. Trouble just found him. So now he was making a *really* hot exit from deep within the jungle with trained guerrillas on his ass. Luckily he'd scouted his escape route days ago.

He could hear the *whop-whop* of the Huey in the distance, the sound unmistakable. Most civilians couldn't tell the difference between choppers, but any military guy could. That shit got ingrained into your psyche. And what he heard now was pure music.

His extraction point was less than a hundred yards away. He couldn't see it because of the thick trees and foliage, but a giant clearing the size of a football field was waiting for him up ahead. And so was his rescue team.

Staccato fire sounded behind him, closer now. A loud thud landed in the dirt to his left. Then another. Then a louder thud into a tree on his right as he raced by. They were lucky shots because with the thick overhang it was damn near impossible to see much. Didn't matter that it was daytime. That triple canopy was so damn dense it was hard to comprehend until you'd seen it for yourself. He didn't have time to stop and return fire. There were too many men after him, and while he was good, he couldn't hold them off forever.

He'd been tasked with blowing up four underground bunkers deep in the jungles of Colombia that belonged to a vicious cartel leader. From what he'd seen firsthand, the war on drugs was a waste of time, but Nesto Valencia was a piece of shit who preyed on the innocent. Foreign travelers, his countrymen, it didn't matter. Cade was more than happy to help purge the asshole's income. Soon the guy wouldn't exist anyway. The CIA wanted to stop Valencia before he grew too big, so they'd coordinated a planned strike to completely wipe out him and everything he owned from the face of the earth.

This was totally off the books and wouldn't go on

Cade's official dust jacket. Classified and all that shit. Valencia had made the mistake of letting some of his men target a student tourist group that just happened to include a powerful senator's niece. She'd been killed and Valencia had become a dead man walking overnight. He just hadn't realized it.

Pulling a grenade free from his jacket, Cade slid out the pin and tossed it behind him without losing any momentum. He couldn't afford to.

As he jumped over a jagged tree root, he pulled another grenade free as a wave of heat and an explosion tore through the air at his back. Shouts of agony followed as he tossed another behind him.

Whop-whop. The sound was louder now. Now that the trees were thinning, he could see daylight and the twin-engine helicopter hovering high above the LZ clearing, but he didn't allow himself any relief. He wasn't free yet. Not even close.

The next explosion sounded seconds later, and as he pulled the canister of blue smoke free from his LBV, there were more cries of pain. Good. He hoped he got all of them.

He'd brought three different canisters, each of which signaled something different. Blue meant that he was coming out hot and they needed to make a fast exit. The only time he would have needed it was if his radio had been busted, but since he'd already relayed to the pilot that he'd been burned, there was no need to signal. Even so, he planned to use the smoke to cover their escape once they hit the air.

Gunfire still sounded in the distance behind him, so he knew he hadn't gotten them all. Sweat poured off him as he burst into the clearing. The Huey rose, but a rope dropped immediately. His legs and lungs burned as he ate up the distance to his freedom. As he reached the dangling line, he immediately hooked the carabiner to the harness he wore. His entire body jerked as the chopper lifted higher and he left the earth far behind.

He didn't let his guard down. The wind whipped around him, the sound of gunfire and shouting into his radio fierce. He twisted just in time to see at least a dozen men spill into the clearing like cockroaches.

As he released the top on the smoke canister, a sharp pain pierced his upper leg, then his shoulder.

"Fuck, I'm hit," he ground out, letting the pilot know even though above him he could hear the backup team returning fire with rapid speed. Adrenaline still pumping through him, he hauled back and threw the canister like a football. Blue smoke rolled everywhere, the color invading the air and whipping around with the wind, completely covering the men below and destroying their visibility.

As he was winched up, he gritted his teeth against the pain shredding through him. Each tug and swing with the wind increased his aching. He couldn't tell if the bullets had gone through, but he'd find out soon enough. After what felt like an eternity, he was finally hauled into the belly of the Huey to find two Marines he'd gone on missions with before, a Navy medic, and an older guy in a suit he didn't recognize. Cade blinked, trying to get his bearing, but his vision was starting to blur.

One of the Marines started applying pressure to his shoulder while the medic ripped open a packet of Quick-Clot and poured it on his leg wound. The unknown man sat there strapped in as he watched with piercing green eyes that made Cade feel as if the guy could see right through to his soul. What the hell? Maybe he'd been hit worse than he realized.

Iciness snaked through Cade as he tore his gaze away and watched the team work. The medic asked him something, but the edges of his vision started to dim as he tried to force his voice to work. *Damn it*, he was going into shock. He wanted to fight it, to resist, but his body won out as cold and blackness took over, sucking him under like an angry vortex.

Cade blinked, opening his eyes to a steady beeping sound. His surroundings quickly came into focus as he glanced around the sterile white room. He was on his back, had an IV attached to his arm, and was lying on an uncomfortable bed with starchy sheets. Groaning in pain, he pushed the sheet off to reveal a blue-and-white hospital gown that barely covered his dick. The white bandage around his leg looked stark compared to his tanned skin, and as he shifted against the bed his arm ached. Yep, he'd been shot twice.

At the sound of male voices outside his room, he glanced around again. It didn't look like a field hospital, but a real one with walls. Where the hell was he? He remembered being in the Huey, then being in a small plane, but the trip was fuzzy in his memory.

His heart rate increased as the door opened. The man from the chopper stepped inside, holding a manila folder. He wasn't wearing a suit now, but slacks and a green Polo T-shirt. His eyes widened a fraction when he met Cade's gaze before he ducked back out, still keeping the door propped open.

He spoke in low tones to someone, then stepped back inside with Colonel Abraham Winters, Cade's commander.

He tried to push up, but the colonel frowned. "At ease, son."

Cade semi-relaxed against the bed but reached for the remote to push his bed up to a sitting position and pulled the sheet over his lap. He was sure the two men didn't want to see his junk any more than he wanted to flash them. When he found the right buttons, he watched the two men out of the corner of his eye as he worked the controller. The movements intensified the aching in his arm and upper thigh, but he embraced the discomfort.

Pain sharpened his senses and pushed out some of the fuzziness. "Where am I?"

"Mexico." Colonel Winters looked at the man who still hadn't spoken, then back at Cade. "This is Lieutenant General Wesley Burkhart. You know who he is?"

Cade nodded. "Head of the NSA."

If the man with dark hair just barely graying at the temples was surprised Cade knew his name, he gave no indication. He just watched Cade with that unnerving stare. Not that Cade would ever show he was uncomfortable. Nope, he stared right back. The man didn't put off evil vibes, but he was a predator. Trained. Just like Cade.

"All right, enough of the staring contest. O'Reilly, listen to what the lieutenant general has to say. He's a straight shooter. Whatever he says, he means, and he has the highest clearance in the country. You can ask or reveal anything to him. I . . ." He paused for a long moment, then cleared his throat. "It's been an honor to have you under my command, O'Reilly." Then he was gone, slipping out the door like a ghost.

Cade frowned at his commander's words since they sounded a lot like that he wasn't going to be working with him in the future. He hadn't screwed up his mission, he knew that much. "Why were you on that Huey? Did something go wrong in the jungle? Did the rest of the mission go off as planned?" Since his commander said this guy had the highest clearance possible and Cade didn't feel like getting into another staring contest, he asked everything on his mind.

Standing at attention with the manila file tucked under one arm, the man looked as though he'd have no problem commanding thousands. "I was on it because I wanted to see you in action. Nothing went wrong; you completed your mission in record time. It was . . . impressive."

Normally he would have gone in with two to three other men for a mission like that; even with the top-secret intel unit, they always worked in teams. But for this mission he'd been assigned to go in alone. It had surprised him, but he'd wanted the challenge, so he hadn't questioned it. Cade nodded, not sure if he was supposed to respond.

"The rest of the mission is also complete. Valencia is dead."

Okay, then. "Why are you in my room and what do you want with me?"

The man pulled out one of the cheap-looking blue plastic seats against the only window and moved it closer to the bed before sitting. "You know a Marine named Sam Kelly?"

Cade nodded, a pang of sadness shooting through him at Kelly's name. "Yeah. Best sniper I ever worked with. I was sad to hear he'd died." KIA in Afghanistan. Cade had done a few missions with Kelly as backup for really hot exits. The finest damn backup he'd ever had, in fact. That man never missed a shot.

"He's not dead. He works for me now but under a new name. If you're smart, and I know you are, you're going to accept the job I'm offering. You're one of the best men Winters has ever worked with. You take directions well, but you're not a fucking machine. You think for yourself and if you don't like an order, you ask questions. I like that. I don't want some moron on my team. You're also twenty-nine. Jumping out of planes and helicopters isn't something you can do long-term. I know you've been thinking about getting out of the Corps when your next term is up."

Sam Kelly was alive? Cade was going to go back to that, but first . . . "How the hell do you know that?" Asking that was as good as admitting the man was right, but Cade was too stunned by the spiel Burkhart was giving him to care.

"Because I've been watching you. It wasn't by chance you were sent in for the Valencia mission by yourself. I needed to see how you'd handle things solo. I could have waited to approach you, but I'm not wasting any more time. I'm putting together a team of men and women with certain skill sets. Black ops, not as many rules as the CIA. I'm offering you a job and under normal circumstances I'd be telling you that your name and past would cease to exist. Since you don't have any family and all your missions have been top secret, you get to keep your name and you'll have an honorable discharge. But if you take this job, as soon as you're healed we're leaving. If the mission calls for it, you might have to adopt a cover ID—you most definitely will sooner or later." He held up the manila folder. "I've got a lot more to discuss with you, but if you're feeling up to it, you can start reading some details on what your new role would be."

Cade nodded as he tried to filter through his pain and everything the lieutenant general had said to him. "I thought the NSA was into cryptography."

The man half smiled. "That's exactly what Kelly said. And we are, but we also do a lot of other things. Read the file while I make a phone call. You hungry?"

He nodded, feeling overwhelmed as the surreal quality of the situation settled in. "I haven't said yes yet, but you told me about Kelly." Clearly that was top-secret information. "What if I don't agree to work for you?"

"You will," he said as he strode from the room, his voice absolutely confident.

Arrogant bastard. As Cade flipped open the file and started reading, he realized the man was arrogant for a reason, because as soon as Cade was capable, he was taking the job.

Chapter 1

Soft target: undefended target, such as a person or place that is vulnerable to a military or terrorist attack.

Maria Cervantes grasped the interior door handle of the SUV limo as her family's regular driver took what would hopefully be the last sharp turn of the night. Either he'd forgotten how to drive or she was sicker than she'd realized. Every little bump in the road made her afraid she'd puke. After being laid up in bed with flulike symptoms for five days and missing work for a week straight—something she'd never done before—she was positive she'd kicked the nasty stomach bug this morning. Now she wasn't so sure.

Nausea roiled in her stomach and she swallowed hard, forcing the sickness back down. *Just a few hours*, she reminded herself. That was all she had to get through, and then she could go back home and pass out.

As the vehicle straightened and slowed, she peered through the divider. At her request she'd asked the driver to keep the partition down. In case she got so sick he needed to pull over, she didn't want to waste precious seconds buzzing him. Either way she was clutching one of the empty silver ice buckets she'd snagged from the minibar in case she didn't have time to warn him.

"We're almost there, Ms. Cervantes." His voice was ridiculously polite despite the fact that she and Nash had known each other for two years.

She knew why, though. He was annoyed with her for going to this party when she was sick. "I swear to God if you call me Ms. Cervantes again I'm going to crawl up there and puke on you. We're the same age, Nash."

"Damn it, Maria—"

She let out a raspy laugh, loving that she'd gotten Nash Larson to curse since it was a rarity. He'd been working for her parents for two years. Before he started working for the Cervantes family, he had done private security work for a year, and for eight years before that he'd been in the Army. Her father, Riel, had needed an outside security company to oversee one of his projects in Mexico two years ago and Nash had been assigned. After witnessing the man at work, her father had snatched Nash away with a hefty pay raise and better benefits. Now he was more or less a personal bodyguard/driver/fix-all man for her parents. While her dad often used Nash when traveling on business as extra security, he hadn't for his current trip since it was so short.

Nash let out a growl of frustration as the vehicle slowed to stop. Maria barely paid attention as she heard him talking to one of the security personnel outside the gated mansion where a very exclusive party was going on. She didn't need to listen, because she knew he was showing off her elegant gold-and-cream-embossed invitation. If it was any other event she would have bailed, but Bayside Community Center, where she worked, needed the donations that would come in from tonight. And there was one potential donor in particular Maria desperately wanted to talk to.

Maria had grown up with incredibly wealthy parents and they'd taught her to give back. They weren't exactly happy with her chosen profession, but they supported her career as a counselor. After getting a bachelor's degree in behavioral psychology and a master's in counseling, she couldn't imagine doing anything else. She was also the current acting director since her predecessor had suddenly died a couple of months ago. Until they found a replacement, she was in charge of the center. She'd thought the added responsibility would be overwhelming, but Maria found she liked the challenge.

Since her parents wouldn't let her arrive at the Westwood gala driving her Prius, she had a chauffeur. Any other night it would have been annoying, but there was no way she could operate heavy machinery right now. She'd stopped taking her over-the-counter anti-nausea medicine so she wouldn't be drowsy, but the side effect was that she was now nauseated. She was just impressed she'd managed to get dressed on her own.

The Westwood family wasn't originally from Miami, but California. They liked to do things over-the-top and a bit garish, but Maria didn't care. They were friendly, donated to local charities, and in addition to three food banks and another community center in Miami, Bayside was one of the recipients of donations from tonight. Which meant Maria had to be here. She was the public face for Bayside, and she took her position very seriously. Though it wasn't the only reason she was here. She also had to meet Joann Hood, an insanely wealthy woman who wanted to "talk numbers" in regards to donating money to Bayside. And this was the only time the eccentric woman could meet Maria. So here she was.

"You look like shit, Maria. As soon as we stop, I'm texting your mother to let her know I'm taking you home." Nash's expression in the rearview mirror was almost scolding.

Despite also being twenty-nine, he sometimes seemed light-years older. She put a hand to her unsettled stomach before continuing. "One hour. That's all I need." Or she hoped it was. "And I'll be fine. Just don't take me through the main entrance." There would be a silly red carpet and photographers hoping to snap shots of some of the politicians and possible celebrities. She definitely wasn't newsworthy, but there would be an extra crush of people there and she knew there was another entrance.

"I wasn't planning to," he growled. "And I'm not letting the valet take the SUV. I'll be waiting in the parking area. Call or text when you're ready and I'll pick you up." The driveway leading to the main house was long and winding. Instead of following the drive to the left where it curved, Nash continued straight until they reached one of the service entrances. There was more security there, but after a quick conversation with someone Nash clearly knew, they were allowed past.

"You know him?" she asked, glad her voice sounded stronger. If she could get some decent face time tonight, it meant she'd get an invite to next year's party and Bayside would be on the list to continue receiving donations. Since it was the first year she'd received an invitation, she wasn't taking any chances by not showing up and insulting the Westwoods. With the economy the way it was, Maria had to look out for her kids. That community center was the only form of family some of them had and she refused to let them down.

"Yeah, when I heard you were sick I called the security team and found out who was on duty. I still don't think you should be here."

Maria sighed, not bothering with a response as Nash pulled up next to a catering van and parked. "Didn't you used to work for the same security company as that guy?" Even though the man at the front gate wore a suit, the one who'd just stopped them had been wearing a black Polo shirt with a familiar security logo and cargo pants. He'd also had a gun strapped to his belt, much like ones the police wore. Definitely not trying to hide what his job was for the evening.

"You know I did. Don't try to change the subject."

"Argue all you want. It's a battle you'll lose."

He muttered something under his breath as he got out of the vehicle. She straightened her long violet gown and glanced down at herself. While she hadn't been able to do much with her hair other than curl it and leave it loose around her shoulders, her dress was so gorgeous it wouldn't matter. Before she could open the door, it swung open and Nash held out a hand for her.

Even though his smile had an almost boyish quality, there was nothing boyish about the man in front of her. His normally relaxed face was drawn into a tight expression and his blue eyes flashed with annoyance. Well, he wasn't her freaking boss and certainly not her boyfriend—though she had a feeling he had a small crush on her, so she tried not to get too angry. Despite his obvious annoyance he held out an arm and helped her from the vehicle.

Normally she wouldn't need help, but tonight she was

taking it. She'd already gotten the okay from her doctor that she wasn't contagious—otherwise she wouldn't have come.

"You—"

"Nash, enough," she snapped, at the end of her rope. She was barely keeping it together and didn't have the strength to argue.

"I was just going to say you look beautiful," he muttered, his ears turning pink.

"Oh, thank you." Not wanting things to get awkward, and because she wanted to get inside as soon as possible, she stepped away and held up her simple clutch purse. "I've got my phone. As soon as I'm ready to leave, I'll call you and meet you right out here." She glanced toward the part of the mansion they were parked outside. There was a security man standing by a side door, clearly waiting for her. In the distance she heard music and voices, but it was fairly quiet where they were. Mansion probably wasn't the right term for this home. It was more like a castle. Sure, her parents were wealthy, but the Westwoods were in a totally different stratosphere. They were like royalty. "You're sure I can go in through there?"

"Yes, I worked it out ahead of time." Nash tilted his head in the direction of the man patiently waiting. "Cormac will lead you into the party and . . ." He glanced down at his cell phone when it pinged. "Your mother is waiting by the ice sculpture of a dragon. It's near the . . . room of weapons?"

"Room of . . . oh, right, tell her I'm on my way." She was so grateful her mother had taken to texting Nash instead of her. The thought of trying to focus on tiny letters now . . . no, thank you.

She was also glad she knew where the weapons room was. Well, sort of. Once she got in the house, she was certain she could find it. The Westwoods were huge history buffs and had an actual room designated solely to display various weaponry from the last two centuries. It was actually pretty cool, if a little weird.

Her heels clicked along the pathway up to an intimidating man wearing all black. His expression was cool and assessing as he took her in. "Normally I'd check you for weapons, but Nash says you're all right." He opened the door for her with a sharp gesture that said she should enter.

Okay, then. They stepped into a kitchen that was humming quietly with activity. Various people were setting up dessert trays and plates, but this definitely wasn't the main kitchen. Maria had been in that one a couple of years ago.

"This way," the security man urged, clearly not liking that he was her temporary escort.

All the food aromas were overwhelming, so she hurried after him but not before snagging a mini-cupcake. She hadn't eaten in hours and sugar probably wasn't the best idea, but she needed something in her stomach. Shoving it in her mouth, she stumbled trying to keep up with the long-legged man. He took her down a lot of hallways and too many turns to count. Dizziness swarmed her as they reached the end of a hallway that emptied out into a room where well-dressed people were all drinking either champagne or martinis. Female servers were walking around wearing ... *holy shit, they were wearing only body paint made to look like tuxedos*. Maria blinked and tried to listen as Cormac gave her directions to the weapons room. Nodding politely, she fought more nausea as he hurried away while talking into an ear mic. Before she'd taken two steps, a woman named Greta Dobbins latched onto her arm.

Maria guessed the white-haired woman was pushing eighty. She was slim, a few inches taller than Maria and had a wicked grip. "Hi, sweetheart. I just saw your mother. She told me you were coming and I'm just so glad. It's amazing how much time you dedicate to that center. Of course I know your dear mother wishes you'd settle down and get married...."

Oh, sweet Lord. Maria's eyes and ears glazed over for a moment as she took in the room. Two sparkly chandeliers hung above them and classical music was being piped in from somewhere. About forty people in long, glittery gowns or tuxedos talked among themselves. She recognized some of them, but not everyone. Pasting on a smile for Mrs. Dobbins, she tried to focus on the woman's face, but bile rose in her throat as clamminess descended over her bare skin. Oh yeah, that cupcake had been a really bad idea.

"Maria, you don't look so good." Without waiting for a response, Mrs. Dobbins practically dragged her across the marble floor to the other side, ignoring the calls of her husband.

"Where are we going?" She had no strength to fight the other woman and just prayed there was an empty bathroom nearby.

Taking Maria by surprise, the older woman opened a door Maria hadn't even seen. It was built into the dark wooden paneling, seamless in its architecture. "We're going to find you a place to rest and I'm going to get your mother. You shouldn't be here. She told me you weren't feeling well, but you look like death warmed over. I know how dedicated you are to that center, but this is unacceptable."

Even though she wanted to argue, Maria knew the woman was right. Her face and hands were clammy, but sweat had started to blossom across her forehead, between her breasts, and down her back. A chill snaked through her body, making her shiver. "How did you even know about that door?"

Mrs. Dobbins chuckled. "Oh, I know a lot about this place. Flora has me over for tea at least once a month. And that's code for martinis, but don't tell Kingsley. It'll just raise his blood pressure and . . ."

Everything went hazy again as the woman chatted away. Maria had forgotten how close Mrs. Dobbins was with Flora Westwood. Even though the woman was a total chatterbox, Maria was incredibly grateful for her kindness now. While she wasn't sure where they were, she couldn't hear the crowd of people anymore and her heels were silent against the carpet runner covering rich wooden floors. Finally the woman stopped in front of a door and peered inside. She let out a breath. "Okay, no one's in here. There's a bathroom right through there." Mrs. Dobbins pointed even though Maria couldn't see past the heavy door. "I'll be back in ten minutes, I promise. Just as soon as I find your mother."

"She's near a dragon ice sculpture." Or she had been. Maria wasn't even sure how much time had passed since she arrived. Or where she now was in the giant house for that matter.

"Make that twenty minutes, then." The woman ushered her into what turned out to be a lavish guest room. It was dimly lit with a Tiffany table lamp, but Maria didn't care about the decor.

Racing toward the door Mrs. Dobbins had pointed out, she hurried inside and barely made it to the toilet before she threw up the cupcake. After a while she was just dry-heaving, her stomach muscles cramping in agony.

The bathroom lights were too harsh, so she crawled to the entry and shut them off. Relief rolled over her at the sudden dimness. There was still a little stream of light from the bedroom, but her eyes didn't hurt anymore. Wanting to call Nash and her mother, she opened her clutch but frowned when she didn't see her phone. The purse wasn't big, so it wasn't as if it was hiding in a compartment. Which meant it had likely fallen out in the SUV. Lord, she couldn't even remember if she'd brought it. Everything about tonight and the last few days was too fuzzy. Cursing, she snapped the clutch shut and struggled to her feet. She shouldn't have come tonight and didn't want to be lying on the floor when Mrs. Dobbins and her mother found her.

As Maria entered the bedroom, she heard loud male shouting coming from the next room. At least three men. Two had accents she couldn't place, but one man she recognized. She hadn't even realized he'd be at the party. She wanted to say hello but was too ill to face anyone and the shouting was escalating.

A low hum of panic threaded through her veins as the shouting suddenly increased in volume. She couldn't make out the words, but then everything got quieter. Curious and worried, she hurried to the shared wall and pressed her ear against it.

"You cannot bomb the Freedom Tower last," the familiar voice said, anger punching through each word.

"We can and will. It is symbolic," an accented voice growled.

"No, the tower is a landmark. If you try to wait it won't work. The police, the FBI, and everyone hunting you will . . ."

Maria wavered on her feet. Bomb the Freedom Tower? Panic gripped her with sharp talons, digging into her chest until it was hard to breathe. Blood rushed in her ears and she shook her head, trying to clear her panic so she could hear better. Straining, she held her breath as a man talked about bombing other Miami landmarks and individual residences. Some names she recognized well. Then there was a vile curse about hating the United States and all it stood for.

When everything suddenly went quiet, she pushed away from the wall. What the hell had she just heard? Terror was like a live thing inside her, pushing back most of her nausea. She had to tell someone what she'd just heard. While she didn't recognize two of the voices, she knew the third one. And it scared the holy hell out of her that a man she knew, a man she *trusted*, was involved with . . . whatever was going on.

Her gaze landed on the door, but she backed away from it. There was no way she could exit through it. What if she ran into one of those men in the hallway? Looking around the unfamiliar room, she hurried to a double panel of ceiling-to-floor curtains. Peering behind one of the thick silk panels, she realized the curtains covered two French doors.

When she untwisted the lock, the sound seemed overpronounced in the stillness even though she knew no one could have heard it. As she slipped outside onto the small balcony, the cool air rushed over her skin and a chill snaked through her that had nothing to do with the weather or her sickness.

Glancing around the expansive moonlit acreage, she looked for a guard or any signs of life. *Are you freaking kidding me?* The place had to be crawling with extra security.

Maria slipped off her heels and hurried across the small stone patio outside the room she'd been in. Immediately her feet hit grass. It was cool under her toes, but nothing could calm her right now. Pure panic raged through her as she hurried across the yard. Even through all the trees, on all sides she could only see a wall of hedges engulfing this place. Heading east across the yard in what she thought was the direction in which Nash had originally parked, she picked up her pace. She still felt shaky and nauseated, but nothing could stop her now. The hair on the back of her neck rose as another fear set in. What if someone had seen her leave that room? Or was watching her right now?

Those men had been serious about the destruction they meant to cause. She had to get help.

When she reached one of the giant hedges, a small sliver of relief slid through her. It wasn't an actual wall, just thick bushes, which she could slip through. At this point she didn't care what was on the other side. She just had to escape from this place and get to the limo. Her phone should be there, and more important, Nash would be able to help.

As she tried to find an opening large enough that she could shove through, a rumble, then a horrific blast filled the air. She spun around, heart in her throat. Not truly comprehending what she was seeing, she felt her stomach pitch when a giant ball of orange flames tore through the sky, engulfing the west and east side of the mansion.

Another rumble ripped through the air as the place

started crumbling in on itself. Her mouth opened, but no sound came out as the knowledge that her mother had been in there pierced through her numbed mind. Darkness edged her vision, but she started to run toward the fire, needing to get to her mom, when another ball of flames tore through the night sky. Her entire body trembled under the impact, heat warming her despite the distance from the building. She blindly reached for something to hold her up but collapsed to her knees as her legs gave way. Tears streamed down her face as, unable to help, unable to breathe, she watched the place implode on itself.

Though she tried to fight it off, the darkness that had threatened to overtake her earlier suddenly claimed her as she passed out.

Chapter 2

Agent: a person officially employed by an intelligence service.

Maria held her phone to her ear as she listened to her dad talking and tried to rein in her tears. The sheets of the hospital bed beneath her were surprisingly soft, and the scent of flowers from the two dozen bouquets and baskets filling her large room gave off a too-sweet aroma. All of it made her want to throw up. And it had nothing to do with her previous flulike symptoms, which her body had finally kicked.

Her mother and hundreds of people were dead, she was in the hospital because the doctors had been worried she might have a concussion—though they'd now ruled that out—and she was barely keeping it together. She also couldn't remember anything from before the explosion. Hell, she couldn't remember much of anything from yesterday. Not even leaving for the fundraiser. But she knew she'd been there because she'd woken in a rumpled formal gown as paramedics lifted her up on a stretcher, talking about how it was a miracle she was alive. Waking up like that had been a nightmare of confusion and panic. Of pure freaking terror.

But the real nightmare was learning her mother was really gone. She'd already lost her older brother in Afghanistan. To lose her mother too . . . she swallowed hard. God, why couldn't she remember anything? The doctors said her mind was blocking out what she'd seen as a defense mechanism and that she might eventually get her memories back. Eventually wasn't good enough.

"We're leaving now, sweetheart. I'm sorry I'm not there with you. . . ." His voice broke, her normally rock-solid father faltering.

"I know, Dad," she said, her own voice thick with un-shed tears. "Just get home safely. Nash is here, so don't worry." Well, he was outside the hospital room, not with her. She closed her eyes as if that could block out the reality of the situation.

Her father said something else, but it barely registered. After they said their good-byes, she hung up and laid the phone on the bed next to her thigh. Her chest ached so bad she just knew it was about to crack open. Her mom . . . no, she wouldn't even think about what had happened.

Not here. Not when she was about to have a break-down of epic proportions.

Forcing her body to obey her when all she wanted to do was curl into a ball and cry until she passed out, she got up. Cool air rushed over her exposed back and back-side as her feet hit the chilly linoleum floor. She wasn't wearing any panties and the hospital gown wasn't cover-ing much of her. She didn't care.

Right now she didn't care about much at all.

Sometime when she'd been asleep her dirty, rumpled gown had been removed from the room. And someone had left a small bag of clothes on the bench by the window. No doubt Nash had brought her something to wear. He'd been in to see her a few times, but she'd asked him to leave each time. She felt like a complete bitch because she knew he just wanted to help, but she didn't care. Nothing could help, and being alone with her pain was the only way she could cope right now.

Feeling as if she were a hundred years old, she'd started unzipping the small brown leather bag when the door opened. As she turned to look over her shoulder, she found Nash, a uniformed police officer, and another really tall, thuggish-looking man entering.

Her eyes widened in recognition. The tattoos were new, but the *thug* was Cade O'Reilly. He'd served in the Marines with her brother. They'd been best friends and her brother, Riel, named after her father, had even brought him home a few times. But that was years ago. Eight to be exact. It was hard to forget the man who'd completely cut her out of his life after her brother died, as if she meant nothing to him.

Cade towered over Nash—who was pretty tall himself—and had a sleeve of tattoos on one arm and a couple on the other. His jet-black hair was almost shaved, the skull trim close to his head, just like the last time she'd seen him. He was . . . intimidating. Always had been. And startlingly handsome in that bad-boy way she was sure had made plenty of women . . . Yeah, she wasn't even going there.

She swiveled quickly, putting her back to the window so she wasn't flashing them. Reaching around to her back, she clasped the hospital gown together. "You can't knock?" she practically shouted, her voice raspy from crying, not sure whom she was directing the question to.

"I told them you weren't to be bothered, but—"

The police officer cut Nash off, his gaze kind but direct. "Ms. Cervantes, this man is from the NSA and needs to ask you some questions. As soon as you're done, the doctors will release you."

"I know who he is." She bit the words out angrily, earning a surprised look from Nash and a controlled look from Cade.

She might know Cade, or she had at one time, but she hadn't known he worked for the NSA. After her brother's death he'd stopped communicating with her. Her brother had brought him home during one of their short leaves, and she and Cade had become friends. *Good friends.* They'd e-mailed all the time, for almost a year straight. Right near the end of their long correspondence, things had shifted between them, had been heading into more than friendly territory. Then after Riel died, it was as if Cade had too. It had cut her so deep to lose him on top of her brother. And now he showed up in the hospital room after her mom's death and wanted to talk to her? Hell no.

She'd been harassing the nurses to find a doctor who would discharge her, and now she knew why they'd been putting her off. They'd done a dozen tests and she didn't have a brain injury. She wasn't exhibiting any signs of having a concussion except for the memory loss, but the doctors were convinced that this was because of shock and trauma at what she'd apparently witnessed.

Nash started to argue, but the cop hauled him away, talking in low undertones, shutting the door behind them. Leaving her alone with this giant of a man.

Feeling raw and vulnerable, Maria wrapped her arms around herself. The sun had almost set, so even standing by the window didn't warm her up. She just felt so damn cold. Because of the room and probably grief. And now to be faced with a dark reminder of her past was too much.

Cade took another step toward her and nodded politely, as if he barely knew her. "I know it probably means nothing coming from me, but I'm sorry about your mother." His voice was deeper than she remembered. Masculine and oddly soothing.

Her first instinct was to snap at him that he was right; it didn't mean anything. But her mother had raised her better than that and she didn't want to lash out at everyone she came in contact with. It made her feel even worse. She knew that was why she'd been doing it to everyone. If she was in pain, she wanted the world to be in pain too. But that was wrong. Plus, she wanted to know why Cade was in her hospital room. "Thank you. . . . So you're with the NSA now?"

Nodding, he took a few steps closer and pulled out something that looked like a wallet. He flipped open the black leather holder to show her his identification. As if she needed the proof.

She looked at it, then at him. Even if it was fake, she would have no clue, but she doubted a Miami police officer would have escorted him into the room if he were a liar. She had a ton of questions for him, like why the hell he'd fallen off the face of the earth eight years ago, but knew now wasn't the time. "Why does the NSA want to talk to me?" She'd talked to the police and even Homeland Security, but she knew nothing about the NSA or why they would possibly want to talk to her. She couldn't remember anything about last night.

How many times did she have to explain that? Instead of returning to the bed she sat on the bench and crossed her legs. She felt ridiculously small compared to him when he remained standing, but she didn't have the energy to walk back to the bed.

"I just want to go over the events of last night, Ms. Cervantes."

Tears burned her eyes as she glanced down. "Really? You're going to call me Ms. Cervantes? That's lame, Cade." Not to mention that hearing "Ms. Cervantes" made her think of her mother, which made her want to cry.

He cleared his throat. "I'm sorry, Maria. What do you remember about last night?"

"Nothing. It's a giant blank, so I'm sorry you've wasted your time." She was tempted to ask him why he even wanted to know, but at this point she figured asking questions would invite more conversation. And that cop had said when they were done, she could go home. Right now she couldn't handle this glaring blast from her past on top of everything else. It was too surreal that the man who had hurt her so badly, the man she'd lost many tears and sleepless nights over, was in her hospital room.

He watched her carefully for a long moment before sliding a plastic chair a couple of feet in front of her. He turned it around and straddled it, the almost relaxed position putting her at ease, though she wasn't sure why. There was something about him that was calming, which was weird because of his large size and her residual anger. She glanced at his tattoos, watching the muscles and tendons flex when he crossed his arms over the back of the chair.

"Tell me what you do remember."

She took a deep, ragged breath and was glad her voice didn't shake when she answered. "I remember waking up in what looked like a war zone. Or what I imagine one would look like. Everything around me seemed to be burning. The Westwood mansion was ... in ruins and two paramedics were putting me in the back of an ambulance. They put an oxygen mask on me and I must have fallen asleep or passed out again, because the next thing I remember I was waking up in a hospital room to find a doctor shining a tiny flashlight into my eyes." She wrapped her arms around herself.

"What's the first thing you remember before that?"

She closed her eyes and tried to concentrate. "I remember ... throwing up." She opened her eyes then. "I was sick for over a week and staying home from work. The last week I've been at home and miserable and my last memory is clutching onto my toilet at home and hurling." A gross image, but he didn't seem to mind and she didn't care what he thought. She started to stand then, needing to get the hell out of there and away from this man and his mesmerizing eyes. And she was pissed he was in her room after he'd ignored her for almost a decade.

When he didn't make a move to get up, fury detonated inside her. Her mother was dead, her father was still out of town, and she had a lot of arrangements to make while she tried not to fall apart. She had nothing to tell the authorities that would be of any use. How could Cade not realize that? If she knew something she'd tell them. Anything to bring her mother's murderer—or murderers—to justice.

"Why were you outside out of the blast zone when the bombs went off?" he asked calmly, still not moving.

Something about his tone rubbed her the wrong way. "What? If I don't even remember being at the party, how the hell would I know why I was outside?" Now she was definitely shouting.

The question was insulting, like something those stupid news reporters asked people after they'd suffered a tragedy. Like "How do you feel now that your home is destroyed and you've lost all your earthly belongings?" Did they really expect people to say, "Great, freaking fantastic!"? Her hands and voice shook as she turned to her bag. She didn't give a crap if she gave him a show of bare ass.

Maria was going home right *now*. Unstoppable tears started falling down her face as she tore her bag open and yanked out a pair of jeans. Not bothering with underclothes, she managed to tug them on beneath the hospital gown as sobs racked her body.

He was saying something in that deep voice, but all she could think was that her mom was dead and she'd never see her again. Never get to tell her good-bye or how much she'd loved her. Never get to feel her mom's warm embrace around her. As Maria pulled out her sweater, she heard the chair squeaking against the floor behind her.

"Maria—"

She whirled on him then, her sweater clutched to her chest. She couldn't see him clearly through her tears, but she lashed out with her top, slapping him in the shoulder with it. It made a soft smacking sound. "Fuck you! You show up after eight years of silence the day after my mom dies with no explanation about . . ." She trailed off, unable to formulate any more words. Her throat clenched impossibly tight as she tried to stop the avalanche of pain.

"Fuck, I'm sorry. Maria, I just—"

Covering her face with her hands, she collapsed onto the bench and didn't bother trying to stop the tears. It was impossible now. She'd known once she let them loose it would be like a hurricane of grief. And she didn't want this man, of all people, to see her so weak. She just wanted him gone.

Taking her completely by surprise, two strong arms wrapped around her shoulders, pulling her into a tight, comforting embrace. Beyond being able to feel embarrassed, Maria buried her face in Cade's chest and sobbed until her throat was raw and she was simply shaking.

She wasn't sure how long she cried like that, clutching him like a lunatic, but she eventually became aware of him rubbing her back in soothing strokes as he quietly held her. Though she knew her tears weren't dried up completely, part of her edginess had eased as she pulled back from him. Probably because she was now utterly exhausted.

When she saw the wet marks on his shirt, embarrassment flooded her as she looked down at her hands. She couldn't even look him in the eye after that insane display. "I'm sorry about your shirt," she muttered as she started wiping the wetness from her face.

"You lost your mom. You don't have anything to apologize for. I'm sorry I just showed up without warning, but ... I requested this assignment. When I saw your name as the only surviving guest, I thought maybe it would make things easier for you. I know it's not much, but I have to talk to you, so why don't you wash your face and I'll see if I can get you some food and something to drink? You might not want to eat, but you need to. It'll help take the edge off your fatigue." His voice was so calm, his expression unreadable as he watched her.

He seemed so solid. Unbreakable. Like the kind of person you could count on in any situation. She'd thought that once; then her brother had died and it was as if she didn't exist for Cade anymore. The dark thought made her frown, but she nodded and stood. "Okay, just give me a few minutes."

"Take your time. I'll get some food."

Once he was gone she stood on shaky legs, as if she'd just run a marathon. It was hard to wrap her mind around the fact that Cade O'Reilly had just walked back into her life. She rubbed a hand over her face. This was too much to deal with.

Her cell phone vibrated against the bed, the sound amplified in the suddenly quiet room, making her jump. In between the hospital's tests and talking to her father almost every hour, she'd been fielding calls pretty much ever since she'd woken.

When she saw the familiar name on the caller ID, she almost rejected the call. But he'd contacted her so many times today she felt she owed it to him. "Andre, hi."

"Honey, I'm so relieved you're okay, but I'm so sorry about your mom." Andre Moran was a family friend, someone she'd made the mistake of going on a couple of dates with.

She cringed at the use of the endearment but kept her voice civil. She knew he was just being kind. "Thanks for calling, but I can't talk long. A bunch of different government agencies need to talk to me and I can't keep them waiting any longer."

"About what? Where's your father? Why isn't he—"

"He's not back in town yet. And I can't talk about anything else." Sort of the truth. "Listen, I've got to go, but someone will let you know about..." She cleared her throat, forcing the words out. "...the funeral arrangements."

After another few seconds of talking, she managed to get off the phone and it rang again. This time it was Wayne Gregory, an ICE agent she was friends with thanks to her work at the community center. Though she was tempted to answer, she set the phone back on the bed and headed for the attached bathroom. She needed to wash her face and try to get herself under control. After she talked to Cade and was discharged, she had too many things to take care of, including contacting the community center and figuring out who was going to be covering for her while she handled her mother's funeral.

At that thought, more tears sprang up, so she splashed cold water on her face. Just a little bit longer and she'd be out of there.

Cade leaned against the wall outside Maria's room and tried to steady his out-of-control heartbeat. Eight years wasn't enough time to make him forget her. The last time he'd seen her, she'd been twenty-one and he'd been twenty-six. He hadn't been good enough for her then and he sure as hell wasn't now.

Volunteering to take such a small role in the NSA's mission to track down the terrorists had surprised Cade's boss. But when Cade had seen Maria's name on their intel file, he knew there was no way in hell he couldn't *not* talk to her.

Maria was petite with luscious curves and unique amber eyes he'd been captivated by from the moment he'd met her. Everything about her features should be too big to be attractive—her eyes, her full bottom lip. The combination, however, was ...stunning.

He felt like an asshole even noticing her right now. On the job he was always in control. Always. He did his duty well and, while he'd worked with attractive women before, he never mixed sex and work. Hell, he couldn't remember the last time he'd had sex. Which probably explained his intense reaction to Maria. He inwardly snorted as he tried to lie to himself. That attraction had always simmered for her, and she was the last woman on the planet he should be noticing. Not after he'd cut ties with her. Not after . . . He abruptly shut down his train of thought and forced himself to focus on the present. He'd nearly drowned in guilt over what he'd done eight years ago. Thinking about it now wouldn't help him any.

Some caterers, hired drivers, and other entertainers not in the mansion when the double explosion went off had survived, but she was the only partygoer who was alive. The NSA wanted to know why.

His gut told him she wasn't involved—not with her own mother being dead. He'd stake his entire fucking career that Maria would never be involved in something so horrific. The raw grief rolling off her had been real. The kind even the best actor in the world couldn't fake.

Out of habit, Cade rubbed a hand over his skull trim. For some jobs he'd grown it out, but this was his preferred cut. Now he wished he hadn't recently buzzed it, because he knew what he looked like. A thug with tattoos and so far below Maria's league it was embarrassing. He'd gotten most of the tattoos after her brother died as a way to channel his pain. Cade's appearance was something he'd always used to his advantage. He was large and scary looking, which was often a plus when he wanted information. When he threatened people they just assumed he could back it up with violence if necessary. Which he could. Of course he'd never threaten Maria.

He'd read the file the NSA analysts had compiled on her from front to back, and the woman was like a freaking saint. She came from wealth but worked at a community center where she donated most of her time and energy. Hell, she even helped out with the accounting department for free when they needed her. Most of that he'd already known, though. He didn't want to grill her for more answers when she might not have them, but he had no choice. And he'd rather be the one talking to her, not some random agent who wouldn't care about making her comfortable.

The city of Miami was in a state of shock over the deaths of so many of its elite. Politicians and some well-known movie stars had been buried in the rubble of the mansion, so it was a media feeding frenzy. Since Maria was the only person to survive, he'd been assigned—well, volunteered—as her shadow until his boss was absolutely positive she knew nothing.

If she was suffering from shock—the doctors seemed to think so since she had no brain injuries—memories of the night could come back later. Probably in the form of nightmares. Or at least that was Cade's personal experience. He didn't know one man who'd been to war who didn't suffer from nightmares or at least vivid dreams.

The assignment to shadow her was considered more or less a babysitting gig, something that most agents didn't want to deal with. He didn't consider guarding her a problem, though. The only thing he worried about was staying objective. Just being in her presence again was already messing with his head.

Sighing, he radioed the Miami PD officer to tell him

he could return to guarding Maria's room. Cade knew the pseudo-bodyguard, Nash Larson, would be there too, and while the guy rubbed Cade the wrong way, he wanted Maria to have extra security. Until she was cleared of everything, and they figured out why she'd survived, he wanted her under constant surveillance. If it was temporarily provided by someone Maria trusted, it would make Cade's job that much easier.

Once the cop and other man rounded the corner at the end of the hallway, Cade stepped away from the door and headed for the elevators. First food, and then he'd hopefully get Maria to talk.

*   *   *

Date: September 25, 2006
To: Cade O'Reilly
From: Maria Cervantes
Subject: Care package

Hey, jarhead (ha!), be on the lookout for a care package. It's big so you won't miss it. Sent you guys a Christmas tree since you can't come home this year and wanted to make sure it got there early. I thought the shipping was going to cost a small fortune, but it wasn't too bad. My mom wanted to send ornaments too, but I wasn't sure if they'd make the trip to A-stan, so I skipped them. But I included string and popcorn baggies. Figured you guys could string popcorn together like Riel and I did when we were kids.

I know e-mail access is hard for you, but if you get a chance, let me know you're okay. I've been worried about you the past couple weeks. BTW, I got the silk shamma you sent me. I think that's the right spelling. Anyway, it's beautiful and so thoughtful, thank you. I'm wearing it everywhere this "winter," but as a scarf, not around my head. It's been in the fifties the past couple weeks, so I've had an excuse to.

I know e-mail access is temperamental over there, but I hope you can write back soon and that you're doing well. I miss you. I'm going to e-mail Riel right after you, but tell my brother I miss him too.

xo,
Maria

Chapter 3

Terrorist act: the calculated use of violence against civilians in order to achieve goals that are political, religious, or ideological in nature.

As he drove down a quiet Miami street, Mihails Balodis glanced over at his friend Oto when the other man's cell phone buzzed once with an incoming message. Perhaps the word "friend" did not accurately describe their relationship. They'd been imprisoned together, had been through hell together after Latvia had gained independence from the U.S.S.R. decades ago and the Baltic States had been plunged into abject poverty. Oto was his comrade, his brother in arms. He trusted no one more than him. Not true, he trusted no one *but* Oto.

Not even the men in the vehicle with them right now. Yes, they followed the same cause and had similar ideals because of their unified hatred of the United States. Many had sworn they would die for Mihails and their beliefs but . . . he still did not completely trust them.

"What is it?" he asked in their native tongue as he pulled up to a stoplight. The Miami sun was close to setting, taking the wretched heat and humidity of the day with it. He hated this city with its flashy people, beaches, and whorish lifestyle. Just like the rest of the country.

Oto frowned at his phone, then pulled out his iPad. "Our contact says there was a survivor from the party. A guest, not a worker. It's on the news. She was found alive—near our exit point."

That could mean nothing, but he wanted to know everything about the woman. No one should have survived that blast. Instead of asking questions he knew Oto wouldn't have answers for yet, he continued driving, following the speed limit exactly as his friend pulled up a news site. They were still getting used to having so much technology right at their fingertips. The younger generations of Latvia had embraced technology, getting their hands on anything they could, often through the black market.

But Mihails was from a different time, and though two of his men were geniuses when it came to hacking, neither Mihails nor Oto had the understanding of it, or the desire, to become too embroiled with its use. Technology had its purposes, however, including being able to look up anything at any time. Oto likely could have looked up the story on his cell phone, but the screens were so small Mihails didn't understand how anyone watched videos on the things.

As he steered the nondescript white SUV into a grocery store parking lot and parked far away from other vehicles, Oto handed the flat-screened device over to him. In the rearview mirror Mihails saw two of his men lean forward. The two in the very back remained where they were, silent but listening.

A tanned blond woman came on the screen, talking about a lone female survivor of the horrific act of terror at the Westwood mansion. Americans knew very little of terror firsthand. But that was about to change. No longer would they live in their protective bubbles where the problems of the world were something they simply watched on the television screen.

"What is she saying?" Janis, one of the men from the back, asked in Latvian. "She is speaking too fast." The man understood some English, but he wasn't as fluent as Mihails and Oto were.

"There's a survivor from last night. She comes from a well-known, wealthy Miami family. She is . . . uh, the reporter is saying she works with poor children. She's being questioned by the authorities and not speaking to reporters." Oto stopped then, watching the screen as a picture of the survivor was displayed.

Mihails stilled at the sight of the traffic-stopping beautiful dark-haired Hispanic woman. Her eyes were a unique amber color, just like his dead sister Alise's. The similarities in their features ended there, as his sister had been tall, lean, and blond, but the eye color was jarring to his senses. He felt such a visceral reaction to those eyes, as if he were looking at Alise.

"Our contact and the news say she is talking to the police. She should die," Oto said in his usual clipped tone. The man believed in killing first and worrying about consequences later.

"No." His immediate response surprised Oto as much as it surprised himself.

His friend's only outward reaction was a slight raising of his blond eyebrows, but that was enough of a reaction from the other man for Mihails to know he'd startled him.

"We have more important targets. Our focus is on

them. We should not divide our resources for someone who may not be important." He detested explaining himself, but sometimes it was necessary.

Oto's lips pulled into a thin line, his eyes growing hard as he subtly glanced behind them without moving his head. Mihails understood what his friend was communicating even though he hadn't spoken aloud. Mihails could never show weakness.

Oto was right. He'd just had a momentary lapse, something that happened when he thought of either of his sisters too often. He turned in his seat to face Janis. "Contact Oskars. He's to go to the hospital. See what he can find out. If she knows anything, eliminate the problem. If he can't eliminate her at the hospital, track her until he can." Without waiting for a response, he turned back around and watched as Oto pulled up the schematics for the home they were about to infiltrate.

They had reviewed this strategy what felt like a hundred times. Everything had to go according to plan, so even if the others didn't like it, he believed in being prepared.

Last night had been a success, since he had eliminated twenty of the prominent men involved in the sexual slavery ring that had killed one of his sisters. It didn't matter that his other sister still lived; she would always have to live with the shame of what had been done to her. If his sister Ieva had known what Mihails would do after she'd told him about her suffering, she might never have told him names. Luckily she had no idea that he and Oto would burn the world down to avenge them.

The collateral damage at the mansion had been worth it. A small part of him experienced remorse, as there had surely been innocent lives taken, but to eliminate so many men who deserved it under one roof had been efficient and necessary.

It would also send a message that this reprehensible crime would not be tolerated. At first the world would not understand the reason for the destruction last night, but after today, it would start to become clearer. At least to some of the American authorities. For that, he was glad. He wanted them to know why so many of their people had been killed. If they had been doing their job in the first place, policing the slave trade and protecting the innocent, Alise might still be alive and Ieva would still be innocent.

The United States had pushed so hard for the fall of the Communist regime and the independence of the Baltic States, but once Latvia had been freed from the Iron Curtain, its economy had shriveled. And no one had stepped in to help his country find solid footing. Especially not those who had pushed to "free" them and inadvertently turned them into slaves. While he'd been working abroad in the U.K., trying to earn a living for his family, his sisters had come to America for work.

And found hell instead. Now he was going to rain hell down on those who had hurt them.

He blinked, pushing those thoughts away as Oto looked at him expectantly. His friend had asked him a question. *Focus,* he ordered himself. His friend's words slowly trickled through the haze of his thoughts. "Yes, we go in right at dusk. Bastard won't know what hit him."

Oto smiled coldly, the look of a man who had killed before and would do so again with no compunction. And Mihails knew that Oto loved Ieva. His friend had never admitted it to anyone, but Mihails knew because of the way his expression changed when he talked about her. It was so slight, the strange softening around the eyes of a man who had never smiled. It was another reason he trusted his friend. This job wasn't just political; it was personal for Oto too. For men like them, there was no separation of the two, something Americans would understand soon.

Mihails looked at the clock on the dashboard of the SUV, then outside. He already knew exactly what time the sun would set. They had planned everything perfectly, synchronizing their watches. Only ten minutes left until they would leave the quiet parking lot.

"Oskars will be at the hospital in five minutes. He will leave a message with you if there is a problem," Janis said quietly from the back.

The three others remained quiet as Mihails nodded and tried not to watch the clock or the setting sun. They had prepared for this, and compared to last night this would be an easier mission, but he had learned never to get cocky. His men were the same. They all had military training and had all been to a Russian prison at one time or another. They understood patience and planning.

As the parking lot lights flicked on, Mihails steered his team back out of the parking lot and onto another quiet side street. Tucked away in a quiet Miami neighborhood with high fences and a security guard, his target thought he was safe. Everyone who lived there thought they were.

The interior mood of the vehicle changed as he pulled up to the security gate. It was almost palpable, the focused readiness of his men.

Mihails had his Makarov in his right hand as Oto rolled the window down using the controls on the center console.

The security man, wearing all-black fatigues, frowned as he looked through the interior of their SUV and started to speak, but Mihails lifted his weapon and shot him in the head. The man dropped like a stone, falling behind the half door of the small security building. A clean kill. One bullet right through his skull. Mihails's suppressor covered what would have been a loud boom.

They had to move fast now. Mihails pulled forward until the passenger door was lined up with the half door. He watched in the rearview mirror as Kristaps slipped from the vehicle and entered the small gatehouse.

Seconds later, the security gate opened up and Mihails pulled through, leaving Kristaps behind to take the man's uniform and act as security until they had completed their mission. It was why Mihails had gone with a head shot. They needed the security uniform as clean as possible. The wealthy people here likely wouldn't look too closely at a uniform or a new guard.

No, the type of people who lived here were more concerned with their own pampered lives. With one act Mihails was going to remind them they were just like everyone else. Breakable.

Chapter 4

Wet work: expression for murdering or assassinating someone; "wet" alludes to the spilling of blood.

M aria stood in front of the virtually inactive nurses' station two floors above her hospital room. It was much quieter on this floor, and while guilt pricked at her that she was being discharged without talking to Cade first, she ruthlessly shoved it down. She didn't owe him anything, and the more she thought about his presence here, the more pissed off she got.

"We're going to get you home so you can rest," Nash said quietly, as if sensing her mixed emotions.

She knew the last thing she should be concerned about was talking to an old friend turned federal agent when she'd just lost her mother, but something deep inside nagged at her. A raw, edgy sensation she couldn't shake. When she was washing her face, she'd had the sharpest flash of knowledge that she needed to tell *someone* ... something. Which was frustratingly vague.

She was mentally and emotionally exhausted, and seeing Cade after so many years had rattled her even worse than she already was. His presence just reminded her of how callously he'd cut off contact with her. How after her brother died and she'd assumed Cade would be the one person there for her, he'd just decided she wasn't important anymore.

"First we need to go to the center." Her voice was still raspy and tired. Maria knew Nash would argue, but she didn't want to go home just yet. Way too many memories of her mother there. She knew she couldn't avoid it forever, but she wanted to put it off as long as she could.

Nash opened his mouth, his boyishly handsome face set in frustration, but instead of arguing, he just nodded. "Okay."

Maria blinked, surprised he wasn't fighting her, then realized he wouldn't right now. Not after everything that had happened. Before she could respond, a broad-shouldered, striking doctor with a warm tan and liberal amounts of white peppering his dark hair rounded the nearest corner and strode down the short hallway toward them, wearing the standard white coat. Dr. José Famosa. Head of neurosurgery and a family friend.

His expression was soft as he came up to her and gathered her into a tight hug. "I'm so sorry about your mother," he said. "I . . . the whole city has been rocked by this horror."

Her throat tight, all she could do was nod into his shoulder. He was about the same height as her father, so at five feet eight, he didn't dwarf her when he hugged her. After a few moments he pulled back and Maria quickly blinked away the threatening tears. "Thank you for discharging me."

His expression darkened before he nodded politely at a nurse who handed him a clipboard. He started scribbling furiously as he spoke. "I don't care what government branch they are. No one has the right to hold any patient hostage when she's ready to be discharged. If you knew something that would help them, you would tell them. They're stupid not to realize it." She could tell he was angry because his accent grew thicker, shakier. Slightly older than her parents, he'd come over from Cuba at ten years old, fleeing the Communist regime after his teacher parents had been killed for being moderates. She knew that was why her father had called him to get her discharged. He had a strong dislike for any government interference.

"Do you know of a quiet exit?" Nash softly asked José.

The doctor looked at him and nodded. "Yes. Reporters were swarming the front of the ER and many of the exits, but the police have been diligent in getting most of them across the street." He handed the clipboard to the nurse, then motioned for them to follow him down a nearly deserted hallway.

The ballet-slipper-type shoes Nash had brought for Maria made soft squeaking sounds against the floor, but the other two men were silent as they headed down the quiet hallway. This was a recovery ward, which explained the lack of activity.

Moments later, José opened a stairwell door for them and motioned inside. "This goes all the way to a parking garage. I don't know where you're parked, but there should be minimal activity in this garage, if any." He looked at Nash sharply. "You can find your vehicle, then pick Maria up from the garage. She's fine to leave, but I want her resting and I don't want anyone recognizing her."

To Nash's credit, he merely nodded. Maria knew he didn't take orders often, but right now she understood both men just cared about her well-being. Something she appreciated. After giving the doctor another quick hug, she and Nash hurried into the stairwell.

"The NSA will probably be angry." Okay, not probably. She didn't know why she even cared, but for some reason she felt guilty about slipping out before talking to the tall . . . sexy Cade O'Reilly.

She hated that after so long he was even better looking than she remembered. After the way he'd comforted her when he hadn't needed to, it made her feel even crappier. She'd felt like a total maniac sobbing against his chest, but he hadn't made her feel stupid. She could justify leaving all she wanted, but right now she just couldn't deal with talking to him or anyone else.

"Who cares? That guy was a dick," Nash muttered, hoisting her bag higher on his shoulder. "You know him?" he asked cautiously.

Maria was surprised he'd waited to ask her, but she nodded. "Yeah. He served in the Marines with Riel. My brother," she clarified, though she figured he understood even though he'd never met her brother. He'd died long before Nash came to work for her father. "It was a long time ago, though." She didn't offer up more than that.

Thankfully Nash didn't push her. "Let me just get you to the center, then your parents' place. Your father will be home by the time you finish at the center and . . . he needs you, Maria." Nash's jaw clenched tight and for the first time Maria realized how absorbed in her own grief she'd been. Nash loved both her parents. Unlike her father, her mom had treated Nash more like a son than an employee, always fussing over him. Maria had always thought it was because she missed her own son so much.

"Oh, Nash, I'm . . ." She pulled him into a tight hug as

they reached the second-stairwell landing. "You're right. I'm sorry."

He was stiff in her embrace, but he gently patted her back before stepping back. "Let's get you out of here. I don't want any of those reporters getting a hint you've been discharged. I know Dr. Famosa won't say anything, but any one of those nurses could leak it."

A shot of adrenaline surged through her. Nash was right. They needed to get out of the hospital as soon as possible. Something else was bugging her, a nagging, dark feeling in the pit of her stomach she knew had nothing to do with her grief. It was almost as if something bad was about to happen.

She just couldn't figure out what.

Cade set the two water bottles and a foam food container on the bench by the window in Maria's room. There hadn't been a police officer outside or her bodyguard. Cade had already had an analyst run everything on Nash Larson. Former Army, clean record, all-around stand-up guy. Cade hadn't been able to figure why the man rubbed him the wrong way until he'd returned and found Maria gone. He didn't like the way Larson looked at Maria in that proprietary way. It had been subtle, but something about it pissed Cade off even though he had no right to care if there was something going on between the two of them.

His focus was on the job. And now finding Maria since she'd clearly left. The bed was rumpled, but her bag was gone. He wanted to be pissed. Under normal circumstances he would be, but she'd gotten under his skin a long time ago. Then when she'd let her guard down, crying against him, it had pierced him. Normally crying women didn't faze him. But her grief had just been so raw it punched right through his senses. He'd lost his mom at a young age and too many friends during his time overseas, so he understood what she was going through on a certain level.

Tracking her down would be a pain in the ass, but easy enough once he pinged her location. He pulled out his cell and had started to text one of the analysts so they could track her cell phone when the bathroom door slowly creaked open.

All the hairs on Cade's arms stood up in alert as the heavy wooden door moved, inch by inch. Withdrawing his weapon, Cade silently sidestepped until he was half-hidden behind the curtain partially drawn around the empty bed.

A dark-haired man wearing tan cargo pants, black boots, and a black long-sleeved T-shirt stepped from the bathroom with a fluid stealth. He scanned the room for signs of life, his gaze landing almost immediately on Cade's partially blocked body and raised weapon.

Instantly the man grabbed the rolling food cart and shoved it toward the bed before yanking open the door to the hall.

Cade blocked the cart and raced after the man, his weapon still clutched in his hand.

He could have wounded the intruder, but he didn't know shit about the man or his intentions and wasn't going to open fire in a hospital. In the hallway two nurses were helping a pregnant woman who'd clearly been knocked down to her feet. The suspect was about twenty yards ahead, shoving people out of the way as he barreled through.

Shouts of alarm filtered down the crowded hallway as

Cade dodged around a man in a wheelchair. "Federal agent, move out of the way!" he shouted, the path instantly clearing as people either jumped back against the walls or were pulled back.

Cade kept his focus on the dark-haired man, who disappeared into a stairwell at the end of the hallway. Though there was a team of agents outside the hospital, he didn't have anyone as direct backup because this was basically a babysitting job.

Apparently Maria knew something or someone thought she did. Or maybe the terrorists just wanted everyone from the party eliminated. Cade wasn't sure. All he knew was that he had to find this guy before he escaped.

He tapped his earpiece once to activate it. "This is O'Reilly. Unknown man escaping down eastern stairwell of main building, two possible exits. Parking garage or Fourteenth Street. Wearing tan cargo pants, black fatigues, and boots. Dark hair. A little under six feet." He'd memorized the layout of the hospital and entire surrounding area, never knowing when he might need it. "Need backup. His intent is unknown, but he was hiding in Maria Cervantes's hospital bathroom. Likely armed." Whether the man was or not, Cade and everyone he worked with always assumed people had weapons. Their lives depended on that assumption.

He received two affirmatives as he made it to the stairwell door. Slowing his pace, he kicked open the door before carefully sweeping inside with his weapon. Pounding footsteps sounded below him, echoing off the walls.

Cade took off again, his heart rate pounding as he sprinted down the stairs. Fear for Maria raged through him as his legs ate up the distance, a new surge of adrenaline spiking through him. That man had been in her room for a reason, and the way he'd fled told Cade it wasn't to give his condolences.

A loud slam from below and a flash of light illuminated the stairwell for a moment. Cade looked over the railing of the second floor to see the exit door into the street swinging open. "He's taken the street exit."

"On our way. We're on foot because of the fucking traffic," Taylor White growled, her normally sweet Southern accent filled with frustration.

Cade didn't respond as he neared the exit. Once again he slowed his pace in case of an ambush. It was unlikely, considering the man was running for his life, but Cade wasn't going to risk a bullet in the head because of carelessness.

With the relative cover of the stairwell, he scanned the area for others as he spotted the man sprinting down the sidewalk. "He's running northwest, heading for Bayshore!" They couldn't let him get that far.

Cars whizzed past them on Mercy Way, but Bayshore Drive was a main street full of vehicles, and with the news coverage, there were even more people at the hospital now. The guy could open fire into the crowd or carjack someone. Hell, he could have a bomb strapped onto him. After last night Cade couldn't take the chance. "Freeze or I shoot!" he shouted, his voice carrying across the nearly thirty-yard gap between them.

The man faltered and stumbled as he looked over his shoulder.

Twenty yards now. Cade's weapon was raised, aimed right at the guy.

"We're behind you," Taylor said, sounding slightly winded.

The guy must have seen the backup, because his eyes

widened and he turned around, darting into the street in an attempt to escape. A truck barreled toward him. For a long moment everything seemed to move in slow motion.

Shit. No. Cade reached out as if he could stop him, but an oncoming truck slammed into the man, sending him flying across the pavement as the vehicle screeched to a stop.

He didn't think it was a suicide attempt; the man had blindly been trying to escape. Weapon drawn, Cade approached the man, who was flat on his back, unmoving. Not even his chest rose and fell. His eyes were open, but Cade had seen enough dead people to guess this man was done for. There was a preternatural stillness only the truly dead possessed.

Out of the corner of his eye, he watched as the driver jumped from the delivery truck. "He just jumped out in front of me! I'm sorry—"

"Sir, step back to your vehicle." Taylor and two other agents hurried onto the scene. As Taylor guided the civilian away, Cade knelt by the man and checked his pulse. There was Cyrillic writing tattooed on his neck, the ink thick and dark.

As he'd suspected, no heartbeat. He sheathed his weapon when he was sure the guy was dead. After a quick search of the body, Cade came away with two blades. No guns, though. Blood had started to pool around the dead man's head, and a cloudy film had already started to seep into his eyes as he stared vacantly into space. *Just great.*

Cade looked up at a newer agent he'd never worked with before. The guy was maybe twenty-three and not part of Cade's elite unit made up of only former military.

"Call it in and get this body hauled away before the locals show up. Run his prints and someone better contact me with a name ASAP." He looked over at Taylor, whom he'd worked with before. He trusted her to follow through.

The tall woman nodded. "I'll call you."

He jumped up and raced back toward the hospital, ignoring the few cars that had already stopped on the street. People had just parked and were getting out of their vehicles to see what had happened. Under normal circumstances he would have stayed to help wrap up the scene and deal with any locals if there were problems, but he had to find Maria.

The dead man had what looked like prison tattoos on his neck, had been carrying two knives, and he'd been in Maria's room.

Cade told himself he'd be this worried about any potential witness, but the thought of seeing Maria again, of keeping her safe, spurred him into moving faster. Whether she could be an asset to the case or not, the woman was in danger. He'd failed her before in ways he didn't want to think about, and there was no way Cade was letting anything happen to her.

* * *

Date: October 6, 2006
To: Maria Cervantes
From: Cade O'Reilly
Subject: re: Care package

Got the Christmas tree and I hate to tell ya, but Riel's already eaten the popcorn. I'm also pretty sure he stole all that jerky you sent me. I've got an idea for ornaments, though, using empty shell casings, soda cans, and small

lightbulbs. I'll send you a picture once we get the
ornaments set up. Everyone's gotten a kick out of us
putting it up so damn early. It was really sweet of you to
send, thanks. It's a nice reminder of why we're in this
shithole. Sorry my e-mails have been sporadic lately, I'm
back on base for a while so you should hear from me
more often. At least for now.

Glad you got the shamma, the amber color reminded
me of your eyes. Will you send me a picture of you
wearing it?

Cade

Chapter 5

Babysitter: a bodyguard.

Lingering in the midst of the growing crowd of onlookers, he watched the scene outside the hospital unfolding with interest. One of Mihails's men was supposed to have taken care of Maria Cervantes, but it looked as if he had failed.

He'd met Oskars once and knew the dead man was part of Mihails's crew. Of course, he might have actually killed her, then been killed afterward. There was no way to find out just yet.

He frowned as an unmarked black van pulled up to the scene where a group of men and women not wearing any identifying badges or uniforms had sectioned off the area. Though the crowd at the hospital was growing, everyone was keeping a respectful distance from the accident.

A team of men dressed in black retrieved the body before putting it in the back of the van. It all happened so quickly, as if they'd choreographed the scene. The news crew on the other side of the hospital hadn't even arrived yet. The way these men moved in so quickly and efficiently told him they had to be working for some government agency in a clandestine capacity.

As the van steered away, two police cruisers were pulling onto the street. One of the cruisers immediately blocked the van's exit, a cop exiting and drawing his weapon, though not raising it at the van. From the other cruiser, a uniformed cop exited and then cautiously approached the van. The window rolled down and after a few minutes of speaking to whoever was inside, the cop waved the van through. Just like that. There had been no questioning of the driver who'd hit the man, nothing. At least not from the men in black.

That was . . . interesting. At the sight of a news van pulling up behind one of the police vehicles, he turned and headed back to one of the parking garages. The last thing he needed was to be seen on camera. He seriously doubted he would even be noticed, but right now he had to be cautious. He pulled his ball cap low and kept his pace steady as he broke away from the crowd he'd been using as cover.

As he walked, he texted Mihails what he'd witnessed with one of his disposable phones. The Latvian would definitely want to know that his man had been killed and then taken away by unknown government men. And he had no doubt that it was the government. Which branch, however, was a mystery.

"I can't believe you're here. You need to be at home resting or . . . something. You just shouldn't be *here*." Leah Davis sat across from Maria's desk, leaning back in the comfortable leather chair that had seen better days. Her long blond hair was pulled back into a ponytail and she wore her standard faded jeans and a V-neck T-shirt. Today's color was blue. Like her eyes.

Maria hadn't actually come to work, but to escape. "I

know. I just didn't want to go home. Because as soon as I pack a bag, Nash is taking me to my parents' house." Which would be filled with constant reminders of her mother. Maria leaned back in her own chair and rubbed a hand over her face. She still couldn't get the strange feeling in the pit of her stomach to go away. Maybe seeing Cade after so long had affected her more than she'd realized. Either that or there truly was something she desperately needed to remember. Because the truth was, the fact that she'd been outside during the blast was odd. She'd had no reason to be where she'd been found.

"Honey, I know. It might be good for you to be surrounded by her things, but . . . if it's too much you know you're more than welcome to stay with me. God knows you've been there for me through bad breakups and my own mom . . ." Her voice and expression were gentle as she trailed off.

It was true. Leah was more like a sister to her. They talked on the phone multiple times a day if they weren't working together, and she couldn't count the number of times they'd drowned their sorrows over glasses of wine because of some loser. Then when Leah's mom committed suicide, Maria had practically lived with her friend until she'd gotten back on her feet. "Thanks, but no. I need to be there for my dad. I just can't figure out *why* I was outside when the explosion went off. It makes no sense." She'd been wondering about that even before the police, Homeland Security, or the NSA had asked her. She looked at Leah imploringly, as if her friend had any magical answers. The not knowing was driving her crazy.

"It's a miracle," Leah said softly.

Maria had no response. Sitting in her office at the center always made her feel better, more grounded. She spent so much time here it was more like home than her actual house. The framed art on the walls had been done by various kids who'd grown up and moved on to become contributing members of society. One had actually become a famous artist. The others were just drawings, sketches, or paintings by kids who'd needed an outlet. Looking at all the art made with love, she swallowed hard.

"Yeah," she muttered, feeling like anything but a miracle. She felt almost guilty that she was alive and so many others weren't. Pushing up from her chair, she stood, ready to head home, when the door to her office opened.

Javier, a sixteen-year-old boy who'd been coming to the center for the last two years, ever since getting out of his older brother's gang, stepped inside. Wordlessly he strode toward her and around her desk and pulled Maria into a tight hug. Tall for his age, he was almost six feet and still growing. With lanky arms he held on, though he was slightly shaking. "We're all so sorry about your mom, Miss Cervantes."

Afraid she'd burst into tears again, she patted his back gently. "Thank you, Javier. That means a lot."

When he stepped back, he blinked rapidly, looking impossibly young for just a brief moment. "Some of us were here last night when the . . . when it happened. We all knew you'd gone to the party and thought . . ." He swallowed hard as he trailed off.

It had taken almost six months to get Javier to open up to her or show any kind of emotion other than anger, but once he had, she'd learned more about his past than she figured anyone knew. She also understood that she and Leah were mother figures to so many of these kids who didn't have one. Now they were more alike than ever before—but at least she'd had a loving mother for so many years. It was something she'd be holding on to. "I'm okay and not going anywhere, I promise."

He nodded, clearing his throat. "If it's okay, most of us want to come to your mom's funeral."

Crap, now she really was going to cry. "I'd really like that." Maria struggled to continue, but thankfully Leah stepped in.

"Come on, Javi. Maria's got to get out of here. She needs rest, but I'll make sure everyone is informed about the service and when Maria will be back." She looked at Maria and mouthed *I'll call you* over her shoulder as she steered the teenager out.

Sighing, Maria decided to suck it up and go to her parents'. It was a Tuesday evening, so it was quiet at the center, but she'd left Nash in the gym with two adult volunteers and a group of twelve-year-olds to help referee their basketball game. Mainly because she'd needed some space from him too and she'd wanted some privacy with Leah. That was one of the great things about her friend: she didn't need to fill silences, but she was always there no matter what. Maria had just wanted to soak up her friend's support and strength while she could. Before she'd taken more than two steps from the desk, her door opened again and Cade O'Reilly strode in.

And he was pissed. Alarm jumped inside her.

She could tell he was trying to mask his anger, but it was clear in the harsh lines of his handsome face. Her heart jumped into her throat at the sight of him and she chastised herself for even noticing. But it was hard not to. The man was huge and sexy. Sweet Lord, why did he have to be so damn good looking? And why did she have to notice? The sleeves of his long-sleeved shirt were pushed up to his elbows, showing off all those tattoos and muscular arms. Arms that had held her gently while he comforted her. Inwardly cringing, she met his piercing gaze. "How did you find me?"

His jaw clenched once before he answered, his expression almost incredulous that she'd asked. "I work for the NSA. Tracking your phone wasn't hard. Why did you leave?"

"I . . ." She thought about lying, saying there had been some emergency, but the lie wouldn't come. "I didn't want to deal with your questions or seeing you. I felt like an idiot after I blubbered all over you and was afraid I'd do it again." His expression softened but she continued. "I'm exhausted and back at the hospital I didn't think I had any answers for your questions then."

He went impossibly still. "What do you mean *then*? Do you *now*?"

Sighing, she leaned against the front of her desk, perching on the edge of it as she wrapped her arms around herself. "It's probably nothing. I still don't know why I was outside the Westwood mansion when paramedics found me. I keep trying to rack my brain, but I can't think of any plausible explanation for why I would ever be outside and that far away from the party. And when I was washing my face at the hospital, I got a flash of . . ." She splayed her hands out in front of her as if that would help explain what she didn't understand herself. "I don't know. I was scared, like I needed to tell someone *something*. And I know that makes absolutely no sense to you, because it doesn't to me either." Maria stopped talking, feeling like she was rambling as he pinned her with that intense stare.

He was silent for a long moment, assessing her, as if he was deciding if she was telling the truth or not. Finally he spoke, his voice grim. "I caught a man sneaking out of your bathroom at the hospital. He was armed with two knives. When he saw me, he ran and died during the chase—an accident, he was hit by a truck. On my way here one of our analysts informed me that according to his fingerprints, he's a known Latvian terrorist. He's worked with various outfits before, but things always end bloody with any group he's been involved with. He likes to kill his victims with a blade. I can't know the specific intent for sure, but he was in your hospital room for a reason. My guess is either you know something or someone thinks you do."

Maria was glad she was sitting down as Cade's words slammed through her, because the blood drained from her face, leaving her dizzy. She didn't know what to make of what he'd just said. Or what the hell she was supposed to do about some dead terrorist wanting to kill her. What did it mean? She'd been so convinced she didn't know anything, but that nagging feeling in the pit of her stomach was growing out of control. Now it was even worse.

"So what happens now? I can't tell you what I don't know. I wasn't lying when I said I don't remember the explosion or even being at the party. I wish I did, though, believe me. Wait a minute, if the man who was in my room is a known terrorist, then it stands to reason his partner or partners would be in Miami, right? He can't be working alone, and if some guy was sent to kill me or whatever—"

Half smiling, he stepped farther into the room, his posture slightly relaxing. "My guys are already looking into all his known associates, how he got into the country, and what he's been doing since he got here."

None of which Cade would tell her, she was sure. "Oh." She still wasn't certain what that meant for her.

As if he read her mind, he said, "From this moment on, I'm more or less your shadow. I know it's less than ideal especially with everything you're dealing with. For that, I'm sorry. You can either fight me and I can tail you twenty-four-seven or you can suck it up and deal with me until we figure out why that terrorist wanted you dead. Because believe me, after reading his file, I have no doubt in my mind you would be if you'd stuck around the hospital. You're a hell of a lot better off having me as your shadow right now." There was a dark note in his tone she couldn't read.

It was impossible to believe that someone wanted her dead. But a couple of days ago she would have said it was impossible that someone could get away with such a horrific act of terror in her city, or that her mother would have died in a terrorist attack. When her brother had died in Afghanistan, it was one of the hardest things she'd ever had to deal with. But their family had always known that his death was a possibility. Someone didn't go to a war zone without that knowledge. The way her mom was killed was too surreal.

And Cade was right. There was no solid reason for a terrorist to be hiding out in her hospital room other than malicious intent. "If you're my shadow, what does that mean? I have a lot of things to take care of, including dealing with my mom's funeral." Her throat tightened at the thought, but at least she didn't break down into tears again.

"Consider yourself in my protective custody. I'll basically be your chauffeur and bodyguard." There he went again with that tone she couldn't read. Everything about him was hard to read. He barely moved when he spoke, keeping his body rigid and under control.

The man in front of her would never be anyone's chauffeur, and something told her he would consider bodyguard duty more like babysitting. But the surprisingly subtle look he raked over her told her he didn't exactly view being her shadow as a chore. She could tell he liked what he saw, even though he was trying not to show it. For just a brief moment, his green eyes filled with something that looked a lot like desire.

For her.

It was hard to be sure, but she'd been on the receiving end of an appreciative male look enough times to recognize it. Maria was surprised she could feel anything other than grief, but a ribbon of awareness curled through her before his gaze completely shuttered, blocking her out again.

Just as he'd cut her out of his life eight years ago.

Shoving those thoughts from her mind, she went over her options. If someone wanted her dead, being guarded by an NSA agent was smart. Not to mention that nagging feeling in her gut. She wasn't sure what it was, but it wouldn't go away. Maria rarely ignored her instincts. So many people did and it was often a huge mistake.

Sighing, she nodded as she pushed up from her desk. "Fine. Nash drove me here, so I need to let him know I'm leaving with you. I need to drop by my house to pick up some things before heading to my parents' home. You can ask all the questions you want on the way. Maybe something will break through," she muttered, frustrated with herself that such a huge block of time was missing from her memory. It was scary not to be able to remember. She also had some questions for Cade and hoped she found the courage to ask them.

"Don't push yourself too hard," he said softly. "Give yourself time. Your memories might come back."

"I hope so." The door opened before she could say anything else and Nash paused in the doorway.

His gaze zeroed in on Cade as the two men more or less sized each other up. The dislike between them was so vivid it surprised her since they hadn't known each other before today.

"Nash, I need to go with ... Mr. O'Reilly to answer some questions." Saying "Cade" seemed too familiar somehow even if they had been friends at one time. "There's been a ..." She struggled to find the right words, still trying to swallow the fact that a terrorist had been in her hospital room.

Cade took care of it for her. "I'm going to be guarding Maria from this point forward. She's of interest to the NSA and we feel she needs our protection. Nothing about her schedule will change, but I will be with her twenty-four-seven." His expression was almost challenging as he spoke to Nash.

Her friend was no better, his glare cutting. "Of interest? What the fuck does that mean?" He stepped into the room, a foot from Cade as they faced off.

Maria didn't feel like explaining everything to Nash right now. Not when she just wanted to get her belongings and go see her dad. He should have landed and would be home soon. Even though she was dreading going to her parents' home, she needed to be there. Stepping between them, she placed her hand on Nash's forearm. "Nash, just let me go with him and get these questions out of the way. If I can somehow help find who killed my mom, I'm going to." Saying the words made her feel stronger. She might be torn up inside, but she desperately wanted to help if she could. She wanted justice for everyone who had been ruthlessly killed.

It was clear Nash wanted to argue, but he nodded tightly. "Fine. I've got my cell if you need me."

Yeah, he definitely wanted to say more. He shot Cade an almost threatening look before stepping out of her office.

Both men hovered behind her, making her feel awkward as she locked up. The walk down the quiet hallways until they reached the side exit was even more awkward, the tension excruciating. The exit door automatically locked behind her. One of the volunteers or employees would have a key card to get back in if necessary, but after a certain time of day the locks were set to stay closed for the safety of everyone.

Maria kept pace with Cade, following him to a black SUV with tinted windows. Nash headed for his vehicle but waited until she and Cade pulled out of the parking lot before leaving. She also noticed that her home address was already programmed into Cade's GPS—which told her he'd planned on her cooperation. She wasn't sure if that should annoy her or not.

"I'm sorry, he's just worried about me, that's all," Maria said into the relative quiet of the SUV. Normally she didn't feel the need to fill silences or apologize for anyone, but she did now. After the way she'd run from the hospital—though now she was thankful she had—then Nash's hostile behavior, she wanted to smooth things over with Cade. If they were going to be spending any amount of time together, things had to be civil.

"He's more than just worried about you," he said, his voice wry. "And no more 'Mr. O'Reilly.'"

"I know, I don't know why I called you that." It was just as lame as she'd accused him of being in that hospital room. She shifted against the leather seat, staring out the window at the passing traffic. Dusk had fallen and the city was bright and vibrant with life. It was just another seemingly normal night in Miami, but nothing would ever be normal again. "So, what questions do you have for me?"

"Why were you at the Westwood party and how did you get there?"

She was fairly certain he already knew the response to both those questions, but she answered anyway. "Bayside Center depends on donations. So that's the main reason I was there. And Nash, who you must know works for my parents, drove me. I was sick for days and was too weak to drive, but I needed to attend the party."

Cade was silent for so long she turned away from the window to glance at him. He had a strong profile, a chiseled jaw that was so defined it seemed almost unreal. It was as if the man had literally been cut from stone and molded into flesh and bone. Absolute perfection. Finally he spoke, but his question surprised her. "What is Nash to you?" His voice was rough, uneven.

She frowned. "I already told you he works for my parents. Well, just my dad now." And that knowledge cut so deep it drew blood. "But he's my friend. Why?" Cade couldn't think Nash was involved with anything, could he? The two men had looked at each other as if they'd wanted to rip each other to shreds.

"Were you two ever involved?"

A burst of anger erupted inside her. "Are you kidding me? How is that important?"

He shrugged in what he might have hoped was an apologetic gesture—though probably not—and shot her a hooded look as they pulled up to a stoplight. Yeah, there was nothing apologetic in his eyes. Just a simmering . . . heat. Right below the surface.

Annoyance and awareness battled inside her for dominance. Her annoyance won out. "You don't get to ask me questions like that. *Ever.*" At one time he would have been justified but not now. Not when it had nothing to do with the terrorist attack.

Gritting his teeth, he turned back to the road and she forced herself to look away from his profile—and to ignore the strange butterflies in her stomach.

Right now she shouldn't be able to feel anything other than grief, and it confused her that this man made her experience something more. Just like when she'd been twenty-one and relatively inexperienced. As she once again looked out the window, she could feel sleep closing in on her. Maria tried not to doze, but her body refused to listen.

Even with everything going on and so many scary unknowns, she knew that she was safe with Cade. It was a bone-deep certainty, and right now exhaustion was winning out against the voice in her head ordering her to remain awake. He'd stopped asking her questions, so she decided to close her eyes for a few minutes. At least until they got to her house. She'd worry about her mother's funeral, terrorists who wanted to kill her, and her memory loss problem later.

*   *   *

Date: October 7, 2006
To: Cade O'Reilly
From: Maria Cervantes
Subject: Picture

All right, what do you think? I had my mom take this picture of me out on the lanai. When I told her I was sending it to you, she said this better be the only type of picture I send because she'd heard about boards where military guys posted naked pictures sent by exes. Can you believe that? I don't know if I'm more disturbed that she knows about those boards or that she thinks I'd send naked pictures in the first place.

You should have seen my dad's face when my mom just blurted that out over dinner. They both told me to tell you hi, BTW. When you and Riel get your next leave, they want you both to come visit. I hope you can.

I can't wait for Christmas break this year. I feel like I've been in college forever even though I'm almost done. I swear the closer I get to graduating, the longer it seems to take. Of course complaining about this to you when you're in a war zone makes me an asshole. How are things over there? I know you can't tell me details, but let me know if there's anything specific you want or need. A bunch of students from one of my business classes are getting packages together for soldiers for the holidays and we can do one for you. I'm already sending you something for Christmas (in addition to the tree), but I figure you won't say no to more things from home.

xo,
Maria

Chapter 6

Post-traumatic stress disorder (PTSD): a condition that may develop after a person is exposed to a traumatic event, serious injury, or the possibility of death; the symptoms vary but include recurring flashbacks, a numbing of memories of the event, and high levels of anxiety; a diagnosis may be given when symptoms continue for more than a month after the event.

Cade had more questions for Maria, but seeing her so peaceful and watching the steady rise and fall of her chest and soft breathing made him show restraint. She'd surprised him by dozing off so quickly, but he knew she needed the sleep. His gut told him she wasn't involved directly, but she had to know something. Otherwise that terrorist wouldn't have been in her room.

The NSA and pretty much every three-letter government agency was working on finding the bastards who'd bombed the Westwood mansion. His job was simply to check out this angle. Though there was nothing simple about being in close quarters with Maria Cervantes.

He still couldn't believe the jackass way he'd asked her if she'd been involved with Nash Larson. It had been unprofessional and not like him. His control was rock solid.

Always.

It was the way he'd learned to deal with life. He'd lost his mom at a young age and been sent to live with her brother and his wife. His aunt and uncle had been religious fanatics, but they'd taken care of him well enough. They hadn't been abusive, so he'd been fortunate in that regard. Still, they'd been adamant that he should be grateful he had a roof over his head, that he shouldn't complain about anything. Translation: He shouldn't expect warmth or love from them. So he'd learned early not to show emotion. Emotion equaled weakness. And any he'd had left when he turned eighteen had been drilled out of him by the time he finished boot camp.

Until he'd met Maria. She'd been twenty-one, so full of life and almost innocent in her view of the world. Home on leave with her brother, Cade had been smitten when they met. But as she was Riel's sister, there was no way in hell he'd have ever made a move on her.

But one night they'd all gone dancing at a local South Beach club, and Riel had left to hook up with some girl, and Cade had been left alone with Maria. They'd danced all night and when they'd returned to her parents' place—where he'd been staying with Riel—she'd kissed him. It had taken him so off guard he hadn't stopped her. Hadn't wanted to stop it until his sanity won out. She'd been surprised that he'd put the brakes on, but she'd also seemed to think it was a good idea. Probably because of her brother. They'd never talked about it afterward, so he didn't know for sure.

He'd left the next day with her brother, headed back to base, then the damn desert. But Maria had stayed in touch with him and it had been impossible not to write back. He wasn't sure when it had happened, but a couple of months after their correspondence started, he'd began to fall for her.

Hard.

Then Riel had been killed in action and everything in his life had gone to shit. The way he'd cut contact with her was fucked up. He knew that. But he hadn't known how to deal with the fact that he'd gotten her brother killed. She'd been devastated, but she hadn't known all the details of her brother's death. To continue their friendship had made him feel like a fraud, a liar. So he'd taken the coward's way out.

Now he was sitting in the same vehicle as her and feeling so far off his game he didn't know how to handle it. All because of a sweet woman with big amber eyes who wore her emotions right out in the open. It was disarming and scary. He still had some of the handwritten letters she'd sent him tucked away back at home in Virginia. And he'd printed off most of their e-mail correspondence. Hell, he'd memorized most of the letters, he'd read them so many damn times. He kept them in his safe along with other valuables. He'd never been able to get rid of them.

He rolled his shoulders once as he pulled down her quiet street. He needed to figure out what she knew and then get on with his job. Volunteering to talk to her had been a colossal mistake, because with her it was impossible to keep his emotions in check. As he neared her driveway, he dreaded waking her up.

When she started making frightened moans in her sleep, his protective instincts went into overdrive. He quickly pulled into her driveway and parked. Her head moved to the side so that it was tilted up toward him and her face was scrunched, as if she was concentrating. And she kept making those little sounds that pierced right through him.

He wanted to reach out and wake her up to comfort her, but paused, trying to figure out what the fuck was wrong with him. Before he had to make that decision, her eyes popped open and for one moment he saw stark fear shining in them. It was so visceral, her eyes almost glazed over as if she wasn't seeing him, but something or someone else.

Then she blinked and looked at him in confusion. Her breathing was erratic as she looked around the front seat, gathering her bearings; then she turned back to him. Those amber eyes were clear again.

"Are you okay?" he asked quietly, unable to stop himself from reaching out and tucking a wayward strand of her dark hair behind her ear. His fingers brushed her soft cheek and for just a moment she leaned into his hand before shaking herself and pulling back. He immediately missed the contact.

"I don't know. I think I must have been dreaming. I was running from something. Or to something. Then there was . . . absolute hell. Just fire and heat and destruction everywhere." Her pretty mouth pulled into a thin line as understanding settled into her gaze. "It had to be the explosion, right? I'm remembering what I saw, aren't I?"

Cade nodded slowly. "It's possible." He'd had enough nightmares of his own from previous missions with the NSA and when he'd been in the Corps to know that.

Sometimes shit came back that he'd never wanted to see in the first place.

She wrapped her arms around herself and rubbed her hands up and down her upper arms as if she was cold. "I'm sorry I fell asleep." He started to respond when an insistent buzzing sounded. Either a text or she'd turned her phone to vibrate and someone was calling.

He'd heard it go off a few times but hadn't wanted to wake her up. Whoever it was, he'd doubted they couldn't wait the twenty minutes it took to get to her one-and-a-half-story bungalow-style home.

Blinking away her sleep, she shook her head and reached down to the floorboard, where her small bag was. She fished her phone out and started scrolling through messages. He watched as her frown deepened and she kept swiping her thumb and finger across the touch screen.

"What is it?"

"I have half a dozen texts from my aunt and dad. My aunt took over like she always does and scheduled my mom's funeral for *tomorrow*. What the hell is she thinking?" she muttered. Maria rubbed a hand over her face, looking exhausted and close to breaking down again.

"Her sister or his?" he asked, remembering what she'd told him about her family through e-mails.

"Hers." She met his gaze, and the pain he saw in the dark depths sliced through him. "They were close and she probably thought she was doing me a favor. Hell, I know she just wants to help me and my dad out, but . . . she was *my* mom. And tomorrow is so soon. Too soon."

Unsure what to say, Cade rubbed the back of his neck out of habit. When he did, Maria tracked the movement of his arm, her gaze growing distracted as she watched the flex of his muscles and tattoos. It was brief, but the spark of awareness from her took him off guard. He doubted she was even aware of it. He cleared his throat, feeling out of his depth with her. "It's one less thing you have to worry about now."

"Yeah, I know. And my dad seems relieved." She sighed and shot off a couple of fast texts, her fingers flying over her screen faster than he'd ever seen anyone do. When she looked back at him, he had to resist again reaching out to comfort her. "It won't take me long to pack a bag. You don't have to come inside if—"

He snorted and opened the door. "I go where you go." Yeah, as if he was leaving her alone. Though he'd scanned the quiet neighborhood as he'd driven up and a team of agents had already canvassed the area not long after the incident at the hospital, he did another visual sweep as he pulled his weapon out. It was after dark and most houses had one or two lights on inside, and the street-lights along the street were bright. Nothing seemed out of place, though he wouldn't technically know. While he hated drawing his weapon in front of her, he'd rather keep her aware of the danger than worry about scaring her. The more aware she was, the more vigilant she'd be if he wasn't around.

As she came around the vehicle to stand next to him, her eyes widened when she saw his gun. "What's wrong?" she whispered.

"Nothing, just being careful. Do you see anything out of place? Any vehicles you don't recognize?" he asked as he placed his free hand on the small of her back. He kept his body half-positioned in front of her in a defensive stance.

He couldn't protect her from everything, but his guard was always up. One of the members of the team who'd checked out her neighborhood had radioed him that they were leaving as he was driving Maria back from the center, so he wasn't worried about a sniper or similar attack, but he believed in being careful.

When he saw the headlights of a vehicle coming down the street, he expertly maneuvered her so they were shielded by his SUV.

"Everything looks normal. It's hard to believe someone attacked our city so brutally just . . ." Trailing off, she stiffened as the vehicle he'd been watching pulled up next to the curb in front of her house. Cade started to push her down so she was completely protected, but she suddenly relaxed. "I know him," she said, answering him before he could ask the question.

"Who is he?" Cade still kept his body in front of hers and his grip on his weapon.

"Wayne Gregory. He's an ICE agent I've come in contact with a few times because of some issues a few of my kids at the community center were having. He's a friend, trust me." She sidestepped around Cade and started across the lawn as a black man in his late twenties, wearing a blue Polo shirt and khakis stepped out from the four-door sedan.

Cade kept pace with her, still scanning the street for other threats. ICE agents were part of the U.S. Immigration and Customs Enforcement Agency, which was part of the Department of Homeland Security. but Cade didn't know this guy. And right now he didn't trust anyone.

"Maria, I'm so sorry about . . ." The man's voice trailed off as he rounded the vehicle, his gaze quickly zeroing in on Cade and the weapon he held loosely at his side. The streetlights gave enough light that they were all illuminated clearly.

The man stopped and half turned in a defensive position, as if readying to get his own weapon.

"Cade O'Reilly, NSA. Maria is under our protective custody." He pulled out his ID and quickly flashed it before tucking it away.

"Wayne Gregory, ICE," he said cautiously, his gaze switching to Maria, who nodded.

"He's telling the truth, Wayne." She'd stopped next to Cade instead of continuing toward the newcomer, which alleviated some of his tension, but not by much.

Cade didn't like her out in the open. He tucked his weapon away as the other man's stance loosened and Gregory crossed over the sidewalk and the lawn to stand in front of them. His body language was nonthreatening, but Cade was still on the defensive.

"I'm so sorry about your mom. I saw what happened on the news and finally got hold of Leah. She said I just missed you, but you were heading home, so I thought I'd catch you." Eyeing Cade cautiously, he stepped forward and pulled Maria into a hug.

To Cade's annoyance, she returned the man's embrace tightly. He had no good reason to feel proprietary, but he didn't like the sight of her in another man's arms.

"Why are you here? You could have called her." Cade's voice was tight as he spoke.

Maria stepped back and they both turned to look at him.

"I couldn't get you on the phone," Gregory said to Maria, ignoring Cade completely. "I can only imagine how much you have to deal with now, but I wanted to let you know I'll help in any way I can. I heard on the news that your mother's funeral is tomorrow, so—"

"It was on the news?" Maria sounded shocked, but Cade wasn't.

That kind of information would have been leaked immediately by someone at the funeral home. The news stations were covering this story like rabid animals.

The ICE agent nodded, his expression grim. "Yeah, there are a lot of funerals tomorrow. I know you must be overwhelmed, but if there's anything I can do, let me know."

"I will. Thank you."

"Listen, I need to get Maria out of here. It's late and she's exhausted." Cade knew he sounded like a blunt asshole, but he didn't care. He wanted to get Maria out of plain sight.

Maria's eyebrows rose and she grimaced apologetically to her friend. "Cade is right—we need to leave—but thank you for coming by. I appreciate it. I promise I'll call you soon." She gave the man another quick hug before Cade practically pushed her toward her house.

Once they were inside, he ordered her to stay in the foyer while he swept the two-bedroom, two-bath house. It wasn't overly large, but it was filled with eclectic art and warm furniture reflective of the kind woman he knew she was. Just being under her roof made him miss her more. She'd still been in college and living at home when they first met.

"Your house is clear. Once you pack a bag we'll go to your father's house. I'm sorry I had to get rid of your friend like that." He wasn't, but he figured he needed to smooth things over in case he'd pissed her off.

"I'm not. I don't want to see or talk to anyone else

right now," she muttered before stepping into the living room and disappearing up the half-hidden stairs to her room. The master bedroom and bath took up the upstairs half-story part of the house. He could hear her moving around for a few minutes, the soft creaks and groans of an older house settling in, but when everything went suddenly silent, alarm settled into his gut.

Following after her on quiet feet, he paused outside the open door, where dim light streamed out. His weapon was drawn, but he immediately sheathed it in his shoulder holster when he saw her sitting on the edge of her king-sized bed with her back facing him. Other than the bed she had a giant vintage armoire and another large dresser situated to make the room seem as big as possible. The floor-to-ceiling curtains had been pulled back, which probably let in a lot of light during the day. He hadn't touched them before because he hadn't wanted to disturb her things, but with her light on and windows open, anyone could see in her room. He didn't like that.

On instinct and overcome by a deep-seated need to protect her, he drew them closed before turning to find her watching him with an annoyed expression.

"What is it?" he asked.

"I feel as if my freaking brain hurts. Every time I close my eyes I see fire and I'm consumed with the need to just run." The mix of frustration and fear in her voice was palpable. "I feel completely useless right now. Other than Leah, my mom is one of the few people I would normally call about something like this." Her voice cracked on the last word.

Cade sat next to her on the bed and nearly jerked back at the sight of the amber-gold scarf he'd given her eight years ago. It was wrapped around the lamp on her dresser, crisscrossed up the base and back down, making it look as if it was part of it. He hadn't noticed it when he swept her room earlier. She'd kept it? *Fuck*. He didn't know what to think of that.

Turning, he stared at a painting of the ocean during what looked like raging hurricane weather. Dark, stormy, and out of control. "My mom was killed when I was twelve. Murdered." The words were out before he could stop himself. He never spoke of her, so he wasn't sure why he did now. Years ago he'd told Maria that his mom died, but he'd never given specifics. "She could never find a decent boyfriend, but she was always looking for one. The last one she had killed her in a jealous rage." And he'd seen it happen. He left that part out, already having told Maria more than he'd told his closest friends.

Maria sucked in a deep breath and laid her hand over his where it rested on his knee. "I'm sorry."

He shook his head, not wanting her sympathy. Especially not now when she was dealing with so much grief. "I'm just saying it gets easier. Or . . . at least you'll eventually be able to compartmentalize the pain." Something she already knew from the loss of her brother, but Cade just wanted to give her some comfort.

"Just not today," she said softly.

"No." Definitely not.

She was silent for a while and even though he wanted to rush her out of there, he refrained. "When did you get all these tattoos?"

He was surprised by the change in subject and the question. Staring at her, he could feel himself being sucked into this tidal wave of . . . fuck if he knew what it was. But it made him feel as if he were drowning. She confused and scared the hell out of him and he knew she wasn't even trying. He wasn't going to answer her. Nope ... "After Riel died."

She sucked in a sharp breath at the mention of her brother but didn't respond. She simply watched him for a long moment, then gently squeezed his hand before standing. "Thank you for telling me about your mom. I feel like I'm so alone with all this, and I know that's not the case. People lose loved ones every day. It just sucks right now."

He nodded. It did suck. And it would for a long time. But Maria was strong and would deal with it. Cade missed the warmth of her hand over his, but he stood and withdrew his weapon again out of habit. He picked up her bag, then motioned toward the door. "If you've got everything, I want to get you to your father's. You'll have a small team of agents monitoring the property and I'll stay either inside or outside tonight. Whichever you prefer." He could have pushed it, but he wanted to give her the options. She needed some control in her life right now, and he understood that. Hell, he wanted to give it to her. Anything to help her cope.

She blinked in surprise as she picked up her purse. "Inside is fine. Their home is large, but don't you need clothes and other stuff?"

"I have a bag in the SUV." He was always prepared on missions. Everyone was. Wherever he went, he had at least three sets of clothes and toiletries.

"Oh." Her surprised expression didn't change, but she just nodded and headed down the stairs.

He followed after her, trying not to focus on the smooth sway of her hips. She moved so gracefully, everything about her calling to him on the most primal level. But she was dealing with so much shit and he was on the job. Something he'd never had to remind himself of before. Not to mention he'd forfeited the right to even look at her like this after he shut her out all those years ago.

Most of the lights in her house were still off, but he made a motion for her to remain by the foot of the stairs. "I'm going to check out the front window, make sure everything is clear."

She nodded and that fearful look he hated bled back into her expression. There was nothing he could do about it, though. After he turned off the light in the foyer and her outside porch light, the house was plunged into relative darkness. The half-open blinds in her living room allowed enough illumination for him to move around easily.

After letting his eyes adjust to the darkness, he moved toward the front windows but kept to the shadows. For a full minute, he peered through the slat blinds, watching any movement from the street. It was late enough that most people in the neighborhood would already be in for the night, but he'd seen two vehicles drive by. One red two-door car, and an extended-cab truck. It was either black or blue. Even with the bright streetlights he couldn't distinguish.

As he started to step back, the truck slowly drove by again. Could be nothing, but he waited, watching as it pulled under an overhanging oak tree across the street from Maria's house. Not directly across, but to the right.

Without waiting to see who got out, he hurried toward the hallway, motioning for Maria. "We're going out the back door."

"Is someone out there?" Her voice shook.

"Maybe. I don't want to take a chance." He didn't

want to get put in a situation where he and Maria were trapped in a house. Not when he didn't know how many men he was up against. If any. The truck could be a neighbor, or someone visiting a neighbor, but he wasn't taking the chance.

As they hurried down the hallway to the kitchen, he handed Maria her bag so he had full mobility. She didn't have any blinds in her kitchen, just sheer curtains that were pulled back, so he had complete visibility of the backyard. It was large, filled with trees and lush foliage, which could be hell if someone was waiting to ambush them, but he had to make a split-second decision and go with his gut.

Once in the backyard, he motioned toward the privacy fence she shared with one of her neighbors. Understanding, she nodded as he silently pulled the back door shut. Without him having to explain, she tossed her bag over the fence and started climbing, her movements nimble and fast. After another visual sweep of the yard, he followed after her.

Crouching low, he held a finger to his lips, then pointed to the back of the neighbor's yard. They had big floodlights on each corner of the house and he didn't want to trip a sensor if they had them.

From the back corner, they raced along the back of the fence to the opposite side, then climbed it into another neighbor's yard. He was thankful this neighbor had a chain-link as opposed to a wooden one.

"What's going on?" Maria whispered as they crept along the edge of the fence toward the back of the house.

"Maybe nothing. Someone drove by your house twice and then parked. I need to be sure they're no danger to you."

"This is insane," she muttered.

Cade didn't know if she meant him or the situation, so he didn't respond. The fence gate squeaked as he opened it, so he didn't bother closing it. Once they neared the edge of the front of the house, he held up his hand in the signal to stop. "Stay here. I'm gonna check it out." Cade didn't bother looking at her before he slipped over to the neighbor's house they'd just crept behind. Using the SUV in the driveway as cover, he looked around it and focused on the truck. It was dark and with the tinted windows, it was difficult to see much inside. It didn't look as though anyone was in the driver's or front passenger seat.

But one of the back windows of the extended cab was rolled down and every few seconds he'd see the bright red glow of someone taking a drag on a cigarette through the window opening. He couldn't see the individual, but he knew someone was there. When he looked at Maria's house, ice chilled his veins.

There was a dim light moving around in the living room. Like someone using a flashlight. Someone was inside, and the person in the truck was likely the lookout.

Cade weighed his options. He could head back the way they'd escaped and make an attack using her back door as a point of entry. But he didn't know how many people were inside. There wasn't time to call in a backup team. Whoever was in her house was likely looking for her or trying to find a way to locate her. Or, hell, maybe they were setting up a trap for when she came home. He'd have to call in a bomb squad to check her house out.

But first, he was going to plant a tracker on that truck, then get Maria to safety. Under other circumstances he would have handled things much differently, but he didn't like leaving Maria exposed and unprotected. So instead of infiltrating her house and taking the intruders on, one-on-one, he took the less risky path. Right now she was his priority, and if something happened to him, she'd be left unprotected. He'd been tasked with guarding her, and he was damn sure going to.

Sticking to the shadows, he headed back the way he'd come but bypassed Maria's hiding spot and raced down the street until he could cross over without being noticed. From there, getting to the truck unseen wasn't a problem. Even with the streetlights, Cade was used to hiding when necessary. There were plenty of vehicles and trees along the street, all providing the perfect cover.

Once he'd reached the yard next to where the vehicle was parked, he hid behind a tree and watched Maria's house across the street. Now he could see a faint light in the upstairs room. Her bedroom. The knowledge that some strangers were in her home, invading her privacy, made a surprising pop of anger surge through him.

Taking a calming breath, he focused on the truck. Now that he was closer and from his angle, he could see into the backseat through the windshield. There was just one shadow, wide enough shoulders to be male, and he could see the same red glow of the cigarette. From the way the shadow was angled, it was clear the man was watching the house. Which was good for Cade.

Ducking down, he crouched and moved out from his hiding place. Staying low, he half crawled his way across the sidewalk and then rolled onto his back when he was directly next to the truck. Slowly, he pulled one of the standard trackers he always carried with him out of his pants pocket. He slid the small switch on, removed the adhesive backing, and reached under the chrome running board. As he did, the hushed sound of two male voices drifted closer.

His heart raced against his chest, his adrenaline pumping overtime as he pressed the tracker into place. When he was sure it would stick, he rolled away and made his way to the closest tree. The moment he ducked behind it, he barely heard the sound of multiple vehicle doors opening, then closing almost simultaneously. He didn't dare move from his spot, though he drew his weapon in case he'd been spotted.

When the engine roared to life and he heard the truck pull away from the curb, only then did he fish out his cell phone. It was time to track these bastards.

*   *   *

Date: October 10, 2006
To: Maria Cervantes
From: Cade O'Reilly
Subject: re: Picture

The scarf looks beautiful. I'm glad you like it. I'm not surprised about your mom, especially not after the stories your brother tells about her. You guys are lucky to have someone who cares so much about you.

If Riel can put up with my ass, you know I'll be there. Wish we'd be stateside for Christmas too. Things here are the same. At least it's not balls hot right now. You don't have to send anything else. What you've done is already more than enough. If I haven't said it enough, thank you. Your packages and letters mean a lot. More than you know. But tell your group that if they do send stuff to others to make sure it's not really perishable items. And if they do send food, make sure it's secured in plastic bags.

Also, books are so appreciated. It's hard to get anything like that here.

How are your classes going? Did you tell your parents your plans for after graduation yet or are you still holding off?

Cade

P.S. I wouldn't say no to those cinnamon sugar cookies your mom makes.

Chapter 7

Off the reservation: unofficial term for when agents of clandestine agencies take on unsanctioned missions or leave the fold.

Wesley Burkhart stared at the carnage in front of him, the floodlights set up in the residential front yard highlighting a gory scene fit for a horror movie. Scott Mullen, former U.S. diplomat who'd once been stationed in various North African countries, had been tortured to death. Though torture didn't seem a strong enough word for the partially dismembered, bloody corpse that had been nailed to a cross and left in the middle of his expansive front yard. The hedges and privacy wall blocked the grisly scene, but a gardener who had forgotten something at the house had alerted the authorities when he found Mr. Mullen.

For some reason, the men who had killed him had left his wife alive and relatively unharmed. She'd been bound and gagged and left in their master bathroom. One of her attackers had broken a few of her fingers in the initial struggle, but her survival was something Wesley found very interesting.

Though not as interesting as the message painted in

blood across the man's front door and carved into his chest. *Westwood is just the beginning.*

As his phone rang, Wesley tapped his earpiece without bothering to look at the caller ID. Every call was important right now. "Burkhart."

"Got Mullen's file," Karen Stafford, one of his senior analysts, said in her standard clipped tone. "It's interesting. I'm sending everything to your e-mail, but some key points—he was forced to retire early from the Foreign Service, had a fairly distinguished career, a lot of unaccompanied assignments."

Unaccompanied meaning he was stationed without his family. From personal experience, Wesley knew those types of assignments were hard on anyone. Knowing better than to interrupt her, he listened as Karen continued.

"Spoke seven languages, really diplomatic, a dream for the Foreign Service, but about five years ago there were rumors that he was involved with the sex slave trade. It was when he was in Yemen. Less than a month after the accusations started flying, he was moved to D.C., then retired six months later. In my opinion, they didn't investigate like they should have because they didn't want the scandal. As soon as he retired he and his wife packed up and moved to Miami. No criminal record there, no issues at all. His wife comes from old money and they've been living comfortably in retirement since moving."

"What were his connections at the Westwood party?"

"There were at least half a dozen men there that he played golf with, but I'm sure there are more. I've got the names of the solid leads and have two junior analysts running the links between them."

"Thanks. You find out anything more on Karklinski?"

Oskars Karklinski. The dead terrorist from the hospital.

"Yeah, I've narrowed down his potential ties to only half a dozen operators who are possibly in the U.S. now."

Wesley rubbed a hand over his face. Six was better than the original twenty terrorist cells they'd suspected Karklinski of working for. The man had done a lot of operations for hire. so narrowing down who he'd been working for was time-consuming. Since his arrival in the United States, he'd been like a ghost. No paper trail whatsoever. Except for the phone they'd found on him.

"What about the phone?"

"I've dumped it and I'm still cross-referencing with all the numbers he dialed or received. There are a lot of them, but I found one call to a pawnshop that's a front for a low-level gunrunner. Small-time but thought it was worth checking out. We're stretched thin, so I let the only available team know and they're on their way to talk to the owner. It's Long's team. Didn't think you wanted me to hand this over to the locals." Her voice held a note of hesitation, likely because she'd made a decision without consulting him. He liked that Karen stepped up; it saved him time and energy and eliminated the need for him to micromanage.

Wesley snorted. Everyone on the ground was working together now to bring down these terrorists, but some things he wanted to handle himself. Especially a lead like this. The owner of the pawnshop would be talking all right. Wesley didn't give a shit about some low-level gunrunner, but if the guy was even remotely involved in the bombing, his life as he knew it was over. "Good work.

Text me the updates." Not bothering with social niceties, he disconnected and had started to call O'Reilly when the man's name appeared on his caller ID.

"Yeah," Wesley said.

"Spotted two unknowns breaking into Maria's house. They left a lookout in their vehicle, but I placed a tracker on it without being seen. No visual ID on any of them. I just texted Stafford the tracker ID and license plate number. We need a team following them ASAP."

Wesley wondered if O'Reilly even realized he'd called the Cervantes woman by her first name. It wasn't like his agent to get personal with any of his jobs, but Wesley knew of the history between O'Reilly and the woman's dead brother. Under normal circumstances he wouldn't have allowed his man to volunteer for the position of guarding her with such a connection, but O'Reilly never asked for anything. He worked like a damn machine, never taking vacations, and he was one of his best men. "We don't have anyone to spare in the vicinity. You have to track them."

"Maria's with me," he said after a slight pause.

"Take her but don't engage unless necessary. Call Stafford to help you pursue them. We need to see where they go. Has she remembered anything?"

"No, but she's trying." Wesley could hear the sound of an engine starting as O'Reilly spoke.

"Good. Ask her if she knows anything about a man who lives in the Gable Estates neighborhood." It was a long shot, but Wesley was looking at any angle he could. He rattled off the address and told him about the tortured body, then said, "Keep me updated with your progress."

His phone rang yet again as he strode toward the front of the house. One of the police techs was motioning him and his own captain over, his arms waving excitedly.

Wesley nodded at Jarvis Nieto, the local Miami PD captain he'd been working with the past few hours, as they headed for the front door, but he tapped his earpiece. It was an unknown number. "Burkhart here."

"The two men behind the Westwood attack are Mihails Balodis and Oto Ozols. They're in the city." The sound of Levi Lazaro's familiar voice jarred Wesley straight to his core to the point he almost stumbled.

His blood chilled at hearing from Lazaro after so long. At one time the man had been one of his best agents. He'd been solid, dependable, a fucking patriot. Then his wife had been murdered and he'd gone off the reservation in search of revenge. Now he was working for only God knew who. This wasn't the time to dredge up any of that, though. Not if his information was accurate. "How good is your intel?"

"Impeccable. And they're not done killing." There was a soft warning note in his voice.

No shit. "Why are you telling me this?"

Lazaro paused so long Wesley glanced at his phone, but the connection was still open. "It's the right thing to do. Killing so many civilians like that . . ." He trailed off, then continued again, his voice harder. "Don't get any ideas. This isn't because I owe you shit. Track those bastards down before more innocent people die." Then he hung up, just like that.

Wesley started to contact one of his analysts to have them trace the number, but he knew it was pointless.

Lazaro had learned from the best. Hell, he'd been the first man Wesley had recruited. After Lazaro's wife had been murdered, though, something inside him had cracked. It was the only reason Wesley hadn't tried very hard to hunt him down—or at all. The man deserved his revenge. And Wesley had been trying his damnedest to find out who'd orchestrated the killing of Lazaro's wife too.

He shelved the knowledge of the two names he'd just been given—though he planned to follow up with Karen in less than five minutes. First he needed to see whatever this tech was so excited about. Tuning out all the background noise of the men and women in various uniforms canvassing the house, he strode up next to Nieto. The dark-haired man was about the same age as Wesley and also had former military experience. Navy too. Which automatically gave him points. So far, Wesley liked working with him. He just cared about finding the truth, not posturing for the media.

"You know what he found?" he asked.

Nieto shook his head, his expression grim. "No, but I'm guessing it's not good."

Nothing about this night was good. Their shoes were silent along the marble floor of the entryway, then along the many polished hardwood floors until the tech, wearing a blue windbreaker type of jacket, stopped in front of an open door.

Looking inside, they found another similarly dressed tech with gloves and shoe covers standing next to a queen-sized bed covered in Polaroid photos. There were hundreds of them. On the wall behind the bed the word "Guilty" was written in crisp black letters. Probably done with a marker.

As he got closer, Wesley's gut twisted at the images.

Each photo had a picture of a naked woman. Some were in cages, others were bruised, bleeding, and splayed out on cement floors, and still others had smiles on their faces—though the smiles didn't reach their eyes. The pictures were disturbing, but unfortunately Wesley had seen worse. Just what the hell was going on here? What did Westwood have to do with Mullen's murder? And who did these pictures belong to? And how was Mullen connected to them, if at all? Fuck ... Wesley scrubbed a hand over his face as he pulled his cell phone out again. He needed to have Karen run the names Lazaro had given him and look for ties to their dead terrorist. Then he needed to make sense of this mess.

Hovering in the dark shadows of her neighbor's house, Maria couldn't stop the shivers racking her body. What the hell had happened to her life?

Cade had just dashed off, leaving her here, and every second that ticked by she was starting to freak out. If something had happened to him or he'd been discovered— her heart jumped into her throat as headlights momentarily blinded her. She scrambled back against the side of the wall, ready to sprint for the backyard.

Until she heard his reassuring voice. "Maria, get in."

Jumping up, she hurried toward the idling SUV, which she now saw was Cade's. "What happened?" she asked as she slid into the passenger seat and shut the door.

"Two men were in your house, not sure why. We need to send a bomb squad over later. Would anyone just drop by your house unexpectedly?"

Bomb squad? What the hell? "No." No one had a key but her parents. "Do you really think they planted a bomb?"

He shook his head as he steered out onto her street and revved the engine. "No . . . hold on." He tapped the earpiece that seemed attached to him, then started talking to someone in clipped, incomplete sentences. Then he pulled out a slim device from his center console and held it out to Maria.

"Hold this."

She did as he said and watched as a map pulled up on the flat computer screen. She'd seen similar handheld devices, and her e-reader was a couple of inches smaller, but this thing was sleek and razor thin. It also didn't have a brand name on it anywhere. It was simple and black. A few seconds later she realized the map layout was of Miami. She knew Cade had a GPS in his vehicle, so she wasn't sure why he needed this map.

"Yeah, it's working. I'll call you if I have an issue. Yeah . . . yeah, okay. Thanks." He tapped his earpiece again, then glanced at her as he sped down another street.

"I put a tracker on the truck of the men who were at your house. Everyone is racing around Miami looking for leads on the bombing and there's not a team to follow these guys, so I'm it. I hate dragging you with me, but it's the way it is."

"Are you freaking kidding me?" She needed to be with her father and she wanted to know what had happened at her house.

"I'm sorry, Maria." She was pretty certain there was more behind his apology than for what he was dragging her into right now. Or maybe that was just wishful thinking on her part.

"When will I get to see my father?"

"You won't be able to stay with your dad tonight, but I'm having a security detail put on him. With Larson protecting him, he should be secure, though. I've seen his file," he said almost grudgingly. "I'm sorry, but without knowing what's going on, your father's house will be the next best place for those men to look." She started to argue, but he cut her off. "Do you want to bring danger to his doorstep?"

That made her shut her mouth but only made her feel even more lost. She couldn't go to her own home or even her parents' house. Those were her two safe havens. Staring at the flat-screen, she watched a red dot moving along a street and realized Cade was using this thing to track the truck. "I need to call my dad."

Cade nodded, his expression grim. "Fine. Make sure he doesn't come by your house, and tell him there's a possibility you might not make it to the funeral tomorrow."

"What?" she shouted. "You'd better lock me up if you think you're keeping me from my mother's funeral." Maria could feel her temper rising with each word, the anger slicing her grief down with an emotion she could easily deal with. There was way too much going on for her to handle and she just wouldn't miss her mom's funeral.

"Maria—" he started, his voice soft and soothing, which was ridiculously infuriating. As if he thought a calm voice would make her change her mind.

"Don't." She was going to the funeral no matter what. "What do you know about these men we're following?"

His fingers tightened on the steering wheel, the muscles in his arms flexing with his frustration. "Nothing yet.

I'm sorry to take you with me, but there's no other choice. Believe me," he said through gritted teeth.

She did.

"Do you know a man named Scott Mullen?"

"It's familiar." The name rang a bell. She frowned, trying to place it as that nagging alarm sounded in her head. "Why?"

"He was murdered and there might be a connection between his death and what happened last night."

An icy fist clasped around her chest as numbness settled through her veins. "Does he live—or did he, I guess—in Gable Estates?"

Cade shot her a sharp look as he slowed to a stop in front of a red light. "Yes, why?"

"It's fuzzy, but I remember his name and . . . another name. Clay Ervin. I feel afraid even saying their names and I don't know why." She wrapped her arms around herself and fought the shudder that racked her. What the hell had happened at that party that she was blocking out?

Cade immediately got on his phone and called someone. After a brief conversation in which he relayed what she'd told him, he got off his cell and gave her a look she couldn't quite define. Ignoring it, she called her dad and tried to explain why she wasn't going to be at his place as planned without breaking into tears. Her father didn't understand, because she barely did herself. She could tell he was hurt, but she didn't have any other choice.

The conversation was painful and when she finally hung up, she shot Cade an angry look. "So, where are we staying tonight?"

"A safe house or a hotel," he said almost absently as

he slowed down and pulled up to a curb a few houses away from the truck they'd been tracking.

The passenger-side door was open and from what she could tell, it didn't appear as if anyone was in it.

Swallowing hard, she took in their surroundings. She'd been concentrating on her phone call and hadn't realized that they'd entered an older, run-down neighborhood with chain-link fences surrounding the front yards of the one-story homes. Each house had bars on the windows. She could hear loud music thumping from one of the houses nearby and there were a few people huddled together, talking over one of the fences, three houses down from where they were parked.

Cade lifted his pant leg and pulled out a small revolver. "You know how to use this?"

Of course she knew how. She was a single woman who lived alone in Miami and worked at a center with kids who often had dangerous relatives pissed at her or her people for trying to give the kids a better life. And pissed often equaled violent. Nodding, she took it even though she didn't want to. "Yeah."

"Good. Stay here and keep the doors locked. If something happens to me, get out of here." Cade didn't give her a chance to argue before he slid from the SUV like a ghost.

She hadn't even seen him withdraw his weapon, but she could see it clearly in his hand as he crept up on the back of the truck. Body tense, he moved along the back, then side and hurried to the open passenger door, weapon drawn. Just as quickly, he sheathed it in his shoulder holster and though she couldn't hear, she saw his mouth move in what looked like an unmistakable curse.

Leaning in, he grabbed a stack of papers from the glove compartment, then headed toward the two men talking to each other by one of the fences. One of the guys saw him, turned, and sprinted away, but the other stayed and talked to him.

After a few minutes, Cade returned to the SUV, his expression grim.

"What happened?" she demanded.

"I got a call from one of our analysts that the vehicle was just reported stolen, and that guy I just spoke to confirmed that three white guys just left it here, then got into a Humvee and split."

"So you have no clue who was in my house?"

He shook his head, frustration clear in every line. "We're going to have the locals pick up the truck and dust it for prints and anything else, but . . . no."

Maria leaned back against the seat, tension still radiating from her body. Tomorrow was her mom's funeral, some unknown men had broken into her house, and she couldn't even go home or be with her family. "So, what do we do now?"

"Wait for the cops to secure the vehicle, then head to a hotel," he muttered as he started the engine. In less than two minutes, a couple of black-and-whites steered down the street, lights flashing. Cade didn't wait to talk to them, just pulled away from the curb and they headed out. After a few moments of driving, he asked, "How well do you know that ICE agent?"

Surprised by the question, she shrugged. "We're friends. A while ago he helped the parents of some of my kids get political asylum. Their families had left horrific situations only to be harassed almost as badly here. They couldn't go to the police to press charges because they were illegal. It was a nightmare. One of the kids finally came to me and I went to Wayne. He bent over backward helping them out. . . . He's a good man, so whatever you're thinking, don't."

"I just find it interesting that not long after he left, someone broke into your house."

Maria took a deep breath and tried to rein in her anger. It was just a coincidence. If a terrorist could sneak into her hospital room, then it wasn't a stretch to imagine one breaking into her house. "Anyone could have found out my address. It's not that hard."

Cade just grunted and kept his eyes on the street, but she could see the wheels in his head turning. Whatever he was thinking, she just hoped he didn't think her friend had been involved with any of this. That just wasn't possible.

*   *   *

Date: October 11, 2006
To: Cade O'Reilly
From: Maria Cervantes
Subject: Cookies

You made my mom's entire year. She and my aunt are making you enough of those cookies to feed a small platoon (is that the right word for the Marines?). Of course my aunt's taking over the kitchen like she always does. Fine with me, though, because I'm eating everything they don't send, lol. I'll send them out this week along with a bunch of books. What kind do you want? Fiction, nonfiction, specific genre . . . ? I could send you some from my romance collection, but I don't think those are your reading style *g*.

Classes are good, but no, not telling them anything yet. In the end I know they'll deal with my choices, but I don't want to have to listen to them try to change my mind for months and months on end. And when I say "them," I mean my mom. I love her like crazy, but she drives me nuts sometimes.

Well, my eyes are about to fall out I'm so tired. I've got class at 7 tomorrow (remind me why I ever thought that was a good idea?), so I'm going to crash. Stay safe!

xo,
Maria

Chapter 8

Collateral damage: damage, injuries, or deaths that are incidental to an intended target(s). Unintended civilian casualties or destruction of civilian property.

Maria stepped inside the quiet two-story house in the middle-class neighborhood Cade had driven them to. He'd originally planned to take her to a hotel but had made a last-minute change and brought her to a safe house. Which was fine with her. She desperately needed sleep and preferred a house to a hotel by far. She wouldn't be faced with random strangers or social niceties. The thought of interacting with people—no, thanks.

"A security team will be arriving in a few hours to guard the place, but only three people know we're even here and I trust them with my life," Cade said as he locked the door behind them. He also set the alarm using a standard-looking keypad.

"Just show me to my room," she said tiredly, hoping she didn't sound ungrateful. Because she wasn't. She was glad to be protected from whoever wanted her dead, but mental exhaustion was pressing in on her. Especially since she knew she had to wake up in a few hours for her mom's funeral. That was going to be hard enough to deal with even if she had a full night of sleep.

"You want to eat first? This place is stocked with anything you want." Concern etched his expression.

The thought of food wasn't appealing. She shook her head. "No, but thank you. I'd just like to take a shower and crash." She picked up the bag he'd set in the foyer, but he took it from her and motioned that she should follow him up a set of stairs.

The house was painted with warm earth tones and had nice furniture, but there were no pictures or anything personal on the walls or shelves. "Does the NSA use this house a lot?"

Cade shook his head as they reached the top of the stairs. "No. This is actually a transitional WITSEC house, but my boss pulled some strings to get us put here."

"A transitional house?" She knew what WITSEC was but didn't understand what he meant.

Three doors down, he held open a door for her and motioned inside. "Sometimes witnesses put into the Witness Protection Program stop over here or other similar locations for a few days before being moved to their permanent location."

"Oh." She let out a sigh of relief when she saw the queen-sized bed with a simple white comforter set with tiny pink flowers embroidered in the soft-looking material. The bed looked like heaven.

"Shower's through there." Cade pointed to the other door in the room. "I'm going to get something to eat downstairs, but I'll be sleeping right next door."

"Okay, thanks. The funeral's at eleven, Cade. I'm not missing it." They hadn't talked about it again, but she was going no matter what he might think. She might not have the energy for much, but this was one fight he'd lose.

"I know, I already talked to my boss. You're going to have to go in disguise, but you're attending." His expression wasn't exactly happy, but he seemed resigned that she was going. Which was good because at least he wasn't arguing with her.

The thought of going in a disguise sucked, but it was better than nothing. She wanted to argue, but she couldn't stand the thought of bringing danger to anyone at the funeral, and if someone truly wanted her dead, it would make sense that they would look for her there. Since most of the bodies—including her mother's—hadn't yet been recovered from the rubble, it was just going to be a ceremony at her parents' church. No urn, no casket, nothing. There was no guarantee all the bodies would be discovered anyway. Many had been obliterated in the blast. That thought brought up another wave of grief.

"Okay," she rasped out. Her throat tightened, making it impossible to speak more, so she just picked up her bag and headed for the bathroom.

Once inside, she stripped and turned the shower to hot. Even though she'd brought her own things, there was shampoo, conditioner, a razor, and shower gel in the tiled stall. Cade hadn't been kidding. This place was stocked. Once the water turned hot, she stepped inside and let the jets pummel her tense shoulders. It didn't help any and when her fingers started to prune from being in the water so long, she got out and made a half-ass attempt to towel-dry her hair.

Next she pulled out the simple black dress she would be wearing in the morning and hung it up to get out the wrinkles. Actual ironing was so not one of her priorities at the moment. The closet was surprisingly large, made even more so with her lone dress hanging there.

Sighing, she tugged on panties, set the alarm on her phone so she'd wake up in plenty of time to get ready, then crawled under the covers. The sheets were cool against her skin, a sharp contrast to the hot shower she'd just taken. Feeling as if she were on a giant cloud, she closed her eyes and tried to block out the images of fire and rubble that appeared each time she did. The scene from when she'd woken with paramedics looking down at her worriedly just wouldn't disappear. The terror, the confusion—it was as if it was seared into her pores and she couldn't shake those feelings or the ever-growing fear inside her. As more thoughts continued to race through her mind, she squeezed her eyes shut, willing sleep to come.

I've got to tell someone. Find a phone. Like, yesterday. *Urgency bombarded Maria as she raced over the grass and across the expansive property. Why wasn't anyone here? Where were the guards? She couldn't go back through the house or else* they *might see her.*

Even thinking of those men's words terrified her. The Freedom Tower. Lord, it sounded as if they wanted to target places all over Miami. But why? Okay, she didn't care why. She just wanted to stop them.

Beneath her the earth began to rumble. Fire and destruction burst through the night sky. . . .

"Maria . . . Maria."

Opening her eyes, Maria realized Cade was staring down at her, his handsome face a mask of concern.

Light from the adjacent bathroom streamed in, giving her enough illumination to make out her surroundings.

His hand was on her shoulder and he'd been lightly shaking her. She glanced down and realized her sheet was pulled over her breasts, covering her. She blinked, trying to orient herself from the nightmare. Sweat dotted her upper lip, and her palms were damp. She wiped at her face as she tried to will her racing heart to slow down. "The Freedom Tower."

"What?" His piercing eyes narrowed a fraction. "Are you okay?"

They had to *do* something. "Someone is going to bomb the Freedom Tower. I don't know when or . . . anything else. I just know they are." It scared her that she didn't know how she possessed that knowledge or who was behind it, but she had no doubt that something was going to happen there if she didn't stop it.

Cade looked torn for a moment as he stood, but he remained at the edge of the bed. "You're sure?"

She nodded. "I dreamed about the explosion. Well, before it. Most of that night is still a blank, but I remember that."

"Do you know who?"

Fury surged through her at the unknown men. Why couldn't she remember more? "No."

"Give me a second." He disappeared from her room but returned five minutes later, still looking tense. "I've informed my boss. Someone's going to look into it. They're also following up on a lead—the one you gave them about Clay Ervin. Looks like you might have been right."

Before she could ask who the man was, Cade shook

his head. "I don't know more than that and the truth is, I might not be able to tell you more even when I do have details."

That pissed her off, but she actually understood. She wanted to help as much as she could, but she also knew they had national security to worry about. Her own curiosity didn't matter when weighed against finding the terrorists behind the bombing and apparent new murder. "I get it," she murmured.

Cade stood there for a long moment, watching her, as if unsure whether he should go or not. Wearing plain black boxers and nothing else, the man looked delicious. Not that she should be noticing him like that. Especially not now.

But it was hard not to when all those muscles, tattoos, and raw sexuality were right in front of her face. It was as if he'd been cut from marble. His body was exquisite, though something told her that if he knew what she was thinking it would embarrass him. But the man had a body that artists or photographers would kill to mold or photograph. There was such a raw sexual vibe he put off.

He exuded a quiet strength and undeniable power. It was one of the things that had originally drawn her to him years ago, part of why she'd decided to start e-mailing him. She swallowed hard, hating how weak she felt at the moment. But she was human and decided to ask for what she wanted. Even if he rejected her. "Will you stay with me? Just until I fall asleep?" She'd been tossing and turning and even though she'd finally fallen into a fitful doze, her eyes were gritty and she felt as if she'd run a marathon instead of sleeping.

His eyebrows rose in surprise, but he immediately nodded. "Yeah, just give me a sec." Once again he disappeared from the room, returning moments later with a gun, phone, and pillow. After placing them on the small nightstand, he started to stretch out onto the floor, but she frowned and pulled back the comforter, still keeping herself mostly covered with the sheet.

"You can sleep on top of the sheet if it makes you feel better," she muttered. Maria was too damn tired to think of sex right now. She just wanted someone to hold her. If that made her weak, then she didn't care.

After a longer pause this time, he slid in behind her. Maria turned her back to him, hoping he'd wrap his arm around her. The bed depressed a little and shook as he settled in. Seconds later, he did what she'd hoped. Pulling her close, his chin resting on the top of her head as he wrapped his strong arm around her middle, he sighed. "This isn't protocol for an NSA agent."

It was hard to read his tone, but he didn't sound put out by holding her. "I don't care." She laid her own arm over his and settled back against his strong chest. The man was so warm he was like a furnace. Considering how chilled and shaky she'd been, this was heavenly comfort. She wished the sheet wasn't between them, but even with it covering her back, she still savored his embrace.

"Neither do I." His voice was almost a whisper, his warm breath teasing her hair.

An unexpected frisson of awareness curled through her at his words, but she ignored it and closed her eyes. She wasn't sure how much time passed as they lay there in the near darkness, but she knew he wasn't asleep. His breathing was steady and reassuring, but he was tense. And ... she could feel his erection even though he'd tried to move his hips away from her. Apparently the man was huge all over.

Something she didn't want to know because it made her think all sorts of things. Like how that thick length would feel thrusting inside her. Her nipples strained against the thin sheet as heat slowly built between her legs. Cade was turned on. Because of her. Finally she couldn't stand it anymore. "Are you . . ."

"Yeah," he said through gritted teeth. Even though his breathing was steady, his voice certainly wasn't.

"You don't have to stay." Even though it was selfish, she still wanted him to. She might not be able to sleep yet, but she felt safe. All because of him.

"I want to."

If she was completely honest with herself, she wanted him with her but not just because of the comfort factor. It had been a long time since she'd had sex or any sort of relationship, but right now the thought of . . . No. She didn't need to do anything stupid. Lord, the man had cut communication with her years ago as if she meant nothing. The thought made her go cold, the iciness invading her veins as she remembered how much she'd cried, not only over the loss of her brother, but of her friendship with Cade.

As if he sensed her train of thought, his grip tightened. "What are you thinking?"

"Why did you stop writing me? The truth." It was like dropping a bomb into the quiet.

He went still, but finally he answered, "When Riel and the rest of my team died, I didn't handle it well. You were a reminder of my best friend, so instead of bringing you down with me, I cut contact. It was a shitty thing to do, I know that. But it was the only way I could deal at the time. I wish I could say it was a youthful thing to do, but

I wasn't that young. I was just mourning. If I could go back ... fuck, I don't know what I'd do, Maria."

When he laid it out in such blunt terms, she actually understood. Still, they'd been friends, with the possibility of more, and she couldn't get rid of the feeling that he was holding something back. She turned over so she could face him. Her sheet slid down, and cool air rushed over her breasts, but she didn't make a move to cover herself. Even with the bathroom light his face was cast in shadows, but she could see enough and she knew he could too. His gaze dipped to her breasts for a moment, and he swallowed hard, but he quickly met her gaze.

"You hurt me." She wanted him to know. "I cried over you and Riel. I lost both of you at once."

His jaw tightened. "I know and I'm so damn sorry. More than you know." His hand settled on her hip, his fingers flexing slightly as his gaze dipped to her chest again. "You deserved better than that. Better than me."

Her nipples tightened even harder, the peaks becoming almost painfully aroused. She didn't just want him looking at her. It didn't matter that he'd hurt her. Okay, it *did* matter, but some primal part of her wanted the release she knew he could give her. She wanted his mouth on her breasts, teasing them until she was begging for more.

Cade sucked in a deep breath, his nostrils slightly flaring, but he didn't say anything else or make a move to touch her. And she wanted him to. Sex should be the last thing on her mind, but she could lose herself in him for just a little while and feel no regret.

"No," he said quietly, correctly reading her thoughts.

"No, what?"

"I know what you're thinking. You'll regret it in the morning."

"How do you know what I'm thinking?" she whispered. And what made him think she'd regret it later?

"Because I'm thinking the same thing."

Oh, damn. Now he was just trying to make it harder on her. He wanted her and she wanted him. The awareness sparking between them made her entire body flush with heat. They might have history and baggage between them, but it didn't take away from the attraction simmering. It had always been there too, even when she was younger. But it hadn't been as potent as it was now.

He let out a low curse, then pulled her to him. Her breasts pressed against his chest as she curved into the strength of his long, muscular body. Maybe she should be angrier at him, and she still was for the way he'd up and cut her out of his life, but damn, she was exhausted and had just lost her mom. She didn't have the energy to hold on to any more anger right now. "Just go to sleep," he murmured in a soothing voice that belied the tension she felt humming through him.

Oh, how she wanted to. But with the press of his erection against her belly, she had a feeling it was going to be damn hard to rest.

Mihails's hands tightened on the wheel of the newest SUV he and his crew had acquired. He didn't think anyone had witnessed them leaving Mullen's home and Kristaps had deleted the video surveillance at the guardhouse, but they all believed in being careful. So they'd ditched the vehicle and found a new one. This was an older model blue Suburban and big enough for his crew.

Before killing Scott Mullen, they'd gleaned more information through torture. Mihails understood that things gained that way were not always reliable, but Mullen had been weak and they'd barely done anything to him before he started talking. They'd only pulled one tooth before he turned on his friends. Pathetic.

Of course, what could one expect from a man who preyed on the innocent? They already had a few names, including Clay Ervin, whose home they were on their way to now. But they'd gained more than that as well. The pain they'd inflicted after Mullen had given up everything he knew had been pure pleasure on Mihails's part. The man deserved everything they'd done to him and more.

But there wasn't time to dwell on that. He had a job to do. After killing Ervin, then the hotel hit, they would hunt down their newest acquired targets.

Oto sat next to him, speaking in rapid-fire Latvian, his expression rigid. Eventually he disconnected and glanced at Mihails. "The woman wasn't there, but there was an SUV with government plates in the driveway. They believe they just missed her and that she likely packed a bag. Her closet was disturbed and she had no makeup or hairbrush in her bathroom."

Mihails knew enough about women to realize if those items were missing, she was gone for the time being. But she could be at her father's house. It would make sense, considering that her mother had died. Something Mihails tried not to think about. His victims had been collateral damage. Nothing more. "What about—"

Already knowing what he was going to ask, Oto shook his head. "They already tried her parents' home. Her father is wealthy and has excellent security. Not the kind our men are equipped to infiltrate on such short notice. But ... there was also a team of government agents watching the home. They were trying to blend in, but our men saw them. They don't know if she is there."

"She likely knows nothing." How could she? Mihails didn't like wasting resources. It had nothing to do with the woman's haunting amber eyes. Because he felt no guilt over hunting her down. At least that was what he told himself.

"Then why is the government guarding her? And our contact said she deserves to die anyway."

Digesting Oto's words, Mihails was silent as he steered through the gated entrance to Ervin's neighborhood. Unlike Mullen's place, this one didn't have a guardhouse. Just a large open gate that had malfunctioned a week ago—thanks to a member of Mihails's crew—and hadn't been repaired yet. "He has his own motives." Motives Mihails hadn't yet figured out. He would soon, though.

Oto shrugged. "We all do, yes? He says the woman isn't who she seems and does more harm than good for her neighborhood."

Mihails knew what the man had said. But it didn't mean he believed him. He grunted in response, not willing to continue this conversation until after Clay Ervin was dead. Oto was acting edgier and that in turn was putting Mihails on alert. Oto had already lost control at Mullen's house, hurting the man's wife when it hadn't been necessary. A couple of broken fingers weren't a big deal, but he didn't like the uncontrollable rage he saw in Oto's eyes sometimes. They had a plan and would stick to it. As they crept down the quiet street of the upper-class neighborhood, he frowned at the sight of an unfamiliar SUV in the driveway. The house had a three-car garage and from the previous recon they'd done, there was *never* a vehicle parked outside. Not at Ervin's house or any in the large neighborhood.

"I don't like this," he murmured.

There was a murmur of agreement from Oto and the others in the back. As he slowly cruised by, his eyes widened when he saw the government plates on the SUV. Without a word, he continued past the house and exited the neighborhood as quickly as possible.

There wasn't an overt connection between Mullen and Ervin. The government shouldn't have been able to link the two men. Not so quickly. It had taken Mihails and Oto years to hunt down the men involved in the ring that had taken his sisters from him. And even though Ieva was still alive, she was so broken she might as well have been dead.

"What now?" Oto asked quietly.

"We return to base and put out feelers, see how much the government knows. And what branch was at Ervin's home." There were many agencies involved in the Westwood case, which Mihails believed would work to their advantage. There was a greater chance for miscommunication.

"What about the hotel?"

Mihails shot Oto a sharp look, not liking the doubt he heard in his friend's voice. "The plan is still on." They would burn that building of evil to the ground, and he didn't care how many people were in it when they did.

Chapter 9

Interrogation: questioning/interviewing suspects, victims, or witnesses with the purpose of gaining information or a confession.

Under most circumstances Wesley would have felt bad about waking up some random guy in the predawn hours, but he didn't give a shit if he had to wake up the freaking president right now. Clay Ervin might have a link to Scott Mullen, and after the file Karen had sent him on Mihails Balodis and Oto Ozols, Wesley wasn't taking any chances with Ervin's safety if he was somehow connected to all this.

For all he knew the guy was a piece of crap, but he could be in danger and he might shed some light on what the hell Westwood had to do with Mullen's murder. Not to mention that they all wanted to minimize any more collateral damage.

Even with the information he'd gained on the two known Latvian terrorists—who were unfortunately very educated and resourceful—he didn't know what their ties were to either men. If any.

But his gut told him Levi's information was good. Levi had no reason to lie to him, and while the former agent might have gone off the reservation, he still had a soul. All those innocent people killed at the Westwood mansion ... Even after all Wesley had seen and done, it was still difficult to digest that yet another massive act of terror had happened on American soil. It didn't matter that the last one was over a decade ago. He hadn't forgotten.

Not to mention that Mihails and Oto were in the United States, which put them at the top of his suspect list until he had absolute confirmation one way or another. They'd entered through Canada using aliases, but once Wesley had ordered a search for them in every online system imaginable, their faces had shown up in multiple facial-recognition software programs.

He knew they'd entered Florida a couple of months ago, but since then, the two men and whoever they were working with had been like ghosts. If they'd been here for months, it meant they'd had a lot of time to plan. Which explained how they'd been able to destroy the Westwood place with such efficiency.

So now he was standing in Clay Ervin's living room while Ervin sat on the edge of his love seat looking nervous and just plain guilty of *something*. The guy had shifty dark eyes that put Wesley on edge.

The man tightened his forest green robe around himself and crossed his arms over his chest. "I already told you, I didn't know Scott very well. We were members of the same yacht club, but that's it."

Information Wesley already knew thanks to his capable analysts. He also knew Ervin was lying. The way he said Mullen's first name was too damn familiar. It was a small thing, but that was how people tripped up. "You were part of the same club for almost five years."

"Yeah, so?" the man snapped, the tension from him almost palpable. "There are a ton of members I don't know personally. It's a big club."

Something had this guy spooked. Something more than an early-morning visit from the NSA. His financials were complete shit. The man was up to his eyeballs in debt, upside down on his mortgage, and would likely lose his house in a few months. Forgoing all that info, Wesley could tell the man was scared. He could see it in his eyes.

That raw kind of fear was toxic and it had been rolling off Ervin since they mentioned Mullen's murder. Considering the sick pictures they'd found at Mullen's house, Wesley wondered if the women were the tie between the two men.

Clearing his throat, Wesley looked at Captain Nieto. Normally Wesley preferred working with members of his own team, but he really liked Nieto. The Miami PD was lucky to have someone like him working for them.

The man's dark eyes narrowed a fraction, as if he read Wesley's mind. Then his lips curved up into an almost wicked smile as he pulled a slim manila folder from the inside of his jacket. "So, your buddy Mullen wasn't just killed. He was tortured. Gruesome too."

Ervin had started to argue that he barely knew Mullen when Nieto placed a picture of Mullen's bloodied corpse on the glass coffee table. It was a shock tactic and one Wesley approved of.

Ervin's face paled a shade as he stared in horror. "Who did that to him?" he rasped out.

Wesley stepped up now, taking over. "Not sure yet. But it's connected to Westwood and it's connected to *this*." He pulled out half a dozen of the Polaroids they'd found in Mullen's home from an envelope he'd been carrying and tossed them onto the table next to Mullen's picture.

Normally Wesley didn't go for the hard push in an interrogation so soon—and this was definitely an interrogation of sorts—but with more innocent lives at stake, he'd do anything to figure out what the hell was going on. If it turned out he was wrong and Ervin wasn't connected to any of this, he'd apologize. But national security was more important than this guy's feelings.

Ervin blinked as he took in the photographs, his face turning even more ashen. But there was also recognition in his eyes as he saw the caged women. "I don't know who they are," he snarled.

"Huh," Nieto started, leaning back in his seat as he looked up at Wesley. "I believe him. And it's a good thing he doesn't know Mullen or have any connection to those women, because the way I see it, whoever killed Mullen did it out of revenge. That crime scene . . ." The big man mock-shuddered as he stood. "We're sorry to have wasted your time, sir, but since you don't know anything, we'll pull our security detail from the house."

Wesley shrugged and started gathering the photos. There was no way they'd pull the guy's detail—though it sure as hell wasn't for Ervin's security. They wanted to trap whoever was after him. Up until this point Wesley had wondered how or if the guy was even involved. But the man knew something. He was neck deep in this shit.

"You can't do that!" Ervin shouted, shaking as he stood up.

"Do what, exactly?"

He swallowed hard, looking back and forth between Wesley and Nieto. "You think Mullen was killed out of revenge? Because of those ... pictures?" He couldn't even say women, or girls.

Something Wesley found very telling. His team of analysts and the team Nieto had working on this case were all circling around the idea that the naked, caged women were at the center of this. Somehow they had to be. Revenge was the only thing that made sense. Hell, wars had been started for less. And revenge was one of the most powerful motivators for someone angry enough. The "guilty" word scrawled on the wall and the other phrase carved into Mullen's skin were there for a reason. "It's possible."

He licked his lips. "Then I need protection."

"Why? You barely knew the guy." Nieto shrugged and had already started walking toward the foyer, as if ready to leave.

"Wait! I'll tell you everything I know, but first I need to speak to my lawyer."

Finally they were getting somewhere. Wesley inwardly smiled but kept his face a mask as he pinned Ervin with a hard glare. "Call him now and tell him to meet you at the police station." This guy was obviously a piece of shit—anyone involved with hurting women was—and Wesley planned to get everything he could out of him before making sure the guy paid for whatever crimes he'd committed.

Cade shifted against the sheets, trying to ease his painful erection. He was going against every protocol there was. Sleeping in the same bed as the woman in his protective custody? Genius plan. It would be one thing if he was simply trying to comfort her, to make her feel at ease. Yeah, it would still be breaking some rules, but he was intensely attracted to her. Had been from the moment they met all those years ago.

It had been easier to ignore the attraction then because she'd been younger and he'd been in the Corps. He'd known there was no possible way for them to have a relationship. Especially not when Maria had been the little sister of his best friend. That was a code he hadn't been willing to break.

Then she'd started e-mailing him. All those letters had been his lifeline on really dark nights. Overseas he'd had more than his share of them too. Hell, all his friends had. It was just the nature of war. He'd never hidden the fact that he'd been in contact with her, and surprisingly Riel hadn't cared. He'd seemed almost glad Cade and Maria were friends. Or maybe that was wishful thinking on his part.

Then things had started to change between them in their e-mails and letters. Slowly at first, their relationship building into something more as the days passed. He'd opened up to her in a way he never had with anyone else. Then his life had gone to shit and he'd pushed her out of his in an effort to simply fucking survive. He'd known if he'd told her the truth about what happened to her brother that she'd hate him and kick him out of her life anyway. He wouldn't have survived that. Not after losing so many damn people in his life. So he knew he shouldn't be lying here with her in his arms. The guilt over his secret was eating him up alive, but hell, the feel of her in his arms threatened to override any guilt. This was Maria, the woman he'd fantasized about for almost a decade. In his arms.

He shifted again and tried to pull his hips back, but Maria snuggled tighter against him, hooking one leg over his hip.

Fuck.

Yeah, he had to get out of here. It was still dark out-side, so maybe he could salvage a few hours and get some rest in his own bed. She'd just asked him to stay until she fell asleep. Which he'd done. Now it was time to relocate.

Slowly he reached back and lightly grasped her wrist, moving her hand so that she wasn't wrapping her arm around him. Next, he tried to do the same with her leg. Grasping her silky-smooth thigh, he froze when she let out a tiny moan in her sleep. And when she practically ground against him, he groaned.

Couldn't help it. She felt so good the sound just es-caped—and woke her up.

Even though it was too dark to see how vibrant her amber eyes were, he could see the confusion in her gaze. Blinking, she looked at him, then down at their practi-cally intertwined bodies. The sheet was tangled between them and he still had his boxers on, but it didn't do much to hide his arousal. Or cover her exposed breasts.

He didn't want to notice them, but he couldn't stop himself from looking. As if drawn by a magnet, he ze-roed in on them. They weren't overly large, but full and round and just enough for him to cup in his hands. Per-fection.

Her breathing grew erratic and he forced himself to look at her face. Desire and hunger were there, so palpa-ble it floored him. He might not be willing to have sex with her—even if he'd never wanted anything more in his life, he just couldn't take advantage of her. Not now. Not after she'd lost so much. And not when he'd never deserve someone like her. Not after what he'd done.

But he could bring her pleasure. Hell, he *wanted* to.

The thought of seeing her expression as she climaxed, and because of him no less, was something he'd fantasized about on more than one occasion. It was primitive, possessive, and yeah, he fucking cared about this woman. He'd never been able to bury his feelings for her no matter how many years had passed. She'd been so sweet and caring to him when he'd been in some of the shittiest places on earth. She'd been his reminder that there were still good things in the world, that people like her were the reason he did what he did. If he could make her feel relief for just a little bit, he was doing it.

Before he had time to argue with himself and leave her room in an attempt to regain his sanity, he covered her mouth with his. She didn't resist for even a moment.

She molded to him, her breasts pressing against his chest, her hard nipples rubbing against him as her tongue met his stroke for stroke in a hungry frenzy. As her hands roamed up his chest, he turned her onto her back so that he was covering her body with his.

He loved the feel of her petite, luscious body underneath him. She rolled her hips against his and he reached between them, tugging the sheet away.

Nipping his bottom lip, she rolled her hips again, her intent clear. He could practically feel her heat, their clothing offering almost no barrier between their bodies.

As her fingers dug into his shoulders, he slid his hand down her flat belly and dipped beneath her barely there panties. He wanted to pleasure her, to taste every part of her. To slowly savor her. He cupped her mound, the silky thatch of her hair soft against his palm. When he felt how wet she already was, he shuddered. But he didn't penetrate. Not yet. First he wanted to work her up to it. Get her so hot and ready she could barely stand it.

Pulling back, he tore his mouth from hers. Her fingers clenched around his shoulders and she made a protesting sound until he started kissing her jaw. She let out a shudder as he worked his way down the elegant column of her neck, teasing and nipping as he went.

When he reached her breasts, he shuddered. "I've fantasized about this. Us," he said, unable to stop the admission. Had he ever. What he'd imagined didn't live up to the reality of her compact yet lush body. The woman was pure sex appeal. And right now she was his. It wasn't real or long-term; he knew that. Not because he didn't want that, but because he didn't deserve her. But for tonight, he was going to give her what she needed.

"Me too." Her voice was still thick from sleep, the raspy quality sexy as hell.

It was as hot as her admission. He was glad he wasn't the only one so affected. His cock pulsed between his legs. What he wouldn't give to sink deep inside her. To thrust until both of them were sated and exhausted.

Slowly, he circled her light brown nipple with his tongue. The tight bud was hard and aroused and the moment his tongue made contact she arched her back, pushing it farther into his mouth. Oh yeah, the woman was reactive. And he wanted to see how far he could push her, to stake a claim she wouldn't soon forget.

As he alternated between her breasts, stroking each nipple until she was moaning and rubbing herself against his hand, he finally penetrated her slick folds and slowly stroked inside her tight sheath.

"Oh . . . yes. Faster." It was a barely audible demand. One he would happily oblige.

He drew his finger out, then pushed two in with his

next stroke. She nearly vaulted off the bed and he increased his thrusting. He barely grazed her clit with his thumb as he stroked into her.

He doubted the pressure was enough, considering the frustrated pants she made, so he blazed a trail of kisses down the rest of her body until he settled between her thighs. Keeping up the rhythm of his fingers, he pressed gentle kisses over her mound and on her inner thighs.

Her legs shook each time he kissed, then licked the soft skin, but he held back from her clit. The sensitive bundle of nerves was swollen and begging for his kiss.

"You're a tease." Her voice was strained, her inner walls tightening around his fingers with each push, telling him how close she was.

What he wouldn't give to feel her clenching around his cock. Though he wanted to drag this out longer, to keep teasing her body, he knew she needed sleep. And an orgasm was the best way for her to get it.

Without any more buildup, he swiped his tongue over her clit, exerting more pressure with each stroke until she was trembling under him.

She slid her hands to his head, running her fingers over his skull trim and gripping him as if she was afraid he'd stop. Then she shattered, her climax ripping through her as she shouted his name. On her lips it sounded like a damn prayer, so fucking reverent it humbled him. Her inner walls continued to clench around him, her gasps and moans incoherent until finally she pushed at his head with trembling fingers.

"No more . . . too sensitive," she gasped.

Though he loved tasting her, he stopped and slowly withdrew his fingers. Crawling up the bed so that he was covering her, he kept his gaze on her face as he slid his fingers into his mouth.

Though it was dark, he could almost swear she blushed as she raptly watched him. God, *her taste*. It was almost enough for him to forget his good intentions. But he hadn't lost his head that much. Yet.

Leaning down, he leisurely kissed her, gently cupping her face as he enjoyed her sweet body beneath him. But when she reached between them and went to stroke his cock, he grasped her wrist and moved off her.

"You need sleep, Maria," he murmured, pulling the covers up to cover her chest even though it pained him to hide all that beauty.

It was almost as painful as the ache between his legs.

She frowned, a flash of hurt in those beautiful eyes. "But—"

He dropped a chaste kiss on her lips. "Sleep now. This was about you, not me. I wanted to do that for you. And I want a hell of a lot more, but . . . you've got a long day ahead of you." Before she could respond, he slid out of bed and strode from the room. Once he was in the hallway, he leaned against the wall and rubbed a hand over his face.

Restraint. He had it. Right? He gritted his teeth and headed for his room. His control was at its breaking point. He was going to take care of himself in the shower and try to ignore the fact that a beautiful, willing woman was waiting for him. Because he wouldn't take advantage of her like that. No matter how much he wanted her. Which was why he couldn't stay with her. He was only human and if he was in that bed any longer, he was going to be inside her.

*   *   *

Date: November 6, 2006
To: Maria Cervantes
From: Cade O'Reilly
Subject: Hey

I'm still getting requests for those cookies your mom sent.
Please make sure you tell her and your aunt thanks for
me. It's getting colder here and of course they're running
low on our supplies (not the Army's, though). I always
thought I'd be a lifer, but some days I think I'd like to do
something else. Just don't know what.

    Got your handwritten letters. About ten came in one
bundle. It's probably weird to say, but they smell like you,
kinda reminded me of the ocean and Miami. Makes me
look forward to leave more than ever. Fucking mail is slow
here, so I'm glad we're e-mailing too. Seeing your name
on my screen makes my day.

    Got a mission tomorrow and I'm not sure how long I'll
be gone, so if you don't hear from me for a couple weeks
don't worry. Miss you.

                                                            Cade

Chapter 10

Bombing: to attack, damage, or destroy with the use of explosive weapons; a tactic frequently used by terrorists.

"She has to know something," Oto said quietly, for Mihails's ears alone, as they strode across the marble floor of the posh hotel lobby. The "she" who he referred to was clear. Maria Cervantes.

Mihails nodded, his jaw tight, knowing his friend had to be correct. After seeing the government vehicle at Clay Ervin's home early this morning, everyone on his team was moving with more caution. Before coming to this hotel they had done reconnaissance of all their intended target sites. As far as they could tell, the majority of the locations were not under surveillance except for one.

The Freedom Tower. As for actual damage, it was unlikely that site would have much impact as a target, but he wanted it destroyed for the symbolism. Eventually he wanted everyone, not just the government agencies, to know why he'd targeted Miami.

It could be a coincidence that the place was under surveillance. Just as it could be a coincidence that the government was interested in Ervin. But Mihails didn't believe in coincidences. He was racking his brain trying to remember all they had discussed at the Westwood mansion.

Until the past couple of days, they had been careful not to speak of any of their plans over the phone. They only discussed things with their Miami contact at prearranged meetings. And even then, Mihails and Oto had been careful with electronic scramblers to block their conversation from potential surveillance. The mansion was the first time they had spoken freely, as they had been alone and the plan was being put into motion minutes after they left. Not to mention that section of the house had been secure. Or he'd thought it had been. To get to that wing, one would have had to possess a knowledge of the layout of the house because it wasn't as simple as opening a few doors or stumbling down a hallway or two by accident. No, someone would have to *know* where they were going.

"Her mother's funeral is today. It was on the news," Oto said quietly as they waited behind a man in a suit that likely cost three thousand dollars. Such an obnoxious waste.

Why was Oto insisting on bringing this up now, when he was already aware of it? It was as if his friend was questioning his ability to make decisions. "I *know*. She will be handled there." Their contact would kill her there or follow her and do it afterward.

"We should send Kristaps instead," Oto murmured.

So that was why he'd brought her up. "Hmm." Mihails glanced at his phone. Kristaps was supposed to check in once he'd eliminated another one of their problems. "He is busy."

Oto was silent and Mihails did not continue, because there was no need. Kristaps had been sent to eliminate Reuben Flowers, attorney to Clay Ervin. They'd had to move up their timeline with Flowers, but if Ervin was talking to the government, it stood to reason that he would involve his lawyer. Men like him wouldn't talk about anything without their legal protection behind them. Flowers had known of what Ervin and his friends engaged in, though whether he'd actually been involved, Mihails didn't know. Either way, his knowledge made him complicit, in Mihails's opinion.

But he did agree that they might have to step up and eliminate the Cervantes woman. Maybe even bring her in alive. He wanted to know what she knew and what she'd told the government. Mihails might have to handle her himself.

Though it wasn't something he wanted to do. He didn't like hurting women. The majority of his team didn't. It was why they'd let Scott Mullens's wife live even when it was clear Oto had wanted her dead. In the end Mihails might have to hand the Cervantes woman over to Oto and give his friend his outlet for rage and get the information they needed. But the thought of doing so didn't sit right with him.

Even though they'd killed men and women at the Westwood mansion, no one had suffered in a blast so instantaneous and destructive. Unfortunately those people had been collateral damage anyway. A necessary part of his mission. And Maria Cervantes was a loose end he needed to deal with one way or another.

The Opulen was an exclusive hotel owned by a very wealthy group of men who would soon die. Well, those who weren't already dead from the blast at the Westwood mansion. Three still lived, but that would soon be changing.

But that wasn't enough for him. He needed them in complete and utter agony before they died. He might even change his rule about not hurting women and target their families. He hadn't brought up the idea to Oto yet, but he'd been rolling it around in his mind.

According to Ieva, this place had been used for select clients with particular tastes. Sick tastes. Alise had been brought here. Not long after her time here, she'd died. Hopefully Ieva would never discover Mihails had been behind all the destruction in Miami, but if she found out, he wouldn't deny it. She deserved justice.

A sharp pain pricked his palms and he realized he was digging his fingers into his flesh. His entire body was taut; he was too tense. Too wired. For the next part of their plan to work, he needed to focus on the endgame. After he'd accomplished what he planned to do, he was willing to die.

Not something many of his enemies could say. But first he had to carry out his mission. The need burned inside him, consuming his every waking thought. For so long he'd been working toward this goal. Now that it was finally within his grasp, he had to take it with both hands.

Oto cleared his throat and Mihails blinked. The man in front of them was gone and a woman behind the concierge desk was watching them expectantly, a plastic smile on her too-perfect face.

"How may I help you, gentlemen?" She even sounded like a robot.

"My brother and I arrived early for our reservation. Aaron and Oliver James." Two of their cover IDs. He pulled out his forged identification and slid it across the shiny surface of the welcome desk. He and Oto might as well be brothers, so posing as relatives was easy.

Her eyes widened slightly as she took his license. "Oh, Mr. James, yes. One of the penthouse suites, correct?"

He nodded and watched as her fingers flew over the keyboard of the sleek black computer. "Thank you for choosing the Opulen as your home away from home." It sounded as if she was reciting a standard spiel. "Do you have any bags with you? I will have them brought to your room immediately."

"My assistant will be bringing our bags in the next couple of hours. Until then we'd like access to our room. I realize we are early, so if it is not possible, I understand." Politeness was often the best way to gain what he wanted.

She gave him a bright smile. "It's ready, so there's no reason for you to wait." Then she was on the phone, asking for assistance.

As if they were so helpless they couldn't use the elevators themselves and locate the penthouse without assistance. Mihails would never understand rich people, but he gave her a professional smile and shot Oto a quick glance.

His partner was scanning the quiet, nearly empty lobby with ever-watchful eyes. No government agents lurking around. Just a lone man with dark hair sitting on one of the thick couches, drinking coffee from one of the delicate white cups with real platinum trim the hotel was known to use, as he read on his tablet. The skylights above let in an abundance of natural light, illuminating the sitting area with the coffee bar. It made the man stand out.

Mihails narrowed his gaze on the man, feeling something trigger his senses. Was something familiar about him or was Mihails being paranoid? Frowning, he took a step forward, meaning to get a better look, when a beautiful woman with dark hair who looked like one of those pinup models from fifty years ago approached the man with a big smile.

Immediately the man stood, sliding his tablet into his jacket pocket as he greeted her. As they left, some of the tension fled Mihails's body. He rubbed the back of his neck. He couldn't let paranoia make him do something stupid.

Since entering the hotel they'd been careful to stay to their pre-laid-out route to avoid cameras. They couldn't avoid all of them, especially the ones in the elevator, but he and Oto could keep their heads tilted down at a certain angle to avoid full facial recognition. Not that anyone at the hotel should be looking at them with interest, but they had planned everything out to avoid as much detection as possible.

Pushing out a sigh of relief, he looked over at Oto to find his friend watching him curiously. He ignored whatever was behind that look and gave a brief nod behind Oto. A man in his twenties wearing one of the crisp hotel uniforms was striding toward them.

Time to head to their suite. Next step, bringing in their explosives without detection.

Levi let the paid escort slide her hand into the crook of his arm as they left the Opulen. His heart was racing, though it had nothing to do with the beautiful woman next to him. No woman had the ability to affect him physically anymore. Not after his wife's death. That part of him had died a spectacular death.

What had him tense was who he'd just spotted. He couldn't believe that Mihails Balodis and Oto Ozols had just checked into the Opulen. His current cover had brought him back to Miami of all places, so he'd been staying at the exclusive hotel. Though a dark part of him wanted to ignore what he'd just witnessed, he couldn't.

His wife might be dead, but her ghost fucked with his conscience, trying to convince him he still had a soul somewhere in his hollowed-out chest.

Keeping his stride steady, he maintained pace with the tall woman with perfectly painted red lips and a body so exquisite he should be rock hard that her hand was on him. Or at least fantasizing about her. *Fuck*, he hated this dead feeling that was eating him alive from the inside out. He was like the damn tin man. Revenge was the only thing that could ease it. Until he had it, he'd never be free.

Hell, he wished all it would take was a beautiful woman to jar this rage loose. To exorcise it somehow. He'd used her as part of his cover over the past week on four separate occasions and she was a good companion. Well educated, could carry on an intelligent conversation with him and the significant others of the contacts he'd been meeting. It was all fake, small talk, but he liked having a partner of sorts. Of course she had no idea he was using her as part of his cover, even though he'd never touched her other than out of politeness.

"My plans have changed. I won't need your services today," he said as they exited the hotel. Without pause he handed his slip to one of the valets. Normally he didn't like giving up control of his vehicle, but there was no other choice at this hotel.

"Okay." She turned slightly into him so that her breast

brushed against his upper arm. It didn't stir any reaction in him but mild annoyance.

"You'll still be compensated." He didn't look at her as he scanned their surroundings out of ingrained habit. If things worked out, he might use her again, but after the next phone call he was about to make, he might have to make a hot exit from Miami. Only time would tell.

"Thank you."

He'd paid for most of her services up front, but this latest meeting had been last minute and he hadn't deposited the money yet. But he would. His cover required that he act a certain way, and that meant hiring escorts. He hadn't slept with her, though. The thought made him nauseated. And not because she was a prostitute. He'd learned a long damn time ago not to judge what any human had to do to survive. He just couldn't stand the thought of anyone who wasn't Meghan touching him intimately.

When the woman shifted next to him, rubbing her breast against him again, he realized she'd spoken and was watching him expectantly.

"I'm sorry?" Shit, he had to get it together. Getting distracted could get him killed. He could deal with dying, but not until he'd avenged his wife's murder.

The woman cleared her throat delicately. "I'm free this evening. No charge."

Levi blinked in surprise at the invitation. He also realized he wouldn't be using her in the future; he needed a true professional. "Thank you, but no. Do you need me to take you somewhere or do you have transportation?"

A flicker of disappointment played in her eyes, but she smiled, showing perfect white teeth. "No."

He nodded once as the valet pulled up with his SUV.

"I'll be in contact soon." A small lie compared to the countless he'd told over the last decade, first with the NSA, then when he'd gone off the reservation, developing his own covers and background stories for various roles.

At that, she gave him a real smile. One that reached her eyes. It made him feel shitty, though he wasn't sure why. As soon as he was on the causeway, he pulled out one of his countless burner phones from a hidden compartment in the center console. This one he'd be ditching seconds after he used it. Even if it was encrypted, he wasn't taking a chance that his former boss somehow use it to track him down. It would be a weak, rookie mistake.

The Opulen was on one of the man-made islands off the coast of Miami and there weren't many ways on or off, so he waited until he was almost back to the mainland to make the call.

"Burkhart here," his former boss barked, his voice raspy, probably from lack of sleep.

After that bombing at the Westwood mansion, the man had probably stolen only a couple of hours of shuteye. "You follow up on that tip I gave you?"

"Yeah." No pause this time.

The last time he'd called, Levi knew he'd stunned the other man. "You find them yet?"

"No," he growled.

"They just checked into the Opulen Hotel. You're welcome." Levi hung up, took out the battery, then tossed all the pieces out the window onto the causeway. He had his own hunting to do.

Chapter 11

Disguise: to modify one's appearance in order to conceal the wearer's identity. Tactic often used by intelligence agencies.

As they drove to the funeral, Maria felt ridiculous wearing a wig and oversized sunglasses, but the short bob that angled down around her chin actually looked real. It was a light honey brown, a much paler shade than her own hair. Even though everything looked natural, she felt as if she were wearing a helmet or a heavy hat.

She'd had to put a small mesh net on to secure her thick hair in place; then Cade had helped her with pinning the fake piece on. He'd done it with such efficiency it was a little scary. Obviously this wasn't his first time with disguises. Which made her feel a little better, but not much.

Self-consciously, she fingered the strands around her face.

"Don't mess with it. No one will know it's not yours." Cade didn't take his eyes off the street as he spoke, but his voice was soft.

"I know, it's just weird." Not that a wig should even be part of her concerns this morning. But it gave her something to focus on besides the grief that had taken up residence in her chest and was weighing her down with each passing second. Waking up this morning and knowing she had to attend her mother's funeral—it was like swallowing shards of glass. The constant struggle not to burst into tears and have a meltdown was making her edgy and shaky.

Surprising her, Cade reached out and took her hand in his, linking his long fingers through hers. When he squeezed gently, tears burned her eyes and she was thankful for her sunglasses. She tightened her fingers around his, the tight vise around her chest easing just a fraction. Even so, she turned to look out at the passing landscape. Everything was a blur.

Other than his help with the wig, this was the first physical contact he'd shown her this morning. After what they'd shared last night, it had taken her off guard when he'd been in strict professional mode this morning. She understood that he was trying to maintain a professional distance and was just doing his job, but that knowledge hadn't lessened the sting any.

She was thankful he didn't pull away now but kept his fingers linked with hers. "So, how will we even get into the funeral?" She'd called her father early this morning, just as the sun had come up, and he'd told her they'd implemented extra security because of the vulture-like media and potentially violent threats. There hadn't been any made, but the majority of the families who had lost someone in the blast were being cautious in case the bombers tried to target one of the funerals. Sadly, she knew that wasn't out of the realm of possibility.

Since she couldn't attend as herself, she was worried about getting in, and she'd forgotten to ask her dad about it. So much was weighing on her mind right now, especially as she struggled to remember what had happened the night of the bombing.

"I spoke to the head of your father's security while you were showering. Mr. Larson has been very helpful." There seemed to be a bite of sarcasm at the mention of Nash, but she couldn't be sure as Cade continued. "We'll be seated near the front and will be surrounded by security, all who are under strict instructions not to call you by name or act as if they know you. You are a distant cousin if anyone asks, but we'll position you so that your back is to most people. You won't be recognizable and you won't be given a chance to speak to anyone."

She turned back toward Cade, tears completely dried. "And you're just telling me now?"

He shot her a sideways glance as he removed his hand from hers to take a left turn into another quiet residential neighborhood, bringing them even closer to the funeral proceedings. Without the feel of his hand in hers, everything seemed somehow worse. She felt sick to her stomach. She didn't want to do this. Didn't want to acknowledge that her mom was really and truly gone. Panic settled in for a moment, but she pushed it back down. She couldn't have a freaking breakdown right now.

"Yes," he murmured.

She gritted her teeth, annoyance filtering through her. It was ridiculous to be annoyed, but she latched onto the feeling, hoping it would overpower or at least temper the pain burning in her chest. That was a stupid hope, but it was there nonetheless. Nothing was going to dilute the agony of attending her mother's funeral. "You can't just leave me in the dark about stuff." Not when it concerned her life and something as important as this.

Her abdomen tightened when she saw the pointed arch of her family's Catholic church visible above the trees and houses. The Gothic cathedral was nestled in one of South Miami's residential neighborhoods. The church shared the expansive grounds with an elementary school and a huge social hall, but there wouldn't be any socializing afterward. Her father would be having only close friends and relatives back to his house after the ceremony, but that was it. Unfortunately she couldn't even attend that. Or maybe fortunately. She didn't feel like making small talk with anyone right now. Not even people she cared about. But she wanted to be there for her dad. Every time they'd spoken on the phone, she'd heard the ragged pain in his voice.

"Listen, the NSA is letting you attend—"

"*Letting* me?" she shouted as a burst of anger and pain popped inside her. "My father's having to deal with all this without me! He's lost his son and now his wife and I'm not even there for him. Do you think that's easy for him *or* me?" She barreled on, not wanting to stop, needing to hold on to her annoyance. "It's not and if you think you're 'letting' me do anything, you're out of your damn mind."

Cade's fingers tightened on the wheel and she had a brief flash from last night as she remembered how he'd stroked her to orgasm with his hands and mouth. She shook her head, shoving the untimely memory away.

"Damn it, Maria. You know what I mean. I'm not used to checking in with anyone. I'm making decisions about your safety and yeah, I'm not going to remember to tell you everything. It doesn't mean I'm intentionally leaving you in the dark. I just want to get you there, then get you the hell out unharmed. Nothing is going to happen to you on my fucking watch." Now he was practically shouting, the slight tremble in his voice at the last couple of words slamming through her like a shock wave.

He was worried about her. Which she knew on an intellectual level. But maybe he was worried for more than just professional reasons. Any lingering frustration seeped out of her in a rush. "Sorry," she murmured.

He sighed, the frustration visibly draining out of him. "You don't have anything to be sorry for. I just ... I'm worried about you being exposed," he muttered as he slowed and pulled down another quiet street. This one was lined with cars along the curbs. Which wasn't normal. The church had a parking lot. A big one. Clearly it had overflowed if people were taking to parking in front of homes.

Cade parked behind a four-door Volvo and gave himself plenty of space so they couldn't be blocked in. Though she knew he'd just ram into a vehicle if they needed to make a fast getaway. She waited as he pulled out his phone and texted someone. Once he received a buzzing response, he nodded at her. "All right, instead of going in through the narthex, Nash is meeting us at the southwest entrance. We'll escort you through a side entryway that's been blocked off."

Maria wasn't even sure where the southwest entrance was, but clearly Cade did. He'd probably memorized the entire layout and architecture of the church and its grounds. "Okay." Grabbing her small purse, she slid out of the vehicle. As her kitten heels touched the sidewalk, a tremble went through her. The pressure on her chest was damn near suffocating. Soon she'd be in a church filled with mourners and would have to listen to people tell stories about her mom and how wonderful she'd been. Which she had been. But the thought of sitting there, of acknowledging that her mom was truly gone ... Crap, how was she going to do this without breaking down?

Before she'd taken a step, Cade wrapped his big arm around her and pulled her tight. He kissed the top of her wig-covered head. "Cry all you want. I've got you and I'm not letting go."

"Thank you," she murmured, needing to hear those words more than she'd realized. Inside she was already shaking apart and even Cade couldn't hold her together. Part of her hated how nice he was being, because he would be an easy target to lash out at. Especially right now when her pain was raking against her insides like razor wire. She wanted to hate him for how he'd cut contact between them eight years ago. It would be a hell of a lot easier if he were an asshole in the present day, if he'd never apologized. But after he'd been honest about why he'd cut and run, how could she hate someone for mourning in his own way? What he'd done was wrong, but it had been a long time ago and clearly he'd changed. Hell, he'd originally requested this assignment to question her. Then when it had turned into more, he began protecting her.

He pulled her close to his chest and just stood there for a long moment as he rubbed a hand up and down the length of her back.

She drew on that strength and finally pulled back. Even if she wanted to, she couldn't stand out there all day. In silence, they walked along the sidewalk with her arm wrapped around his waist and his around her shoulders. She was thankful he wasn't keeping his distance anymore. She soaked up the feel of his big body pressing against hers. Without trying, he was such a comfort. Cade was tense and she knew he was on alert, looking for any potential threats. For that she was grateful because she could barely see past the tears blurring her vision. She didn't want to do this. How was she going to get through this?

Her shoes clicked along the sidewalk until they reached an iron gate that led to a private garden she'd been in before. Cade put his body in front of hers, but before he'd even reached over it to unhook the latch, Nash appeared from seemingly out of nowhere. The foliage in the garden was thick, creating a quiet tropical oasis, making it easy for anyone to hide. Something she wouldn't even have thought of a few days ago.

"Hey, Nash," she said quietly as they stepped into the garden.

She heard Cade snap the latch back into place behind them as Nash pulled her into a hug. "I'm sorry you're dealing with so much shit on top of . . ." He trailed off as he stepped back. He looked severe in his black suit, crisp white shirt, and black tie. She could see his small earpiece when he turned to look at Cade. "Everything's set up. You two will go in through the west entrance, down the aisle until you reach the third row back. I've already got two men in place. They'll sit on either side of you. When the service is over, you'll leave the way you came. Everyone else will be going out through the main entrance, so this should work." He glanced around as he spoke, taking on the same tense stance as Cade. "I don't like her being out here like this. Let's go."

Cade just grunted in agreement and slid his arm protectively around her shoulders again. It might have been her imagination, but there was something almost possessive about the way he held her tight. And it didn't escape Nash's ever-watchful gaze either.

But he didn't comment. Instead he spoke quietly into his earpiece as they headed down a winding stone path that led right through the middle of the garden. Once they were across, the garden opened up onto the west side of the church where a private parking lot was situated. The main one where all the mourners would be parking was on the opposite side. She'd never been in this area before, but she recognized her father's Mercedes. The silver SUV shone under the bright sun.

"Your dad wanted to see you before the service." Nash's voice had a rough edge to it today and she knew this had to be hard for him too.

Cade had started to say something when the driver's-side door opened and her father stepped out. Maria immediately left the two men and hurried to her father. The tears that had been building finally broke free, but she didn't care as her dad pulled her into a tight hug. She knew how much he was suffering and she was glad to finally be able to hug him, to mourn with him.

"How private is this parking lot?" Cade scanned the limited number of vehicles in the small lot.

"It's been secured. No one other than family is getting in this way," Nash said.

Cade hated having Maria out in the open, especially in a place where there were so many trees and other places to hide. If someone wanted, they could have set

up early in one of the cathedral towers with a sniper rifle. He expected that Nash's team would already have secured it, but he didn't know all the details of what they'd
done. At that thought, Cade automatically glanced up.

"The towers have been swept and secured," Nash said
tightly, obviously understanding. "We were here early
this morning and the church has been very cooperative.
They love the Cervantes family and are doing everything
possible to make sure today is as smooth as possible." A
short pause. "The wig is good. I recognized her because
I know her so well, but most people won't be able to tell.
Especially not with those glasses."

Cade nodded, his gaze straying to where Maria stood
with her father. It looked as if they were both crying, and
he tried not to let the sight of her in pain affect him so
much. It was a fruitless effort.

He'd rather get punched in the nuts than see her griev-
ing. This morning he'd ordered himself to keep things professional. The hurt in her eyes had been palpable and he'd
wanted to kick his own ass for putting it there. For adding
to what she was already dealing with. But he'd needed to
set up some damn boundaries. For both their sakes. Someone wanted to hurt her, and they needed to know why.

"She remember anything else?" Nash asked quietly,
though Cade knew he had an earpiece in.

He shook his head, still not completely comfortable
opening up to the man even if he was with her family's
security. The guy's record was clean and he seemed to
truly care about her, but Cade didn't care. To him, everyone but the men and women he worked with were the
enemy right now. And while the rest of the security team
had passed standard vetting from the NSA—otherwise

Maria wouldn't be here—he definitely couldn't risk some-one random overhearing. "How many people are here?"

"A few hundred. Riel had to tighten the list of mourn-ers allowed. He doesn't want his daughter at risk. But people are still showing up. My team's having to turn them away."

He shook his head. "Bet that's fucking fun."

Larson made an annoyed sound, then straightened when Maria stepped back from her father and looked at them. "See you inside," he murmured before heading toward Riel Cervantes.

Cade made his way to Maria, who tried to wipe away her tears under her sunglasses. He quickly fished out a tissue and handed it to her. She seemed almost surprised, though it was hard to tell with the shades, but she mur-mured thanks and took it from him.

She pushed her sunglasses up for a moment, and the sight of her red-rimmed eyes was a jolt to his system.

Against his better judgment, he pulled her against him once again and headed for the entrance. He wanted to give her a moment to compose herself but didn't want to keep her outside longer than necessary. Not when he hadn't done the securing himself. Larson's team might be good, but he didn't know them.

As they stepped into the side door, Maria turned and buried her face against his side. Her body shook as she tried to hold her tears in. He just held her tighter. Fuck being professional. He'd tried that this morning, but there was no way in hell he could keep his distance from her today. Not when she needed him.

Oh yeah, he was a total masochist, because whatever happened between them was going to end badly. A woman like Maria had the ability to completely strip him of his control and shred his heart. They were from two different worlds and if she knew the truth about him, she'd hate him. Which would destroy him—but his heart wasn't listening to his head right now.

He just wanted to protect her from all the pain she was experiencing. The only small silver lining was that there was no coffin. Since the bodies hadn't been released, and in some cases, some might never be recovered, there wouldn't be a symbol for her to look at. It probably wouldn't make things any easier for her. When she tried to muffle another sob, he tightened his grip, hating how helpless he was to shield her from any of this. He might be able to defend her physically, but there was nothing he could do to protect her heart from breaking right now.

He narrowed his gaze on the back of the woman's head. Even with the light brown, almost blond hair, it had to be Maria. The hair was different, obviously a wig—a very good one because it looked real—but his gut told him it was the bitch.

That giant tattooed guy sitting next to her gave her away. All his tats were covered up because of the suit, but he recognized the man. And he looked like a street thug. But he wasn't. No, the man worked for the government, so he had to have decent training. Of course he'd seen the agent in action, so he knew he was skilled.

Getting to her here would be impossible, though he'd temporarily toyed with the idea. He didn't have a death wish, though. Unlike the men he worked with, he wasn't hell-bent on some cause he would die for. No, he was in this for one very important reason. He loved money. People who said money couldn't buy happiness were fucking stupid and had obviously never been poor. Not truly. Not the kind of poor where you had no idea where your next meal was coming from or where you would sleep at night.

Unfortunately, taking out Maria would be tricky, with her lethal shadow. Not to mention the extra security sitting next to her and the team of men sitting behind her.

Yes, her father wasn't leaving her safety to chance at all. Speaking of, he turned back to where Riel Cervantes stood at the front of the church, speaking quietly into a microphone about how much his late wife would be missed.

Fucking spare me.

His wife had died instantly; it wasn't as if she'd suffered. All those wealthy people didn't know shit about true pain. The rich kept getting richer and people like him had to struggle to get to where they were. Even Maria; she might try to make herself feel better by giving back to the poor in her community, but she always had her parents' money to fall back on. Money she hadn't earned. Right now she was an obstacle in his way. Her and that community center. Soon enough she'd be out of the way and he could finally make the money he'd worked so hard for. It was what he deserved.

Glancing around, he eyed each of the exits. If he had to guess, he'd say that Maria and her shadow wouldn't be leaving through the narthex. They hadn't come through that way, because he'd been waiting for her. No, they'd take one of three other exits, if he had to guess. As soon as the ceremony was over, he'd make his way to the end of his pew as quickly as possible and try to catch up with her.

While he might not be able to do any damage here, he had another plan. One she wouldn't see coming. He'd be able to track her without worrying about avoiding detection from a trained operative. Then when the time was right, he'd strike and eliminate her.

Chapter 12

Command center: central location for processing data, giving orders, and supervising a critical situation.

M aria might have felt stupid keeping her sunglasses on, but as she used Cade to block her, covertly looking over his shoulder at the crowd of mourners, she saw she wasn't the only one. There were more than a handful of famous people in attendance, and the shades were so typical of many in this crowd. For once, she didn't think the act of wearing them was pretentious.

The artificial barrier over her eyes made her feel saner. Even having a small way to block out the rest of the world was a comfort. Her pain was hers and she didn't want to share it with anyone else.

Except maybe Cade. That thought was terrifying in its own way. She shouldn't be leaning on him for anything. Not after the way he'd disappeared on her when her brother died. But he was here now and even though it was for his job, he was an incredible comfort.

Her aunt was speaking now as the service finally wound down. Maria had loved hearing everything different friends and family members had to say about her mother, but her heart could only take so much. It was like nails being pounded into her chest with each person that got up on the podium. One more person solidifying that yeah, her mom was gone for good and that this wasn't some nightmare.

It was real and horrifying and she just wanted to curl into a ball and cry, blocking out the rest of the world. She didn't want to hear any more damn words. She just wanted to leave and be alone in her misery.

After sobbing in the shower this morning until she didn't think she had any tears left, she wished she could be numb. But she wasn't. No, she wasn't that lucky. Every second that passed was agony.

Closing her eyes, she leaned her head against Cade's shoulder. His arm had been around her the entire service and he tightened it as she moved in. His spicy scent wrapped around her, just as much a comfort as his physical presence. She didn't even know where to go with the feelings he evoked in her. It was as if he calmed part of her when she needed it most. He just had that rock-solid, steady thing about him. The type of man you could depend on for anything. It was deceiving, though, and despite that she tried to remind herself of that, it didn't matter. She soaked up all his comfort without reserve.

Finally, after what felt like an eternity, her aunt stopped talking and the priest wrapped things up very quickly. That was out of character, but Maria had a feeling her father might have said something beforehand. He could be forceful like that. He wouldn't want anyone preaching at his wife's funeral and wouldn't be shy about making that clear.

She was vaguely aware of the crowd starting to stand and shift toward the middle and outer aisles. Instinctively she stood, but her knees were shaky. Emotionally exhausted, she felt as if she'd just run a marathon for how weak she was.

Cade moved up beside her impossibly fast. He kept his hand at the small of her back, another possessive gesture that didn't go unnoticed.

"We're going out the same side exit," he murmured as they followed after a couple of the security members walking to the outer aisle. It was the quickest route.

Glancing around, she watched as people slowly made their way to the back of the church. She spotted so many people she knew, including her best friend and a handful of kids from the center. Just seeing them made a fresh wave of tears well up. She knew they must be wondering why she wasn't at the funeral and hoped Leah had made something up. The only person whose opinion mattered was her dad's, and he knew she was there. Eyes burning, she prayed for the security men in front of her to move faster. Her chest ached as she tried to stifle the sobs she'd been holding in since the moment they arrived. It wouldn't do for her to break down and make a spectacle of herself, drawing attention to her and Cade. She didn't care about personal embarrassment, but right now she knew she needed to remain unnoticed for safety reasons.

A big echo from the back ricocheted through the church as something slammed into the stone of the entryway. It was followed by a startled hum of voices that seemed to grow louder. Maria glanced in the direction but couldn't see anything over the throng of heads. As they reached the end of the pew, Cade placed a hand on her shoulder, signaling for her to stop as he stepped forward and started talking to one of the security men who'd been in front of them.

Even though the guy wouldn't be able to see what was going on either, he had an earpiece and it seemed as if he was relaying what had happened. Their voices were too low for her to hear over the rest of the din of people murmuring among themselves.

When she saw her father standing by the middle altar hugging her aunt, she thought she would lose it. Seeing her father cry was too much. The icing on the shittiest cake in the world.

Cade was still talking to one of the men and Maria knew if she tried to talk to him, she'd break. She clutched onto the forearm of one of the other security men and pointed to the exit. Her throat tightened, making it impossible to speak. It ached so badly from trying to hold back her tears.

He understood, though, because he nodded and hustled her away, his expression sympathetic. Seconds later they were outside. Bending over at the waist, she placed her hands on her knees and tried to drag in a deep breath. As air filled her lungs, she felt less light-headed but not much better than she had inside.

"Can I get you anything?" the man asked softly as he stood next to her. She'd seen him around the grounds of her parents' home before but couldn't remember his name.

She shook her head. "No, thank you." Her voice was raspy, unsteady as tears clogged her throat.

"Maria." At Cade's tight voice she stood to find him barreling out the side door, his expression dark.

"Don't," she snapped, unable to handle any chastising. She'd been with a security guy, so it wasn't as if she'd just run outside without any protection.

Before he could respond, her friend Leah hurried out the door, followed by two annoyed-looking security guys. When she hugged Leah, the men stepped back and she heard Cade mutter something under his breath about the weak security, but at least he didn't try to stop her.

"Is this a new look?" Leah asked, her voice watery and her eyes red.

Maria let out a harsh, shaky laugh. "Not exactly."

"I didn't realize it was you at first, but then I saw him," her friend said quietly, nodding behind Maria.

Right. Even if she was in disguise, Cade definitely wasn't. "Thanks for coming."

She snorted. "As if that was ever in doubt. Honey, I'm so sorry about your mom. What do you want me doing right now? I want to help you any way I can."

Maria shook her head. "Just keep doing what you're doing at the center. That's the biggest thing you can do right now."

Leah nodded and took Maria's chilled hands. "That's a given. Do you want me to bring meals over? Do you need help with—"

"I need Dr. York's contact info," she said abruptly. That he could possibly help with her memory loss problem just popped into her mind. It was a long shot, but at this point she was willing to try pretty much *anything*. This helpless sensation of not being able to remember was too much. She had to get her memories back from the night of the explosion. The need clawed at her insides. Her mother's murderers would be brought to justice. Something important hovered at the corners of her memory. She just had to dig it out.

Leah's blond eyebrows furrowed together, but she nodded. "Okay. I'll text you the information in a sec. I've got it stored in my phone."

"Thank you—"

"Maria. We need to leave *now*." Cade's firm hand landed on her elbow. She looked up to find a hard expression on his face. Not directed at her exactly, but he was annoyed.

"I know. I just—"

"Maria?" She looked up at the sound of a familiar male voice calling her name.

"Fucking security," Cade muttered as he moved to stand in front of her, blocking her from the man heading her way.

Andre was a family friend and knew her fairly well. She should have known the wig wouldn't fool everyone. She nodded at him but let him cross the ten or so yards to meet her instead of making a move toward him.

"I'll text you right now. Call me if you need anything. Or if you just want to cry. I don't care if it's the middle of the night and you want me to bring ice cream and a bottle of wine over, I'm there." Leah dropped a quick kiss on her cheek before hurrying away.

"Cade, he's fine," Maria murmured, low enough for Cade to hear as she placed a hand on his forearm.

He ignored her as he positioned himself in front of her.

"I knew you wouldn't miss the funeral. I don't understand why your father said you weren't here," Andre said as he reached her and Cade. He gave Cade a confused look. "Who are you?"

"He's ... a friend." Maria completely stepped out

from behind Cade's protective stance. "Thank you for coming, Andre. I'm sorry I won't be able to be at my father's after this, but I appreciate you attending today. Both my dad and I do." She felt so lame doing the polite small talk but knew she had to be civil.

The majority of the people had come because they truly cared her mom was gone. She couldn't forget that even through the piercing agony searing her chest.

"Of course," he said quietly.

A new rush of people exited the side door and Cade let out an angry curse, earning a surprised glance from Andre. When Maria spotted Wayne Gregory among the crowd of mourners, she frowned. She hadn't realized he was attending, though she did appreciate it. Still, if she had to make small talk with any more people, she was going to collapse.

Luckily Cade didn't give her a choice. He held firmly on to her elbow. "We have to leave now. Excuse us." Cade didn't give either one of them a chance to respond as he steered her toward the stone walkway.

Unfortunately they had to head past all the people milling out. She turned her face toward Cade's chest as they passed Wayne, letting Cade guide her. She avoided looking at everyone she recognized and getting caught up in a conversation. Not that Cade would have let her stop anyway.

He was moving her along at such a fast clip she could barely keep up. She nearly stumbled in her heels, skating past a couple of the mourners, but Cade didn't even let her apologize as he whisked her away.

"Slow down," she snapped.

"I should throw you over my shoulder and carry

you." There was a barely contained note of anger in his voice.

Why the hell was he angry with her? She'd just come from her mother's funeral. But she didn't question him as they backtracked their original route. She was half jogging by the time they reached the truck and he unceremoniously shoved her into the passenger seat.

"What the hell's the matter with you?" she practically shouted as he slid into the driver's seat.

"You were too exposed. Why'd you leave like that?" His voice was sharp as he started the engine.

"I wasn't alone. I had a security guy with me."

"Some fucking security." Now the rage was there, but not directed at her. Still, she could see it simmering beneath the surface of those green eyes.

"What happened?"

"Some idiot knocked over one of the big vases of flowers and people apparently forgot how to fucking walk. They started using the side exits. And security couldn't *maintain* them." There was a definite bit of sarcasm behind those words as he put the vehicle into gear and pulled away from the curb.

"What were they going to do, shoot them?" Her voice was wry.

Some of the tension eased from his shoulders as he gave her a ghost of a smile, but his profile was still hard as he drove them away from the church. "Why'd you leave like that?"

"I was about to have a breakdown for the fiftieth time and needed to breathe. I didn't want a bunch of people staring at me if I started sobbing uncontrollably. I needed some air." She understood he had security concerns, but she wasn't trained for a situation like this. She was barely hanging on to her sanity right now.

Now his expression completely softened and he shot her a quick glance as he pulled up to a stop sign. Reaching out, he cupped her cheek, his gaze intense as he watched her. His big hand was so gentle it stunned her. The feel of his callused palm against her skin was startlingly reassuring. "And I need you safe," he whispered.

Well, hell. She couldn't get angry at that.

Just as quickly he dropped his hand and returned his attention to the street. As he drove through the quiet residential streets, she tried to get ahold of the jumbled mess that her mind was right now. But it was no use. Today had been awful and last night . . . "Why'd you leave so suddenly last night?"

Cade's hands jerked slightly on the wheel, but he didn't respond. Just looked in the rearview mirror before pulling into a small parking area next to a local park. There was no one around and no cars anywhere, but he still scanned the area diligently before putting the SUV into park and looking at her.

He cupped her cheek again in that sweet way of his and his eyes dipped to her mouth. For a moment she saw a flash of raw, unrestricted desire in his eyes. He leaned forward a fraction but stopped himself. Still, he didn't drop his hand, just lightly rubbed his thumb over her cheek. The action was so soft, but it was in opposition to the hunger burning in his gaze. "Last night was . . ."

He seemed to struggle with his words, as if he wanted to say the night before had been a mistake. She was glad he didn't. She could tell he didn't plan to take things any further between them, though. But she didn't have a problem acting on her need. She just wanted a few minutes—okay, hours—of pure pleasure. Something to wash away, or at least mute, the grief burning out of control inside her. Cade was the only one who could help her temporarily forget. She knew this wouldn't be about a relationship or anything long-term. He'd already shown her that he had no problem walking away. So right now she didn't feel bad for wanting to use him just a little bit to help ease her grief.

"Cade . . ." She swallowed hard, trying to find the right words as her gaze strayed to his mouth. She wouldn't bother hiding what she wanted. Without thinking she licked her lips.

The radio was off and she guessed the windows were bullet resistant or something because she couldn't hear anything outside, not that there were any people nearby. It made the silence in the vehicle deafening, their increasingly ragged breathing the only sounds.

"Maria . . ." There was a wealth of regret in that one word. His hand still cupped her jaw, and his fingers flexed against her skin, the rough pads of them sending a shiver through her.

She refused to accept whatever he was going to say. Leaning over, she brushed her lips against his. Just to test his reaction. After last night she knew how much he wanted her, but she was still feeling vulnerable and yeah, insecure. When their mouths touched, it was like something igniting between them. She felt it all the way down to her toes.

A spark of fiery hunger shot through her as he took over, completely dominating the kiss, his tongue invading her mouth. His hand slid back and cupped her head in that way she loved. Craved.

His other hand quickly sought out her hip as she

clutched his shoulders to steady herself. It was pointless. She was a quaking mass of nerves and untamed energy. Nothing could steady her now. As her fingers dug into his hard muscle, he tugged her over the center console and in a few moves she was straddling his lap. She lost one of her shoes in the process. Her dress pushed up her thighs, but he shoved the material farther until it was bunched against her waist.

The cool air from the air-conditioning rolled over her bare skin, but as his big hand roamed over her backside, digging into her soft flesh, a blast of heat surged through her, making her nipples tighten and her inner walls clench with an unfulfilled need. The man could get her hot in seconds flat.

The windows were darkly tinted—probably illegally—so she wasn't worried about anyone seeing them. Hell, she wasn't worried about anything at the moment and she knew she should be. Her only concern was feeling him inside her. Because if he was thrusting deep into her she wouldn't be thinking about anything else. She wouldn't be battling her grief. She didn't care if she was using sex as a temporary Band-Aid.

As his tongue danced against hers, she slowly started grinding against him. The feel of his erection rubbing over her covered mound was delicious. It didn't matter that his pants and her flimsy panties were in the way. The friction against her clit was mounting each time he rolled his hips, rubbing harder and harder against her.

When cool air rushed over her back, it registered that he'd tugged the zipper of her dress down. She hadn't even felt him move. Hadn't even been aware.

As the simple black boat-neck dress loosened and fell

down her body, he leaned back so that their lips weren't touching anymore. She immediately felt the loss, but as she looked at his face and saw the hunger in his gaze as he stared at her breasts, another wave of heat punched through her. She grew even damper as he practically devoured her with his eyes.

He didn't even unhook her bra, just shoved the lace cups down and latched onto one of her breasts with his hungry mouth. The abrupt action took her off guard. Arching into his mouth, she held on to his shoulder and head as pleasure swamped her. She loved the feel of his buzz cut. It was soft against her palm.

He lightly pressed down with his teeth on her hardened nipple as he flicked his tongue against the already sensitized bud over and over. The tender lashing had her body trembling out of control. It wouldn't take much to push her over the edge.

When his hips surged up again, that thick hardness rubbing against her clit, she let her head fall back and began moving against him. The sensation of his erection hitting her sensitive bundle of nerves in just the right spot, over and over, had her entire body pulling taut.

She told herself to stop, but it was impossible. She had absolutely no self-control. It was as if she'd turned into some primal being who only cared about pleasure.

Because pleasure drowned out everything else. Things she wouldn't let herself think about now. If she did, she'd sink into the pain and might never claw her way out.

Suddenly he switched breasts, making sounds of pleasure as he sucked on her other nipple. As his covered cock continued stimulating her clit, she let free what had been building inside her. The orgasm swept through her, the tingles reaching all her nerve endings. As her climax built, her thighs tightened around him.

She buried her face against his neck as it crested higher. His hands slid up and down her back as he held her through the release. As she came down from her high, she inwardly cringed even as she inhaled that spicy familiar scent she loved so much.

"I'm sorry," she whispered, feeling embarrassed. She'd just jumped him, then come against him like a cat in heat.

"What the hell for?" he growled, pulling her back so she had to look at him.

With her breasts on display and her clothes tangled around her, she could feel her face heat up and knew she must be crimson. What the hell was wrong with her? She felt like a hot freaking mess, minus the hot part. God, she was just a mess, plain and simple, doing this right after the funeral. "For ... attacking you." She trailed off as more heat flooded her face. Internally she winced, feeling selfish. What if he felt sorry for her and was just ... She covered her face with her hand, unable to look at him. "If ... this was some kind of pity thing, I really am sorry and just, God, I'm sorry and—"

"Maria! Look at me." His voice was harsh and demanding.

Internally berating herself, she met his gaze.

"That wasn't about pity. I'm going to come inside you. *Soon*. But I'm going to take you in a bed where I can do a hell of a lot more than a frantic fuck." There was a raw, guttural sound to his words, and his face was slightly flushed but not from embarrassment like hers. He was incredibly turned on, the desire written all over his face.

She nodded and tried to think of a response, but a soft

buzzing cut through the air. Frowning, she looked around for her purse, but when Cade cursed she realized it was his phone.

He fished it out of his pocket and swore again when he looked at the caller ID. "Perfect timing," he muttered.

Maria quickly slid her dress back up her arms and eased off him as he answered his cell. She straightened her clothes and listened to the one-sided conversation. By the time he was done, she had a feeling she wasn't going to like what he had to say.

When he ended the call, his expression was grim as he turned to her. "That was my boss. There have been a couple new developments. Looks like we might have a lead on the suspected bombers and he wants me to be part of the direct assault team."

Nodding, she swallowed. "Oh." What more was there to say?

"I hate to drag you anywhere but the safe house, but you'll be under the protection of four trained agents while I go in with the rest of the team. You won't be close to the action, but you'll be in the vicinity. We don't have any teams set up off-site and I don't trust you with any other agency. I'm sorry but we just don't have time to take you anywhere else right now or I swear I would. If we bring these guys down, you'll be safe again. No more hiding."

It made sense that his boss would want him, especially if they'd found the terrorists. Then they wouldn't need whatever knowledge she had buried in her memories anymore. While she was glad they might have found the terrorists, a small, completely emotional part of her was bereft. What did this mean for her and Cade now? Once they caught the bad guys, there would be no reason for him to be with her anymore. She could go home and try to grieve and just deal with everything that had happened. She *should* be relieved. It wasn't as though she envisioned a future with him or wanted anything long-term. Not after the way he'd bailed on her before.

Instead a new ache settled in her chest. "Good, let's go, then." Her voice was raspy and she felt a new onslaught of tears coming so she looked out the window.

A tense silence settled between them like a wall. "I swear I'll come back to you after this assault."

As tears tracked down her face, she kept her head turned out the window. "Sure." It was all she could squeeze out.

"Maria . . ." Just when she thought Cade might continue, he sighed and steered the truck away from the curb as they headed to wherever the suspected terrorists were.

*   *   *

Date: November 7, 2006
To: Cade O'Reilly
From: Maria Cervantes
Subject: re: Hey

Don't worry? Yeah, okay. I'm going to be biting my fingernails until I hear back. But I'm glad you told me. It's easier knowing this way. I'm glad my other letters made it. I wasn't sure if they'd gotten lost in the mail. I'm looking forward to you guys coming back too. Miami in the spring is perfect. You'll miss the humidity and it'll be warm enough for the beach. And I've got some new places I want to take you and Riel to, including a couple food trucks. Which might sound gross, but trust me, I found some jewels last month, including a Middle Eastern one. Not sure if you'll even want that type of food when you get back, but it's pretty good.

So, what would you want to do if you got out? There are so many opportunities and you're still young. Maybe something in law enforcement? Or do you want something totally different?

I look forward to all your e-mails too. They're usually the highlight of my day. Miss you and I'll be praying for your mission.

xo,
Maria

Chapter 13

Tactical team: a highly trained small law enforcement unit that uses military-grade weapons and engages in high-risk operations, including hostage rescue and counterterrorism maneuvers.

Mihails carefully slid the blasting caps into the last half brick of C-4. He, Oto, and two other team members had strategically placed the explosives around the spacious penthouse suite. They'd secured them to all of the load-bearing walls to inflict maximum damage. Next they'd be moving on to another of the penthouse suites, then down ten floors, where one of his men had checked in under an alias. After they'd placed similar explosives on that floor, they would move to the floor right above the lobby.

Three strategic areas of the building guaranteed to make the place implode on itself and pancake down, layer upon layer, until it was just a heap of rubble. But he would call in a bomb threat this time, only giving the people inside enough time to escape. Maybe ten minutes. He was sending a message to the owners of the Opulen, but there was no need for collateral damage today. Not like at the Westwood mansion. That had been unavoidable, but he didn't relish the thought of taking more human lives. He wasn't a monster. Not like the men who'd hurt his sisters and countless other women.

Even with the bomb threat, it would be impossible for the police to make it to the island in time. And if they somehow did, his lookout would tell him of their presence and he would detonate everything before they arrived.

As he stepped back into the middle of the main living room, his phone buzzed in his pocket. All their phones for this mission were burners, but he'd designated initials for each member of his team. When K came up on his caller ID, he knew it was Kristaps. The other man had taken care of a problem for them and was now their lookout. If he was calling, it couldn't be good.

"Yes?"

"It is a nice day to go parasailing." An amenity the hotel offered to its guests. In this case, it was a code for "get out now" and use a boat as a means of escape instead of the recently stolen SUVs they'd acquired. Since they'd already wiped the vehicles down, he wasn't worried about DNA or fingerprints being left behind.

His heart rate increased a fraction, but he kept his voice calm. "Yes, it is. Will you be joining us?"

A pause. "No." Which meant it would be too difficult for Kristaps to meet them without exposing either himself or the rest of the team.

"See you soon, then." If all went well, Kristaps would meet them at their previously designated rendezvous point, but if he was captured, Mihails knew he wouldn't talk. None of his men would. They'd all planned for this. Each one was prepared for the consequences, and in this case, the American justice system was so weak and flawed that going to prison here was nothing to be feared.

After he disconnected, Mihails placed his earpiece on the rectangular table behind one of the couches. He would leave it to be destroyed in the blast. While they wouldn't be able to raze the hotel to the ground now, they would still be setting off the current charges. There was no way these would go to waste.

"Everyone leave your phones. It's time for plan C," he called out. The place had impressive insulation and, with the layout of the hotel, he wasn't worried about any neighbors overhearing since they didn't have any. Not to mention that civilians were the least of his worries now.

At this point he didn't know how bad the situation was, but for Kristaps to call meant it was serious. They could have less than five minutes to get out. And it was almost a guarantee that one or more government agency would be monitoring incoming and outgoing calls in the vicinity. If they remotely suspected something, it would have been the first thing they did before descending on the place. So even though he and Kristaps had spoken in code, it wasn't much of a cover if the government knew their identities. Not that he was sure they did or even had eavesdropping capabilities. He hated not knowing at this point, but now the only thing they could do was try to get out of the Opulen alive and finish the rest of their objective.

Moments later Oto and his two other men emerged from other rooms. They tossed their phones onto whatever was closest to them.

Wordlessly, they all converged on the two suitcases his other men had brought. He and Oto pulled out the standard uniforms the security members at the hotel wore. Simple black suits, white button-down shirts, and black ties. They also had fake badges that might not hold up under scrutiny, but for their current plan, they would be perfect. Once he called in a bomb threat, people would be running around and not paying attention to badges. The other two men changed into blue maintenance uniforms.

As soon as they were dressed, they discarded their clothes on the floor and Mihails grabbed his burner phone. He'd be ditching it soon, but he had one more call to make. Moving quickly, he kept pace with Oto as they made their escape. He and his friend headed toward the east elevators while the other two men went to the west-side elevators.

Once they'd descended to the floor directly above the lobby, they exited and Mihails pressed SEND on a number stored in the throwaway phone.

"Opulen Hotel, how may I help you today?" a chirpy female answered.

The hallway was empty as Oto pointed toward the stairs. Mihails nodded and kept his voice low as he spoke. "In five minutes your beautiful hotel will be rubble." Not exactly true, but they would do some damage. Without giving her a chance to respond other than a gasp, he continued. "If you don't clear out everyone, you will all be dead. The clock is ticking. Leave or die."

She gasped and started to say something, but he ended the call and tossed it into the stairwell. For all he knew, law enforcement had already moved into the hotel and were doing sweeps. The unknown was making him edgy. But they hadn't been able to bring in a big team for this op. It was too difficult to get eyes in this hotel without arousing suspicion. The owners were paranoid—

because of their own illegal activities—so Mihails had needed to play this operation right. Unfortunately his lack of sight around the perimeter was now hurting him.

As they reached the floor that would lead to the lobby, a piercing alarm went off, the wail echoing in the stairwell. They bypassed the current floor and continued to the underground parking garage. He was sure that panicked guests would be running around everywhere soon.

There was a door in the garage that emptied out near the pool area. They would have to ascend another set of anterior stairs once they went through it, but from there, escape would be a straight shot to the hotel-owned marina. All they would have to do was retrieve their boat and they would be free.

Cade stood in the oversized van next to Burkhart and another member of his four-man tactical team. Maria sat against one wall between two well-armed men Cade trusted with his life. She'd been quiet on the drive over, and he hated that he'd had to drag her here, but anyone he trusted to watch her—and there was no way he'd entrust her safety to local law enforcement—was on-site at the Opulen Hotel. There'd been no other choice and she seemed to understand, even if she was withdrawn. Not that he blamed her. Fuck, he hated that she was here. And he hated that he'd been dumb enough to touch her.

Again.

It was as though he couldn't stop himself. The hunger he experienced around her was intense, making him out of control. He looked away from her, scanning where she'd be staying.

The van they were in was their on-scene command center. Computers lined one wall with two very dedicated analysts sitting in small swivel chairs reviewing angles of the Opulen video cameras and running various data such as the incoming and outgoing phone calls made in the last hour in the direct vicinity. Considering that they were on an outlying island off the coast of Miami, it was easy to pinpoint calls. Eavesdropping was impossible at this point, but they were hoping to get a pattern or something from the calls as the tactical teams surrounded the outlying areas of the hotel.

Burkhart hadn't told him the tip about the terrorists had come from Levi *fucking* Lazaro until he'd arrived on-site, but now that he was aware of that, Cade was more amped up than ever. No matter what choices Lazaro had made, he wouldn't lie to men and women he'd worked side by side with before. Cade knew it in his gut.

He'd always thought Lazaro had gotten a shitty deal when his wife was murdered. No one—at least no one Cade knew within the company—blamed the guy for wanting revenge. But that wasn't important now.

Once the NSA had hacked the hotel's Wi-Fi cameras, they'd started running a facial-recognition software. So far it hadn't picked up either Mihails Baolodis or Oto Ozols in the last twenty-four hours of fast-forwarded footage. But that didn't mean anything. The men were trained and would know how to avoid detection or disguise their appearance. Of course disguises only went so far with the type of software the NSA had. But if they'd been in the hotel previously doing recon, they might not have been as careful while learning the layout of the security cameras. Not that that helped the NSA right now, because they didn't have hours and hours to dissect the footage. They needed a hit now.

If the terrorists were here, they'd have a hell of a time getting away. The main road had been blocked off, eliminating exit on land, but there were other ways to escape. Including sea or air, and with just the NSA and FBI working this op, they couldn't cover the entire damn island—which encompassed the personal residences of some of the highest-per-capita-income individuals in the damn country. If they tried to search any of those residences without a warrant, they'd be met with a giant fuck-you and follow-ups from attorneys. For all they knew, the terrorists had already escaped the hotel and outlying areas.

"Fuck," Burkhart muttered.

Cade turned to look at him, alert. "What?"

His boss tapped his earpiece. "Someone called in a bomb threat to the front desk. The hotel is evacuating."

Burkhart turned to one of the analysts, but before he could ask the question the others wanted to know, the petite woman with jet-black hair said, "Only one call was placed to the front desk in the last couple minutes. . . ." She trailed off as her fingers flew across the keyboard at warp speed. Numbers, words, and other data popped up on the screen directly in front of her; then, "Throwaway phone. I can eventually trace where it was bought and track funds unless it was bought with cash, but it won't do us any good now. . . . Wait. There was a call to this number five minutes *before* the outgoing bomb threat."

Cade glanced at Burkhart, who gave him a hard look. There were a dozen different scenarios that played out in his mind, but the simplest, the one that made the most sense, said that whoever had placed the bomb threat had received some kind of warning call. The tactical teams show up; then a bomb threat is made? No fucking way. He'd done enough operations like this to be secure with his instinct. And his gut said the bad guys were here.

The threat might be fake, designed to cause a panic, but after the destruction at the Westwood mansion, no one would take that chance.

"Evacuate the hotel now. No one goes in!" Burkhart shouted into his phone at someone as he hurried from the van, using the side door.

Cade quickly looked at Maria to see how she was holding up before he focused on Ortiz, one of his team-mates for this operation. "You ready?"

He nodded, his M-4 at the ready as he headed for the door at the back. Sunlight filtered in, bathing two of the computers in light as he stepped down from the vehicle.

Cade followed but stopped in the doorway and looked at Maria. "I'll be back soon. You'll be safe, I swear." No one was getting in this damn van. It was the command center, but if the shit hit the fan, everyone in the van was under orders to get off the island. One of the reasons he'd made sure Maria was stationed inside it, even if her presence was irregular.

She nodded, her eyes red-rimmed and slightly puffy. She'd cried on and off in the truck on the way over, though she'd tried to hide it, and he could see the pain etched so clearly on her beautiful face. "Don't worry about me. Just be safe."

He paused, not used to anyone being concerned about his safety. He was well trained and his boss and various teammates all looked out for one another, but they didn't worry. Not like the way he could see she did.

He hated that today of all days he had to leave her. What he wouldn't give to stay and comfort her, but he couldn't.

His boss had assigned him as point man of this four-man team, and if he could be instrumental in bringing down the fuckers who had killed Maria's mother, he wanted to be part of that. He hadn't been able to save her brother, but if he could give her some small peace in this way, he would.

As he dropped to the ground outside the van, Ortiz shut the door and they turned to face Bell and Freeman, two other operators he'd worked with before. Bell was former Delta, sent in as extra support, but the other two were Black Death 9 agents just like Cade. Normally their jobs were covert and off the books.

Except today. Today they were going to dominate their objective in broad fucking daylight.

Cade tapped his earpiece. They'd all programmed theirs to one channel. "Testing."

All three men nodded in unison.

Cade quickly glanced around the parking lot next to the hotel. He didn't have a full view of the front but knew teams were in place helping people get out after that bomb threat. He'd seen the flood of guests and employees hurrying out the main doors from one of the analyst's video screens. Normally they'd be sweeping and clearing the building, but with the impending danger and so many of the teams helping the civilians to safety, everyone was staying outside. Soon they'd create a perimeter in case that bomb threat was real.

"Let's go, then." They headed across the lot. The sun beat down on them as they hurried, single file, sweeping around the back of the hotel toward the pool area.

Each team had a designated objective. Theirs was to

secure the small marina the hotel owned. While the Opulen hadn't given them complete access to their hotel, they were being cooperative enough and had ordered all employees to evacuate to one location in the northwest parking lot. Of course that bomb threat had moved Cade's team's time frame up, so they had no clue if there were still employees lingering at the marina.

His team was about to find out, though.

As they bypassed the empty pool area and neared the marina, Cade scanned the front dock that ran parallel to the water. Clear.

The main dock had seven different very long docks attached to it, with about a dozen boats of varying sizes tied to each one.

"Ortiz, take the farthest on the east, Bell, you take—"

Pop, pop!

For a fraction of a second they stilled at the unmistakable sound of gunfire. A roaring engine followed a split second later. He could hear what direction it was coming from, but there were too many boats blocking their view. Using hand motions, Cade signaled that he and Ortiz would take the second-to-last dock and the other two should take the very last.

As he and Ortiz raced down the evenly spaced wooden planks, Cade held up a hand signaling that he was slowing down when they neared a Grady White.

Once he reached the edge of the front of the boat, he used it as cover to peer around it. Fifty yards down, two men were boarding a Donzi that two other men were already on. The speedboats were incredibly fast and if they made it to open water, they could get away if the NSA's air support didn't stop them.

Cade recognized Mihails and Oto immediately from

their pictures. The boat engine was running, the water churning behind it as the boat idled.

His entire body went tense. "I have the tangos in sight. Anyone else have eyes?" No way in hell were their targets getting away.

"Affirmative," Bell and Freeman said in unison. "We're about fifty yards down, using a boat as cover. I only see four," Bell continued.

"Same here. Take them alive if you can, but use lethal force if necessary." The NSA wanted intel from the terrorists, but not at any cost. Their people came first. "We take them now. Let's roll." There was no time to call in another team.

The engine revved once as he and Ortiz moved from hiding.

Weapon raised, he looked down the reflex sight of his M-4 as they ran. "Drop your weapons! Hands in the air!" he shouted as they sprinted toward the boat.

The four men froze before they all swiveled in Cade's direction. Out of the corner of his eye, he could see Bell and Freeman on the parallel dock, moving in sync with them. His and Ortiz's boots pounded against the wood as their legs ate up the distance to the speedboat.

As they neared it, he could see a man lying prone on the ground, blood pooling around his body. Must have been the shooting victim.

The two men he didn't recognize dropped from sight, but the one Cade recognized as Oto lifted a semi-automatic rifle and opened fire, spraying a volley of bullets in their direction.

Cade automatically dropped to his belly. The explosion of noise around them was deafening. Wood splintered everywhere, but he tuned it out as he lifted his weapon and returned fire. From his location he was trapped in position, but so were the terrorists. It was impossible to get a straight shot, so he aimed at the front of the boat.

Chunks of fiberglass and plastic exploded into the air as he and Ortiz hit their target, but the boat reversed, splintering apart the dock as it swiveled and pulled away.

Jumping up from his position, he opened fire on the quickly retreating boat. Oto was still returning fire, but his shots were wild, ripping up the dock as he alternated between Cade and Ortiz and the other two tactical team members.

Cade looked down his sight, focusing on the driver, but another of the terrorists stood up, a rifle in hand, blocking Mihails. Cade fired, hitting the unknown terrorist in the chest. The guy dropped like a stone.

At the same time Ortiz grunted and fell back, landing on the dock with a hard thud. Shit. Cade dropped out of line of sight again and bent over the other man.

"Just my vest," he rasped out. "Get those fuckers." Ortiz was already starting to push up. Their tactical vests were level-four armor, designed to stop even rifle rounds. Even so, it felt like getting slammed in the chest with a sledgehammer. It would leave a bruise, possibly even crack a rib or two.

Trusting that Ortiz was telling the truth, Cade tapped his earpiece, switching channels as he turned and jumped back up, running to the end of the dock as the boat sped away. "Four tangos on a speedboat, making a fast exit. Heading west. Boat is orange with two thick yellow stripes down the side. Made by Donzi. Civilian down, don't know the status yet," he shouted to Burkhart as he ran.

He and his other two teammates still returned fire, but this particular speedboat had wicked capabilities and was already eating up the water with impressive speed. Some could go up to a hundred miles an hour. Cade knew that because the FBI used them for maritime operations.

Lowering his weapon when it was clear they were out of range, he cursed, heading back toward the fallen civilian. Burkhart was shouting orders at someone in the background but hadn't responded to him yet.

Finally he said, "You hit any of them?"

"At least one." Cade bent to the body of the man wearing white pants and a blue Polo shirt. Blood covered the shirt, soaking it completely through. Cade checked the pulse, surprised to find a faint heartbeat. "Shit, we need medical, ASAP. An employee was hit, but I've got a faint pulse."

Moving fast, he started unhooking his tactical vest, the Velcro making tearing sounds as he ripped it off. He pulled off his long-sleeved black T-shirt and held it to the man's chest as Bell and Freeman raced over.

"Check on Ortiz," he said without looking up.

Before either of them responded, a shocking blast ripped through the air. Cade's head snapped up as a ball of orange-and-black smoke blew out the top floor of the hotel. Glass shattered and debris flew out in all directions, pieces landing in the ocean a hundred yards away.

A jolt of terror shot through him. The wreckage could do some serious damage falling from that height, and Maria was to the east of the hotel. Freeman had already moved onto Ortiz, so Cade looked up at Bell. "Will you hold the pressure?" he asked, indicating the civilian.

Bell nodded, already falling to one knee as Cade shot

up and raced back the way they'd come. "Burkhart!" he shouted into his earpiece.

When his boss didn't answer, raw fear punched through him like a blast of adrenaline. He had to get to Maria.

*   *   *

Date: December 23, 2006
To: Maria Cervantes
From: Cade O'Reilly
Subject: holidays

Can't believe it's almost Christmas. I'm counting down the days until I'm in Miami in spring. Bring on the white sand beaches and cool beers. If they cancel our leave I think Riel will lose his shit. He's going more stir-crazy than I've ever seen him. Probably because they've had us locked down on base lately.

How're things at the house? Your mom and aunts driving you crazy for Christmas? Can't believe they sent us more cookies. I shared with our team, but Riel and I kept a stash for ourselves this time. Did you get the Christmas gift I sent? Shipping over here can be a PITA, so I wasn't sure if it'd make it in time. Computer time's almost up, talk to you soon. Miss you.

Cade

Chapter 14

Situation report (SITREP): an intermittent report of the
current high-risk situation.

Maria jumped in her seat, her entire body jerking at
the explosion. She swallowed hard as she watched
the horrific display on one of the van's video screens.
Instinctively she closed her eyes, wanting to block it out,
but more images of fire and destruction flickered through
her mind like a horror movie.

A rumble.

Orange fire illuminating the night sky.

The mansion imploding.

Her mother . . .

"Are you okay?" a male voice asked.

Maria's eyes flew open. Her stomach twisted, her
mouth filling with saliva as she fought back a wave of
nausea. She looked up to find the two men Cade had left
to guard her, watching her with concern. Feeling weak
and pathetic for all of two seconds, she swallowed hard.
But screw that.

She wasn't weak. Today she'd said good-bye to her
mother forever and now she was sitting in a van full of
strangers when the top of the Opulen had exploded. All

she cared about was finding out if Cade was all right. *Oh God, what if...* Her throat tightened. Hell no. She couldn't even go there.

She ignored the question and stood. Her legs trembled, but she forced herself to focus on the two men. They were here to protect her and would have information on the man she cared about way too much. "Where's Cade?" She hated that her voice shook.

It was subtle, but they shot each other a quick glance before looking at her. The shorter of the two cleared his throat. "We're not patched into his radio feed, but we've got to go outside for a sec. Stay put."

Before she could respond, the two men disappeared out the back doors. The two analysts at the computer bank completely tuned her out as they clacked away on their keyboards. Feeling utterly helpless and useless, she scanned all the screens. A huddle of hotel employees were all sectioned off in one parking lot. Men and women wearing military-style fatigues or jackets with FBI emblazoned on them were milling around in each screen. It looked like chaos, but everyone was moving around with precise movements, as if they knew exactly what they were doing.

A familiar figure caught her eye as her gaze jumped from screen to screen. Eyes wide, she froze as she saw Cade running across one of the parking lots. It was a side angle, but his shirt and vest were off and he was bloody. For one agonizing moment, her heart stopped.

Since no one was paying attention to her, she slipped out the side door instead of using the back ones. The bright sunlight was jarring, leaving her unfocused as she scanned the area. She spotted Cade almost immediately about twenty-five yards away talking heatedly to the same older man who had been in the van with them earlier. Burkhart.

There was so much noise outside, people talking and shouting, a wailing siren coming from inside the hotel, and a whole other cacophony of sound. She ignored it and everything around her and ran straight for Cade. As she neared him she realized that the blood wasn't his. Or at least she didn't think so.

"We need you here!" Burkhart shouted at Cade, not bothering to hide his anger even when she reached the two of them.

She wanted to punch him for yelling at Cade when he looked like this. "Are you okay?" she asked as she skidded to a halt. She ignored the other man, her eyes taking in every inch of Cade's bloody torso as she fought back panic. "Is that your blood? What happened?" Her adrenaline pump from earlier was in a free fall.

"I'm fine," he said softly. He started to raise his hand to touch her. Then his jaw tightened as if aware they weren't alone.

Nonetheless she still scanned him again, trying to tamp down the fear coursing through her that he could have been injured. That blast . . . she mentally shook herself. He was alive and standing right in front of her.

Cade did the same, examining her from head to foot, clearly making sure she was uninjured. "Are *you* okay?"

She nodded, her throat tight. "Yeah." She desperately wanted to ask about the blood but knew this wasn't the time.

"You got her?" a voice asked from behind her.

She turned to find the two men who'd left her in the van standing only a couple of feet behind her, their expressions tense.

"Yeah, go where you're needed," Cade said, interrupting whatever Burkhart had been about to say.

His boss sighed. "Damn it, O'Reilly, I need you here. They can handle her, take her to an off-site location and keep her safe."

Even though she had a dozen questions, a burst of annoyance popped inside Maria. She didn't like being talked about as if she didn't exist. "I'm standing right here."

The man didn't spare her a glance, just stared Cade down while they had some sort of confrontation with only their eyes.

Cade took a step closer to her but kept his focus on Burkhart. "You don't like this, fire me."

Maria sucked in a sharp breath, not exactly sure what was going on, though she could guess. "Cade, if you need to stay—"

Burkhart grunted in annoyance. "Fine, go. Contact me when you reach the safe house. I hope you know what you're doing." Without waiting for a response, he turned on his heel.

Cade didn't seem bothered by his boss's response as he turned to her again. She was surprised when he reached out and cupped her cheek gently. "You sure you're okay?"

She covered his hand with hers. "Me? Whose blood is that? Are *you* okay? And what's going on?" She gestured behind them to the smoke billowing out of the top floor of the hotel.

"This isn't mine and we don't need to be here. I want you away from all this. Let's get you out of here." Though his voice was soft, his expression was hard, determined. She felt as if she was seeing a different side to him. He was in straight battle mode as he continued. "There are teams of people handling this. Despite what my boss thinks, I'm one man and you need protection."

But she didn't want to be a burden to him and she definitely didn't want him to put his job at risk for her sake. "Cade, listen—"

"Come on." He gently took her elbow and steered her through a mass of people, but at least she didn't see any trauma units set up.

"Were there any injuries?" She ignored some of the curious looks they got, though she guessed they were because of Cade's shirtless, bloody state.

He paused but didn't slow his pace. "Not from the blast. We're pretty sure everyone got out in time, but won't know for sure until we've done a full sweep." He pointed toward where an unmarked ambulance was parked on the far side of the parking lot. "We're past there."

"A sweep? What about other bombs? And why don't I see any local law enforcement?" There were only FBI and she assumed everyone else was NSA or something similar. What she didn't see was anyone wearing Miami PD gear.

He kept his hand on her elbow as he steered them past the ambulance. His vehicle was three spots down, behind two darkly tinted SUVs. "We've got trained bomb techs, but we'll send in a robot first. And the reason there aren't any local law enforcement personnel is that we had to move fast and didn't need any extra red-tape bullshit to deal with. We've worked with the FBI before and are trained for situations like this. We have our own trauma teams."

"Well, what about your job? Why did you tell your boss he could fire you?"

He pulled open the passenger door and held on to the frame of it while she leaned against the seat, wrapping her arms around herself. Though he wasn't actually touching her, he completely caged her in. She could feel his body heat and that spicy scent of his wrapped around her, rising above even the smell of soot. Though she wanted to feel his arms around her, she knew he was holding back because of the blood. "Because I don't give a shit if he does. No one will protect you like I can and I'm not letting you out of my sight. If he doesn't like it, fuck him. Besides, he's not going to fire me. We've worked together for too damn long."

His words took her by surprise, but she still needed to know. . . . "Why?" Damn it, her voice shook.

His green eyes darkened, his expression going molten hot. "Because . . . I care about you, Maria. Probably more than I should." The last part was raspy, almost a whisper, and he said it like a confession.

"I care about you too." Damn it, no, she didn't. She couldn't. Not when things between them hadn't worked before. Unfortunately the feelings he evoked in her were like nothing she'd ever experienced. Back when they were friends—and had just started down that road to more than friendship—she'd been giddy every time she opened her e-mail and saw a message from him. Now that she was older, those feelings seemed magnified by a hundred. She shouldn't be telling him she freaking cared for him. She should be shoving him away and trying to save herself from more heartache.

"You shouldn't," he snapped before turning away from her with an abruptness that left her feeling cold.

She swallowed hard and struggled to find her voice. What had just happened? Watching as he went to the backseat and pulled out a small duffel bag with clean clothes and wet wipes, she let her anger free and jumped out of the vehicle. "What the hell, Cade? I *shouldn't?*"

His jaw clenched tight as he wiped the blood from his abdomen. He didn't stop there, though, but continued wiping his chest, arms, and even hands. This time when her throat tightened it was for a different reason. His arm muscles flexed as he moved with that sinful, liquid grace. And those long fingers brought up memories of how he'd expertly played her body. Lord, she felt as if she was on an emotional roller coaster with him. He told her that he cared for her, then pushed her away. Now she couldn't stop devouring him with her eyes and remembering how amazing his mouth and hands had felt caressing her breasts and . . . Damn it! His raw appeal should be the last thing on her mind.

But it was impossible not to notice the beauty of the man, the way his muscles and tendons flexed under the bright sunlight. The sinewy strength that pulsated off him should be illegal.

"Are you ignoring me now?" she demanded, her temper starting to simmer.

He tugged on a black T-shirt that did little to cover his delicious tattoos and turned to face her, but his expression was unreadable. "No, I'm just . . . You've been through a lot with your mom. I don't want to take advantage of you." He might be saying one thing, but there was something else she wasn't understanding. Something between the lines that she just couldn't translate.

"Take advantage? I'm the one taking advantage of you. You haven't even . . . you know." She felt lame not being able to say the words.

"That's not what I mean. You make me feel out of control!" He pushed out a ragged breath, the words seemingly torn from him, and she saw a crack in that hard veneer he was trying so desperately to put up. "I shouldn't even be guarding you because of my feelings. . . . Fuck!"

So that was the root of his problem. Or at least part of it. "Yeah, well, the feeling is mutual!" she shouted back, angry at herself for wanting this man when he'd hurt her so badly before. Even though her emotions were completely out of control, his presence was still the only thing keeping her grounded. That just pissed her off even more, but she didn't see the point in fighting it. Not when she knew their coming together was inevitable.

He just watched her, those green eyes piercing in their intensity. Finally he leaned forward slowly, as to give her enough time to pull away before brushing his lips over hers. The action was soft, almost chaste, but it soothed something deep inside her.

She reached for him, tugging on his shoulders as she melded her body to his. He didn't resist and she savored the feel of her breasts pressing against his hard chest.

After a long moment, he sighed and pulled back. "We need to go."

She nodded, the knot in her chest easing ever so slightly. Grief and fear still burned deep inside her, but with Cade next to her she felt as if she could deal with anything.

As he steered them out of the parking lot, she looked behind them. She hated that she might be taking him away from where he was needed, but the most selfish part of her was glad he'd been so adamant about coming with her. Until they figured out what she knew, if anything, she wanted him by her side.

"One of the men in the van got excited at one point, saying there had been a sighting of the terrorists." They'd actually used technical terms like "tango" and some other jargon she didn't understand, but she'd gotten the gist of it and figured out that tango meant target.

"Yeah. I shot one, but—"

"What?" Her head whipped around to him. "Is that whose blood is on you?"

He shook his head as he rolled down his window and flashed his ID to one of the uniformed FBI agents manning the bridge. The guy quickly waved them through. A weight she hadn't even realized she'd been holding on to lifted off her shoulders as they left the site. For all they knew, there were still more explosives hidden.

"No, they shot a marina worker but got away by boat—for the moment. We've got eyes in the sky right now. Should be able to track them soon, especially since one of them is wounded."

Or dead. Her brother had always told her what a great shot Cade was. She had started to respond when her cell phone buzzed. When she saw the name on the caller ID, she immediately answered.

Cade shot her a few curious looks while she talked and he drove down the highway. He pulled off at a different exit than she assumed he would, then realized he was probably going to take a different route. The night before he'd driven them around in so many circles there was no way anyone could have followed them. Not without Cade seeing them.

When she finally ended her call, she looked at him but couldn't read his expression. His profile had that impenetrable, stoic look she was becoming familiar with. He might hate her plan, but she hoped he at least listened to what she had to say before making a decision. *Here goes nothing.*

Cade resisted the urge to stand up and pace. Instead he sat still on a wingback chair, trying to force himself to stay calm. It was hard when he and Maria were at the office of a doctor he didn't know much about and she was basically sedated.

Not by drugs, but she was stretched out on a pale green chaise longue with her hands clasped lightly over her middle. It was almost too cliché for her to be practically lying down at a psychiatrist's office, but here they were.

When she was in the command center van, she'd reached out to Dr. York, a man who worked with a lot of kids at Bayside Community Center. The doctor had been out of town when the Westwood mansion was bombed, but he had just arrived back in Miami.

While Cade was secure in his ability to protect her, he didn't like having her anywhere but the safe house at this point. An analyst had run York's information and the guy appeared clean—and Cade had checked him for weapons, much to the man's annoyance—but he wanted Maria somewhere secure.

After she first told Cade that she wanted to come here, it had been clear she'd expected an argument. But he was fine with the idea of hypnotherapy and had seen it used more than once successfully. When the mind was utterly relaxed, it was amazing how many memories could be retrieved.

Of course Burkhart had been all over this idea, which had just pissed Cade off. He was still angry that his boss had tried to pull him from Maria's detail even if he understood why. Burkhart had seen that Cade was getting too involved, something he'd never done before. He'd always been able to keep his distance from any asset. But Maria was way more than that. If he truly thought he might put her in harm's way by continuing on as her guard, he'd pull himself faster than Burkhart ever could. But he wasn't distracted enough that he couldn't do his job. Hell, if anything he was more focused on her safety than anything else.

"What do you see now, Maria?" Dr. York's soft voice matched his small, wiry frame. Everything about the gray-haired man was nonthreatening. After he'd put Maria in a trancelike state, he walked her through the steps she'd taken the night of the bombing: from arriving there by a driven escort to how sick she'd been feeling. So far her memories matched up with the scant information she'd relayed to Cade.

With her eyes closed, Maria frowned, stress lines bracketing her mouth. "A hallway. Not secret, but it's not open for public use. Mrs. Dobbins says it's okay if we use it. But I don't want to go any farther...." She trailed off in a whisper, her entire body tensing and her hands balling into fists. A tear trickled down the side of her face, carving a path along her delicate cheek.

The sight was like a punch to the face.

"You have to," the doctor said soothingly.

The hell she did. Cade started to say something, but the doctor shot him a sharp look. The man had already warned Cade that he needed to be quiet while he was in here or he would make him leave. Cade nearly snorted at *that* thought. Clenching his jaw, he nodded tightly as the doctor turned back to her.

York sat next to her, leaning slightly forward, his rimless glasses pushed back on his head. "Why don't you want to go any farther?"

"I . . . don't know." Her voice sounded almost broken, her face growing even paler.

"Yes, you do, and you need to go in there."

She swallowed loudly, the sound over-pronounced in the quiet room. Restless, she shifted against the chair. Whatever she was reliving, clearly she was afraid of what was coming. "I'm opening the door. Mrs. Dobbins is gone and it's just me now."

"What do you see?"

"A nice room, but I don't care about any of it. I just want to throw up. And sleep. I'm so tired my eyes hurt."

"This is just a memory, Maria. You're not actually sick and you're not tired. Look at your surroundings and tell me what else you remember."

Cade had to hand it to the guy, his voice was incredibly soothing. It had a melodic quality that was managing to even calm him. It was no surprise that he had such a high success rate with hypnotherapy. Cade might hate that Maria was putting herself through this, but damn it, they needed this information. Even with the identity of the terrorists revealed, there could be more that they were missing.

"I got sick and dozed in the bathroom for a while. I don't think it was very long, because when I woke up I heard voices. Male voices."

Cade sat up straighter, but the doctor never wavered. "Can you see who is speaking?"

Eyes still closed, she frowned, her expression frustrated. "No. They're shouting, though. From . . . next door. They want to hit . . . someone, more than one person, where it hurts. First they want to bring down the hotel, to destroy the place of evil with fire and destruction, but that's not enough. They have to pay financially . . . the port." Her breathing grew more erratic as she lay there.

"The port?" Cade asked without thinking, wanting to know everything.

Her head tilted to the side in his direction, but she didn't respond.

Dr. York scowled at him but spoke to Maria. "Did they say anything else?"

"I don't know." Now her breaths were coming in short, rapid bursts. "I need to tell someone what I heard, but I don't want to look anymore. I don't want to see!" She clutched the couch beneath her, her knuckles white.

Cade stood, wanting to comfort her, but the doctor held up a hand without glancing his way.

"Maria, take a deep breath. I'm doing to count backward to one from five. When I reach one, you're going to open your eyes. Do you understand?"

She nodded, her breathing ragged. "I can't be here anymore. I can't. . . ."

Dr. York counted backward in that agreeable voice and the second he said, "One," Maria's amber eyes snapped open. She blinked, her breathing growing steadier as she looked between the two of them. When her gaze landed on Cade, tears glistened in her eyes. "I feel sick."

Shit. Moving fast, he grabbed the ridiculously expensive looking gold-colored wastebasket next to the doctor's desk and brought it to her. Thankfully it was empty.

She clutched it, holding it in her lap as she stared at it for a few long moments, her breathing ragged. Finally she shook her head and set it down next to her, but Cade didn't move from his position next to the chaise. "I think I'm okay. I'm sorry I couldn't keep going. It's like there's a block in my brain. I . . . I was afraid to remember more, I think."

"Don't worry—you were helpful." The mention of the hotel could be a reference to the Opulen, and the port might mean the Port of Miami. Unfortunately the place was vast. Still, if the port was important, it could help out the NSA to narrow down any future targets.

"Do you remember any of our conversation?" Dr. York asked.

"Yes, but it's more like sensations. I remember what I felt like. The fear, the terror, just not . . . what I saw or heard. But . . ." She looked at Cade, then the doctor. "Sometimes when I close my eyes I see fire and destruction. I think it's the bombing. Is it normal that I'm having flashbacks?"

The bombing must have happened right after she overheard that conversation. It would explain her fear to even go in the room, because after she left it, she would have seen the mansion destroyed with her mother inside. Her subconscious was trying to protect her.

Dr. York nodded. "It's very normal. Until you recover all your memories without aid, it's likely you'll continue to get them. They might become more intense and while I would never insist, it wouldn't hurt you to talk to a professional when you're ready. And if not with me, I can recommend a few very good doctors."

Maria gave a noncommittal shrug and went to stand. Cade slid an arm around her and helped her up. He had some questions for her but wanted to wait until they were alone. Even if the guy was a doctor and bound by doctor-patient confidentiality and had signed the twenty-page confidentiality agreement from the NSA that Cade had given him, he still didn't want to discuss anything else in front of the guy.

A ghost of a smile touched her lips. "I can walk on my own."

Cade just shrugged. He liked touching her. Okay, more than liked. He was starting to crave the feel of her, and having her pressed up against him like this wasn't a chore. Unfortunately his need for her compounded the damn guilt he felt for all his past mistakes. His insides were like a constant battlefield. "You feel okay to get out of here?"

She nodded. "Yes. Thanks for letting me do this."

He inclined his head, though really, he'd only brought her here because she'd been so adamant about it.

After thanking the doctor for his help, Maria and Cade left. As he drove back to the safe house, he couldn't escape the tingling sensation at the back of his neck. He hadn't felt it when they were on the way to the office, but something was bothering him now. Something that told him danger was near, and even though he was positive they weren't being followed, that subconscious warning just wouldn't abate.

Sighing, he rubbed the back of his neck, as if that could get rid of the awareness. He just needed to get Maria to safety. That was all.

*   *   *

Date: December 25, 2006
To: Cade O'Reilly
From: Maria Cervantes
Subject: re: holidays

Merry Christmas! Sorry I didn't get to respond yesterday. I
didn't get home until late. My mom had us running around
looking at Christmas lights, attending two parties, a boat
parade, and midnight Mass. . . . Some holiday break. I
wish you guys were here with us, and yes, my mom and
aunts (that's plural!) are driving me and my dad crazy. My
mom is so insistent that I learn how to cook, but then
when I'm in the kitchen, she shoos me out. Probably
because I eat more than I pay attention, but really, can
you blame me? All I know is, when I find the right guy,
he's going to cook for me.
    I showed the family the picture of your tree. I love how
you made lights out of the bullet casings, very creative.
And you look pretty good in your fatigues.
    Ran into some friends from school when we were at
the boat parade. That was a madhouse, but really
beautiful. I hope you'll get to see it sometime. One of the
guys asked me out on a date, but I said no. At the risk of
making things awkward between us . . . I said no because
it felt wrong when I have feelings for you. I've written and
deleted this e-mail about fifty times, but it's been almost a
year and I can't deny it any longer. At first it was just a
little crush, but all our e-mails have changed that for me.
I'm more honest with you than I've ever been with
anyone. If you don't feel the same, then just ignore this
and nothing will change. Okay, that's a lie, it'll probably be
super awkward for a while, but it's a risk I'm willing to
take. But if you do have more than friendly feelings for
me . . . God, I don't even know. I just wanted to let you
know how I feel.

xo,
Maria

Chapter 15

Bang and burn: demolition and sabotage operations.

Mihails glanced behind him before taking a sharp turn into the opening of a new canal. If he hadn't already known about it, he would have missed the turn-off hidden by brush and a half-fallen cypress tree. He was only aware of its existence because a gunrunner contact had told him of it—in exchange for a favor, of course.

After their initial getaway from the Opulen, they'd switched boats twice, then spent the next few hours hiding in a mansion that had gone into foreclosure a few months ago. Such homes were common in Miami. They'd preordained the place as their first meeting spot in case the hotel operation went south. Some of his men thought his planning was overkill, but a time like this was a reminder of why he was so meticulous.

He'd heard the helicopters in the distance as they'd ditched the Donzi and it was a miracle they'd been able to get away. After that point, it was a matter of waiting out the searchers. Miami was a big place and it had been easy enough to hide since they'd had a location already scouted out.

With dusk falling, it would be next to impossible to track them now even by satellite. So if for some reason the government somehow pinged them from the sky—though he couldn't see how they would—Mihails would lose anyone in the intricate web of channels in this swampy area south of Miami.

As he steered them into the inland waterway, he slowed the boat even though every fiber in him wanted to gun the engine. The channels were complex, and even with the map they had, he knew it would be easy to get lost.

"How's he doing?" Mihails asked Oto quietly.

"Just lost him." Oto shook his head and stood, stepping away from the fallen bodies of both their comrades. One had died on-scene immediately after being shot, but Janis had been hit twice, once in the upper arm and another in the gut. The stomach wound had done him in. And his death had been slow and painful.

Mihails was just surprised Janis had lasted as long as he had. They'd been too far from the rest of their men to get medical help, and taking Janis to a hospital had been out of the question. Hospital staff had to report gunshot wounds. There were too many CCTVs in Miami and far too many government agencies hunting for them. He wasn't positive the government knew their identities yet, but if they did, he and the others wouldn't have made it half a mile inland without being brought down.

He'd hated seeing his friend suffering but had been hopeful Janis might be able to hold on long enough until they met up with their medic. Janis had been loyal and dependable. His loss would be felt by all of them. But it wasn't to be.

Mihails had seen and caused so much death that it was becoming easier to deal with. That scared him more than anything. He knew his cause was just, but sometimes he questioned himself. . . . No, there was no time for doubts.

Crickets chirped from the nearby banks, and other animals moved almost soundlessly through the water, small ripples of movement the only sign of their presence. It was impossibly quiet in the swamps. Because of the cooler weather, the air was crisp and fresh smelling, an almost sweet scent permeating everything. He looked at the GPS bolted onto the dash of the speedboat and turned left at the next small opening into another waterway channel. At least neither the boat nor the GPS had been seriously damaged in their escape. It was a miracle and he cursed that incompetent marina employee who had slowed them down.

The stupid fool had wanted to talk, refusing to let the four of them make their quick escape. Shooting him had been the only option, and the shot had alerted that team of agents. Now it was just him and Oto until they could be reunited with the rest of their team.

"What about the bodies?" Oto scanned the banks, alert for danger as he asked what Mihails had been debating himself.

He paused as he weighed their options. "If we dump them here they'll never be found." According to his gunrunner contact, this was the perfect place for dumping bodies. They would be eaten by alligators in less than a day. Which meant no DNA leads or any way to trace these men back to their crew. It would be much easier to dispose of them here than deal with them once they docked.

"Agreed. I'll remove any weapons or ammo."

Mihails nodded and kept his gaze on the GPS. The sun had finally disappeared behind the horizon, so he'd turned on a small light at the front of the boat. The soft green glow illuminated their movements, but the GPS was the biggest help. It showed water depth and possible obstructions in the waterway.

"Either our contact sold us out or the woman knew about the hotel," Oto said as he worked.

It wouldn't have been financially viable for the man to betray Mihails. And he was too afraid of him and Oto anyway. "We need her alive if possible."

"Yes. Finding out what she told the government will be easy enough once we have her." A bite of anger ran through Oto's words.

Mihails ignored it. He didn't care for torturing women, but he would let Oto do it if she refused to talk. She'd already ruined one part of their plan and he had to know how much she was aware of. If they had to change their attack strategy, that was fine, but until he was sure what she knew, he couldn't risk moving forward. He retrieved one of his burner phones from his bag and turned it on.

This one had no numbers programmed into it, but he had the necessary number memorized.

"Hello?" His contact picked up on the second ring, his voice cautious.

"It's me. Have you located the woman?" Mihails had been positive the other man could, but at this point he was having doubts.

"Yes, I managed to put a tracker on her at the funeral. She's been to a few places since then, including the hotel." Mihails noticed that he didn't use the word "Opulen," probably because the government was monitoring the airwaves for mentions of certain keywords.

Surprise shot through him as his heart rate picked up. "She was there?"

"According to my map, she was in the vicinity, during the time of . . ." He trailed off and Mihails understood why. He cleared his throat. "Afterward, she went to a doctor's office and now she's at a residence. I've tried searching but can't find out who the owner is."

"What's the address?"

A pause. "Why?"

He gritted his teeth. Explaining himself was not something he was accustomed to. "I have different resources and will see if I can discover the owner. In the meantime, track her down, but do not eliminate the problem. We need her alive."

Another pause. "I will try."

His words weren't convincing, but Mihails didn't respond as the man continued. "I'm on the other side of town but should be there in half an hour. I'll do reconnaissance but won't move in until about three this morning."

"Good." Dawn and the hours directly before were the smartest time to conduct any operation. It would give them the element of surprise.

After he gave Mihails the address, they disconnected. Mihails glanced at Oto as he slid Janis's weighted body over the side of the boat. It made a soft splash that seemed overpronounced in the quiet canal. A twinge settled in his chest. He would send Janis's mother compensation once this op was over. "He has outlived his usefulness," he said, referring to the man they'd been using.

Oto nodded as he hefted the other body up and over.

Decision made, Mihails texted Fedor with the address and ordered him to kill their problem and bring the woman in alive. She might be protected, but now that they had an address, he was confident in his man's ability to bring her in. No more screwups. Once he received the reply that it would be done, he tucked the phone into his pocket and savored the small bit of relief coursing through him.

The hotel strike might not have gone off as planned, but he and Oto were still alive and could be very effective even with a limited team. The bastards he was hunting would never know what hit them.

Burkhart slid into the backseat of the waiting SUV. After hours of dealing with the Opulen blast site, he still had more shit to deal with and not enough hours in the day. If only he could clone himself. It still wouldn't be enough, though. Not with all the crazy going on.

His driver, a trained agent, maneuvered his way toward the bridge that was their only exit off the island, while Burkhart opened his slim laptop. He didn't even have time to drive himself because of all the reports he needed to scan. Most of the time his analysts or his assistant just gave him a rundown of key points, but he still had to follow up.

As he pulled up the most updated file on Clay Ervin, his cell buzzed. He didn't bother to look at the caller ID as he tapped his earpiece on. Right now everything was important and he'd missed a shitload of calls the past couple of hours.

"Ervin is dead," Captain Nieto said, not bothering with any greeting.

Shit. "How? Where?" Ervin was supposed to have been in holding. That was who Burkhart was on his way to see.

"When he found out his attorney was dead, he asked to make a phone call for another attorney. His new attorney made it clear that if we weren't going to charge him with anything, he was a free man. Thirty minutes later, he was released from holding."

Shit, shit, shit. "Who was his attorney?"

"Piers Tennyson the Fourth." Nieto's voice was dry.

"That sounds familiar." Burkhart pulled up another file on his computer, one filled with a list of names. He recognized the name because it just sounded pretentious.

"He's a high-priced attorney who represents a lot wealthy people in South Florida. Including the owners of the Opulen. . . . I heard about what happened today. Any injuries or deaths?"

"We didn't lose anyone." *Thank God.*

"Good."

"Where was Ervin found and how was he killed?" Burkhart's mind was racing as he asked the question. Tennyson was the attorney to the owners of the Opulen. That's why he recognized the name. He was also on the list of guests who had been scheduled to attend the Westwood party but never made it. Those were some interesting ties. It could mean nothing, but Burkhart wanted to know more about the man immediately.

"Shot twice in the back of the head, close range. He was dumped in an alley in an abandoned neighborhood. We wouldn't even have known about it, but the DEA had a bust and the body was discovered in the cleanup."

"Thanks for the info. By the way, did Ervin call anyone else other than his attorney while he was there?"

"Hold on." Burkhart could hear Nieto talking to someone in the background. A minute later he was back on the line. "Got the call log and he didn't actually call his attorney. He called the cell number for a man named Paul Hill. He's—"

"One of the owners of the Opulen." Burkhart frowned. "That's interesting."

"Yeah." There had to be a connection somewhere. He just wasn't seeing it. But he would. "Thanks for the call."

"No problem. If you need help with anything, let me know."

Burkhart continued frowning after they disconnected and he pieced together what he'd just learned. Tennyson was supposed to have attended the Westwood party and he had a connection with at least a dozen of the attendees there, if his client list was up-to-date. He probably knew more attendees than that, though. Ervin's own attorney had been killed, and once his new attorney got him free, Ervin had been killed also. But not tortured like Flowers or his friend Scott Mullen.

A quick hit. It had to mean something as important as the more gruesome deaths.

Burkhart rubbed the back of this neck. Hell. He had a headache just thinking about all the possible connections. Sighing, he dialed his assistant. He wanted to find out everything there was to know on the owners of the Opulen Hotel. She'd already been running checks for him, but this was going to take priority. If they had something to hide, they were going to be very sorry.

Chapter 16

Safe house: a house in a secret location, used by spies or criminals in hiding.

Maria knocked lightly on Cade's bedroom door. When he didn't answer, she opened it a fraction. "Cade?" Still no answer.

Even though she knew he was more capable than most of taking care of himself, a heavy dose of fear slid through her. And after everything that had happened over the past couple of days, she wasn't worried about invading his privacy. She opened the door wider but stopped when she heard water running. Her relief was instantaneous. Of course. He was taking a shower. They'd had a long, tiring day and he'd only been able to clean off with wet wipes earlier. The man simply hadn't had a break.

On their way back to the safe house, he'd ended up taking half a dozen calls and they'd barely spoken two words since he'd made sure the house was secure. He'd been as attentive as he could and had made sure she had dinner, but he'd been attached to his phone and laptop. She'd tried to wait to talk to him but had finally given up and gone to take a shower and change into her pajamas.

He wasn't being rude; he was simply focused. She understood that this was his job. He might be tasked with protecting her, but he was still trying to bring to justice the monsters who had massacred so many innocent civilians, including her mother. She'd only come to see him now because she'd wanted to talk to him before going to bed.

Okay, maybe more than talk. After what they'd shared with each other and the way he'd started to open up, she wanted to know what was going on in his head and if he saw any sort of future between them. No matter how much she tried to convince herself that she could just settle for something physical and brief, she knew that wasn't true. That just wasn't her. Maybe if this was someone else other than Cade, but she couldn't settle for less than everything from him.

The timing was probably all wrong, but when would it be right? When this was over? When he'd moved on to the next assignment and wasn't part of her life anymore? No, she wasn't waiting to do this. When he'd cut contact with her before, she hadn't pushed hard for answers from him. She'd been too damn hurt by his callous rejection of their relationship. Now, with eight years and more insight into Cade and who he'd become, she knew there was more to why he'd cut and run. More than he'd admitted. She planned to find out what it was.

She stepped inside the room, but nerves took hold deep inside her, fastening onto her insecurity with sharp talons. She couldn't help wondering if she was stupid to put herself out there for him. The thought of sleeping alone was so damn depressing it brought on a fresh wave of tears. She angrily blinked them away.

But she didn't want just *anyone* to hold her right now. She only wanted Cade.

Moving fully into the room, she shut the door behind her. Acting braver than she felt, she stripped off the light pajamas she'd put on earlier and headed for the attached bathroom.

Oh God, if he rejected her . . . The thought made her body go ice-cold, the flash streaking from her face all the way to her toes. Goose bumps skittered over her skin at how vulnerable she was making herself. But she shoved her doubts away. She knew he wanted her. Physically they didn't seem to have any issues. She'd felt the proof of his desire more than once, and after the way he'd pleasured her, she wanted to give back to him tonight. To get lost in his arms and magnificent body so that she could forget everything—especially the heavy grief weighing on her chest—for just a little while.

The bathroom door was already cracked open a couple of inches, white steam billowing out from the small gap. Taking a deep breath, she pushed the door open and stepped inside.

The layout was similar to the bathroom attached to her bedroom, only this one was slightly bigger. To her left there were two big sinks with a long rectangular mirror above them. To the right was a door to a linen closet.

And straight ahead was the shower. A wall made of thick glass blocks blurred out the big man behind it, but she could see Cade's outline standing under the pulsing jet of the overhead shower. There was no shower door, just the enclosure. His head turned as she took another step inside.

She couldn't make out much, but she wasn't surprised by how alert he was. "It's just me."

A long pause. "Is everything okay?"

Feeling slightly braver, she took a couple more steps inside, the tile cool against her feet. It was a sharp contrast to the warmth of the steam pulsing through the room. She crossed her arms over her chest as she closed the distance to the shower. "Yes. I'd like to join you if that's okay." She swallowed hard, shocked she'd managed to say the words.

While she'd had a few lovers, she'd never been the aggressor. It just wasn't in her nature. But now she wanted to grab onto Cade for as long as she could have him.

After what felt like an eternity but was really only a couple of seconds, he spoke. "Yes."

The invisible band around her chest loosened, allowing her to breathe again. Nervousness for an entirely different reason settled in her stomach as she stepped forward. Her fingers skated over the cool ridges of the glass blocks. The sensation grounded her as she stepped over the small ledge and into the humid shower.

Her gaze caught Cade's the moment she entered the enclosure, his green eyes practically electric as they took in her nakedness. Water sprayed all around him, his big body deflecting it, but she barely noticed the wetness hitting her skin.

She'd never felt as vulnerable in her life as she did then, waiting for him to say something. He devoured every single inch of her bare body with a hunger so clear she couldn't stop a tremble from rolling through her.

As he looked, she did the same. So far she'd always seen him partially clothed, but now ... The top part of one arm was a complete sleeve of interwoven Celtic designs that were so beautiful and intricate she could only imagine how long it had taken the artist to tattoo them. On his lower forearm was a Celtic cross with a circle around it and what looked like names scripted parallel to the circle. She'd noticed part of it before but hadn't wanted to stare at him. Now she was looking her fill. On his other upper arm he had the Marine Corps eagle, globe and anchor.

His arm muscles were taut, the tendons pulled tight as he clenched his hands into fists. His chest and abs were muscular planes of perfection. Seriously, a man should not be able to look that good. And ... She sucked in a breath as her gaze landed on his hard length. He was absolutely magnificent. Long and thick, and all she could think about was how he would feel as he pumped into her. Would he be sweet and gentle? Every fiber of her being told her absolutely not. And she hoped not. She didn't want that now. Imagining the sensation of him inside her made her grow even wetter. Just staring at his naked body was like looking at a piece of art. The man was simply breathtaking.

"Maria." His voice was strained, her name coming out shaky.

She didn't look him in the eye, knew if she did she'd lose her nerve. That wasn't going to happen. Stepping closer to him, she slid her palms down his defined arms as she skimmed her mouth over the middle of his chest. He was all hard muscles, his strength palpable and a little overwhelming. Kissing him ever so lightly, she took pure pleasure when his giant body shuddered. She loved that she'd dragged that reaction from him.

One big hand reached out and landed lightly on her bare hip. His fingers flexed and for a panicked moment she thought he'd push her away. But he didn't. Instead his hips rolled once, his cock pulsing against her abdomen.

She could smell whatever body wash he'd used and inhaled the fresh, clean scent as she moved lower down to the ripped planes of his abdomen. There wasn't a bit of fat on the man. He was all beautiful, hard lines and striations.

True perfection.

The tattoos could have taken away from all that stark beauty, but they just made him that much sexier. Lord, she was so lost over this man, who had not only protected her with his body but put his job on the line for her. How could she not be falling for him? Deep down she was afraid to hope for more than a short affair with him. It would be hot and intense and in the end possibly rip her heart out. Maybe not, but she was simply terrified to think this could be more than just sex. Okay, she hoped it could be more but had no clue what he was thinking.

She continued sliding her hands down his arms as she bent lower, blazing a trail of kisses along his body. He made a rough, raspy sound when she reached his lower abdomen, and his fists clenched.

"Maria." There he went again with her name, that deep timbre reverberating through her and making her absolutely crazy. His hands were now on her shoulders, those long fingers flexing. Again, she thought he might push her away, but when she took the top part of his cock between her lips, he just clenched tighter.

Kneeling on the tile, she felt more powerful than she ever had as she took him fully in her mouth. In past relationships, this had been part of bedroom play, but not something she craved. With Cade she found that she desperately wanted to taste him. The thought of giving him as much pleasure as he'd given her was a powerful aphrodisiac. It was damn near addicting.

Water rolled over them, the splashing sounds fading into the background as she took him in her mouth, over and over. Each time she took him deep, he made strangled, gasping sounds. He removed his hands from her shoulders and she felt immediately bereft, but when she heard two hard slaps, she realized he'd slammed his palms against the tile and glass walls.

Oh yeah, she was pushing him past his point of control. His entire body was trembling, that show of desperation so out of character it made her nipples pebble even tighter.

When she reached around his body and dug her fingers into the hard flesh of his backside, he moved so fast she barely had a chance to catch her breath as he pulled her up against his body. He buried one hand in her hair and wrapped the other around her back, his hold dominating and impenetrable.

His mouth crushed over hers, ravenous as he devoured her. His kisses weren't sweet or gentle, but hard and demanding. Exactly what she wanted. She wrapped her arms around his neck, pressing her breasts up against his chest, and he just gripped her tighter. The friction of their bodies sent spirals of pleasure through her.

Dragging his hand from her hair, he fisted her hips and hoisted her up. Without pause she wrapped her legs around him. The skin-to-skin contact was pushing her into sensory overload. She'd fantasized about Cade way too many times in the past. To be with him now was almost too much.

The cool tile hit her back, the sensation doing nothing to dim the scorching heat that had overtaken her. When he tore his mouth from hers, she started to protest, but he dipped his head to her neck, kissing and nipping her skin in erotic little strokes with his tongue and teeth.

She arched against him, wanting more—she was desperate for him. It was as if she could crawl out of her skin right now. Her entire body hummed with a pent-up need and he hadn't even touched her most sensitive areas yet. The way he made her feel was insane.

Cade rolled his hips, his hard length rubbing against her abdomen as she slid against the tile. As she ran her hands up over his head, gliding her fingers over his wet skull trim, he froze.

Oh no. He wasn't stopping. She'd kill him. "What's wrong?"

He lifted his head back, his expression tight, his eyes filled with too many emotions to translate. "Condom."

She blinked as the word pushed through the lust-filled haze of her mind. God, where was her head? She nodded. Yes, they would use one. If it meant leaving the shower, fine. But she wanted to come back here later.

"Don't have one." The way he barely pushed the words out told her how close he was to losing that thin thread of control he was grasping.

"I'm on the pill and I was tested at my last visit, and

it's been . . . a while for me." She had irregular periods and the pill was the only thing that kept her hormones in balance. She didn't want to put any pressure on him or be stupid, but if he was clean too . . .

The tendons in his neck pulled tight as he spoke. "I'm tested every six months for the job and I'm clean. But we can stop. Hell, we can—"

She covered his mouth with hers. Cade wasn't a liar. She trusted him more than she'd trusted any man she'd ever dated. If he said he was clean, he was. And it touched her that he hadn't even questioned her either.

Her tongue stroked against his as she enjoyed his taste and teasing. Those playful strokes quickly turned heated, though, as he reached between their bodies.

He cupped her mound in a purely possessive hold, running a long finger against her slit. "You're so wet," he murmured as he pulled back, feathering kisses along her jawline. He was slowing the pace and she couldn't decide if that was a good or bad thing.

Her inner walls clenched to be filled and he wanted to slow down? When he slid a finger inside her, she arched against him again, her entire body pulling tight.

"I want more than your finger."

"What exactly do you want?" He slid another finger inside her as he nipped that sensitive spot where her neck and shoulder met.

She trembled at the action. "You."

"Tell me," he whispered, the words a low demand.

She felt her face heat up, but she wasn't holding anything back. Not now. "I want your cock inside me."

He made a rough sound of approval and pulled his hand away. Her lower abdomen tightened in anticipation as he grabbed her hips and thrust into her.

Closing her eyes, she clutched onto his shoulders as he filled her. Her inner walls stretched and molded around him until all she was aware of was Cade.

He remained still, buried deep inside her, his breathing as ragged as hers. Then he raised his head and started slowly moving.

She opened her eyes to find him watching her with that intense green gaze. He was so hard to read sometimes, but now she could see all the hunger and desire burning right at the surface.

Reaching between them, he slowly rubbed her clit as he increased his thrusts. She held on to his shoulders as that normally elusive release was already pressing at her, insistent and ready to be set free. It was as if he knew her body better than she did. She responded to him in a way she never had with anyone else.

As he increased the pressure against her sensitive bundle of nerves, he also increased his rhythm inside her. His thrusts became harder and more unsteady until finally her climax slammed into her. It was so unexpected she let out a sharp cry, his name ragged on her lips.

It moved through her body like ripples across a lake, each one getting wider and wider, pushing out to all her nerve endings. She buried her face against his neck, crying out his name as the pleasure continued to overtake her.

As her orgasm ebbed, the sensation turning into tiny tendrils that brushed against her oversensitive body, he let out a loud groan. His drove into her over and over, her name a moan on his lips as he emptied himself inside her.

He still didn't move but held her up against the wall,

his breathing slowly steadying against her neck as they both got their breath back.

She wasn't sure how much time passed, and she didn't really care. Even with all the horror going on around them, she'd felt impossibly safe, and yes, cherished, in Cade's arms. It was a strange sensation, but one she embraced. Eventually he stepped back and she let her legs unwrap from around him. They felt rubbery and she faltered as her feet touched the slick floor.

But he held on to her, guiding her directly under the still-pulsing showerhead. Closing her eyes, she let him maneuver her until she was turned around, her back pressed against his chest. The water rushed over her, completely soaking her hair and body.

When she heard a soft *snick*ing sound, then felt his hands gently massaging her scalp, she realized he was washing her hair. In that instant it hit her how much she'd fallen for Cade. *Again.* So hard and far, there was no way she could walk away from him. She didn't want to. The problem was, she had no idea if he felt the same. After what had happened between them before, she had her doubts. Even if he hurt her, she wasn't going to walk away before they had a chance to see if things could work between them.

*   *   *

Date: December 26, 2006
To: Maria Cervantes
From: Cade O'Reilly
Subject: re: holidays

I'm glad you said no to that guy, and for full disclosure, I've written and deleted the same type of e-mail about a hundred times. I look forward to your e-mails more than a "friend" should and I want more than friendship. Asking you to wait for me, though, seems fucked up. I have no clue what I'm going to do when my time to reenlist comes up. More and more I'm thinking about getting out, but I don't know at this point. Even though it is selfish . . . I don't want you to see anyone and I'm definitely not interested in anyone else. Haven't been from the moment I met you.

Cade

Chapter 17

Grenade launcher: a weapon that launches a grenade with more accuracy, higher velocity, and to greater distances than an individual could throw it by hand.

Cade pulled Maria's back tight to his chest, his arm wrapped securely around her waist. She snuggled tighter against him, wiggling her ass over his growing erection. Pulling her even tighter to him, he kissed her neck, savoring the soft appreciative sounds she made. He *should* be sated. But that seemed an impossible feat around her.

After their shower they'd dried off, changed, and grabbed some food downstairs and then she'd jumped him again. Not that he minded. He'd wanted her again pretty much from the moment they'd *left* the shower, but she'd been through a hell of a lot and he wasn't sure how much she could take tonight—this morning. God, it was already two a.m. How had that happened?

She wiggled against him and laughed under her breath when he let out a low growl and nipped her shoulder. "Don't tempt me," he murmured.

"I was just seeing if it was possible that you were already hard again." Her voice was raspy, probably because she was exhausted. And he wouldn't be responsible for keeping her up any longer. She'd been through so much already; her body needed time to rest. Even if she didn't care, he did.

"You're naked and in my arms—what do you expect?" He could definitely go another round, but he also liked simply holding her. The stillness inside him was unexpected. For the first time in as long as he could remember, he just felt at peace. Which was insane, considering the job he was working. It had nothing to do with their being at a safe house either. His mind was working overtime, as always, but something deep inside him was just . . . calm. All because of the woman in his arms.

Which shouldn't surprise him. He'd felt that searing calm eight years ago when talking, e-mailing, or writing long handwritten letters to her. He'd let his guard down with her in a way he hadn't with any other woman. Then he'd fucked everything up.

She let out a soft sigh but didn't make a move to turn around. That alone told him that she was too tired for more. She tightened her arm over his, linking her fingers through his, and despite how he felt holding her, a knot formed in his chest.

Guilt.

It never went away. No matter how much he tried to box it up or pretend it didn't exist, the truth was, it was his fault Maria's brother was dead. He'd wanted to tell her before she went down on him in the shower, anything to stop what he knew what was about to happen. But once her lips had wrapped around him, there had been no turning back and he'd been completely lost to her.

He was also a little selfish. Fuck yeah, he could admit

it. He wanted Maria, just for as long as she'd keep him. She was too good for him, and once he finally confessed the truth, she'd probably hate him, which was no less than he deserved. Part of him wanted to see that hatred and anger in her gaze, to have it directed at him because he deserved it. He deserved to pay penance for what he'd done. But for now, she was his. He'd been sacrificing for his country in one way or another since he was eighteen, and right now he just wanted to hold on to some happiness for himself.

Even in shitty circumstances, lying here with Maria made him happy. A weird fucking concept.

"Do they have any news on the terrorists? Did what I told you at Dr. York's help?" She asked one question after the other, the tiredness in her voice evident, even though her mind wouldn't let her sleep just yet.

He knew she was fighting sleep, but if she wanted to know, he'd tell her anything that wasn't classified. "No news on the bastards. They ditched their first boat, and switched at least once, but probably a couple times after that first ditch. It's like they just disappeared." Even though he was angry about it, he didn't regret leaving the scene to take care of Maria. There was nothing he could have done there that another teammate couldn't.

"I thought you guys used satellites and stuff," she said sleepily, her fingers loosening around his hand.

He paused for a moment, weighing what he could say without wading into a gray area. "We do, but our options failed." It had been a giant cluster fuck of failures. Some days it didn't matter how much technology they had at their fingertips; some events were just unavoidable.

The FBI helicopter designated for the mission had been parked on the Opulen's private helicopter pad, and one of the rotors got clipped by falling debris from the explosion. They'd had backups about a mile away, but the Donzi had been too damn fast. The satellite the NSA had originally wanted to use hadn't been in reliable working condition, and with the last-minute operation, there was no way that could have changed.

However, the aerial drone the NSA had utilized had been able to follow them to another marina. A much bigger one that took up almost two miles of space. The NSA had lost a visual of the men, then never got them back. With the number of boats going in and out of the other marina, it had been impossible to even attempt to track one of them. They'd tried, but with the drone and the two helicopters, it was three eyes in the sky trying to narrow down one vessel out of hundreds.

A needle in a stack of needles.

But he didn't tell Maria all that, because she didn't need more to worry about.

"What about the port I mentioned? Do you think it's the Port of Miami?"

"It's possible." Anything was possible at this point. They needed to narrow down the motivation of the terrorists more than anything. Doing that would hopefully give them answers about future targets. Because this wasn't about religion or money. According to Burkhart, the pictures left at Scott Mullen's house were sick but telling. A bunch of naked women kept in cages and other horrific images he didn't even want to think about—not a good thing.

From the file the NSA had started on Mihails Balodis and Oto Ozols, they knew both their parents were dead and that Oto didn't have any other living relatives. Mihails, however, had two sisters. Unfortunately there was no information on either of them. It was as if they'd completely fallen off the grid years ago after getting work visas for the U.S. It wasn't a stretch to think this had something to do with one of them. Not with those fucking pictures left behind.

"I swear I can hear the wheels in your head turning." Maria's voice was soft, soothing, and fading fast.

He chuckled lightly. "Sorry." Cade closed his eyes, trying to shut off his thoughts and get some sleep. He needed to be sharp for Maria and for himself. For all he knew he'd be called in by Burkhart in a few hours. His boss might have given him a short reprieve, but he knew the other man well enough that if he wanted to pull Cade from a job, he'd do it. Cade intended to soak up every moment of this time alone with Maria.

She squeezed his hand lightly, and a few seconds later, her breathing completely evened out. The soft rhythm told him she'd finally fallen asleep. Only then did he allow himself to fade too. The alarm on the house was secure and he had enough weapons to hold off a small army until backup arrived.

Wearing a long-sleeved black T-shirt and black pants, he opened the back passenger door of the car he'd stolen and slipped out. He'd disabled the dome light so he didn't give himself away to anyone who might be awake and looking out their window. He doubted anyone would be up at this time, but he was always careful. And since he was carrying a bulky weapon he couldn't hide anywhere on his person, he really couldn't afford to be seen.

The tracker he'd placed in Maria's purse had remained at the same residential address for the past six hours, but he'd been waiting for the right time to strike. Women took their purses with them everywhere and they typically left them in their bedrooms or kitchens at the end of the day. While it had been tricky, it had been easier slipping the tracker into her purse than placing it on her person.

The quiet hours before dawn were always the best time to conduct any type of infiltration. Standard operating procedure was to attack an enemy when his guard would be down. His time in the Army had taught him that. It had also taught him a lot more. Though he'd hated every second of it, the time he'd spent in had paid for his college. Which was the only reason he'd joined. It had all been part of his plan to become who he was now.

Unlike Maria's family and so many of Miami's elite, he didn't come from money. He had to work for what he had, and very soon he'd be taking a well-deserved payday. He just needed Maria out of the way first.

There was no way in hell she'd ever consider selling the community center, and he wanted that property. Wanted what it could give him.

It was kismet that the bitch had placed herself in Mihails's line of fire. That man was terrifying in a way he didn't want to even think about.

He dismissed those thoughts and hurried down the sidewalk, careful to stick to the shadows of the quiet street. With no innocent reason to be in this neighborhood at this hour—and carrying such an obvious weapon—he had to be careful. The area was middle-class, and any concerned citizens would absolutely call the police if they spotted him.

He'd parked the next street over from the address but had done reconnaissance earlier. There hadn't been any cars in the driveway, but he'd seen an SUV in the garage when he looked through a side window. Getting close enough to the house had been nerve-racking, but he hadn't had a choice. Not when he'd told Mihails he would take care of Maria. Some days he regretted getting in bed with Mihails, but it was done and he couldn't complain too much when he'd been nicely compensated. If it wasn't for his ability to occasionally and discreetly run guns, or more important, smuggle in high-powered, illegal weapons, their paths would never have crossed.

Mihails was an extremist. Not a religious nut, because he wouldn't do business with people like that. No, he had standards. But Mihails was an extremist nonetheless and would die for what he believed in. People like that made him nervous because they could be unpredictable. He preferred people who valued money above all. It was much easier to calculate their moves and speak to their motivation.

Nearing the corner to the street Maria was on, he slowed his pace when he reached the four-way stop sign. It had a slight reflection under the streetlight and half-moon. He peered down her street, his heart beating an erratic thump against his ribs as he scanned the street for any vehicles he hadn't seen earlier.

There didn't appear to be any, but he ducked across the street just the same. He wouldn't approach from the front, so when he got to the other side, he kept walking and only stopped when he reached the next street over. Making his way down yet another quiet street lined with palm and oak trees, he hurried through the yard positioned directly behind the house Maria was in.

He stayed as close to the fence as possible, hoping he wouldn't trip any floodlights. He only allowed himself a small sigh of relief after he'd scaled the fence into her backyard.

It was sparse, with no patio furniture in the small tiled back area. There wasn't even a grill. Nothing. Only a single oak tree in the corner of the yard, its leaves completely still in the almost preternatural quiet.

He hated how damn quiet the evening was, but this was when he had to strike. Since he knew she would have a guard and the place had a security system, his attack would be swift, brutal, and very violent.

It was the only way.

Escaping would be a pain in the ass, but he wouldn't be leaving the way he'd come. No, he had another vehicle waiting and a carefully planned exit. This wasn't the first time he'd done something like this.

Reaching into his back pocket, he pulled out a black mask and tugged it over his face. Once it was secure, he picked his weapon back up and hurried across the backyard.

Positioning himself directly below the bedroom where her beacon had been immobile since she'd settled in at the residence, he lifted his grenade launcher onto his shoulder and aimed.

He could have used an automatic grenade launcher but had opted for the handheld version. It was slightly less powerful but much easier to transport and it was unnecessary to use a tripod to set it up.

His hand steady, he narrowed in on the window and pulled the trigger of the single-shot weapon. The large round grenade exploded from the barrel with a whoosh that nearly knocked him back despite his solid stance.

An explosion of fire and noise lit up the night sky. The burst of orange was brilliant, but he had no time to enjoy the destruction. Lowering the weapon, he reloaded once more and pulled the trigger again, firing into what was likely the kitchen.

The loud boom that rent the air as wood and brick splintered everywhere made him stumble back. He didn't stick around to enjoy the beauty of his work. He dropped the weapon, not caring that he had to leave it behind. He'd wiped it down before he left his home and he'd been wearing gloves the entire time. Turning, he raced back across the yard. In seconds, people would be rushing outside and calling the police. It would be easy enough to blend in and act like a concerned neighbor once he lost his mask and gloves.

Hurrying, he pulled himself up on the fence and froze when he found himself staring down the barrel of a long suppressor. His throat tightened, his heart nearly jumped out of his chest in raw fear, but before he could speak, he was flying back through the air.

Then blackness.

Chapter 18

Blitz attack: a sudden violent attack with a concentrated effort on a target.

M aria's eyes flew open as the entire house shook, a deafening blast ripping through the air. Confusion and fear pumped through her veins like jagged lightning. She started to shove up, but Cade jerked her backward, his big arm snagging around her waist. Instinctively she started to fight but stilled as another explosion rocked the house. Freezing in raw fear, she toppled off the bed with Cade.

Their house was under attack! Her sleep-addled brain was still fighting through the fuzziness of coming from a dead slumber to *this*, but she quickly realized what was going on.

Her ears hummed and her entire body trembled as Cade tucked her underneath his body. "Stay down!" he shouted before he grabbed their mattress and pulled it off the bed frame.

She hunkered low, not caring that she was naked, and watched him move with incredible efficiency as he used the nightstand to prop the mattress up over them. Next, he pulled out the bottom drawer to reveal three guns. He checked the chamber of the smallest one, then slid it to her. "There's no safety. Just aim and pull the trigger," he said as he pulled out the other two guns.

Facedown, she reached out and took it but didn't move otherwise. The smooth wood was cold against her naked body, but that was the least of her worries. She tried to remain calm as she wondered if the house was about to be attacked again. Even though she was internally freaking out, she didn't ask questions as Cade secured his weapons. He was focused and it was clear he had a plan. Or she really hoped he did.

Jaw tight and muscles pulled taut, he climbed over her, keeping his body directly on top of hers as he slid one of the closet doors open. Reaching in, he grabbed a small black duffel bag and tugged it out. He rolled off her as he unzipped it and shoved a T-shirt at her. "Put it on, we're getting out of here."

Still flat on the floor, she tugged it over her head as he pulled on a pair of cargo pants. He tucked one of the guns in the back of his pants but held the other firmly in his hand. "Stay behind me and do exactly what I say." His green eyes were sharp, emerald flecks.

Throat tight, she nodded. Hell yeah, she'd do whatever he said. The smell of smoke teased her nostrils, but it wasn't suffocating. And there hadn't been another explosion after the second one.

Yet.

For all she knew, those two explosions were just the beginning. Had someone set the house on fire? Or thrown bombs or ... grenades or something inside?

Using the tilted mattress as a cover, Cade crawled

to the edge of it. Weapon drawn, he peered out first; then without turning around he motioned for her to follow.

She held on to the gun he'd given her in a tight grasp and crawled with it, her knuckles dragging along the wooden floor as she held firm. Since it didn't have a safety, she was careful not to put her finger near the trigger. Not unless she absolutely had to. She might not want to use it on someone, but the cold steel felt damn good in her palm. If this was the only thing between her and a terrorist trying to harm her or Cade, she didn't think she'd have a problem using it.

When they reached the bedroom door, Cade half stood, his back pressed against the wall as he slowly turned the handle with one hand. Just as carefully he opened the door, then swept out into the hall with his gun. From her position on the floor she watched as he froze for a second, his eyes going wide, before he turned back to her.

He motioned that it was safe and pointed to the right. The direction of the stairs.

Nodding, she stood and stepped out into the hallway. The acrid scent of smoke curled around her, the crackling sound of . . . Her eyes widened as she took in the left side of the hallway.

Or what had once been there.

A gaping hole stood where the last bedroom in the hallway had once been. The bedroom *she* had been in. The actual floor had been ripped away too, leaving a whole lot of nothing. She could see the downstairs through the giant crater in the floor.

Feeling frozen, she tried to move, to look away. It was

like something out of a nightmare. If she hadn't gone to Cade's bedroom tonight, she would have been in there during the explosion.

Dying orange flames flickered around the edges of where the wood and plaster had splintered right apart. The scent of smoke invaded her, and the sight of the flames . . . Suddenly she remembered *everything*. What she'd heard.

And the ultimate betrayal of a family friend. Her throat tightened as bile threatened to suffocate her. She swallowed hard, reliving the conversation she'd overheard the night of the party. The night her mother had died. How could he be involved with terrorists? It didn't make sense. An icy vise squeezed around her chest as she thought about how close she'd been to him after the bombing. More than once. That bastard had come to her mother's funeral when he'd been involved.

A red haze of rage threatened to take over, but a tug on her upper arm jerked her back to reality. She turned to find Cade holding his finger to his lips, then pointing to the stairs. His expression was tight as he dragged her with him.

She shoved her growing horror aside and buried it deep, right next to all the other crap she was trying desperately not to think about. As soon as she was able she'd tell Cade what she remembered. And later, when she was alone and had the luxury, she'd think about how she'd almost died tonight. For now, she just wanted to get the hell out of this place in one piece.

Cade pushed her behind him as they descended the stairs, his movements so fluid and practiced it was impressive to witness. It also made her glad this man was on her side.

As they reached the bottom of the stairs, he scanned in both directions down the hall, his weapon raised and ready. After a few seconds he motioned again for her to follow. She felt numb as she descended the last couple of stairs. How the hell was this really happening? An uncontrollable tremor rolled through her as her feet touched the main floor.

Smoke trailed down the stairs after them, the lingering scent making her sick. Another pump of adrenaline punched through her. They had to get out of there *now*.

Cade pulled her close, his fingers wrapped around her upper arm as he propelled them down the hallway toward the living room. "It looks like the attack came from the backyard, but I don't want to go out through the front in case there are more men waiting. We're going to exit through a window."

"Okay." Her voice shook, matching her insides.

He gave her a sharp look. "We're going to get out of this alive." The promise in his voice was all she needed to hear.

"I believe you."

He nodded once, then continued down the rest of the hallway. Seconds later they were crouched down next to one of the big bay windows on the side of the house. Cade pulled back the thick curtains, the sliding sound of the ring clips seeming incredibly loud in the room. She could see the neighbor's lights on, but it was still dark enough that they wouldn't be exposed. Especially since they didn't have a backlight to illuminate them.

"I'm going to go out first, check for danger, and then you're going to follow. Use your gun if you have to. And if I tell you to run, fucking *run*. Do not wait for me or try to help me. If you get the chance, you make a break for safety."

Deep down, she knew she couldn't leave him behind no matter what the situation. But she knew enough not to tell him that. They didn't have time to argue about it. He put his life on the line every day, often for people who would never have a clue. She wasn't leaving him. But she nodded. "Okay."

Those piercing green eyes narrowed a fraction, as if he'd read her mind, but he didn't respond. The window opened soundlessly and he slipped from the room like a ghost, his movements so smooth it still surprised her that such a big man had that ability.

Moments later, his head popped back up. "Come on," he whispered.

She could hear sirens in the distance, and the neighbor's house next door had all the lights on as she climbed over the edge of the window with much less finesse than Cade. The second her bare feet came in contact with the soft grass, she said, "Andre Moran. In case I don't get to tell you later." Meaning in case she didn't survive this. "You met him at the funeral. He was there the night of the attack. I heard him talking to those men and he's involved."

Cade nodded once, his expression hard as he put his hand on the small of her back and started guiding her toward the front of the house. The sirens were growing louder now. Some of her fear started to fade, but not much.

That icy numbness had taken root deep inside her as she tried not to think about the fact that someone her family had trusted, had invited over for dinner numerous

times—someone she'd gone on a couple of dates with—
had been involved in such a horrific act of terror, which
had taken the life of her mother and countless other in-
nocents. That bastard had been at her mother's funeral
and pretended to care.

Cade continued to scan all around them as they hurried down the side of the house. When another light
from the neighbor's house switched on in the backyard,
Maria's chest constricted. The new light source illuminated a man wearing all black barely twenty feet from
them. He was moving down the edge of the chain-link
fence on *their* side of the yard, a gun in his hand.

She shoved at Cade, wrapping her arms around him
in a full-body tackle.

Cade grunted in surprise as he flew backward, but
with incredible agility, he twisted in midair.

Pop. Pop. Pop.

The night erupted with a blast of gunfire as Cade shot
at the other man. The sound was so close to her ear she
cried out. Her heart lodged in her throat as she landed
on the ground with a thud, Cade falling on top of her. All
the air whooshed from her lungs, but she scarcely felt the
impact.

"Stay down," Cade ordered, his voice low and angry
as he shoved off her.

Disoriented, she rolled over and saw the man in black
lying on his back. Cade had shot him three times. She'd
seen the gun in the other man's hand and wondered if
he'd even gotten off a shot. If he had, she was thankful
he'd missed both of them.

Her gaze trailed after Cade, watching as he raced to
the fallen man and kicked away his weapon. He checked

the man's pulse, then hurried away toward the back of the house and disappeared from sight.

Fear clawed at her, telling her to go after him, but she didn't. He was trained and she didn't want to get in his way. Still, that knowledge did nothing to diminish the raw agony tearing away her insides. The thought of anything happening to Cade shredded her apart. What if there were more men with guns waiting? What if . . . No, no, no. He would be okay. He had to be. She refused to accept any other outcome.

The sirens she'd heard earlier were piercing now. Turning in the other direction, she watched as a police car zoomed down the street, then out of her line of sight. Seconds later a fire truck pulled right up next to the curb. Help had arrived.

Unfortunately she didn't feel any relief and wouldn't until she knew Cade was unhurt.

*   *   *

Date: December 31, 2006
To: Cade O'Reilly
From: Maria Cervantes
Subject: Happy New Year

Happy New Year's (Eve)! I'm sure it'll be a lot happier once you're stateside . . . and I plan to make sure you get the welcome back you deserve. Now that we're being open about everything, it feels good to be even more honest with you. Do you know how many nights I've stared at the ceiling thinking about you and that kiss? Some days I wondered if I imagined it.

I'm sure this is wishful thinking, but I hope your night is quiet with no "fireworks." I know I never said it before, but in case the implication wasn't clear enough, whatever your decision when you decide to stay in or get out, I'm okay with.

In a couple hours I'll be heading out with some friends to a low-key party. Basically it's going to be a bunch of psychology nerds like myself playing beer pong and ringing in the New Year. Until now I've never cared about that New Year's kiss tradition, but I wish you were here to share one with. But don't worry. I won't be kissing anyone else. Miss you.

xo,
Maria

Chapter 19

Clandestine operation: an intelligence operation intended to be secret.

Cade stood at the rear of Burkhart's SUV but kept himself positioned so that he could see Maria clearly. She sat in the back of one of the ambulances with a blanket wrapped around her. Even though she wasn't injured, he still wanted her looked at in case she went into shock and he didn't want her around while he spoke to his boss.

"What have they found on Andre Moran?" Cade asked.

"The team is still tearing apart his life, but so far it looks like he'd bought up all the property around the community center where Maria works as part of a huge real estate deal. The purchases weren't under his name, but a shell corporation. It looks as if his plan was to sell all the properties in one deal and make a fortune. No one even knew this was in the works, but there's a big developer looking to put in a pseudo–shopping center. A bunch of Starbucks and other shit that the neighborhood is apparently perfect for, not that that's important. We're sending a guy to talk to the developer to see if he knew what Moran was up to, but I doubt it."

"So, why was he helping terrorists, and what was his issue with Maria if she just worked there?" Because the bastard had specifically targeted her.

"This is just a guess, but Maria's predecessor there left the property to her. The will is still in probate, but very soon Maria will be the owner of the building and the land. From our initial digging, there were multiple offers made on the center—to her predecessor—and they were all declined. If something happened to Maria before she made a will, there would be a scramble not only to find someone with her credentials to take over in a timely manner, but to figure out who the building would be passed on to. It would likely be her father since he's her closest living relative—but he was supposed to attend the party too, so maybe Moran had planned on the entire Cervantes family dying. If that had happened, say someone offered money for the property in the interim. The state could take over, citing any number of bullshit issues, bank the money, and let it earn interest while her lawyers figured out whether to relocate or whatever. Or say it passed to one of her relatives. Why would they want to hold on to a property with an immediate buyer? Honestly I don't fucking know and we may never know. From what we've found, it looks like money is his number-one priority.

"Since he's got unverified ties to some pretty big criminals in Miami, it's not a stretch that he fell into bed with Mihails for pure monetary gain. And if he had the chance to get the last piece to his little real estate puzzle from her death . . ." Burkhart shrugged. "This is just a theory, but my gut tells me I'm right."

Cade let out a savage curse, barely containing his rage that Maria had been put in more danger. "So, why—"

"Why didn't our guys find this? It wasn't in the first pass through his records because he knew how to cover his tracks—but he was definitely into shady dealings. Possibly smuggling high-powered weapons." Burkhart's expression was grim as he glanced back at what remained of the safe house. Half of it had been completely blown away.

The majority of the damage had been done by the initial explosion from the grenade launcher Cade had found in the backyard. Once the firefighters arrived, they'd put out the slow-moving flames.

Now that Moran was dead—apparently shot by the man Cade had killed—they couldn't question him. Either of them. But the prints they'd run for the other man came back as belonging to a Fedor Lukovs. The man had previous ties with, big surprise, Mihails Balodis.

Cade frowned as he digested what his boss had told him. It amazed him how greed made people do the shittiest things. "Moran was at her mother's funeral." Cade was unable to cover the disgust in his voice. "I . . . think he might have placed a tracker on her. Maybe her purse or her person." He sighed, rubbing a hand over his face, hating that this was likely his fault. He hadn't thought anyone had been close enough to her at the funeral to do something like that, but clearly he was wrong. "It's the only way to explain how he found us." Because they hadn't been followed. Of that he was positive. And there hadn't been any trackers on his SUV. He always checked, but a team had done another sweep as soon as they arrived, and it was clean.

"Makes sense. The room she was in was the one targeted. Which meant he was pretty positive of her location." Burkhart was silent for a long moment as Cade waited for him to ask the question he'd known was coming. "Why wasn't she in her room?"

Cade met that hard stare, unflinching. "She was in mine."

Burkhart's gaze flicked to where she sat on the edge of the ambulance's rear deck. "I figured, since she's just wearing one of your shirts." There was a note of censure in his boss's voice.

If this had been a typical occurrence—though if it was, he'd be out of a job—or anyone else other than Maria, Cade might have felt guilty. "Say what you need to say."

Burkhart lifted his shoulders. "I've never known you to get involved with an asset." When Cade didn't respond, just tightened his jaw, his boss continued. "She's been through a lot. She's vulnerable right now."

At that, Cade swallowed hard. He already knew that. But he'd fallen so damn hard for her. He looked away, his eyes automatically seeking Maria out. She was nodding politely at something the female paramedic said. "She's more than an asset and I didn't take advantage of her." Would never, *could* never.

"I know you wouldn't. Just . . . be careful," Burkhart said softly, the tone out of character. "And answer me honestly. If it was anyone else, I'd pull them, but you've got one of the best records. Will this compromise your ability to do your job?"

Cade shook his head. "No. I wouldn't do that to *her*." If he thought his judgment was skewed enough to put Maria in danger, Burkhart wouldn't have to pull him, because he'd do it himself.

Burkhart just gave him a long look before he tapped his earpiece. And Cade let out a sigh of relief. While his boss gave one-word answers to whoever was on the other end, Cade headed to the ambulance. As he arrived at the back, another paramedic strode up with a folded pair of light blue scrubs: pants and a top. He handed them to Maria before he and the other woman walked away, giving them privacy.

"How are you feeling?" Cade asked, even though it was a stupid question.

Her amber eyes widened as she clutched the clothes to her chest. "Me? You shot someone. How are *you*?"

"It's not the first time. Seriously, are you . . ." Words felt so inadequate. Her mother had been buried the afternoon before and then they'd just barely survived a very violent hit.

She shook her head. "I don't know what I am. It's all too surreal. I feel like I'm watching someone else's life. Or an action movie. I know I'll crash later and have to deal with all this, but more than anything, I'm just glad we're both alive."

His throat tightened. He could have lost her. That was unacceptable. If Burkhart got a lead on where these fuckers were, Cade was going to be part of the team that brought them down. Even though he didn't want to leave her side, things had gotten very personal after this attack.

"Moran was in the backyard. He's dead." He hadn't told her about the other body yet because he'd wanted to wait after what she'd told him about Moran. A tech had used one of the NSA's handheld fingerprint scanners and identified him almost immediately. Burkhart might be pissed that he'd told her, because he hated sharing information with civilians, but she had a right to know.

She sucked in a sharp breath, and uncaring about appearances, he closed the last few inches between them. He slid his hand behind her head, holding her possessively as he wrapped his other arm around her and held her tight. "I'm sorry, sweetheart," he murmured against the top of her head.

She wrapped both hands around him tightly, letting the scrubs fall to her lap. Resting her head against his chest, she let out a shaky breath. "I know what I heard, but I thought maybe . . . I was wrong. He was friends with my parents. I don't understand why he'd be involved with those guys or why he'd come here." She suddenly pulled back, a frown playing across her face. "I didn't hear any more gunfire."

"I didn't kill him and neither did anyone else here. They'll still have to run the ballistics, but it looks as if the man I took down killed Moran."

"I'm not sad he's dead, but why? From what I remember overhearing, he was working with those guys."

Cade shrugged. "I can't say for sure and we might not ever know, but he likely outlived his usefulness. It's usually how things like this work. Moran wasn't part of their crew. He's obviously been helping them with something, but since he wasn't one of them, it could be as simple as Mihails and Oto tying up loose ends." He'd tell her everything Burkhart had told him later, but for now he didn't want to bog her down with even more information about a man she'd trusted. Not to mention that he wasn't even sure if he could tell her about Moran's motives just yet.

She shivered and though he wanted to pull her back into another embrace, he took the blanket wrapped around her shoulders and completely unfolded it before holding it up. "You can change here if you want."

"Thank you," she murmured, her expression full of exhaustion and contemplation.

He glanced around, making sure no one was paying attention, even though she was completely blocked with the blanket. Some primal part of him didn't want anyone to see what he considered his.

His.

He nearly snorted at the thought. She might be for now, but when she learned the truth of what had happened to her brother, she could very well hate him. But a small, stupidly hopeful part of him had started to wonder if maybe she could forgive him. Maybe even ... yeah, not going there.

"I'm done, thanks."

When he looked back, she was neatly folding his shirt. A smile tugged at his mouth, catching him by surprise as he watched her. It smelled like smoke and was dirty, yet she folded it with such precision and care.

"So, what happens now?" As she met his gaze again, he could see the exhaustion lines around her eyes.

He started to respond when she stiffened, looking past him. He turned to find Burkhart striding toward them.

"We've found three abandoned cars in the area," he said to Cade after a polite nod at Maria, then focused solely on Cade. "One a block from here and it has Moran's prints on it. So far there's nothing useful inside, but one of the analysts dumped the contents of the burner phone he had on him. One of the only two numbers from the call history is sending out a signal right now. A very isolated area. No CCTVs or ..." He trailed off, not about to give any more details, and Cade knew his boss wouldn't in front of Maria.

His heart rate accelerated at the news. It could be nothing or it could be the break they'd been waiting for. Mihails Balodis had been caught on facial-recognition software programs when he entered the country and when he entered Florida, but that was months ago, and until yesterday at the marina, the man had been practically a ghost. There were ways to screw up the program and maybe he'd been doing that to stay off the grid. Or he'd just been lying incredibly low. An isolated base of operations would certainly help with that.

"I'm setting up a team now. I want you as lead. I have a place we can take her—completely off the books." Burkhart wasn't ordering him, something Cade appreciated.

He didn't want to leave Maria, but a big threat to her had just been eliminated and if he could help bring down the bastard who had killed her mother— He *had* to do this for her. "Give us a sec?"

His boss nodded, already tapping his earpiece again as he left them to talk.

"You want to go." Maria's voice was soft as she wrapped her arms around herself.

He nodded, placing his hands on her hips and pulling her close. He didn't want anything between them, even imaginary barriers, and he couldn't tell if she was putting them up. At this point he didn't give a shit about propriety as he cupped her cheek. "I don't have to."

She laid gentle hands on his chest, her expression wry. "Yes, you *do*. And I don't want to hold you back." The worry in her eyes was stark, but she meant what she was saying.

It made him love her even more. He almost jerked at the thought.

Love.

Shit. Yeah, he did. He'd been fighting the truth to himself, knowing it was too soon and just plain stupid. "They need to pay for what they've done." And he needed to atone for previous sins. Maybe he could do that by bringing down the men who'd killed her mother. Maybe then she'd forgive him once she learned the truth about him.

"What will happen to me now?" Now a shot of fear crept into her expression.

After the NSA and local cops had shown up, she told Cade everything she remembered from the night of the Westwood explosion. Now they had covert operatives watching over the locations she'd heard specifically mentioned. The NSA and FBI were also following up on a ton of other avenues—including trying to locate the suddenly missing owners of the Opulen Hotel—but they were taking Maria's statement very seriously. After the attempts on her life, they'd be stupid not to.

"You'll still be protected." Frowning, he turned to find Burkhart still talking. From his angle, Cade couldn't see his earpiece but knew his boss had it on. He probably slept with the damn thing. Cade looked back at her and dropped a quick kiss on her head. "Just give me a sec." No matter how badly he wanted to bring the terrorists to justice, he had to know for sure who would be watching over Maria. Otherwise he couldn't leave her.

As he approached, his boss tapped his earpiece off immediately. Before Cade could ask the two questions he needed to know—where would Maria be staying and who would be watching her?—Burkhart motioned toward the fire truck with his head. "Come on."

Rounding the front of the truck with Burkhart, Cade

saw a black SUV right behind the sectioned-off area across the street. It was next to the curb, the parking lights on as it idled. All the neighbors had been ordered back into their houses, so there weren't any civilians around and the SUV didn't have government plates. "Who's in there?" he asked when it was clear Burkhart was heading straight for the vehicle.

His boss just grunted. As they reached it, he rapped his knuckles on the driver's-side window.

When it rolled down, Cade didn't bother to hide his shock. "Holy shit."

Jack Stone, a man he'd worked with in the past—a deadly fucking operative who'd retired a year ago—gave him a small nod. His pale eyes seemed to glow in the darkness. "Been a while, O'Reilly."

"Yeah." He glanced back toward the ambulance to see two armed agents hovering protectively near Maria before he turned back. "I thought you retired."

"I did. I'm in Miami for personal reasons." Of course no further explanations.

Cade looked at Burkhart, who shrugged. "I knew he was in the area, so I called him as soon as you contacted me about this." He pointed over his shoulder. "Ms. Cervantes will be safer with him than with anyone else."

That was probably true, but ... "Where will you be staying?"

Jack gave him an assessing look, then finally spoke. "I'm in town because my wife, Sophie, wanted to see her best friend after the Westwood bombing. Her friend's parents were supposed to have been there." His jaw tightened at that. "We're staying at her friend's parents' home. It's well secured, so in a few hours, once the sun is up, Sophie and I will take Ms. Cervantes over there. The residence has no ties to her or the agency. She can't bring anything personal with her, including her cell phone."

It had been destroyed in the blast, so that wasn't a problem.

"She can use mine in case of an emergency or just to contact her family or you," Stone added.

It was a good plan to keep her safe, and being sure of her security was the only way Cade would be able to do his job. Since they still weren't positive how they'd been tracked to the current safe house, he was more apt to let Maria leave with someone who had no ties to the agency. Not to mention that Stone was lethally efficient. And as long as he had a way to contact her, Cade could live with it. "Okay. Let me go over everything with her first."

Mouth pulled into a grim line, Burkhart nodded.

Levi rolled down the window of the rented SUV as he pulled up to the guard's station at Alexander Lopez's mansion. The arms dealer was cautious and actually likable, for a criminal. Unlike so many men and women Levi had been forced to work with over the past decade, Lopez had a moral code of sorts. He didn't run drugs or people and he wouldn't deal with those who did. The world wasn't black and white and Levi could deal with Lopez's shades of gray.

An armed guard stepped from the guardhouse, looked him and the woman in the passenger seat over, then nodded as someone spoke into his earpiece. Levi couldn't hear what the individual had said, but the guard was clearly listening to someone.

"You're clear," the man said before stepping back into the small structure, which Levi knew had bullet-resistant windows.

Levi also knew he and his companion would be searched for weapons as soon as they parked. Just standard procedure.

Lopez often acted as a go-between for parties who wanted to conduct business. His home was considered neutral ground, and most people in their line of business respected that. Well, Levi wasn't in anyone's business. Right now this was all a job to him whether he worked for the NSA anymore or not. For almost a year and a half he'd been following one lead after another, picking up one thread when another hit a dead end. It was seemingly never ending, but he was getting closer to finding out why his wife had been murdered.

And who was behind it.

He swore he could taste how close he was.

"I've been here before. Who are you meeting with?" the woman sitting next to him asked.

Despite his earlier decision not to use her, he'd decided to hire this woman again. She went by the name Jasmine, but he knew her real name was Allison. Even though he'd tried digging deeper into her past, he hadn't been able to find out how the hell she'd ended up in the escort business. Sadly, there weren't that many options to choose from: bad family life, bad boyfriend talked her into it, she needed the money to eat—he guessed it was one of those three choices. At twenty-four, she was smart, exquisitely beautiful, and shouldn't be selling her body for money. Hell, no one should. He wanted to remain unaffected by her, but before he left town he wanted to talk to her about getting out of the business. "You know Lopez?" he asked, ignoring her question.

She shrugged, the action casual. "Not really. I've serviced some of his clients before."

"What do you think of him?" He slowly steered the vehicle down the long winding drive, wanting to draw out this conversation if she had any information on Lopez.

"He's not so bad. I know what he does but he doesn't hurt women." That right there said it all. It was probably how she gauged whether someone was "not so bad" or not.

"What about Paul Hill? Do you know him?" The man Levi was supposed to meet at Lopez's house. They'd been supposed to meet at the Opulen, but after the shit storm earlier, Hill had canceled.

It was subtle, but her expression tightened ever so slightly. "I've never met him."

A nice, vague answer.

"But you know of him?" he asked as he parked the SUV.

"I know that many women in a line of work similar to mine go into his hotel and never come out." Her voice was icy, her expression remote.

His eyebrows rose as he filed the information away. If that was true, he was surprised Lopez was letting the man onto his property. Levi didn't respond and she didn't speak again as armed guards opened their doors.

After they were thoroughly checked for weapons, including his vehicle, they were shown into the marbled entryway of Lopez's home. Well, one of his homes. An oversized, gaudy sculpture of a nude woman cupping one of her breasts with one hand while the other was between her legs was the first thing they saw upon entry.

"So classy," Allison/Jasmine murmured, and despite himself, he smiled.

"No accounting for tastes." He kept his voice just as low.

Moments later, Alexander strode out wearing a brightly colored Hawaiian button-down shirt, khaki pants, and flip-flops. He nodded politely at Levi's escort, then looked at Levi—though Lopez knew him as Isaiah Moore. "Hill isn't coming."

Levi tensed, annoyance filtering through him, but he kept his stance casual. "Why not?"

The other man glanced at the two guards standing at two of the entrances. Then he looked at Levi's companion. "Sweetheart, why don't you escort my men to the terrace? There's a beautiful view and a full bar." It wasn't a suggestion.

Levi didn't look at her but kept his gaze on Lopez, his expression deadly. "No one touches her."

Lopez rolled his eyes as if the thought was absurd. Once they were alone, he motioned that they should head up the marble stairway behind him. A minute later Levi found himself sitting on a long leather Chesterfield couch in the other man's office. He accepted a scotch to be polite, but it remained untouched on the table next to him.

Lopez leaned against the front of his desk, his arms crossed over his chest in the first gesture of nervousness Levi had ever seen from the man.

That was when he realized he needed to start the conversation. "Why isn't Hill meeting us and why didn't you just contact me to let me know the meeting was canceled?" He didn't like wasting his time.

"Hill is into dirty shit. I didn't realize it until yesterday when . . . a concerned party informed me that it would be beneficial to my life span if I didn't do business with him anymore."

"Dirty shit?"

"He's apparently selling people, among other things, and I don't touch that. But ... he's also on a hit list. He actually canceled on me first, but it was right after I heard that he's being hunted. My guess is, he's gone into hiding."

"Heard from whom?"

Lopez shrugged, placing his hands on the desk on either side of him. "Anonymous tip. Doesn't matter. I'm not doing business with him and you shouldn't either. He's been seriously down low about his dealings until now. I can't believe I didn't know..." He trailed off, shaking his head.

It took all Levi's control to rein in his anger. He didn't like to work with scum, but Hill had been a solid lead. "What about his business partners?"

"They're on the same list."

Well, shit. He thought he was one step closer to finding Meghan's killer. Tightening his jaw, he took a deep breath. He refused to hit another dead end. "Tell me how to find him."

Chapter 20

Shock and awe: a military doctrine meaning rapid
dominance. A technique using an overwhelming display of force to paralyze your target's perception of
the battleground.

Cade looked down at the flat-screen of his handheld
device. The aerial drone the NSA had in place had
picked up four heat signatures in the isolated cabin
they'd discovered thanks to Moran's discarded cell
phone. It was impossible to distinguish between human
and animal, but they were ninety-nine percent sure the
men they'd been hunting were inside. The cell signal was
still working and the figures had been moving around at
different intervals.

This was swampland in the middle of the Everglades;
far enough away from civilization that no one would
bother the terrorists out here. Instead of coming in with
a full assault team, Burkhart had decided to send an
eight-man team, Cade leading them.

There were only two ways in and out of here. By airboat or driving the long, winding, dusty road that led to
a paved road—which eventually led back to some semblance of civilization. Considering that they hadn't seen

many vehicle tracks on the way here and the aerial view didn't have a visual of transportation other than an airboat tied to a dock, it looked as if the terrorists had been coming and going by boat.

Out of instinct, Cade checked his weapon again, then ran a hand down the front of his armor. He was armed, protected, and ready to go. Nevertheless, adrenaline pumped through him at rapid speeds.

Cade and his men had been dropped off two miles away near the start of the dirt road. Then they'd trekked in on foot. After leaving the destruction of the safe house—and Maria in Jack's capable hands—he and Burkhart had met up with the rest of the team his boss had handpicked. They'd geared up at a warehouse the NSA had decided to use as a temporary base of operations, flown to the Everglades on helicopters that landed in a field in the middle of nowhere, and then had been driven another ten miles to the drop-off point. The operation was moving faster than normal, but so far everything was going smoothly.

More agents were driving in from Miami, but Burkhart had wanted to move as fast as possible on this lead. Since he was the boss, there'd been no bureaucratic bullshit red tape to hack through.

"The Semtex is in place," Ortiz said, his voice low over their linked comm.

Despite Ortiz's having been hit in the chest at the Opulen, his body armor had saved him from being truly injured. The man was bruised, but nothing more. Cade was surprised he didn't have broken ribs. He'd volunteered for this assault and Burkhart had given him the all-clear, so that was good enough for Cade. Hell, they didn't become Black Death 9 agents by being fucking pussies.

"Any movement on the water?" he asked, just as quietly.

Ortiz and another man had been assigned to rig the boat with Semtex before the rest of the men made their move. It was all part of the plan. If possible, Burkhart wanted to bring the men in alive. The NSA had to know how big the threat against Miami was. And they all wanted to know the *why* of the attacks. They might have an idea, but they needed specifics.

"Just gators."

A ghost of a smile tugged at his lips before Cade set the small device down next to a cypress tree. "Everybody get in position."

The cabin itself had about fifty feet of open space surrounding it from all sides. It would make a surprise ground assault difficult, but not impossible. Especially not with his team's weapons of choice.

Cade stayed where he was, behind a giant cypress tree, waiting a few seconds before checking in. "Ortiz, you ready?"

"Affirmative."

"Freeman?"

"Affirmative."

"Bell?"

"Affirmative."

They were the three men on the team who had very specific tasks and they had to work in sync with one another for this plan to work.

"Alpha Team?" he asked, waiting for the reply from the rest of the group. Once the other four responded in the affirmative, he pulled his M-4 up, ready to infiltrate. "Three-two-go."

On the word "go," the dawn sky lit up with a brilliant

shower of orange-and-red fire, the ball of black smoke mushrooming in a giant cloud as the airboat was incinerated.

Using hand launchers, Bell and Freeman shot tear gas through two windows, on opposite sides of the cabin. Almost immediately two blasts, then shattering glass rent the air.

"Flash bangs!" Cade shouted, moving from his position behind the tree.

He'd taken two steps when he saw the simultaneous discharges light up the interior of the place. Like a well-oiled machine, the entire team converged on the cabin, completely circling around it.

The destruction of the boat combined with the incapacitating gas and flash bangs was all part of their shock-and-awe tactic for this operation. It was difficult to engage a true rapid-dominance approach all the time, but for this assault, the circumstances had been damn near perfect.

Shouts of agony came from inside. A man tumbled out of one of the shattered windows, a weapon held loosely at his side as he fell to his knees.

Though he'd been trained to shoot to kill, Cade fired at the man's right hand. They wanted these men alive for questioning. His aim was deadly, blood splattering as the pistol fell from the terrorist's grip. The man raised his hands, clawing at his eyes—a result of the concentrated tear gas.

"Securing the tango now," one of his men said as Cade continued toward the front of the cabin. The door flung open. Another man exited, one hand wiping at his red, splotchy face as he raised a SIG. It didn't matter that the guy probably couldn't see for shit. He could get off a lucky shot.

Reflex kicked in. Cade fired, aiming to miss major arteries, but if the guy didn't drop the weapon, he was going down. *Pop. Pop. Pop.* A bullet ripped through the terrorist's shoulder, upper arm, then outer thigh.

His body jerked and the weapon tumbled to the floor, the man shouting in agony. He should be thanking Cade for not killing him.

"Tango down," said one of his men, followed quickly by another.

Including the target Cade had just incapacitated, that made four. He didn't let himself relax, though. Not until this entire place was secure.

On his knees, the terrorist Cade had shot met his gaze, dark eyes filled with hatred. His face was swollen from the gas, the redness streaking down his cheeks in what looked like bee stings. As the SIG fell from the man's fingers, Cade spotted something else in the man's other hand.

Understanding kicked in like a full-force body blow. The device he held was a small black box with a flashing red light. As it tumbled to the wooden porch, another light turned green.

Cade had seen that type of detonator before. "Dead man's switch!" he shouted, putting one bullet through the man's head. "Pull out!" he yelled as the man toppled over.

Through his earpiece he heard curses as they all jumped into action.

He only got five strides in before the explosion ripped through the air. The force of the blast shook the ground, but didn't lift Cade into the air as he'd expected. His legs burned as he ran for cover, his entire body tense as he dove behind a tree. There wasn't a shock wave as he'd expected, the explosion almost muted in intensity.

"Alpha Team, check in." Once he had confirmation all his men were secure, he peered around the tree. The target who'd set off the bomb was a charred lump on the porch, but one of the other terrorists was moving on the ground, his arms secured behind his back, wooden debris littered around his body.

"Am I the only one, or was that blast weak?" Ortiz asked, voicing what Cade was thinking.

"Everyone move back another fifty feet. Now." He'd been in situations before where an initial blast would go off, then another a few minutes later. Those tactics maximized damage, taking out operatives and first responders if they let their guard down.

Cade raced along the underbrush, weaving in and out of trees with ease, the damp ground making squishing sounds under his boots. As he came to a stop, another explosion tore through the swampy area. Through the trees he saw black smoke billowing upward in a whoosh.

Shit. None of the remaining targets would have survived that. After everyone checked in once again, he radioed Burkhart. "Send in a cleanup crew," he said, even though his boss had seen everything from the aerial view.

"Any survivors?"

"I doubt it, but we'll do a preliminary sweep."

Burkhart let out a harsh curse, before he said, "See you in ten."

The line went dead before Cade could respond, but there was nothing to say. The leads they'd hoped to gain were gone. They might find something useful in the rubble, but it could take hours or days to find anything. And time wasn't a luxury they could afford.

*   *   *

Mihails looked down at the cell phone only he and his men had the number for. It was one of their emergency phones. The text came from one of the men at the cabin: 9-1-1. That meant only one thing. They'd been compromised and would set off the prerigged explosives that acted as their last resort. There was no other meaning for that signal.

"The cabin was discovered," he said quietly to Oto, who was driving, and Kristaps, who sat in the backseat. Kristaps had managed to avoid detection at the Opulen and had escaped once everyone cleared out.

Immediately Mihails began making new plans, deciding the best path for them now. Mourning the loss of his men wasn't an option right now. If they were truly dead, they'd died for a cause and Mihails would respect that. He had to. This mission was far from over and he wouldn't have let his men die in vain.

Oto let out a vicious curse, one Mihails agreed with. They had accomplished so much. The Westwood hit alone was impressive, but it wasn't enough.

As of now he had to assume the worst: The cabin was decimated and all his men were dead. And he couldn't reach Fedor or Moran. It was possible that Moran had killed his man and was now in hiding, but that scenario was doubtful. No, with the cabin's location known, it meant the government was closing in on them. How much did they know?

"We need to find out what they know and we need leverage." Oto's words mirrored what he'd been thinking himself.

They had different safe houses around South Florida, but the Everglades location had been the most secure. Or he'd assumed it had been.

When he didn't respond, Oto continued. "Hill and his partners are in the wind—for now. We should take the Cervantes woman, find out what she's told the authorities, then use her if we need her. Until our contacts have reported about Hill's whereabouts, we should go after her. Or Hill's lawyer."

Mihails agreed. Going after the woman would be their first order of business, but he wanted to take Tennyson too. According to the early-morning local news, Clay Ervin had been found murdered in a rough part of town. Since the man was wealthy and well known, his death had been deemed important enough to report. The news had also mentioned that he'd been held by the police only hours before his murder and that he'd been seen leaving the station with Piers Tennyson. An attorney for monsters. "We'll take both. First the woman, then Tennyson. If we apply enough pressure, he'll talk." Torturing a man like that would be a pleasure. He would be all bluster until the pain started. In Mihails's experience, it was always the same with men like that. And Mihails had no problem implementing brute force to discover the whereabouts of Paul Hill.

"Her friend Leah Davis doesn't live far from here," Kristaps said, the first words he'd spoken since they left the Everglades.

Even thinking that they could have been in the Everglades when the cabin was discovered sent an icy chill snaking down Mihails's spine. Turning around as Oto continued driving steadily down I-95, Mihails looked at Kristaps.

The other man was looking at his computer. He turned it around for Mihails to view. "The address from her file. We could be there in less than ten minutes."

Mihails nodded and plugged the address into their GPS. Miami was large and even though they'd been doing reconnaissance of the city for the past few months, they still needed help navigating places. And he'd never prepared for the Cervantes woman. He still knew relatively little about her except what information he'd managed to gather from Andre Moran. Since the government was protecting her, his men had been careful not to do scarches of her name. Those types of searches would send alerts to the authorities, and even though his men were good at covering their tracks, it hadn't been a risk he'd wanted to take. Not when Moran had been more than willing to provide information on her.

Taking Maria Cervantes's friend wouldn't guarantee her cooperation, but it would be a start in the right direction. And the Davis woman was the easier target, compared to Maria's guarded family. According to Moran, she and the woman were more like sisters than coworkers.

Yes, this would be the best option right now. Especially since Maria had just lost her mother. She would be feeling even more protective of those closest to her.

The drive to the woman's neighborhood was quicker than expected. There weren't as many people on the street this early. While he didn't like conducting an operation without planning, they were well armed and one untrained woman would be no match for them. He just hoped she was alone. Otherwise any companion would die.

After driving down the street a few times, they decided to go for the hard approach. The risk was higher, but they didn't have the luxury of time and planning. Oto pulled into her driveway and once they were positive no one was watching—as sure as they could be—they all exited the vehicle.

"I'll take the front. Oto, you take the back. Kristaps..." He pointed to the east side of the house. On their drive-bys, he'd seen that it had more windows.

Waiting on the front porch of the one-story cottage, he tensed when he heard a loud bang, then a breaking of glass. Oto and Kristaps were in. A piercing alarm went off, the sound shattering the quiet. Heart rate increasing, he glanced down the street once more. There was no time to waste.

The front door was flung open and a pretty blond-haired woman with wide blue eyes slammed right into him. Oto and Kristaps were right behind her, their expressions grim. Without pause, he swung out, hitting her across the jaw.

She didn't make a sound as she slumped to the floor. Bending down, he hauled her up and threw her over his shoulder. The slim woman wore a dark blue robe over blue-and-white-polka-dot pajama pants. "Grab a few clothes from her room and her cell phone," he ordered Oto, who immediately nodded and disappeared down the hallway.

Scanning the neighborhood as he hurried to the vehicle, he was pleased to see they didn't have any witnesses. Not that he cared at this point. They'd be ditching this vehicle as soon as they could. Kristaps got into the passenger seat while Mihails slid into the backseat. Carefully he placed her next to him. Despite hitting her, he didn't want her injured more than necessary. After an inspection of her jaw told him that he hadn't broken it, he secured her wrists in front of her with flex ties, then did the same to her ankles before he strapped her in.

When the driver's-side door opened and Oto slid in, he heard the blare of the alarm before the door slammed shut. The vehicle jerked to life and as they reversed, he spotted two neighbors walking out onto their lawns, phones in hand.

"We've got to ditch this vehicle now," Mihails said even though he was almost positive Oto was on the same page. They'd always been like that. After they found new transportation, they would reach out to Maria with her friend's phone. Whether the Davis woman would be co-operative or not remained to be seen, but Mihails would force her to call her friend no matter what. Maria needed to hear her friend crying, in pain, so perhaps if she fought them it would be better for their outcome.

Chapter 21

FUBAR: fucked up beyond all recognition.

Burkhart waited until Cade ended his phone call before asking, "She okay?"

Cade nodded, his expression unreadable. Well, to anyone who didn't know him. Burkhart had never imagined O'Reilly would get so attached to an asset during an operation. Now he worried it was going to come back to bite his trusted operative in the ass. Of course he'd never thought Jack Stone would retire and marry, but his best damn agent had done just that a year ago. Now O'Reilly had insisted on calling Jack so he could check on Maria before they went any further with the investigation.

Normally Cade was so damn focused on a job that everything else faded out for him. He'd always been like a machine. Not now.

Burkhart didn't want to lose Cade. He tilted his head at the Miami PD interrogation room where their interviewee waited. "Good. Let's do this."

After the raid in the Everglades, Burkhart's team was running the DNA of the dead terrorists and scanning the entire site for anything useful. The one thing they knew for certain was that neither Mihails nor Oto had been in that blast. All the terrorists had been visually identified by the team seconds before they'd had to run and take cover. And until his team came up with something solid from the destruction site, Burkhart had another angle he wanted to hit.

And hard.

New evidence had recently surfaced in Clay Ervin's murder, and instead of sitting on the evidence, Jarvis Nieto had called Burkhart. The Miami police captain was a good man, looking at the big picture, something Burkhart was thankful for. Local law enforcement didn't always hold the same view as the NSA when it came to joint cases. Considering that the NSA and FBI had kept them out of the loop on the Opulen operation, Burkhart was surprised, but thankful, to have received Nieto's call. He'd decided to bring Cade along for multiple reasons, the main one that he didn't want him heading over to Maria's safe house. But Cade also looked intimidating. It was a psychological thing and Burkhart loved playing psychological warfare, even on the most subtle levels.

Whether the man waiting in the interrogation room would even acknowledge the fear to himself, it didn't matter. It would be there, lingering at the forefront of his brain, his most primal side aware that Cade was a scary bastard who could break a man in half.

Piers Tennyson shifted in his chair as the door opened, his icy blue eyes landing on Burkhart, then trailing past him to Cade as they both stepped inside. For a brief moment, fear flashed in the man's gaze at the sight of Cade.

The seasoned operative hadn't cleaned up after the morning raid, so he was still wearing his military-style fatigues. With his tattoos and pistol strapped to his belt, he put off a lethal appearance.

Tennyson sat up straighter, casually resting his arm on the table. The sleeve of his charcoal gray suit, only a shade darker than the man's hair, shifted, revealing an obnoxiously expensive watch. His expression was smugly relaxed as he eyed Burkhart. "Why am I here? By the time I'm done with you and this department—"

"Shut the fuck up," Burkhart said quietly. Yelling at a man like this wouldn't work. "I don't work for the Miami PD and I'll keep you here as long as I see fit," he said as he slid his ID onto the table.

Tennyson's icy eyes widened a fraction as he pushed the ID back to him. His hands weren't cuffed since he wasn't under arrest. Yet. "What does the NSA want with me?"

"I want to know where Paul Hill is."

At the mention of Hill, Tennyson's mouth tightened just a fraction. "Why do you think I know?" Not an answer. He didn't move a muscle, made sure to keep his body language neutral. That alone was telling; he was trying to give off the vibe that he was unaffected.

"You're his attorney."

He lifted one shoulder casually. "Exactly. I'm not his mother."

Burkhart didn't have hours to loosen this guy up. There simply wasn't time when he was searching for two violent terrorists who might strike anywhere in Miami at any moment. Hill was definitely connected to them and he was going to find out exactly how. He pulled a small video screen out of his pocket and set it on the table.

Tennyson eyed it but didn't respond. Behind him Cade hadn't made a sound, but it was clear the older attorney was very aware of his presence too. Burkhart had read up on this guy and from all accounts he was normally cool under pressure. On the surface he appeared to be right now, but Burkhart could see past that thin veneer, could see the fear that had bled into his gaze.

"Before you open your mouth and lie to me, I want you to see something." Burkhart swiped his finger over the screen, punched in the code to unlock it, then pressed PLAY before turning it around and sliding it across the table.

The video had been taken outside, from the end of an alleyway, but the lighting was pristine. It showed a man wearing dark gloves driving down a deserted alley, stopping, getting out, and looking around. When he was positive no one was watching, he opened the trunk of an older-model sedan, pulled out the body of Clay Ervin, then dragged him next to an abandoned Dumpster. As the man stepped away, he glanced around his surroundings again, more nervous this time, before hurrying back to the vehicle.

By now Tennyson had paled considerably, his hands clasped together tightly on the table in front of him as he tried to retain control of himself.

"It's amazing how clear phone videos are now. I saw three perfect shots of your face, all verified by our facial-recognition software. Not to mention we've got a witness who saw you dump the body. And the plates on that car you were driving belong to your gardener. We've already got him in questioning and he confirms that he's let you borrow his car multiple times. He's letting us search it for trace evidence. You'll also be happy to know we've secured a warrant for your residence and as we speak, the Miami PD is executing it." Letting his smugness show, he leaned back in his seat and stared the piece of shit down. "Now tell me where Paul Hill is."

His lips thinned and for just a second, Tennyson looked down at the table before meeting Burkhart's gaze. "I want to make a deal. Full immunity—I didn't kill Ervin, just disposed of the body. And I can prove it."

This was the part of the job Burkhart hated, but if he could locate Hill and subsequently stop a terrorist cell from unleashing another level of hell on South Florida, he'd do whatever it took.

After saying good-bye to her father, Maria handed Jack's phone back to him and started to head to the lanai outside, where his wife, Sophie, and her friend Hannah were having coffee. She took two steps, then stopped. Through the wide double French doors of Hannah's parents' house, she could see the two women sitting together on the wooden swing bench talking and laughing. It sent a pang through her chest. She turned back to Jack and tried not to feel intimidated by the intensity of those pale eyes staring back at her. The man was like a wolf, a predator, watching her. It wasn't that he was doing anything offensive, but everything about him was, well, a little intimidating. She knew her reaction was strange considering that Cade was bigger physically and covered in tattoos, but she trusted Cade. More than trusted him. She didn't know Jack except for the fact that Cade had vouched for him. While that mattered immensely, this man still put her on edge.

"Would you mind if I made another call?" she asked.

He shook his head and handed her back the phone. "Why don't you just hold on to it? You can make as many calls you as you like. It's encrypted, but don't tell anyone—"

"Where I am. Yeah, I got it. Trust me, I don't want

anyone shooting a rocket launcher at me again," she said, half smiling as she took it. He'd already drilled it into her head on the drive over earlier. After nearly being blown up in the safe house, she had no problem keeping her whereabouts secret. She didn't have a death wish and there was no way she'd put other people in danger.

Since arriving at the spacious home in a gated neighborhood not far from her parents' house, she'd showered, changed into clothes provided by the NSA, and tried to get some sleep—at Mrs. Young's insistence. Hannah's mom had been so kind, the petite Asian woman reminding Maria of her own mom. She wasn't sure if that made her feel better or worse, but she hadn't been able to sleep, so she'd decided to venture out of the guest bedroom.

Almost immediately she'd run into Jack in the hallway with Cade on the line for her. It warmed her heart that Cade had called to check on her. She'd understood that he'd wanted to be part of the team to bring down the terrorists, but she felt lost without him. Everyone here was still a stranger to her; it didn't matter how nice they were.

She wanted to be with Cade, to feel those strong arms tightening around her with the unspoken promise that everything would be okay. Even if it wouldn't, he made her feel safe. She was still slightly sore from their lovemaking, a physical reminder of how badly she wished he were here. But it wasn't just him she missed; she wanted to be with her family, her friends. She hated that she wasn't there for her dad. And she'd barely spoken to Leah since everything had happened.

It seemed as if an eternity had passed since she'd woken in that hospital room, when in reality only days had passed. She'd felt so damn disconnected then, hadn't wanted to see or speak to anyone. Now she desperately wanted to talk to her best friend.

She'd been holding off because she *didn't* want to break down, but seeing Sophie and Hannah together was too much. Dialing the number she'd memorized long ago, she headed toward the kitchen, her sandals making soft slapping sounds against the hardwood floors. The scent of coffee grew stronger as she reached the swinging wooden door. Pushing it open, she made a beeline for the waiting coffeepot and mugs in the massive, professional-grade kitchen—which made sense since the Young family owned two successful restaurants.

On the fourth ring, she remembered this wasn't her phone. When she called her dad he'd told her it had appeared as an unknown number. That was probably why Leah wasn't answering, because her best friend's phone was practically attached to her. Maria could leave a message, though. As she waited for the voice mail to kick in, the phone line connected. But all she could hear was breathing.

She frowned, wondering if the connection was bad. "Hello?"

"Maria Cervantes?" a male, accented voice asked.

Her stomach pitched as a flashback of that night slammed into her. That horrible, horrible night. Even though he wasn't yelling now, she immediately recognized his voice on her most primal level. She wanted to deny the truth, but the instantaneous fear that followed hearing her name on his lips was so visceral, she started to slightly shake. "Who is this?" Her question came out as a harsh whisper as her surroundings fell away. Everything seemed to disappear as reality started to sink in. There was only one reason for this man to have her best friend's phone. With her free hand, Maria clutched the counter for support. This wasn't happening. It couldn't be.

"I take it you got my voice mail." He sounded pleased.

"What voice mail?" Oh God, had they hurt Leah? Maria tried to banish the thought, but horrible images popped up in her mind. Men who'd killed hundreds of people had no soul, no conscience. They could do anything to Leah.

A short pause. "You didn't receive a voice mail?"

"No," she managed to push out past the tightness in her throat. "What have you done to my friend? Where is she? I want to talk to her. Please don't hurt her," she whispered, her throat tightening in agony on the last words.

"One moment." She heard muted movement, then Leah's trembling voice. "Maria?"

"Oh my God, Leah. Are you all right? Where are you?" Her words were coming out as a harsh whisper as she struggled to talk.

"I'm ... okay. They haven't hurt me. They want ... they want ... Don't give it to them! Swear it to me, Maria. Don't do what they say—"

She was abruptly cut off, the line going silent for a long moment. Fear pumping through her veins, Maria looked at the caller ID and saw the line was still open. A moment later, the same man came back on the line. "Your friend is brave but very stupid. You will trade yourself for her or the next time you see her, she will be in pieces. I will start by mailing you her foot. Next I'll mail you—"

"Stop, please," she whispered. She didn't need the details. She'd give them what they wanted. After losing her brother and her mom, she wasn't losing someone else she loved. No way. Of course, that didn't mean she was going to blindly walk into a trap either. She could let them think that, though. "Just tell me what you want."

"I simply want *you.* You have twenty minutes to meet me. Alone. If I see a hint of law enforcement, she dies." He rattled off the name of a park near South Beach.

"Even if I break every speed limit law, I can't be there by then. I need an hour." She actually could get there, but she wasn't above lying.

"Twenty minutes or I'll start cutting her up now."

"Damn it! Give me thirty! I swear I'll be there. I . . . I have to sneak away from my guards. If you want me, you'll give me half an hour." Beads of sweat rolled down her back even though her body had turned icy, clammy.

Another short pause. "Thirty minutes and no longer. Come alone. If I see anyone with you, or if I even think you brought backup, I'll blow her head off and leave her at the park. And next time, I'll target your father." The line went dead before she could respond.

Her body started shaking as she set the phone down. *Shit, shit, shit.* She wasn't sure who that had been: Mihails Balodis or Oto Ozols. It had to be one of them, though. She'd heard the same voice the night of the explosion and had seen the pictures of the terrorists later, but she had no clue which was which. Not that it mattered. The only thing that did was that they had her friend.

And would kill her unless Maria traded herself. Maria knew there was a great possibility she would die, but she couldn't let Leah get cut into pieces or . . . Shaking her head, she shoved that thought away.

Now she had to focus. A tiny part of her knew she should tell Jack right away, but she also knew that the second she did, she'd be put on lockdown. That wasn't happening. So far Jack had given her privacy because this house was secure. He wasn't treating her like a prisoner or someone who needed babysitting. He had no reason not to trust her, to think she would try to run out on him. She would use that to her advantage.

She shoved the phone in the back pocket of her jeans and as quietly as possible, she started searching the kitchen. Opening drawers, she stopped when she found one with a bunch of knives and other silverware. She picked out three paring knives that were all securely sheathed. She tucked one into her sock, one into the back of her pants, and the third, the smallest, she tucked up under the bottom band of her sports bra. If they did a thorough search of her person, which they no doubt would, they'd find the weapons, but she had to try. She wasn't even sure she'd get as far as meeting them, but in case it came down to that, she had to be prepared. After she called Cade, though, she didn't think things would ever get that far.

Hurrying to the mudroom attached right off the kitchen, she glanced over her shoulder, positive that Jack would walk in at any time. Hannah's parents had left not too long ago, heading to one of their restaurants for an early-morning meeting with their staff, and she'd seen where they'd left their keys; on a silver hook rack right next to the door that led to the garage.

Even though she felt a twinge of guilt for what she was attempting, it wasn't enough to make her stop. Leah was her best friend. Maria paused for only a moment before snagging the set of keys with a Mercedes key fob. Then she yanked the door open. A beeping sound immediately went off. *Beep, beep, beep.* It paused, then continued in that same pattern.

Panic punched through her as she slammed her palm against the garage door opener and raced for the only car in the garage. Jack had mentioned something about a targeted alarm system. It was how the French doors to the lanai were able to remain open, but the rest of the house was on lockdown. He'd told her in the hope of reassuring her that no one could sneak up on them. She hadn't even been thinking about that.

Jumping in the front seat, she started the engine and reversed, barely clearing the rising door. The tires squealed as she swiveled around in the circular driveway and jerked the car into drive. She yanked her phone out, ready to call Cade, when the phone started ringing in her palm. The noise made her jump just as she saw Jack in her rearview mirror racing toward his parked car. Oh yeah, he was pissed.

She slammed her foot on the gas and made a sharp turn into the Young's neighborhood. She knew this area like the back of her hand. It was where she'd grown up.

She answered the phone when she saw Sophie's name on the caller ID and put it on speaker so she could drive with both hands.

"What the hell are you doing?" Jack shouted.

"It's not what you think! One of the terrorists called me. They have my best friend, Leah, and gave me half an hour to meet them. They want to trade me for them."

"You can't do that," he snapped.

"I *know* that. I also know that the second I told you about the call you would have put me on lockdown. I'm not letting my friend die. I'd planned to call Cade as soon as I was on the road." Cade would be pissed, but that was something she'd deal with. She knew the NSA had resources she couldn't even imagine and would be able to target these guys long before she ever got to the park. Maybe using a satellite or drone or something.

But just in case they couldn't, she'd had to leave. She couldn't just sit around and let her best friend be murdered. All she wanted to do was show up near the park and let them see her. They'd *have* to show themselves then. Then the NSA or FBI could bring them down. She didn't mind being bait if she knew there was backup coming. But there was no way Cade, or probably Jack, would have let her do this and she hadn't been prepared to waste time arguing her case when she was doing this no matter what.

He let out a curse, but said, "Are they using the last number you called on my phone?"

"Yeah."

"I'm calling you back in two minutes. Answer the fucking phone!" The line went dead, but closer to five minutes later he called her back.

"Jack?"

"Yeah, you're on with me and Burkhart." His voice was strained.

"Maria, we're tracking your friend's cell as we speak," Burkhart said. "It's at the park they told you to meet them at, so they weren't lying. We don't have a visual yet, but we have a team on the way. We'll bring your friend home safely. Do not continue any farther to the park. Pull over right now. Jack is going to pick you up." There was no room for argument in his voice.

Maria looked in the rearview mirror as she pulled up to a four-way stop, her heart still beating out of control. "You swear you'll keep her safe?"

"We'll do everything in our power. I promise. I know you think we can use you as bait, even visually, but it's not happening. All we needed was their location and now we have it. They fucked up and we're going to bring them down. Right now we need you safe. *Cade* needs you safe."

Even though she was feeling wildly irrational, she knew they were right. When she'd heard Leah's scared voice, it had shredded her insides. But she wasn't trained and even though she could defend herself well enough, she was no match for any of these men. And there was no guarantee that giving herself up to them would save Leah anyway.

"Maria, pull over right *now.*" Cade's voice came over the line, angrier than she'd ever heard him.

Right about now she felt like a total fucking maniac for running off the way she had done. Rubbing a shaky hand over her face, she waited for the third car at the stop to go, then pulled out into the intersection. "I'm so sorry, I'm going to—"

Her body jerked violently as a car rammed into the back of the Mercedes, sending the phone flying from the center console to the floorboards. She scrambled to grab the wheel, but the car rammed into her again. The airbag popped out, punching into her.

Her head slammed back against the seat. Panicking, she pressed on the gas and turned the wheel, trying to get away, but the other car increased its speed, forcing her onto the sidewalk. Metal creaked and groaned as she demolished a stop sign, the vehicle shuddering under the impact. There was a fire hydrant in front of her, leaving her nowhere to go.

Hands shaking, she looked in the rearview mirror,

ready to attempt to reverse into the car, when she hit the hydrant. Glass shattered.

She screamed as shards covered her. Over the phone speaker Cade was shouting her name. She tried to respond but was cut off as two big hands reached through the broken window and started choking her.

Blindly she fought, clawing and tearing at the immovable grip. She couldn't see her attacker's face, but he was too strong. As darkness edged her vision, she managed to get her seat belt free, but it was too late.

Blackness consumed her.

Chapter 22

Kidnap: taking someone away illegally by force.

Cade watched the handheld video screen as Ortiz tore out of the parking lot. There was no way in hell Cade could drive right now. Not after watching from a crystal-clear satellite feed as Maria's limp body was dragged out of a car and shoved into a waiting one.

Adrenaline jagged through him, wild and out of control, but internally he kept his emotions in check. Barely. Acting from an emotional place could get him killed. Or worse, Maria or one of his teammates.

"We're going to get her back," Ortiz said quietly as he drove.

"No doubt," Freeman murmured in agreement from the back.

Yeah, Cade hadn't exactly been super stealthy back at the safe house with his affections toward her. Word had spread quickly and he didn't give a shit what the others thought about his relationship with her.

Maria was his. As soon as this operation was over and she was safe. Safe and alive . . . fuck, he was going to tell her everything. If she rejected him, he'd deal. Hell, if she rejected him, at least it meant she was alive to do so. That was fine with him.

He ignored the tremor that snaked through him. Being so far away and helpless to do anything was eating him alive from the inside out.

"If they'd wanted her dead, they'd have done it at the crash site." This time Jack spoke, the statement blunt, with no emotion. He'd insisted on coming on this mission after Maria had run out on him. And Burkhart had given Stone the okay—not exactly surprising. Those two had always had a tight relationship and Stone was well trained. The former agent had met them at a neutral point and ditched his vehicle. Cade wanted to be pissed at him for losing Maria, but he knew how stubborn she could be.

The man spoke the truth, something Cade knew on an intellectual level. But it didn't matter. These terrorists had wreaked unspeakable horror. Now Maria was in their hands.

"How's the feed?" Burkhart's voice came over the speaker of the SUV's navigational system.

"Perfect." Cade was glad he sounded strong. Burkhart hadn't wanted to let him go on this mission, but had relented. Good thing too, because Cade had been considering punching his boss—something he would have regretted immensely later on.

They had multiple eyes in the sky right now, including a satellite and two drones. In addition to Cade's team they had five other four-man teams in the direct vicinity of Mihails's moving vehicle. At any time, Cade or his men could move on them, but they wanted the assholes alive.

Getting Maria back alive was Cade's priority, but the NSA wanted Mihails and Oto. They needed to know if other bombs were placed around the city and how many operatives they had working with them. Right now it didn't bode well that they'd taken Maria.

It made them appear desperate. And desperate men who'd proven their penchant for violence were the worst type of enemy—because they were unpredictable. Considering that the team at the cabin had blown themselves up rather than face capture, the NSA wasn't risking that again.

They would move on the terrorists only when the timing was right. Even though Cade hated keeping his distance, hated that his team could attack the terrorists right now but weren't doing so, this was the best plan.

"Tennyson gave up some interesting information on Hill and his partners," Burkhart said as Ortiz took another left turn. It was hard for Cade to focus on what his boss was saying when his insides were being shredded at the thought of Maria being harmed.

On their video feed there were red dots that indicated where the other team members were in relation to them and the tangos. Right now his own team was two fucking blocks from Maria. Sweat trickled down his back. *Don't focus on that,* he ordered himself.

"What'd he say?" Cade asked. Just as Tennyson had been about to talk, he and Burkhart had been called away by an emergency call from Jack.

Cade still couldn't believe Maria had just taken off like that. He wanted to shake some sense into her, but after losing her mom she had to be feeling raw, emotional, and just not thinking clearly. If someone kidnapped and threatened to kill someone close to him, Cade knew he wouldn't sit back and do nothing either.

"Paul Hill and his business partners have been running the biggest sex slave ring we've ever seen. They're doing business with Saudi Arabia, various South American countries, Eastern European countries—everywhere. What Tennyson has told us so far . . . it's fucking sick. These bastards cater to every . . ." For Burkhart to pause while talking told Cade all he needed to know.

Cade's body went ice-cold. *Maria.* "What do Mihails and Oto want with Hill?" If it was a business takeover, it was a violent one. Cade wasn't apt to pray, but for the first time in forever, he did. It was bad enough Maria was mixed up in this, but if they might use her for—

"They want him and everyone involved with his business dead. Mihails's sisters were taken by Hill's group years ago. One died, but one survived."

"Tennyson told you that?"

"No, one of our guys found the location of Mihails's only living sister twelve hours ago. London's Metropolitan Police are talking to Ieva Balodis as we speak. She won't leave the house, but she's being cooperative. She gave us the reason why Mihails is so bent on vengeance once they informed her of Paul Hill's connection—and she's horrified by what her brother is doing. She told him what happened to her and her sister, but I get the feeling she had no idea what kind of man her brother is. She didn't even know he was a criminal. And Tennyson backed up what I'd already gleaned from London's report about Hill."

Cade kept his gaze on the video screen, thankful Ortiz was such a skilled driver. The man moved in and out of traffic with a fluid ease that spoke of a lot of training. "So, why was Ervin killed? What's the tie-in for Tennyson dumping his body?"

"After the death of Scott Mullen, then Reuben Flowers, Ervin panicked and called Paul Hill. The pictures left at Mullen's murder site had already solidified Ervin's fear because of their ties to Hill's business. Hill got Tennyson to represent Ervin. Then when he was free, Hill shot Ervin himself. And Tennyson's got him on video. He says he's got more than that on video as part of his insurance if Hill ever tries to kill him."

"Is he telling the truth?" On-screen, the vehicle transporting Maria pulled into a packed parking lot, but the various angles of the feeds almost guaranteed they wouldn't lose her.

Ortiz followed anyway, easing some of Cade's growing tension at being too separated from her. He took a sharp turn behind a strip of shops and drove parallel to their Dumpsters as he headed for the back entry to the other parking lot. Cade's pulse sped up, his heart racing out of control. They were so damn close to Maria now.

"He gave up one of the videos as proof that he didn't kill Ervin, but he wants immunity in exchange for the rest of the videos. He's also got the names of more people Hill is doing business with, bank account numbers, a whole lot of shit we need to bring Hill's organization down."

"Mihails did all this to avenge his sisters." Cade tensed as he watched one of the men transport Maria's limp body to a waiting SUV.

She was still alive. Otherwise they wouldn't be moving her at all. He grasped onto that thin thread of hope buried deep inside him and held on tight. Almost in unison, the other men slid into the vehicle and it drove away. His fists clenched into tight balls. She was so damn close.

"Looks that way."

"Why Westwood?"

"A couple dozen men involved in the ring were there. Hill was supposed to be there too."

"Did you guys catch the license plate of the SUV?" Cade asked, switching topics.

"Yeah, calling it in to the locals to leave the vehicle alone."

Cade pushed out a small breath of relief. Sometimes the smallest thing could fuck up an operation. Right now these terrorists were untouchable and Cade and his team couldn't have a local cop pull them over for speeding or some other infraction. No, these men needed to make it to wherever their destination was, because once they stopped moving, Cade's team was saving Maria and bringing them down. He knew what the NSA wanted, but he didn't give a shit if they lived or died. "How's Leah?"

"Shaken up, but physically unharmed."

"Good." They'd found Leah Davis tied up in a public restroom with her cell phone tucked in her pocket. She'd been bait for them because they'd obviously known Maria would either call for backup or be monitored by law enforcement. They hadn't needed to leave her alive, though; they could have killed Leah or kept her and left just her phone, but they hadn't done either. It was an interesting choice for such violent men. That humane decision gave him a sliver of hope that they'd get Maria back alive. He clutched onto that like a lifeline because he refused to consider a world without her in it.

*   *   *

Mihails glanced around their surroundings as they left in their newly acquired vehicle. The Cervantes woman was still unconscious, her head lolling on his shoulder. He wanted to throttle Oto for hurting her so badly. She could have passed out from fear or shock, but Mihails didn't think so. The way his partner had choked her was too much.

"You shouldn't have been so rough with her," he finally snapped as Oto pulled onto I-95.

He didn't care that Kristaps was in the vehicle and would be privy to their disagreement. There was no other time to have this discussion. They would have to lose this vehicle soon, then switch out with another one yet again, before heading to their final destination. They had to make sure they weren't being tailed.

Oto flicked him a hard glance in the rearview mirror. "She's breathing."

Yes, but if she was so damn terrified that she went into shock when she woke up—if she woke up—she wouldn't be cooperative. And torturing someone in shock was pointless. Something Oto knew.

"I can't get hold of Ieva. She always answers my calls," Oto said, the change in subject a surprise. But it would explain Oto's sudden surge of anger and the way he'd choked Maria.

Frowning, Mihails texted his sister. The time difference was five hours from Miami to London, so it was early evening for her. The place he'd bought his sister in the district of Kensington was well secured and he had groceries and other necessities delivered if she didn't want to the leave the house. Which until recently had been the case. But she'd been getting counseling and seemed almost happy some days. He knew she'd made some friends and assumed that had made a difference in her. When she didn't immediately return his text, he brushed aside the tension building in him. "She could be sleeping or showering. It means nothing."

Oto just grunted and Mihails reined his anger in. Now wasn't the time to lose it and stir up strife between them. He could keep Oto on a leash if he kept Maria away from his friend. Mihails had spent a small fortune to get her. After leaving Leah Davis tied up and unconscious at South Pointe Park, he'd known her cell phone signal would draw the authorities there like feral dogs.

While they were getting ready, he'd had one of the best hackers in the world break the encryption on the phone Maria had called from. Tracking it had been a long shot because he hadn't been sure she would even keep it on her person. The hacker almost hadn't been able to do it—and had charged Mihails an extra fee for his trouble. Mihails had kept the hacker waiting for the moment he received a call from her.

His patience had paid off in the end. Or it better. While his funds were great, he couldn't afford to waste resources for something that might not be worth it. It would make him appear weak in front of his men. With the edgy way Oto had been acting over the past week, he definitely couldn't afford that.

Now they had Maria and she would tell them everything she'd relayed to the authorities. It was possible she didn't know everything; how deep their plans went. If she didn't, they could move forward. And if she had told them too much, they still had time to change their plans. Now they had a hostage if the authorities got too close.

Feeling as if he was in the crosshairs of a sniper, he glanced out the tinted window of the stolen vehicle. No, they'd been careful and after they placed the explosives at the Port of Miami, they would soon be in international waters. The Cubans would provide them with sanctuary if they required it.

Chapter 23

Infiltration: the secret movement of an individual (or small group) penetrating a target area with the intent to remain undetected.

Maria opened her eyes and tried to blink away the grit. She attempted to lift her hand to rub them and realized she couldn't move. Her wrists were secured by flex ties to a plush accent chair. When she attempted to lift her legs, she couldn't move them either. In a rush, she remembered what had happened as she took in her surroundings.

The vehicle running her off the street. Someone punching through the driver's-side window. Big hands choking her. She swallowed and winced in pain. Her skin was definitely bruised, and so was inside her throat. Oh yeah, that memory was all too real. Looking around, she saw that she was on some type of boat. A yacht maybe because the space was luxurious.

The room was a strange triangle shape and there were portholes on either of the walls. Sunlight filtered through them, bathing the striped blue-and-brown silky-looking duvet on the bed in light, but she couldn't see anything other than blue sky outside. Not only that, the room was swaying and she knew it wasn't because she was disoriented. They were moving. It was almost indiscernible but she could feel the soft rumble of the engine.

Nausea rolled through her. If they were on a boat, it meant she'd been kidnapped and her captors were taking her out of the city. It also meant Cade and the NSA hadn't been able to track her. Hope died an agonizing death inside her.

At the same time, a jolt of adrenaline shot through her veins, clearing the cobwebs from her head. She didn't have time to panic or feel sorry for herself. Wiggling her body as best she could, she tried to see how much give there was in the restraints. None with the ankle ties—and she belatedly realized they'd discovered the knife stashed in her sock. She couldn't feel anything tucked into the back of her pants or in her bra either. Crap. They'd found all her weapons. Not that they would do her any good, considering that she could barely move.

Wiggling one of the wrist ties, she had a smidgen of room, but not enough to pull her hand out. The other one was completely restricted, almost to the point where it was cutting off her circulation. Her hand was slightly numb, but not tingly like when it fell asleep. Soon it would probably go completely numb, though. Which told her she hadn't been tied up that long.

At the sound of the door handle twisting, her head snapped in that direction. When a man likely in his forties with blond hair and rage-filled blue eyes stepped inside, she instinctively tried to scoot back, but there was nowhere to go. Her inner alarm bells were going off like crazy. This man was dangerous and would have no problem hurting her. She could see it clearly in his gaze.

"I see you're awake," he said in a light accent. Not the man she'd talked to on the phone.

She recognized this one from the NSA's pictures, though. Oto Ozols. Terrorist, murderer. So she must have talked to Mihails Balodis. Eyes wide, she didn't say anything.

The man's jaw tightened, the jagged, faint white scar on his cheek vivid under the track lighting of the room.

"Can you speak?" he demanded, taking a menacing step toward her.

"Yes," she rasped out, her voice not sounding like her own. It was hoarse, like a longtime smoker's. The attempt at speech wasn't overly painful, but it was uncomfortable. Her throat already felt swollen.

"Good. Because you're going to tell us everything we want to know. . . ." He trailed off as another man walked into the room.

Mihails Balodis. She recognized him immediately, from the picture she'd seen. He was actually handsome — for a murdering terrorist.

He was also tall, with blue eyes and blond hair. His eyes weren't dead exactly, but he was still scary. He said something to Oto in a language she didn't understand. His words were harsh, angry. Oto said something back, his tone just as furious. Mihails didn't respond, just stared at him until Oto gritted his teeth and stormed out.

Then Mihails turned back to her, pinning her with his icy stare.

Maria wished the floor would just open up and swallow her. Trying to move back in her chair was a fruitless effort. It didn't matter how small she wanted to appear; she was in his line of sight and there was no escape.

"You know who I am?" he asked as he went to sit on the edge of the queen-sized bed.

She tracked his movements from her chair, not letting him out of her line of sight. It wasn't as if she could do anything to defend herself, tied up as she was, but if he was going to hurt her she wanted to see the blow coming. "I do. Mihails Balodis." Her voice was still so raspy.

When she spoke, his lips pulled down a fraction. His gaze flicked to her neck for a moment. "I'm sorry about your throat."

Unable to stop herself, she let out an almost maniacal laugh, made worse by her hoarse throat. "You're sorry?" She snorted in disbelief, not wanting to hear his lies. She just wanted to know what he wanted. Obviously there was a reason she wasn't dead yet.

"I *am* sorry. Oto shouldn't have handled you so roughly."

"What about killing my mother?" She tried to shout, but the question was harsh and shaky. "Are you sorry for that?" Rage like nothing she'd ever known built inside her, wanting an outlet. The man who'd killed her mother was right in front of her. What she wouldn't give to put a bullet right through his black heart. She thrashed against her bindings, but it was useless. With willpower she didn't realize she had, she forced herself to stop, knowing she would only tire herself out. Right now she needed her energy. She had no clue what they had in store for her, but she had to be alert. And for all she knew, he probably liked seeing her struggle. Sick bastard.

For a moment she thought she saw a trickle of guilt on his face, but his expression hardened. "How did you know about Clay Ervin or the hotel?"

She hadn't known about the hotel beforehand, but

she chose not to tell him. However, she decided to be somewhat honest. She had no reason not to be. "I overheard you shouting at the Westwood mansion. I was sick and needed privacy in one of the back bedrooms."

His expression remained stony. "How did you even get there?"

"A friend—who you murdered—showed me. She left me and went to get my mother so they could—" Her voice broke and she looked away from him. She hated that she couldn't turn away or leave altogether, but she didn't even want to see his face right now. Taking a few deep breaths, she tried to push all her rage and agony down. She couldn't have a breakdown while talking to this monster. Staying composed was necessary to her survival.

When she looked back at him, he was frowning, likely racking his brain trying to remember that night. After her flashbacks everything was crystal clear for her. She just wished she'd remembered everything sooner.

"Why didn't you come forward earlier? Why not turn in Moran? Why let him . . ." He trailed off and she realized what he'd been about to say. Why let Moran attend her mother's funeral?

She fought the burn of tears, blinking rapidly. "I didn't remember," she rasped out. "I blocked everything out. From shock, probably. When Moran tried to kill me at the safe house, the explosion triggered something in my memory. . . . Why haven't you killed me? Why send Moran to kill me? You had the chance when you ran me off the road." She didn't want to die, but she wanted to know what game he was playing. His friend had nearly choked her to death. She wanted to know why Oto had stopped. There wasn't much information she could give them.

"Moran wasn't supposed to kill you. And right now you are useful, so I'm letting you live. What else did you hear?"

"The Freedom Tower. I heard you shout about its symbolism." It was a small target. That was what Cade had told her. She could give this information away and not feel guilty about it.

"What else?"

She frowned. "I didn't *hear* anything else."

He watched her carefully, his expression grim. "I don't believe you."

"It doesn't matter what you believe," she said, sounding a hell of a lot braver than she felt. She swallowed, trying to clear her throat, even though it did no good. Not with the bruising.

Sighing, he stood and went to the door. With his back to her, he spoke. "Tell me what else you heard. I don't want to let Oto hurt you, but I will."

Her stomach dropped as she imagined what kind of pain the other man could put her through. Probably in ways she couldn't fathom. "You know what you talked about that night. Why ..." She trailed off, realizing he must not remember everything. He'd been shouting, angry, and he hadn't actually *mentioned* the Opulen, yet law enforcement had shown up. He obviously thought she'd told them about the location. Maybe he was questioning his memory. She decided to change tactics, hoping she could appeal to his humanity—not that she was certain he even had any. "Why are you doing this? You killed so many innocent people."

He straightened and turned back to face her, his hands tightening into fists as he glared at her. There was so much rage and anger there. "I'm doing this for my sisters. They deserve justice after what was done to them.

After they were abused, raped—worse than raped. Monsters used them and thousands of women for their own sick pleasures. No one, certainly not your government, stepped in to stop it and it's been going on for years. On your soil! They had to have known about it. Now the world will see what happens when the United States turns a blind eye to atrocities."

She didn't know how to respond, but he didn't seem to expect an answer as he continued ranting. "Decades ago your fucking country pushed and pushed for the fall of Communism. Then you left my country in a state of economic turmoil! My sisters had to look for work elsewhere, and the same country that nearly destroyed mine destroyed both of them!" He was all-out shouting now, but it was as if he wasn't even seeing her. Just raging words he'd likely said hundreds of times before. It was almost like a practiced speech. One he obviously believed.

If it was true, she felt terrible for what had happened to his sisters. But to kill so many people in the name of revenge? There was no way to justify that.

Eventually his breathing evened out, but the anger still glittered in his blue eyes. "Your country mourns over a few school shootings. You know nothing of real pain. But you will." At that chilling announcement, he turned and opened the door. He stepped out into the hallway, looked to his left and right, then froze.

Quickly he moved back into the room, his body rigid, and shut the door firmly behind him. Sensing something was wrong, she swallowed hard as he pulled out a radio. In a language she didn't understand, he spoke into it in low, savage undertones. No response. He tried again three more times. Still no response.

Jaw clenched tight, he pulled a switchblade out of his

pocket. The sharp blade sprang free and she flinched as he took a step toward her. Pulse racing, she tried to scramble away, but the chair wouldn't budge.

Ignoring her, he lifted the blade and . . . cut her wrist free. Moving quickly, he started to cut all her bindings, freeing her other wrist and both her ankles. What the hell? Once she was free, he grabbed her by the upper arm and yanked her to her feet.

He started to say something, but she hauled back and head-butted him.

He shouted in agony as her skull connected with his nose. Blood sprayed everywhere.

She surprised herself, but the action was just instinctual. Working where she did, she'd taken so many self-defense courses she'd lost track. But this move her brother had taught her years ago when they were kids. Ignoring the pain that shot through her head from the impact, she tried to yank her arm free.

His fingers dug into her flesh, making her cry out in pain. He yanked her tighter to him instead of letting her go as she'd hoped. Kicking out, she started to struggle but froze when he pressed the blade to her throat. An icy shiver rippled through her.

"I can't get hold of my men, so you are coming with me. One wrong move and I slit your throat." Turning her toward the door, he kept her in front of him and wrapped his arm around her neck, putting pressure on her already tender throat.

She heard the click of the knife as he folded the blade in and for one brief moment contemplated fighting him again. Then she felt the muzzle of a gun press into her side. Another bit of ice slithered through her veins, making her incredibly aware of her own mortality.

"Open the door," he ordered, his voice an animalistic growl as he used her as a human shield.

Trembling, she did as he said. Slowly she stepped out into what was a narrow hallway with a polished wooden floor. The walls on either side were lined with expensive art, but on the left wall she saw portholes like the ones in the bedroom. Only these were a little bigger. They were definitely on a yacht, out at sea.

"What now?" she asked, her voice trembling. She didn't want to grasp onto the hope surging through her, but the fact that he couldn't get in touch with his men was a good thing. Maybe Cade had found her after all.

Mihails's grip tightened as he directed her down the hall. The muzzle of the gun dug harder into her side. "Walk."

It was difficult to move with him pressed so tightly against her, but she forced her feet forward. As they neared another door on the right, he slowed, his hold around her neck tightening.

Coughing, she instinctively started to struggle, bringing her hands up to his arm to relieve the pressure. Her fingers dug into his arm like claws. His arm loosened a fraction. Sucking in a gasp of air, she started to turn when the gun went off.

Chapter 24

Military phonetic alphabet: all branches of the United States armed services currently use the ICAO (International Civil Aviation Organization) alphabet for radio communication; the current alphabet was adopted by the U.S. armed services in the 1950s.

Twenty minutes earlier

"This is the best way," Jack said to Cade as the four-man team hurriedly stripped down to nothing, their feet bare against the wooden floor of the NSA's forty-five-foot cabin cruiser.

For a long moment Cade didn't respond as he grabbed one of the specially made wet suits. They were designed to mold to their bodies like a second skin and retain heat.

After being tracked all over Miami, Mihails and his team had finally stopped at a large, well-populated marina. People didn't just dock their boats and yachts here; a lot of them lived here too. Lots of families. Which was why Burkhart had ordered this operation completely under the radar. They didn't need any more civilians caught in the cross fire.

Cade might understand that, but he didn't like it. He'd wanted to go after Maria when the men were transporting her to their yacht. Maria was literally thirty yards away from him on a yacht the NSA had linked to a shell company. He had no clue how she was doing. If she was even still alive. What was happening to her . . . He shook off that thought. He wouldn't do her or his team any good if his focus was split.

The NSA was prepared for pretty much damn near any scenario. The cabin cruiser was a prime example. After coordinating with the marina owner, they'd managed to get this boat docked close to the yacht without anyone being the wiser. Cade and his team had been on it before docking, so if Mihails had lookouts they hadn't spotted yet, no one had seen the NSA team boarding.

Even the FBI was in on this operation. While the NSA was monitoring from the sky, the FBI had other plainclothes men and women on the ground near the yacht. They were all professionals, not like those idiots portrayed on TV wearing visible earpieces. No, these agents knew how to blend in. People's lives—Maria's life—depended on it.

"How would you feel if it was your wife?" Cade finally asked Jack as he pulled the side zipper up to his armpit, cursing the way his hand shook. Actually *shook*. Lifting his arms above his head, he twisted back and forth, making sure the synthetic neoprene material fit well. He knew Maria wasn't his wife, but he still loved her. And he wanted the chance to tell her that. Hell, he wanted more than that. They deserved a shot at happiness.

"Sophie was kidnapped last year. Her kidnapper called me and I had to listen to him cut her with a knife and threaten to do worse." Jack didn't look at him as he checked his own wet suit, but an uncharacteristic note of rage threaded through every word.

Cade raised his eyebrows. Maybe that was why the other man had retired. "Did you kill the fucker?"

"Yep."

"Good." He strapped two blades on, one against each outer thigh, then slid his Glock into his gun belt and secured it. It was one of the few firearms that could be submersed in water and still shoot well. Next he visually checked his belt to make sure it had everything he might need. For the most part he just needed a weapon and his hands. In hand-to-hand combat, he had no doubt he could take down any of these fuckers. Not arrogance, just a lot of damn training and experience. Since the NSA wanted at least some of these guys alive, they'd provided a few other choice methods with which to incapacitate them.

Cade and the other three men finished gearing up at the same time, the energy in the cabin high. They were all ready to go.

Ortiz passed out the waterproof earpieces to them. For this op, he was team leader. Cade didn't give a shit who was in charge as long as he was able to bring Maria home. The truth was, once they were on that yacht, he'd do any damn thing to save her, even if it meant losing his job. If he had to break the rules for her, he would.

Once they'd all put them in, Ortiz tapped his. "Testing."

They all nodded. The channel had been preprogrammed so they had a private frequency, but they wouldn't be talking unless absolutely necessary.

"You guys know the drill. O'Reilly, you're taking the

aft deck, Stone, the main deck. Freeman, you've got the wheelhouse and I'm taking the sundeck." Ortiz looked at all of them, waiting for affirmative nods.

They'd all been over this and had been given a layout of the three-level yacht, but this was a last-minute op. It didn't hurt to be overly prepared. Once they made it on board, they would move inward, neutralizing targets— eliminating if necessary—and sweeping each level until they found Maria and secured all the terrorists.

They strode out of the master suite into the interior cabin to find Burkhart and four analysts with computers set up at the round dining table.

"The engine's started. You guys are clear out the back. It's time to move," Burkhart said, his expression tight.

Shit. They had to move *now*. It would take more than a few minutes for a vessel of that size to be ready to leave, but if the engine had started, Cade and his teammates needed to be on it before it left the dock. Otherwise Burkhart would implement the backup plan, and that gave Maria a substantially less chance at survival.

The aft of the NSA's cabin cruiser faced away from the yacht, and if Burkhart said they were clear, they were. Falling in line behind the other three men, Cade put the thought of Maria aside and drew on years of training to focus on the job at hand.

One after the other, they slipped into the chilly water. Even with the thermal insulation provided by the suit and the protective dive slippers, the drop in temperature was still a shock to his system.

Using the dock as cover, the four of them swam steadily until they reached the yacht.

"We're ready," Ortiz said quietly, his words barely discernible over the hum of the engine.

"Oscar, Sierra, go now. No visible tangos," Burkhart said. For this mission they'd gone with the simplest of codes to identify one another using the phonetic military alphabet. Ortiz was Oscar, Stone was Sierra, Freeman was Foxtrot, and Cade was Charlie. Normally Cade was Oscar because his last name was O'Reilly, but with two *O*'s, he'd been designated C.

Immediately Jack and Ortiz dove underwater, heading for the front of the vessel. The adrenaline pumping through Cade was like nothing he'd ever experienced. Jagged and out of control.

"Foxtrot, Charlie, go."

Like a starter pistol signaling a race, the command shot Cade into action as Freeman dove underwater, heading to the port side of the boat. Unlike the others, Cade was taking the aft and didn't have far to go. He also didn't need to employ a handheld grappling hook like the others. The small device was a smaller version of what the Navy SEALs used—and not on the market anywhere. With three hundred psi behind it, the others would have no problem scaling the vessel.

From his position, Cade was too low in the water to see if there were guards, but if Burkhart gave the all-clear, he believed him. Once Cade was directly behind the boat, he hoisted himself up onto the flat aft deck and withdrew his Glock. He still couldn't see anything because of his position. Weapon drawn, he ascended the west set of stairs and was able to scan the outer dining area. It was clear.

All the terrorists were likely belowdecks where the guest cabins were. They wouldn't want to expose themselves outside. Not when they knew they were being hunted by every law enforcement agency. No, they'd remain hidden until they hit international waters. At least. And even then they'd want to keep out of sight of any drones or satellites tracking them.

Hating that he was leaving a wet trail behind him, but knowing there was nothing he could do about it, Cade hurried across the smooth wooden floor toward the set of stairs leading to the lower deck. The traction from his dive shoes prevented him from slipping. Even better, they were noiseless.

Heart racing, he silently descended the stairs. He could hear the soft murmur of male voices as he reached the bottom step. According to the diagram, there were two guest cabins in the back part of the lower deck. His team had designated that as sector twelve.

The voices stopped and a set of footsteps lightly padded toward him. Flattening himself against the small wall between the stairs and hallway leading to the two cabins, he sheathed his weapon. Their goal was to incapacitate the terrorists before they could alert any of their friends. If there was a chance they might alert the others, Cade's team had the authority to use lethal force.

When a blond-haired man stepped into his line of sight, Cade immediately struck, landing a vicious blow to the man's temple. It was a dangerous move, one that could kill a target if done wrong. The tango didn't even cry out as he slumped to the floor.

A sliver of relief slid through him as he recognized the man as Oto Ozols. Cade had started to pull out one of the syringes the NSA team had provided when another man stepped out into the hallway from one of the rooms.

The dark-haired man's eyes widened for a fraction of a second before he reached for his pistol.

Cade was faster. Withdrawing one of his blades, he launched it at the man's chest before he'd even drawn from his belt holster. It embedded deep, the crimson stain of blood spreading around the man's green T-shirt before his knees had even hit the floor. His mouth opened. He gasped out a noise before falling face-forward.

Internally cursing, Cade stabbed the syringe into Oto's neck, then swept the two rooms. Both were clear of tangos, but there was a shitload of Semtex stacked along the full-sized bed. Thankfully not charged to blow.

He retrieved his blade, then dragged the dead man into the nearest room. Moving quickly, he shoved him in the empty, small closet. There wasn't time to clean up the blood trail, but it was minimal.

After securing Ozols's arms, he carried him into the guest room. Placing him facedown on the floor on the opposite side of the bed so he was hidden, Cade secured his feet and gagged him. The drugs should keep him unconscious for at least an hour, but Cade wasn't taking a chance. As he stood, he snagged his radio and turned it all the way down to level one.

He tapped his earpiece. "One tango down, the other secure. Viper two unconscious in sector C." Mihails had been dubbed viper one and Oto viper two. Easy to remember. "Echo situation in sector C." Meaning he'd found explosives.

Withdrawing his Glock again, he internally smiled when Ortiz, Jack, and Freeman all checked in. Each of them had brought down at least one tango too.

"Wheelhouse secure," Freeman said, and Cade could practically hear the grin in his voice.

They now had complete control of the vessel. According to the aerial reports, there should be only one bastard left.

"No sighting of the eagle or viper one," Ortiz said.

That bastard had Maria. Cade was certain of it.

And he was going to find her. Sweeping out into the hall, he hurried down the narrow walkway. At the first door, he paused and listened at it. When he didn't hear anything, he eased it open, weapon in front of him.

Empty.

As he started to step back out, he heard another door opening. Without pause he ducked into the room he'd just checked. With no portholes, the room was near pitch-black. He left the door cracked open only a splinter wide. Pressing up close to the wall, he watched the hallway.

"Walk," a man ordered, his voice a guttural growl.

A second later, Maria came into view, moving under her own power. Harsh relief that she was alive slammed through Cade. An instant later, ice-cold flooded him as he saw the pistol pressed to her side.

Slowly, quietly, he withdrew his own blade. While he wouldn't mind shooting Mihails, a blade would work better. Less chance of Maria getting caught in the cross fire. Because he planned to get up close and personal with Mihails.

The fear on Maria's face as she passed by him, not even knowing he was there to save her, flayed him alive.

Taking out this bastard would be the best thing he'd ever done. As they moved by the room, Mihails pulled out his radio. Cade immediately turned off the one he'd stolen.

Once they'd passed his line of sight, Cade sent up a silent prayer for Maria's life. He didn't give a shit about himself; he just wanted Maria to survive this.

Easing the door open, he stepped out behind them, his heart in his throat. He could reach out and touch Mihails.

"What the hell?" the man muttered.

Cade realized he'd seen the faint water trail.

Mihails started to turn back around, moving the gun off Maria. In that moment, Cade instantaneously grabbed Mihails's head using his left hand and sliced the blade across his throat with his right. Blood sprayed everywhere, the arterial drench a geyser over the wall.

The gun went off, wood splintering in the explosion.

Maria screamed as Mihails dropped to the floor like a stone. Crimson liquid pooled around him. Kicking the weapon away, Cade bent to check the man's pulse. He knew it would take a minute for Mihails's heart to stop and did it as a precaution.

"Cade!" Maria shouted.

He heard the fear in her voice, the warning note. Driven by instinct, he dove, tackling her by the legs as bullets ricocheted around them, the staccato sounds deafening. Wood splintered and glass shattered. Rolling, he lifted his Glock.

Pain slammed into him, fire licking down his arm. The need to protect Maria, to keep her safe, overrode everything else. He could hear Ortiz shouting into his earpiece. Everything funneled out as he focused on the dark-haired tango taking aim again from down the hallway.

Cade fired. *Pop, pop, pop.*

Two to the chest, one to the head. The man dropped before he could get another shot off, his weapon falling to the floor with a clatter.

"Cade." Maria scrambled out from under him, her

eyes wide as she looked at him. She attempted to put pressure on his shoulder, but he pushed her off.

He didn't know if the danger was over yet. She couldn't be exposed like this. Fear clawed at him, razor-sharp blades stripping away at his insides, completely dulling his pain. "Get in that cabin and lock the door," he ordered, shoving her in the direction he wanted her to go.

She looked at him as if he were crazy, but when she moved he thought she was obeying. Instead she grabbed Mihails's fallen gun. At a whisper of sound, she raised it at the same time Cade rolled back over, his own weapon drawn.

Immediately he lowered it when he saw his team.

"Mihails is dead. The other tango came from the engine room. Haven't secured it yet," he told Ortiz as he attempted to sit up. His shoulder ached in agony as he moved, but he wasn't going to just lie there helpless.

Ortiz nodded as he continued past him, leaving red footprints tracked from Mihails's blood.

Jack knelt next to Cade.

"He needs medical help now," Maria snapped, her hoarse voice tinged with fear.

"I'm fine," he muttered as he leaned against the wall. It hurt but he'd been injured worse than this. And he didn't want her there. He wanted her away from all the death and blood.

"We're heading back to the marina. He'll have help in less than five minutes," Jack said as he withdrew one of his knives. *That meant Freeman was driving the vessel. Good.*

With practiced efficiency, Jack cut away the neoprene suit at the shoulder without even grazing Cade's skin.

Maria helped peel the sleeve off his arm. Once it was

free, she stripped off her shirt and wrapped it around his shoulder and under his arm to slow the bleeding. Jack pulled it tight and knotted it.

A ridiculous possessiveness built inside Cade at the sight of her wearing nothing but a bra and pants. It didn't matter that the sports bra covered more than most bathing suit tops.

She cupped his face with her palm. That was when he saw the tears in her eyes. "Thank you for coming for me," she rasped out.

He covered her hand with his. "Maria . . ." His gaze landed on her bruised neck. "Did they hurt you? Do you . . . need medical attention?" He didn't want to ask the other question. She hadn't been alone with the terrorists that long on the yacht, but . . .

"Ozols choked me in the car. I think they were going to do worse, but you showed up. . . ." Her voice cracked on the last word as she trailed off.

Not caring about his injury, he lifted his good arm and tried to pull her close.

"Your arm!" she admonished, but buried her face against his neck anyway.

Grunting at the discomfort, he wrapped his arm around her shoulders and looked at Jack, who was busy talking to Burkhart over their radio frequency. Cade had been half listening to the conversation and knew by now that the engine room was clear, all the terrorists neutralized and accounted for. The only thing they needed to do now was clear the explosives and make sure there weren't any more rigged on the boat.

"Burkhart and the medics are coming down now," Jack said as he gently pulled Maria back.

Cade didn't want to let her go but knew he needed to.

Until they'd secured this boat, he wanted her away from it. Hell, he wanted her completely away from the marina. "You're going to go with some agents. They'll keep you safe until I can get back to you," Cade murmured, weakness overtaking him with each second that passed. Maybe he'd lost more blood than he thought. Or maybe he was just dizzy with relief that Maria was okay.

She nodded and batted away some errant tears. "What about you?"

"He's going to be taken to the nearest hospital," Jack said. "Come on, let's get you up." He stood and looped his arm under Cade's shoulders.

Cade was taller, so he leaned into Jack. The pain and weakness hit him all at once like a full-on body blow. *No way.* He'd been shot worse than this. He had to stay awake. His body didn't listen to his brain. He stumbled, his knees giving out as blackness engulfed him.

Chapter 25

Two days later

Holding two to-go coffee cups, Maria opened the hospital door to Cade's room and pushed it open with her hip. As she entered the room she jerked to a halt at the sight of Cade standing next to his hospital bed shirtless, his jeans unbuttoned and unzipped.

And he was definitely commando, the proof of that clear. Even with, or maybe because of his bandage, he looked even sexier.

"Like what you see?" he asked wickedly, a grin teasing his lips as she met his gaze.

She ignored the heat spreading across her cheeks. "You *know* I do. Did the doctor discharge you?" He was supposed to have come by an hour ago, but when no one had shown up, she'd gone to get them coffee.

"Yeah." He picked up his collared shirt off the bed. Wincing, he slipped it over his head. The bandage around his shoulder pulled with the movement.

She cringed watching him and wanted to offer to help but knew he wouldn't take it. She'd already tried more than once the past couple of days and she'd quickly learned that he was crabby when he was injured, not wanting anyone to do anything for him. Closing the distance between them, she asked, "Are you sure you should be leaving?"

"There's nothing else they can do for me. I was lucky."

He'd been more than lucky. It was an absolute miracle. The bullet had gone right through his shoulder, missing anything major, and while she didn't understand most of the medical-speak from the doctors, the important thing was that he wouldn't lose any mobility. Which meant his injury wouldn't affect his career. For that, she was grateful. She might hate that his job put him in danger, but he clearly loved it and was good at it. If that had been taken away from him, it would have killed her.

"Thanks for the coffee." He plucked one of the cups from her hand and brushed his lips over hers. The kiss might have been nearly chaste, but she felt it all the way to her toes. She wanted to lean into him, to discard her cup and wrap her arms around him. Well, she wanted more than that. She craved to feel his naked body against hers again. With his injury, however, she wasn't pushing anything. Of course he'd tried a couple of times, but until the doctor discharged him she hadn't been willing to risk injuring him.

"Hold that thought for another hour," he murmured, his voice pulling her gaze up to meet his.

The lust she felt was mirrored in his electric green eyes. Mesmerized by that intense stare, she found it impossible to look away.

At the sound of a throat clearing, she jerked around, nearly sloshing her coffee.

Wesley Burkhart stood in the doorway in a dark suit, a crisp white shirt, and a dark tie. His expression was unreadable, which wasn't a surprise. From the limited time she'd spent with the man, he was like a closed book. Stepping inside, he shut the door behind him. "How're you feeling?"

Cade just grunted in response, which apparently his boss took as a good thing because he half smiled.

"What's up?" Cade asked.

"I know you're taking some time off, but I wanted to give you a couple updates in person before I head out of town."

Maria blinked in surprise. She hadn't known Cade was taking time off. She'd been too nervous to broach the subject of them or the future, especially since he'd been shot. And he'd been a bit of a bear the past couple of days. She was positive the nurses would be glad to have him out of the hospital.

Cade wrapped his good arm around her, pulling her tight to his side. She leaned into his embrace, holding on to his waist as she waited for Burkhart to speak. She loved that Cade wasn't afraid to show that he cared for her. No matter what happened between them, his actions in front of his boss and other people meant so much to her.

"Paul Hill has been indicted on over three hundred separate charges. He and his partners turned on one another pretty damn quickly, each wanting to cut a deal. He'll never see the light of day again and neither will they. The state's attorney will likely ask for the needle for him. Not sure yet about his partners. Ozols still isn't being cooperative, but he and his crew are going away forever too. He's definitely getting the death penalty and I don't even think he'll be fighting it. He's refused all legal counsel. So have his men."

"What about the rest of their plans?" she asked. Cade

had told her the NSA had found explosives and a detailed map of the Port of Miami along with blueprints laying out the schematics of two hotels downtown. Apparently the hotels had also been used by Paul Hill's disgusting network. Now the owners of those hotels were also under investigation.

"All the explosives have been accounted for and each target thoroughly swept. They hadn't got that far in their plan yet. Westwood was horrific, but it could have been a lot worse for Miami. Ozols actually seemed . . . relieved after we told him what was happening to Hill and his partners."

Most people would never know how much worse the devastation could have been. The NSA and FBI had decided to keep what they could out of the media. Maria was still coming to terms with everything and knew she'd never get over the loss of her mom. But she was glad the nightmare was over.

"Did we ever find out how Maria was tracked?"

A hard smile crossed Burkhart's face, the glint in his eyes lethal. "A very talented hacker exploited a weakness on Jack's phone, but he won't be a problem ever again."

Maria felt a chill go down her spine at that blunt statement. It wasn't hard to read between the lines. "Thank you for everything," she said to Burkhart. She was just one person and she knew that she could easily have been considered collateral damage in the NSA's effort to bring down the terrorists. While she knew Cade didn't consider her that at all, she also understood that if his boss had wanted, he could have made any decision in regard to the terrorists and excluded Cade in everything. But he hadn't.

He simply nodded and did that same grunting thing Cade had, before focusing on Cade. "Can I talk to you a sec?"

It was slight, but she felt Cade tense next to her. Even though she didn't want to leave the warmth of his embrace, she stepped aside. "I'll give you guys some privacy." Without waiting for his response, she hurried from the room.

Once outside she leaned against the wall and texted Leah, her dad, then Nash. Her father wanted to have dinner at his house tonight with her, Cade, and other family members. Nash was included and she'd already invited Leah but wanted to make sure her friend was still coming. In between staying at the hospital the past couple of days, Maria had spent as much time with her dad as possible. He was a wreck, and would likely never get over the loss of his wife. There was just no cure for that kind of grief. Time would dull the edge of pain, something Maria kept trying to remind herself. It didn't help much, because that ache still sat heavy in her chest. She missed her mom so damn much. Being around Cade certainly helped, but she wondered if soon she'd have a new ache when he moved on to his next mission. Things had been so intense between them, but he'd left once before and she still wasn't sure why. Oh, she knew what he'd told her before, but deep down, she felt he was holding something back from her. With everything going on, there hadn't been much time to question him. Nothing was stopping her now. Unfortunately she wasn't sure if she wanted his answer.

When the door to his room opened, she straightened and pushed away from the wall. Burkhart held it open for her with a half smile. "He's all yours."

She wished that were true. Inside she found Cade lifting his duffel bag from the bench by the window. Immediately she went to him and grabbed it. "I don't care how grouchy you get, I'm taking this."

"Grouchy?" His eyes widened, but he let her take it.

"Seriously? You've been a total terror from the moment you woke up at the hospital." She couldn't fight the smile tugging at her lips as she said it. Once she'd been positive he was going to be fine, it had been a little humorous to see him acting so out of character.

His ears actually turned red as he rubbed a hand over his skull trim. "I haven't been that bad," he muttered.

"Hmm."

"I just don't like being sick or laid up." He slung an arm around her shoulder.

"Clearly," she said as they headed for the door. "Is everything okay with your boss?"

"Yeah, he just wanted to go over some work stuff." There was a hesitant note in his voice she couldn't read.

"Oh." She was such a wimp. She had half a dozen important questions she wanted to ask and couldn't force the words out.

He paused at the door and leaned against it. Plucking the bag from her hand, he dropped it on the floor and tugged her close, his fingers flexing around her hips. "What is it?"

She placed her hands over his chest, savoring the feel of his raw strength. "Nothing, I . . ." She didn't want to do this here. He was recovering from a gunshot wound. Not the best time to ask about their future. She knew exactly what she wanted from him but wasn't sure he was ready for anything serious. Not with his type of job. "Let's get you out of here."

He looked at her for a long moment, as if searching for something. "Shit, Maria. I wanted to wait until we were out of the hospital to tell you, but I love you. You don't have to say the words; I just need you to know how I feel. I had strong fucking feelings for you eight years ago, but now it's different. More."

Pretty much everything he said funneled out after "I love you." "You love me? Why didn't you tell me two days ago? I love you too!" She hated that her words came out all angry sounding.

He shook his head. "Wait. There's something I need to tell you." Fear seeped into his gaze then, so potent she nearly stepped back from the force of it. His fingers flexed tighter on her hips, as if he read her mind. "It's about when Riel died."

A heavy weight settled in the pit of her stomach. "Okay."

"When we were in Afghanistan, we were on a routine mission—I can't tell you where or for what—using intel from one of my contacts. This guy was part of the local police and my friend. I *thought* he was. Everyone told me you can't trust *anyone* but your own team over there...." He released one of her hips and rubbed a hand over his face.

Her heart twisted at his pained expression when he looked at her again. "We walked right into an ambush and got pinned down by insurgents. It was a fucking nightmare. We were ... in a remote location and I called in air support, but they didn't make it in time. By the time they got there, I was the only one alive. I should have died, not Riel or my men. I trusted the wrong person and got all my friends killed." He dropped his hands and if the door hadn't been behind him she was pretty sure he would have backed up from her. Guilt poured off him in waves.

She felt terrible for him, but fury detonated inside her. "That's why you cut contact with me, isn't it? Not that bullshit you told me before?"

His expression tight, he nodded. "I understand if you ... don't want to see me again."

"You're such an asshole!" He flinched and she realized he thought she meant because of what he'd told her. "Not because of what happened. Riel told me more than once how hard it was to trust people over there. Did you intentionally or willingly go into an ambush?"

"Of course not," he muttered.

"Were you written up or demoted for the operation?" Meaning, had his superiors deemed him in the wrong?

"No." His jaw clenched tight as he watched her, clearly understanding where she was going.

"You're human, Cade. *Human.* It tears me up that my brother died, but I can't believe you've been carrying that guilt around for so long when there's nothing to feel guilty about. I just can't believe you cut contact with me for eight freaking years." Her heart twisted at all the time they'd lost. "If you weren't injured I'd punch you."

"I deserve it." From his tone she realized he meant because of what he perceived as his wrongdoing. Before she could respond, he continued. "It's my fault, Maria." His voice was raspy, unsteady. "I still have nightmares about ..."

The pain in his voice took all the steam out of her anger. "Oh, Cade." She linked her fingers behind his neck, plastering her body to his, mindful of his injury.

He tentatively slid his arms around her waist, but the fact that he was touching her was good. "You trusted someone you shouldn't have. There's no rule book for war and I can't even imagine how hard it is to make the types of decisions you and Riel had to on a daily basis, knowing that you held lives in your hands. You became a Marine because you care about your country, and you would never have deliberately put your men in danger; I know that. Now you're working for the NSA, dedicating even more of yourself. Clearly they think the same thing about you. They wouldn't have hired you otherwise. You're one of the bravest men I know, Cade."

The guilt etched on his face tore at her insides, but she knew that if she didn't get this out now, she never would. "You hurt me badly when you just cut me out of your life like that. You were one of my best friends and we'd just admitted our feelings to each other. Then Riel died and . . . nothing." It sliced her up if she thought about what a dark place she'd been in eight years ago.

He gently cupped her face, rubbing his thumb over her cheek once. "I regret it. More than you know. I . . . I should have just told you, but I'd fallen for you. Hard. The thought of losing you after I lost so many people in my life. I didn't think I'd survive it." The truth was in every line of his face.

Her throat tightened as she imagined how hard that had been for him, to literally lose all his friends, then to be worried about losing her too. She could still see fear in his expression as he dropped his hand back to her waist. As if he expected her to reject him now.

She tightened her grip on him. "I'm not angry at you and I'm never going to hold you responsible for something that you couldn't have prevented. Trusting the wrong person is not a crime. Look at me; I thought Andre Moran was a trusted family friend. So if you think this confession is going to push me away, you're wrong. I love you, Cade. Nothing will change that."

He swallowed hard and pulled her closer. "Really?" The hopeful note in his voice was too much.

She couldn't believe he'd held on to this for so long, that it had kept them apart. "Yeah. Since we're getting everything out in the open, I don't want anything casual. I don't know how we're going to make things work with us living in different states, but I want to try."

A slow grin spread across his face. "I wasn't sure what your reaction would be to what I told you. Truthfully I'm a selfish bastard. I wasn't even sure I was going to tell you about Afghanistan. And I don't want anything casual either. It's why I've taken off the next couple weeks. I don't want to do anything but spend time with you—if that's what you want."

Pure relief poured through her. "That's exactly what I want. And no matter what happens between us, no running or hiding—ever. I'm a big believer in communication, and if you have a problem or are afraid of something or whatever, talk to me."

"I can do that—I *will* do that. And I know it's probably too soon, but I've already talked to Burkhart about taking a job at one of our Miami offices—something you'll have to sign a confidentiality agreement about since I'm not supposed to tell you unless we're married. It would mean less travel and while I'd still take rescue missions, I wouldn't do any undercover work anymore. Nothing black ops."

It took a moment to digest his words. He'd told his boss this even before their conversation, *before* his confession to her. Which meant at least on a subconscious level he'd trusted her enough to lay himself bare, to hope that she'd forgive him—not that he needed any forgiveness from her. Not for her brother. He certainly wasn't running now. "That's a huge decision. Are you sure?" She didn't want him to make a decision like that now, coming right off an intense operation.

With one of his hands, he cupped her cheek, his green eyes intense. "I've never been more sure of anything in my life. When Mihails took you, I knew I'd give up *any-thing* to be with you. I know long distance can work, but I don't want to start our relationship that way. I want to wake up to you every morning. I've never felt this way about anyone, Maria. And . . . I know I won't again. I never stopped caring from you. Not for eight fucking years. When I saw your name on that survivor list, fuck, I think I knew even then I wasn't letting you go again. We deserve a chance."

Tears burning her eyes, she leaned up on tiptoe and kissed him. Yes, they did. The fact that he was willing to uproot for her told her everything she needed to know. He loved her as much as she loved him.

Epilogue

Zero dark thirty: after midnight and before dawn.

Six months later

Cade eased open the door to the house he shared with Maria. He quickly disarmed the alarm he'd had installed, then reset it. It was after midnight and while he could have taken a flight home tomorrow, he'd hopped on a red-eye because he'd wanted to get home to her.

Home.

It was still a strange concept. He'd never felt at home anywhere except with her. Even his house in Virginia had never been one. It had been a place he slept at when he wasn't on missions. This place with the woman he loved was everything to him.

She was everything to him.

This last op had only been a week long, but it felt like an eternity being away from her. The house was quiet and even though she'd told him earlier that she'd wait up for him, he had a feeling she'd probably passed out reading, as she so often did.

He left the lights off since he could navigate through their place blind and hurried toward the stairs. Opening the door at the top, he paused in the doorway, unable to fight his grin. Sure enough, the lamplight cast a low glow on their room and Maria was asleep with a book open across her chest. Wearing one of his old Marine Corps T-shirts, which was ridiculously big on her, and nothing else, the woman looked like pure sex.

As quietly as he could, he put his bag by the end of the bed and stripped off his clothes. His body was practically rejoicing at the thought of sleeping in a soft bed instead of a crappy cot in a warehouse full of a team of NSA field agents and analysts—in the middle of the damn desert. He loved his job, but field ops weren't something he wanted to do forever. Hell, he *couldn't* do it forever even if he wanted to. It was why he'd been assigned as one of the NSA liaisons to work with local law enforcement and the feds. Miami was a hotbed of activity, so he'd been insanely busy here the last five months. And the work was fulfilling.

Burkhart had pulled him in for this recent job, but Cade had a feeling it was because he'd wanted to gauge how much Cade missed travel. Which he didn't. It was difficult to want it when he had Maria back home waiting for him.

Before getting into bed, he pulled something out of his bag he'd been holding on to for the past couple of months. The second the bed dipped under his weight, Maria's eyes flew open. Smiling softly at him, she closed the book and moved it to the nightstand before snuggling closer to him. "I missed you," she said as she hooked her arm and leg over him. Her voice was thick with sleep.

"I missed you too." He covered her mouth with his,

stroking her lips open with his tongue in soft, teasing strokes.

When she pushed on his shoulder, rolling him over so she could straddle him, his entire body pulled taut with need. She slid down his body, her heat rubbing over his hard length, and he realized she wasn't wearing any panties.

She grinned down at him, as if reading his mind. "I wanted to be ready for you when you got home," she said as she tugged her shirt over her head.

His brain nearly short-circuited at the sight of her petite, tan body on his. He couldn't wait to devour her. But first ... "Close your eyes."

Her lips pulled into a slight frown, but she closed them. Taking a deep breath, he lifted her left hand up from his chest and slid a diamond ring onto her ring finger. Before he'd told her to open them, her eyes flew open and zeroed in on her fingers. She let out a tiny gasp and lifted her hand, staring at the solitaire diamond.

"I was going to put it on you while you were asleep," he murmured, his heart beating overtime. He'd wanted to propose for months but had been trying to wait until the right time. On the flight back he'd realized there would never be a perfect moment. And he wanted everyone to know she was taken. "Marry me?"

"Yes." Smiling, she covered the small distance between their bodies and kissed him, hot and hungry.

Rolling his hips against her, he shuddered at the feel of her pressed to him. Maria had given him everything he'd never realized he was missing. A home, a family, a love so intense it awed him, and he couldn't wait to spend the rest of his life with her.

ACKNOWLEDGMENTS

I owe a huge thanks to my editor, Danielle Perez. Thank you for pushing me to make this book shine the way it's supposed to. I'm also incredibly thankful to the entire team at NAL: Christina Brower, Jessica Brock, Ashley Polikoff, Katie Anderson, as well as cover illustrator Blake Morrow. You all do so much behind-the-scenes work and it's very appreciated. To my agent, Jill Marsal, thank you for your continuing guidance and support.

As always, thank you to Kari Walker for reading the early version of this book (and all my books). I would be lost without you. Tanya Hyatt, assistant extraordinaire, I'm eternally grateful for everything you do. Without your help I wouldn't get to write as much as I do. For my husband, who not only puts up with my erratic schedule, but is my sounding board and go-to research guy for all things military. It goes without saying that any mistakes in the book are my own. For my readers, I'm so thankful for all of you. Thank you for reading my books. I'm also thankful to God for so many opportunities.

Don't miss the first book in the exciting
Deadly Ops series by Katie Reus

TARGETED

Available now from Headline Eternal.

Prologue

Marine Corps Scout Sniper motto: one shot, one kill.

Sam Kelly could see his GP tent fifty yards away. He was practically salivating at the thought of a shower and a clean bed. But he'd settle for the fucking bed at this point. He didn't even care that he was sharing that tent with twenty other men. Showers were almost pointless at this dusty military base in hellish sub-Saharan Africa anyway. By the time he got back to his tent from the showers, he'd be covered in a film of grime again.

Four weeks behind enemy lines with limited supplies and he was also starving. Even an MRE sounded good about now. As he trekked across the dry, cracked ground, he crossed his fingers that the beef jerky he'd stashed in his locker was still there, but he doubted it. His bunkmate had likely gotten to it weeks ago. Greedy fucker.

"There a reason you haven't shaved, Marine?"

Sam paused and turned at the sound of the condescending, unfamiliar voice. An officer — a lieutenant — he didn't recognize stood a few feet away, his pale face flushed and his skin already burning under the hot sun. With one look Sam knew he was new in-country. Why the hell wasn't the idiot wearing a boonie hat to protect his face? Hell, it had to be a hundred and thirty degrees right now. Yeah, this dick was definitely new. Otherwise, he wouldn't be hassling Sam.

Sam gave him a blank stare and kept his stance relaxed. "Yes, sir, there is. Relaxed grooming standards." *Dumbass.*

The blond man's head tilted to the side just a fraction, as if he didn't understand the concept. God, could this guy be any greener? The man opened his mouth again and Sam could practically hear the stupid shit he was about to spout off by the arrogant look on his face.

"Lieutenant! There a reason you're bothering my boy?" Colonel Seamus Myers was barreling toward them, dust kicking up under his feet with each step.

The man reminded Sam of an angry bull, and when he got pissed, everyone suffered. He was a good battalion commander, though. Right now Sam was just happy the colonel wasn't directing that rage at him. Guy could be a scary fucker when he wanted.

"No, sir. I was just inquiring about his lack of grooming." The officer's face flushed even darker under his spreading sunburn. Yeah, that was going to itch something fierce when it started peeling. Sam smiled inwardly at the thought.

"You're here one week and you think you know more than me?"

"N-no, sir! Of course not, sir."

The colonel leaned closer and spoke so low that Sam couldn't hear him. But he could guess what he was saying because he'd heard it before. *Stay the fuck away from Sam Kelly and the rest of my snipers or I'll send you home.* Rank definitely mattered, but to the colonel, his few snipers were his boys, and the man had been in more wars than Sam ever wanted to think about. Sam had seen and caused enough death himself to want to get out when his enlistment was up. That wasn't too far off either. He'd been to Iraq, Afghanistan, a few places in South America that weren't even on his official record, and now he was stationed in Djibouti, Africa. Or hell, as he liked to think of it. He loved his job and he loved his country, but enough was enough. Sam just wished he could figure out what the hell he wanted to do if he got out of the military.

He watched as the colonel started talking—loudly—to the new guy. Getting right in his face as only a pissed-off Marine could. Sam almost felt sorry for the guy, but what kind of stupid fucker didn't know that since the environment here was so dirty that staph infections were rampant, grooming standards were *different*? That was one of the reasons he and a thousand other guys his age had relaxed grooming standards in the bowels of this hellish place. But they also cut him slack because he was a sniper. Sometimes he had to blend in with the populace, among other things. He might be stationed in Africa, but he'd just gotten back from—where else?—Afghanistan. He'd stayed holed up for days in that dank cave just waiting—

"Sergeant, in my tent. Now."

Sam blinked and realized Colonel Myers was talking to him. He nodded. "Yes, sir."

The colonel was still reaming out whoever the newbie was, but Sam always followed orders. Looked as though that shower was going to wait. The walk to the big tent in the middle of the base was short.

As he drew the flap back and stepped into the colonel's tent, he stilled when he spotted a dark-haired man leaning against a table with maps on it. He looked as if he thought he had every right to be there too. Interesting. A fly landed on Sam's face, but he didn't move. Just watched the man, ready to go for one of his weapons if need be. He didn't recognize him and he wasn't wearing a uniform.

Just simple fatigues and a T-shirt that stretched across a clearly fit body even though the guy had to be pushing fifty. There was something about the man that put Sam on edge. He was like a tiger, coiled and waiting to rip your head off. The man's eyes weren't cold, exactly, but they were calculating.

Carefully the man reached for a manila folder next to him and flipped it open. He glanced down at it. "Sam Kelly. Originally from Miami, Florida. Grew up in foster care. No known family. One of the best damn snipers Myers has ever seen. Sniper school honor grad, aptitude for languages, takes orders well, possibly a lifer." He glanced up then, his green eyes focusing on Sam like a laser. "But I don't think you're a lifer. You want a change, don't you?" The man's gaze was shrewd, assessing. Sam didn't like being analyzed, especially by a stranger. And the guy didn't even have an accent, so he couldn't place where he might be from. Nothing in his speech stood out.

Who the hell was this guy? And how the fuck did he know Sam wanted a change? It wasn't as if he'd told anyone. Sam ran through the list of possibilities. He'd been on different operations before, sometimes working for the CIA for solo things, and he'd been attached to various SEAL teams for larger-scale missions, but he'd never worked with this guy before. He did have Sam's file, though—or Sam guessed that was his file in the man's hand. He could just be bluffing. But what would the point of that be? He dropped all semblance of protocol since this guy clearly wasn't a Marine. "Who are you and what do you want?"

"You did some good work in Cartagena a few years ago." He snapped the file shut and set it back on the table.

Sam just stared at him. His statement said a lot all by itself. That mission wasn't in his official jacket, so this guy knew classified shit and was letting Sam know it. But since he hadn't asked a question or introduced himself, Sam wasn't inclined to respond.

The man's lips quirked up a fraction. As they did, the tent flap opened and the colonel strode in. He glared at the man, cursed, then looked at Sam, his expression almost speculative. He jerked a thumb at the stranger. "Whatever this guy tells you is the truth and he's got top-secret clearance." He snorted, as if something was funny about that, then sobered. "And whatever you decide . . . Hell, I know what you'll decide. Good luck, son. I'll miss you." He shook Sam's hand, then strode out of the tent.

Miss him? What the hell was he talking about? Sam glared at the man in front of him. "I asked you once who you were. Answer or I'm out of here."

The stranger crossed the short distance and held out his hand.

Sam ignored it.

The man cleared his throat and looked as if he was fighting a smile, which just pissed Sam off. "I'm Lieutenant General Wesley Burkhart, head of—"

"The NSA. I know the name." Sam didn't react outwardly, but the gears in his head were turning. "What do you want with me? I thought you guys were into cryptography and cyber stuff."

"We are, but I'm putting together a team of men and

women with a different skill set. Black ops stuff, similar to the CIA, but with less ... rules. I want to offer you a job, but before I go any further, you need to know that if you come to work for me, Sam Kelly will cease to exist. You will leave your past and everything in it behind."

Sam stared at the man, overwhelmed by too many feelings. Relief being one of them. Leaving his identity behind didn't seem like such a bad thing at all. Finishing the rest of his enlistment in shitholes like this wasn't something he looked forward to. He'd seen and caused so much death that sometimes he wondered if God would ever forgive him. The idea of wiping his record clean was so damn appealing. Maybe this was the fresh start he'd been looking for. Except ... he touched the hog's tooth hanging from his neck. He'd bled, sweated, and starved for this thing. For what it represented. It was part of him now. "I'm not taking this off. Ever."

The other man's eyes flicked to the bullet around his neck, and the corners of his mouth pulled up slightly. "Unless the op calls for it, I wouldn't expect you to."

Okay, then. Heart thudding, Sam dropped his rucksack to the ground. "Tell me everything I need to know."

Chapter 1

Black Death 9 Agent: member of an elite group of men and women employed by the NSA for covert, off-the-books operations. A member's purpose is to gain the trust of targeted individuals in order to gather information or evidence by any means necessary.

Five years later

Jack Stone opened and quietly shut the door behind him as he slipped into the conference room. A few analysts and field agents were already seated around the long rectangular table. One empty chair remained.

A few of the new guys looked up as he entered, but the NSA's security was tighter than Langley's. Since he was the only one missing from this meeting, the senior members pored over the briefs in front of them without even giving him a cursory glance.

Wesley Burkhart, his boss, handler, and recruiter all rolled into one, stuck his head in the room just as Jack started to sit. "Jack, my office. Now."

He inwardly cringed because he knew that tone well. At least his bags were still packed. Once he was out in the hall, heading toward Wesley's office, his boss briefly clapped him on the back. "Sorry to drag you out of there, but I've got something bigger for you. Have you had a chance to relax since you've been back?"

Jack shrugged, knowing his boss didn't expect an answer. After working two years undercover to bring down a human trafficking ring that had also been linked to a terrorist group in Southern California, he was still decompressing. He'd been back only a week and the majority of his time had been spent debriefing. It would take longer than a few days to wash the grime and memories off him. If he ever did. "You've got another mission for me already?"

Wesley nodded as he opened the door to his office. "I hate sending you back into the field so soon, but once you read the report, you'll understand why I don't want anyone else."

As the door closed behind them, Jack took a seat in front of his boss's oversized solid oak desk. "Lay it on me."

"Two of our senior analysts have been hearing a lot of chatter lately linking the Vargas cartel and Abu al-Ramaan's terrorist faction. At this point, the only solid connection we have is South Beach Medical Supply."

"SBMS is involved?" The medical company delivered supplies and much-needed drugs to third-world countries across the globe. Ronald Weller, the owner, was such a straight arrow it didn't seem possible.

"Looks that way." His boss handed him an inch-thick manila folder.

Jack picked up the packet and looked over the first document. As he skimmed the report, his chest tightened painfully as long-buried memories clawed at him with razor-sharp talons. After reading the key sections, he looked up. "Is there a chance Sophie is involved?" Her name rolled off his tongue so naturally, as if he'd spoken to her yesterday and not thirteen years ago. As if saying it was no big deal. As if he didn't dream about her all the damn time.

Wesley shook his head. "We don't know. Personally, I don't think so, but it looks like her boss is."

"Ronald Weller? Where are you getting this information?" Jack had been on the West Coast for the last two years, dealing with his own bullshit. A lot could have changed in that time, but SBMS involved with terrorists—he didn't buy it.

"Multiple sources have confirmed his involvement, including Paul Keane, the owner of Keane Flight. We've got Mr. Keane on charges of treason, among other things. He rolled over on SBMS without too much persuasion, but we still need actual proof that SBMS is involved, not just a traitor's word."

"How is Keane Flight involved?"

"Instead of just flying medical supplies, they've been picking up extra cargo."

Jack's mind immediately went to the human trafficking he'd recently dealt with, and he gritted his teeth. "Cargo?"

"Drugs, guns . . . possibly biological weapons."

The first two were typical cargo of most smugglers, but biological shit put Keane right on the NSA's hit list. "What do you want from me?"

His boss rubbed a hand over his face. "I've already built a cover for you. You're a silent partner with Keane Flight. Now that Paul Keane is incapacitated, you'll be taking over the reins for a while, giving you full access to all his dealings."

"Incapacitated, huh?"

The corners of Wesley's mouth pulled up slightly. "He was in a car accident. Bad one."

"Right." Jack flipped through the pages of information. "Where's Keane really at right now?"

"In federal protection until we can bring this whole operation down, but publicly he's in a coma after a serious accident—one that left him scarred beyond recognition and the top half of his body in bandages."

Jack didn't even want to know where they'd gotten the body. Probably a John Doe no one would miss. "So what's the deal with my role?"

"Paul Keane has already made contact with Weller about you—days before his accident. Told him he was taking a vacation and you'd be helping out until he got back. Weller was cautious on the phone, careful not to give up anything. Now that Keane is 'injured,' no one can ask him any questions. Keane's assistant is completely in the dark about everything and thinks you're really a silent partner. You've been e-mailing with her the past week to strengthen your cover, but you won't need to meet her in person. You're supposed to meet with Weller in two days. We want you to completely infiltrate the day-to-day workings of SBMS. We need to know if Weller is working with anyone else, if he has more contacts we're not privy to. Everything."

"Why can't you tap his phone?" That should be child's play for the NSA.

His boss's expression darkened. "So far we've been unable to hack his line. I've got two of my top analysts, Thomas Chadwick and Steven Williams—I don't think you've met either of them." When Jack shook his head, Wesley continued. "The fact that's he's got a filter that *we* can't bust through on his phone means he's probably into some dirty stuff."

Maybe. Or maybe the guy was just paranoid. Jack glanced at the report again, but didn't get that same rush he'd always gotten from his work. The last two years he'd seen mothers and fathers sell their children into slavery for less than a hundred dollars. And that wasn't even the worst of it. In the past he hadn't been on a job for more than six months at a time and he'd never been tasked with anything so brutal before, but in addition to human trafficking, they'd been selling people to scientists—under the direction of Albanian terrorists—who had loved having an endless supply of illegals to experiment on. He rolled his shoulders and shoved those thoughts out of his head. "What am I meeting him about?" *And how the hell will I handle seeing Sophie?* he thought.

"You supposedly want to go over flight schedules and the books and you want to talk about the possibility of investing in his company."

Jack was silent for a long beat. Then he asked the only question that mattered. The question that would burn him alive from the inside out until he actually voiced it. The question that made him feel as if he'd swallowed glass shards as he asked, "Will I be working with Sophie?"

Wesley's jaw clenched. "She *is* Weller's assistant."

"So yes."

Those knowing green eyes narrowed. "Is that going to be a problem?"

Yes. "No."

"She won't recognize you. What're you worried about?" Wesley folded his hands on top of the desk.

Jack wasn't worried about *her*. He was worried he

couldn't stay objective around her. Sophie thought he was dead. And thanks to expensive facial reconstruction — all part of the deal in killing off his former identity when he'd joined Wesley's team with the NSA — she'd never know his true identity. Still, the thought of being in the same zip code as her sent flashes of heat racing down his spine. With a petite, curvy body made for string bikinis and wet T-shirt contests, Sophie was the kind of woman to make a man do a double take. He'd spent too many hours dreaming about running his hands through that thick dark hair again as she rode him. When they were seventeen, she'd been his ultimate fantasy and once they'd finally crossed that line from friends to lovers, there had been no keeping their hands off each other. They'd had sex three or four times a day whenever they'd been able to sneak away and get a little privacy. And it had never been enough with Sophie. She'd consumed him then. Now his boss wanted him to voluntarily work with her. "Why not send another agent?"

"I don't *want* anyone else. In fact, no one else here knows you're going in as Keane's partner except me."

Jack frowned. It wasn't the first time he'd gone undercover with only Wesley as his sole contact, but if his boss had people already working on the connection between Vargas and SBMS, it would be protocol for the direct team to know he was going in undercover. "Why?"

"I don't want to risk a leak. If I'm the only one who knows you're not who you say you are, there's no chance of that."

There was more to it than that, but Jack didn't question him. He had that blank expression Jack recognized all too well that meant he wouldn't be getting any more, not even under torture.

Wesley continued. "You know more about Sophie than most people. I want you to use that knowledge to get close to her. I don't think I need to remind you that this is a matter of national security."

"I haven't seen her since I was eighteen." And not a day went by that he didn't think of the ways he'd failed her. What the hell was Wesley thinking?

"It's time for you to face your past, Jack." His boss suddenly straightened and took on that professorial/fatherly look Jack was accustomed to.

"Is that what this is about? Me, facing my past?" he ground out. Fuck that. If he wanted to keep his memories buried, he damn well would.

Wesley shrugged noncommittally. "You *will* complete this mission."

As Jack stood, he clenched his jaw so he wouldn't say something he'd regret. Part of him wanted to tell Wesley to take his order and shove it, but another part—his most primal side—hummed with anticipation at the thought of seeing Sophie. She'd always brought out his protective side. Probably because she'd been his entire fucking world at one time and looking out for her had been his number-one priority.

He'd noticed Sophie long before she'd been aware of his existence, but once he was placed in the same foster house as her, they'd quickly become best friends. Probably because he hadn't given her a choice in being his friend. He'd just pushed right past her shy exterior until she came to him about anything and everything. Then one day she'd kissed him. He shoved *that* thought right out of his mind.

"There's a car waiting to take you to the flight strip. Once you land in Miami, there will be another car waiting for you. There's a full wardrobe, and anything else you'll need at the condo we've arranged."

"What about my laptop?"

"It's in the car."

When he was halfway to the door, his boss stopped him again. "You need to face your demons, Jack. Seeing Sophie is the only way you'll ever exorcise them. Maybe you can settle down and start a family once you do. I want to see you happy, son."

Son. If only he'd had a father like Wesley growing up. But if he had, he wouldn't have ended up where he was today. And he'd probably never have met Sophie. That alone made his shitty childhood worth every punch and bruise he'd endured. Jack swallowed hard, but didn't turn around before exiting. His chest loosened a little when he was out from under Wesley's scrutiny. The older man might be in his early fifties, but with his skill set, Jack had no doubt his boss could take out any one of the men within their covert organization. That's why he was the deputy director of the NSA and the unidentified head of the covert group Jack worked for.

Officially, Black Death 9 didn't exist. Unofficially, the name was whispered in back rooms and among other similar black ops outfits within the government. Their faction was just another classified group of men and women working to keep their country safe. At times like this Jack wished the NSA didn't have a thick file detailing every minute detail of his past. If they didn't, another agent would be heading for Miami right now and he'd be on his way to a four-star hotel or on another mission.

Jack mentally shook himself as he placed his hand on the elevator scanner. Why was Wesley trying to get under his skin? Now, of all times? The man was too damn intuitive for his own good. He'd been after him for years to see Sophie in person, "to find closure" as he put it, but Jack couldn't bring himself to do it. He had no problem facing down the barrel of a loaded gun, but seeing the woman with the big brown eyes and the soft curves he so often dreamed about—*no, thank you.*

As the elevator opened into the aboveground parking garage, he shoved those thoughts away. He'd be seeing Sophie in two days. Didn't matter what he wanted.

Sophie Moreno took a deep, steadying breath and eased open the side door to one of Keane Flight's hangars. She had a key, so it wasn't as though she was technically breaking in. She was just coming by on a Sunday night when no one was here. And the place was empty. And she just happened to be wearing a black cap to hide her hair.

Oh yeah, she was completely acting like a normal, law-abiding citizen. Cringing at her stupid rationalization, she pushed any fears of getting caught she had to the side. What she was doing wasn't about her.

She loved her job at South Beach Medical Supply, but lately her boss had been acting weird and the flight logs from Keane Flight for SBMS's recent deliveries didn't make sense. They hadn't for the past few months.

And no one—meaning her boss, Ronald Weller— would answer her questions when she brought up anything about Keane Flight.

Considering Ronald hadn't asked her over to dinner in the past few months either, as he normally did, she had a feeling he and his wife must be having problems. They'd treated her like a daughter for almost as long as she'd been with SBMS, so if he was too distracted to look into things because of personal issues, she was going to take care of this herself. SBMS provided much-needed medical supplies to third-world countries, and she wasn't going to let anything jeopardize that. People needed them. And if she could help out Ronald, she wanted to.

She didn't even know what she was looking for, but she'd decided to trust her gut and come here. Wearing all black, she felt a little stupid, like a cat burglar or something, but she wanted to be careful. Hell, she'd even parked outside the hangar and sneaked in through an opening in the giant fence surrounding the private airport. The security here should have been tighter—something she would address later. After she'd done her little B&E. God, she was so going to get in trouble if she was caught. She could tell herself that she wasn't "technically" doing anything wrong, but her palms were sweaty as she stole down the short hallway to where it opened up into a large hangar.

Two twin-engine planes sat there, and the overhead lights from the warehouselike building were dim. But they were bright enough for her to make out a lot of cargo boxes and crates at the foot of one of the planes. The back hatch was open and it looked as if someone had started loading the stuff, then stopped.

Sophie glanced around the hangar as she stepped fully into it just to make sure she was alone. Normally Paul Keane had standard security here. She'd actually been here a couple of weeks ago under the guise of needing paperwork and there had been two Hispanic guys hovering near the planes as if they belonged there. She'd never seen them before and they'd given her the creeps. They'd also killed her chance of trying to sneak in and see what kind of cargo was on the planes.

When she'd asked Paul about them, he'd just waved off her question by telling her he'd hired new security.

One thing she knew for sure. He'd lied straight to her face. Those guys were sure as hell *not* security. One of them had had a MAC-10 tucked into the front of his pants. She might not know everything about weapons, but she'd grown up in shitty neighborhoods all over Miami, so she knew enough. And no respectable security guy carried a MAC-10 with a freaking *suppressor*. That alone was incredibly shady. The only people she'd known to carry that type of gun were gangbangers and other thugs.

So even if she felt a little crazy for sneaking down here, she couldn't go to her boss about any illegal activities—if there even were any—without proof. SBMS was Ronald's heart. He loved the company and she did too. No one was going to mess with it if she had anything to say about it.

Since the place was empty, she hurried across the wide expanse, her black ballet-slipper-type shoes virtually silent. When she neared the back of the plane, she braced herself for someone to be waiting inside.

It was empty except for some crates. Bypassing the crates on the outside, she ran up inside the plane and took half a dozen pictures of the crates with the SBMS logo on the outside. Then she started opening them.

By the time she opened the fifth crate, she was starting to feel completely insane, but as she popped the next lid, ice chilled her veins. She blinked once and struggled to draw in a breath, sure she was seeing things.

A black grenade peeked through the yellow-colored stuffing at the top. Carefully she lifted a bundle of it. There were more grenades lining the smaller crate, packed tight with the fluffy material. Her heart hammered wildly as it registered that Keane was likely running arms and weapons using SBMS supplies as cover, but she forced herself to stay calm. Pulling out her cell phone, she started snapping pictures of the inside of the crate, then pictures that showed the logo on the outside. In the next crate she found actual guns. AK-47s, she was pretty sure. She'd never actually seen one in real life before, but it looked like what she'd seen in movies. After taking pictures of those, she hurried out of the back of the plane toward the crates sitting behind it.

Before she could decide which one to open first, a loud rolling sound rent the air—the hangar door!

Ducking down, she peered under the plane and saw the main door the planes entered and exited through starting to open. Panic detonated inside her. She had no time to do anything but run. Without pause, she raced back toward the darkened hallway. She'd go out the back, the same way she'd come in. All she had to do was get to that hallway before whoever—

"Hey!" a male voice shouted.

Crap, someone had seen her. She shoved her phone in her back pocket and sprinted even faster as she cleared the hallway. Fear ripped through her, threatening to pull her apart at the seams. She wouldn't risk turning around and letting anyone see her face.

The exit door clanged against the wall as she slammed it open. Male voices shouted behind her, ordering her to stop in Spanish.

Her lungs burned and her legs strained with each pounding step against the pavement. She really wished she'd worn sneakers. As she reached the edge of the fence that thankfully had no lighting and was lined with bushes and foliage behind it, she dove for the opening. If she hadn't known where it was, it would be almost impossible to find without the aid of light.

Crawling on her hands and knees, she risked a quick glance behind her. Two men were running across the pavement toward the fence, weapons silhouetted in their hands. She couldn't see their faces because the light from the back of the hangar was behind them, but they were far enough away that she should be able to escape. They slowed as they reached the fence, both looking around in confusion.

"Adónde se fue?" one of them snarled.

Sophie snorted inwardly as she shoved up from the ground and disappeared behind the bushes. They'd never catch her now. Not unless they could jump fences in single bounds. Twenty yards down, her car was still parked on the side of the back road where she'd left it.

The dome light came on when she opened the door, so she shut it as quickly as possible. She started her car but immediately turned off the automatic lights and kicked the vehicle into drive. Her tires made a squealing sound and she cringed. She needed to get out of there before those men figured out how to get through the fence. She couldn't risk them seeing her license plate. Only law enforcement should be able to track plates, but people who were clearly running weapons wouldn't care about breaking laws to find out who she was.

She glanced in the rearview mirror as her car disappeared down the dark road, and didn't see anyone in the road or by the side of it. Didn't mean they weren't there, though. Pure adrenaline pumped through her as she sped away, tearing through her like jagged glass, but her hands remained steady on the wheel.

What the hell was she supposed to do now? If she called the cops, this could incriminate SBMS and that could ruin all the good work their company had done over the past decade. And what if by the time the cops got there all the weapons were gone? Then she'd look crazy and would have admitted to breaking into a private airport hangar, which was against the law. Okay, the cops were out. For now. First she needed to talk to her boss. He'd know what to do and they could figure out this mess together.

ALSO AVAILABLE FROM

NEW YORK TIMES BESTSELLING AUTHOR

Katie Reus

The first book in the Moon Shifter series

Alpha Instinct

Ana Cordona has been a strong leader for the few
remaining lupine shifters in her pack. But with no Alpha
male, the pack is vulnerable to the devious shifter Taggart,
who wants to claim both their ranch and Ana as his own.
When Connor Armstrong comes back into her life,
promising protection, it's *almost* enough to make Ana
forget how he walked out on her before—and she
reluctantly accepts his offer to mate.

Taggart and his rival pack are not the only enemies.
A human element in town is targeting shifters. Their plan
not only threatens Ana and Connor's future—but the
lives of the entire pack.

'A wild, hot ride'
New York Times **bestselling author Cynthia Eden**

facebook.com/eternalromance

ALSO AVAILABLE FROM
NEW YORK TIMES BESTSELLING AUTHOR

Katie Reus

A Moon Shifter series e-novella

Lover's Instinct

Lupine shifter Nikan Lawless has it bad for
Esperanze Cordona, the sweet and curvy woman who
only views him as a friend. But when Nikan is assigned
to act as Esperanze's bodyguard during a weekend
education conference, he knows it's the perfect
opportunity to seduce her.

Nikan cancels one of their hotel rooms, giving them time
to get to know one another in a whole different way. But
when a man from Esperanze's past shows up in need of
help, Nikan must shield her from dangerous rogue
shifters, all while trying to prove that they're destined
to be mates.

'Impossible to put down . . . Ms. Reus bangs
out a top-quality story'
Fresh Fiction

facebook.com/eternalromance

ALSO AVAILABLE FROM

NEW YORK TIMES BESTSELLING AUTHOR

Katie Reus

The second book in the Moon Shifter series

Primal Possession

As his pack's second-in-command, lupine shifter Liam
Armstrong is used to giving orders—not taking them.
That works fine until he meets December McIntyre.
Liam knows the human is his intended mate the moment
he sees her, but December is too strong-willed to accept
his protection. December has every reason to mistrust
shifters after one killed her youngest sibling.

Things get even more complicated when a radical hate
group targets all humans known to sympathize with
paranormal beings. When December is attacked in the
bookstore she owns, she reluctantly turns to the only
person who can help her: Liam.

'You'll look forward to visiting this world again soon!'
Romantic Times

facebook.com/eternalromance

ALSO AVAILABLE FROM

NEW YORK TIMES BESTSELLING AUTHOR

Katie Reus

The third book in the Moon Shifter series

Mating Instinct

For centuries, powerful lupine shifter Jayce Kazan has managed to stay away from humans...until he meets Kat Saburova. While Jayce shares his passion with the human seer, he refuses to make her his bondmate— a refusal that causes the end of their relationship.

A year later, an attack that left Kat near death has resulted in another lupine shifter turning her. Furious that he wasn't the one to save her, Jayce is determined to show Kat that he is the one she should rely on...

'Reus has an instinct for what wows in this perfect blend of shifter, suspense, and sexiness'
New York Times **bestselling author Caridad Piñeiro**

facebook.com/eternalromance

ALSO AVAILABLE FROM

NEW YORK TIMES BESTSELLING AUTHOR

Katie Reus

A Moon Shifter series e-novella

His Untamed Desire

Lupine shifter Daphne's recent move back home
has given her a chance to show sexy jaguar shifter Hector
just what he's been missing. Turns out Hector knows just
what he wants, and how to protect what's his—whether
Daphne wants his protection or not.

But with tensions between vampires and shifters on the
rise as pregnant shifters disappear all over New Orleans,
Hector's got more than Daphne to worry about—his sister
could be the next victim. When Daphne underestimates
her stalker's persistence, it might be too late for Hector to
keep both of the women he loves safe.

'This series keeps getting better and better'
Joyfully Reviewed

facebook.com/eternalromance